FOR BETTER FOR WORSE

Jane Beck

Matador
9 Priory Business Park,
Wistow Road, Kibworth Beauchamp,
Leicestershire. LE8 0RX
Tel: (+44) 116 279 2299
Fax: (+44) 116 279 2277
Email: books@troubador.co.uk
Web: www.troubador.co.uk/matador

ISBN 978 1780882 277

British Library Cataloguing in Publication Data.
A catalogue record for this book is available from the British Library.

Typeset by Troubador Publishing Ltd, Leicester, UK

Matador is an imprint of Troubador Publishing Ltd

Printed and bound in the UK by TJ International, Padstow, Cornwall

For Fiona

With my sincere thanks

AUTHOR'S NOTE

Although this book is based on a real life event the story that I have woven around it is a work of fiction. Any resemblance to actual persons, living or dead, is purely coincidental.

ACKNOWLEDGEMENTS

I would like to thank the following people who have given me advice on artistic/technical aspects of the book. Philipp Fehl who introduced me to Bernini's wonderful Ecstasy of Santa Teresa in the church of Santa Maria della Vittoria in Rome and to Professor Simon Schama CBE who, many years later, explained the significance of her voluminous robes in his BBC TV programme The Power of Art. Philipp's two daughters Kathy Fehl and Carolyn Coulston for giving me permission to use his 'Viennese story'. Martin Hale, British Embassy Vienna, for insight into the role of the consular service for British travellers in Europe. Kevin McCarron who, unlike many lawyers, cuts to the chase in the shortest possible time and never fails to come up with an answer. John Neighbour, HB Accountants, for jogging my memory towards Estate Duty. Harry Bingham and Jeremy Sheldon for help at Writers Workshop. My son Max for sorting the computer technological glitches with patience and good humour and for his valuable insight into the workings of the male mind! Finally to Jeremy Thompson and the staff at Matador who masterminded the final production.

CHAPTER ONE

October 1962

If only we could have stayed in Portofino. For months after their holiday ended the thought buzzed constantly around Liz's head. But if they hadn't been en route to Rome they wouldn't have been in Portofino anyway, so staying wasn't really an option. She should have insisted on more leisure and less action. Why did she suggest they go to Rome in the first place? The list of thoughts was endless and futile and there was no future in 'if only'.

'Is it OK to stick to the coast road?' Paul left Genoa and pointed the car towards La Spezia.

'Well, you could join the autostrada. It might be quicker, but it won't be nearly as picturesque.' On a first trip to Italy Liz could think of more exciting things to see than speeding cars on a motorway. She looked again at the map. They hadn't even stopped in Genoa and the rest of the journey could become a list of places they would tick off as they passed through. It was then that she spotted Portofino and ran the word slowly around her mind, adding an Italian accent for good measure. The longer she thought the more desirable it sounded.

'Let's have lunch in Portofino. It's a tiny diversion, won't take more than five minutes. Come on, Paul, you've been driving through France like an express train. What about an hour off?' She glanced across at him with what she hoped was a winning smile. Normally she didn't do feminine wiles, but if that's what it took to get Paul to stop driving then what the hell.

'OK you win. Sing out when you see a sign. I keep forgetting we're on holiday.'

Liz thanked God with a silent alleluia; with luck she might even manage to stretch that hour. She turned her attention quickly back to the road.

Fifteen minutes later they were parked. 'I'll just have a quick look at the map before we eat, if you don't mind.' Paul spread the map over the bonnet of the car leaving her no alternative but to kill time by staring at his back. The ridge of his spine, clearly visible under his shirt, reminded her of the number of times she'd run her fingers along the length of it. To be alone with him was a rarity and she had an overwhelming desire to drag him away somewhere quiet, tear off his clothes, kiss every last vertebrae and give him the siesta of his life.

Four years ago she wouldn't have thought it possible to see so little of someone once you were married. But Paul seemed always to be somewhere else; running the business or sorting out its problems. They had a flat in the hotel he managed and if there wasn't a member of staff needing his attention there was a guest inviting him for a drink, under the general guise of discussing a booking. The line between work and leisure had become so blurred it was virtually non-existent and there were times when she felt excluded from the major part of his life where all the fun and action was.

Most of her girl friends had the occasional moan about their husbands, but nobody admitted to having real problems and, as far as she knew, none of them ever thought seriously about splitting up as she had in some of her lowest moments. Was she expecting too much? Was it a fact that life for others appeared to be more exciting than ones own? But for the next two weeks she had him almost to herself so maybe she should stop the self-pity and make the most of it.

She tapped him lightly on the shoulder. 'Do you think those tables on the quayside are waiting for customers?'

Paul got the message and began to fold up the map, but not his plans for the rest of the journey. 'If we press on to Viareggio and stay the night it will be a fairly short run into Florence tomorrow and we can spend a few hours there. I'd rather not hit Pisa just as the light's fading. What do *you* think?' At long last they began to walk towards a table.

'Sounds good to me. I've always wanted to *explore* Florence.'

'It's less than three hundred miles from Florence to Rome. If we can reach Florence by mid-morning we could stay until early afternoon then we'll have plenty of time to reach Perugia by early evening.'

The diversion was Liz's idea. Kate, her best friend, was studying Italian in Perugia where she had a small apartment and had invited them to stay the night on the last leg of their journey.

Even on holiday once he got behind the wheel Paul didn't know when to stop. Each day he focussed on a specific goal and it seemed to Liz that he treated each journey in the same way he tackled the rest of his life, with his 'to do' list at his elbow.

'*Please* tell me it was worth the detour,' she said when finally they were sitting down and had ordered lunch. She waved an arm first towards the picturesque villas clinging for dear life to the sloping hillside and then in the direction of the sleek yachts and local fishing boats anchored in the exquisite little bay.

Just at that moment the waiter appeared with a plate of antipasti and a couple of cold beers. An assortment of cured meats; bresaola, salami and Parma ham, plus a few artichoke hearts and large black olives which glistened in the sunlight. It was their first real taste of Italy. Paul grinned at her across the table piling a plate with antipasti before handing it across.

'Well it's a bit picture postcard, but you were right to persuade me to stop, and I guess this is as good a place as any - and better than most,' he added seeing the smile on her face begin to slip. He rubbed his hands together anticipating a lunch he knew he'd enjoy. 'This looks good. Here's to the rest of the trip.'

'I'll drink to that.' Liz lifted her glass with her right hand and crossed the first two fingers of her left underneath the table. The glass was so cold the warm air condensed on the surface and trickled down the outside in slow, fat drops.

'A pity Rex Harrison isn't around to add a bit of extra glamour. Didn't he put this place on the map?'

'I think he bought a villa here when he was married to Lilli Palmer, but since he had six wives altogether I for one don't need that kind of glamour; and anyway, since I'm having lunch with you; who needs Rex Harrison?'

Perhaps all marriages were like theirs under the veneer of togetherness? How would she know? Brought up by her widowed grandmother after her parents were killed during the Second World War she'd never had the opportunity to observe a marriage at close quarters and consequently had no first hand experience to use for comparison. When Paul mentioned casually that his old friend Bruno and his wife were going to be in Rome, Liz had pounced as swiftly as a falcon spotting a ferret, seeing it as an opportunity for a holiday just for the two of them.

Paul and Bruno had been friends since they'd grown up together in Vienna. Their comfortable, trouble-free childhood brought to an abrupt end by the Anschluss when, after a long economic depression, Austria held out welcoming arms to Germany in the expectation of sharing in that country's economic recovery. Paul and Bruno were seventeen and soon learned the harsh reality of being Jewish in a country where non-Jews were the new élite. Life in Vienna became insupportable for anyone who had Jewish blood in their veins and a month later they both left; Paul for the UK, Bruno for the US. Both knew they were lucky to escape with their lives.

Bruno, now an art historian, was coming to the end of his sabbatical in Rome and had promised his university a book on Roman sculpture, creating an expenses-funded trip to the continent of his birth as well as the opportunity to indulge his passion. They'd last seen him in London five years ago. Paul had driven Liz up to Hampstead where Bruno and Anna had been staying in the house of a friend. They'd reached out and welcomed her as warmly as if she'd been a member of their own family. This was a revelation to Liz who'd grown up with a scarcity of relatives and she'd been devoted to both of them ever since.

'I hope everything's alright at home.' Paul broke off a chunk of bread and used it to mop olive oil from his plate.

Liz already felt guilty at leaving the children behind and didn't want to be reminded. Maria, their Austrian au pair, the daughter of one of Paul's family friends, had recently moved in to help care for six months old Emma and was more than capable of looking after both children. If all else failed there was a hotel full of staff who were always sneaking in for a quick peek at the new baby and who could be relied upon in a crisis. Unlike his young sister, Marcus was old enough to realise that his parents had gone away without him. She'd tried to keep in touch by putting a map in his room, marking their route and sending him a daily postcard so that Maria could help him plot their progress.

If Paul started talking about work it wouldn't be long before Antonia's name came up, the one person that Liz was desperate to leave behind. If only she were simply Paul's business partner, Liz would think more kindly of her. But there were times when she acted more as a surrogate mother using any excuse to drop into the flat, usually unannounced. 'Oh! You're having dinner! I'm sorry, I didn't realise!'

'Shall we make a move then?' Paul drained the last of his beer and pushed back his chair. They both took a last lingering look around the quay and up the hillside. 'It's a pity we can't stay longer,' he said, putting an arm round her, but at the same time turning towards the car. Liz said nothing.

As soon as they were seated she held out her hand for the map. Paul always drove when they were out of the country. He was a terrible passenger, although always quick to reassure Liz it had nothing to do with her driving. He'd had years of experience motoring around Europe and could slip seamlessly from driving on the wrong side of the road as he always described it in England. 'Keep to the coast road until we reach La Spezia,' Liz said, 'after that you can join the autostrada.'

They continued the journey mostly in silence, the coast road was tortuous and there was a steep drop down to the shore. Every so often Liz caught a glimpse of one of the Cinque

Terre villages built on fringes of the rugged coastline. She wished they had time to explore one or two of them. They looked like a patchwork quilt, their multi-coloured houses threaded through with medieval passages.

Paul drove as he did everything else - fast. Liz braced herself every time he took a bend at a speed slightly in excess of comfortable, but they'd covered so many miles together she knew better than to ask him to slow down.

They'd been travelling for about thirty minutes when they heard the roar of motorbike engines coming from behind and Paul slowed fractionally as they were overtaken by a couple of carabiniere. Both machines had their lights on and pulled in front of the car, braked and signalled Paul to stop.

'What's up now I wonder?' Paul stayed behind the wheel and watched the two men climb off their bikes and walk slowly towards them. Liz wondered if it was their thick coats that made them look so bulky; feeling they weren't a pair you'd want to argue with.

One of them began to speak in totally incomprehensible rapid Italian. Paul held out both his hands in a gesture of helplessness. 'Inglese,' he said, 'no comprendo.' The man jerked his head slightly to the right and Paul climbed reluctantly out of the car. The men walked round the vehicle in opposite directions scrutinising it, glancing occasionally at Paul. One of them aimed a kick at the front offside tyre. Liz saw Paul's shoulders tense and prayed he wouldn't lose his temper at the assault on his beloved car.

The bulkier of the two stopped by the boot and signalled to Paul to open it. Paul complied and then stood helplessly as the man pulled out pieces of luggage, which he dumped on the road without ceremony and a couple of novels Liz had brought along in case she found the time to read. Well you never knew. The man took them out one at a time and holding them by the spine shook them vigorously.

At the back of the boot was a large cardboard tube containing a print that Paul was bringing as a present for Bruno and his wife. The man took it out, held it against his ear and shook it before handing it to Paul. He made movements with both hands indicating he wanted Paul to open it. Paul twisted the lid and slowly eased out the print, opening it to show that it was a harmless landscape. The man looked hard at Paul, his expression difficult to read. He held out his hand for the tube, shook it firmly again, tapped the base with the tips of his fingers and handed it back.

Paul slowly re-rolled the print, replaced it and watched as the man wrote rapidly on what appeared to be some kind of form. When he'd finished he handed the form to Paul pointing to some figures he'd written at the bottom. Paul shrugged, fumbled in his back pocket for his wallet and pulled out a L10000 note. The man stowed the money in a leather pouch attached to his belt, handed Paul the top copy from his pad of forms, touched his cap briefly and signalled to Paul to move on. There was no other traffic on the road.

'Well, what was all that about?' Liz asked, sighing with relief as Paul replaced their luggage, got back into the car, started the engine and they drove away.

'Search me! I'm sure I wasn't speeding. Maybe they thought we were smuggling drugs or currency or weapons or all three. Thank God I bought one of Klimt's landscapes and not one of his more erotic studies or they might have suspected we were importing porn.' Paul laughed. The print, An Avenue in Schloss Kammer Park, had hung in Bruno's parents' flat and as a child he'd seen it almost every day. Inevitably the flat had been looted under Nazi occupation and the print disappeared, together with most of their other possessions.

They drove into Viareggio just as the light was fading. It had none of the charm of Portofino and Liz disliked it on sight. Through the gathering dusk she saw a promenade of hotels interspersed with restaurants which stretched away in front of them. On the other side of the promenade the ubiquitous pines shaded a pavement which ran along the edge of the beach. *It could have been Eastbourne*, she thought, but said nothing to Paul in case he agreed with her and decided to press on to Pisa.

They never booked in advance: just stopped anywhere which

took their fancy at a time when they'd had enough driving or arrived at a place they'd like to explore. Paul slowed the car. 'Sing out when you see somewhere that looks possible.' He shot a quick glance at Liz.

'Oh just pull in when you see a likely space.' She knew from past experience that by the time she asked him to stop they would be well past the only available parking slot.

'What's the Italian for room with bath?' Paul asked when he finally stopped in front of a likely hotel.

'Una camera con bagno.' Liz spoke slowly for his benefit as she climbed out of the car to stretch her legs. 'You go ahead and do the business. I'll stay here and wait.' She breathed in deeply, filling her lungs with the warm evening air which smelt of the sea and cooking.

As she waited in front of the hotel, a dark blue Jaguar with GB plates pulled in behind their own car. Liz glanced idly across at it then looked again a bit harder. The driver was so short he could scarcely see over the steering wheel and Liz wondered if he needed a big car to boost his ego. The woman sitting next to him had a pinched, long-suffering look as if she were in constant pain or putting up with a situation she wasn't enjoying. Liz decided she must be the wife thinking a mistress would look happier.

Before she could speculate further, Paul reappeared and gave her the thumbs up before walking round to the boot and removing their bags. He said, 'Good evening,' to the driver of the Jaguar who had already taken a large suitcase from his own car and was waiting for his wife to join him. Liz picked up her overnight bag and smiled in the general direction of the other couple, thinking, *what's the betting those two will be joining us later given half a chance?* She saw the woman's mouth tighten slightly and reckoned it could be a smile for all she knew.

'Pity the English found the place.' She said to Paul as they reached their room and started to unpack.

'I bet she doesn't think we're a legal couple,' Paul replied. 'If they're in the dining room when we go down to dinner I shall ask you to marry me - loudly!'

'You'd better be careful, I could just say no.' Liz threw a nightdress on the bed and made for the bathroom.

'If you do I might just forget we're together and leave you behind. Who knows what gorgeous Italian creature I might come across in Florence?'

They were both laughing as Liz turned on the bath taps. For the life of her she couldn't understand why Paul had this hang-up about being older. There was a fifteen year difference in their ages and Liz didn't give it a second thought, but there were times when she thought it might just be an issue for him. She'd known him to get a bit edgy when they were out with her friends, most of whom had husbands a good ten years younger than Paul.

He was the first into the bath and held out a hand for her. She'd been waiting for this since lunch time and didn't need encouraging. What with the children and now the addition of Maria, to say nothing of Antonia popping in and out, any kind of intimacy had to be planned with almost military precision.

Liz closed her eyes and wallowed in the water, which was exactly the right temperature. A friend had given her some Floris bath essence for Christmas, which she'd been hoarding for a special occasion and she'd sprinkled it in with abandon. She inhaled the smell of jasmine and stretched out her tired limbs. She sensed that Paul was relaxed and happy because their journey was going to plan and, with any luck, they would be in Rome by Thursday evening. Concentrating exclusively on Paul deepened her contentment. She wasn't listening for the children in case they woke up and best of all she wasn't expecting the intercom to summon Paul to some crisis - real or imagined.

The bath was large and old with plenty of room for the two of them and above all they had time. This being Italy, there would be no nonsense about the dining room closing at nine o'clock sharp and if they didn't fancy eating in they could always wander off and find a trattoria.

Liz traced a line up the outside of Paul's left leg with her right big toe luxuriating in the physical contact. 'I'm so happy,' she said on a long sigh, mentally crossing her fingers at the same time, hoping desperately the happiness would last.

'In spite of not staying in Portofino?' Paul's voice interrupted her thoughts.

'So you noticed!' She opened her eyes in surprise.

'Sometimes you can be very transparent.'

'Mmm, remind me never to play poker with you.'

'We can always come back to Portofino sometime and stay for longer.'

'You mean we *might* just take another holiday?' Liz kept her tone light but couldn't help wondering if Paul might have had enough of her company by the end of two weeks. Would he be able to forget the demands of work, to say nothing of his partner? Was there a future which would include her? If he was able to tell that she'd have liked to stay in Portofino were there other thoughts of hers which he'd managed to interpret? Was she an open book with whom he might become bored?

He leaned past her and pulled out the plug and Liz stopped contemplating the future. They dried each other on a shared towel and Liz felt her nerve endings jumping in anticipation. She took his hand, dragging him over to the bed. 'Come and show me some action!'

'You're sex crazed!'

'Are you complaining? Would you rather change me for a prude? The woman in the Jag., for instance.'

'That's hardly a fair comparison.'

'Count your blessings. I bet she's never had an orgasm in her life!'

'Talking of orgasms . . .'

'All this talking!' Liz kissed his mouth closed.

The English couple were walking into the dining room as they came down to dinner an hour later. Paul took her hand. 'Shall we see what Viareggio has to offer before we decide where to eat?'

'Oh yes *please*,' Liz didn't want to share her precious dinner with anyone other than Paul leave alone such an unpromising couple, 'and you can still ask me to marry you, unless you've changed your mind,' she added.

They walked hand in hand into the warm Italian evening. Liz was ravenous. It seemed a long time since the antipasti. *I'm holding Paul's hand* she thought with a kind of wonder and couldn't remember the last time she'd done so. More importantly they were both in the same time frame; tuned in to each other. This was a moment to treasure. If life was like this all the time it would be absolutely perfect.

CHAPTER TWO

They were down to breakfast the next morning by seven thirty. Their bags were already packed and Liz, after choosing a postcard of the Leaning Tower of Pisa from a stand in the hotel foyer to send to Marcus, went on ahead to order leaving Paul to pay the bill. Ten minutes later, they sat munching away in silence. Paul buttered his roll as if he were on automatic pilot, his mind already halfway to Florence and it wasn't until he was pouring coffee that he realised the owners of the Jaguar had approached their table.

'Mind if we join you?' The man said and pulled out a chair for his wife before Paul could answer.

'Please do.' Paul half rose and shot a sideways glance at Liz.

'We're Joe and Kathleen,' he said and then, 'from Yorkshire,' he added, in case they hadn't picked up on his accent.

'We looked out for you last night,' Joe began, 'thought we'd see you in t'dining room.'

'Sorry you missed us,' Paul said. 'We decided to have a look at Viareggio. See what it had to offer.'

'Did you find owt exciting?' Kathleen wanted to know.

'Well we discovered a trattoria where a lot of the Italians were eating. It seemed a good enough recommendation to us so, we decided to join them.' Paul explained. 'We tried a delicious local speciality cacciucco.'

'What's that when it's at 'ome?' Kathleen asked.

'Well it's a kind of robust fish soup, or maybe stew would be a better description,' Paul answered. 'Lots of shellfish, octopus, tomatoes, garlic; no frills, just very rustic and tasty.'

Kathleen recoiled slightly when Paul mentioned octopus. '*He* can't stand garlic,' she said, nodding in Joe's direction.

'I miss my egg and bacon more than anything.' Joe sounded wistful.

'We'll soon be 'ome now,' Kathleen reassured him, as if he were a small boy bored with the journey. She sipped orange juice gingerly, little finger well cocked and mouth puckered as if she found the taste too sour.

Paul asked if they were on holiday and Joe explained they'd been staying in Parma. 'Kathleen fancied a look at Pisa,' he confided, 'although we've got a leaning tower in Chesterfield, so I don't know why we're botherin'.'

It began to dawn on Paul why Kathleen looked so long-suffering.

'Some friends of ours 'ave a flat in Parma,' Joe went on, 'and lent it us for a couple of weeks.'

'Was it a good trip?' Liz asked. She'd made little contribution to the conversation so far and Paul was grateful for the intervention.

'It were all right except for t'bacon,' Kathleen chipped in.

'Bacon?' Liz and Paul spoke in unison.

'Well we tried all over to buy some. We don't speak much Italian, so it weren't easy. Nearest thing we could find were that thin it shrivelled up to nothing when we fried it.'

Paul daren't look at Liz. It didn't take a mind reader to realise that Joe and his wife had been buying Parma Ham and frying it to go with their breakfast eggs. Out of the corner of his eye he saw Liz stuff the last of her breakfast roll into her mouth and suspected she was trying to stifle her laughter. He glanced discreetly at his watch and began to make noises about the long drive to Perugia. Liz picked up the cue, drained the rest of her coffee and pushed back her chair.

'I hope you'll excuse us for rushing off. Enjoy the rest of your trip and good luck with the bacon!' she said as they made their escape.

Their speculation about the couple lasted all the way to Pisa. Their home life, their love life, the children. 'Only possible if you believe in the Immaculate Conception!' Paul said. They wondered idly what Joe did for a living. Liz plumped for scrap metal, Paul favoured a chain of butchers shops. They went on and on until all the possibilities were exhausted.

They turned onto the autostrada before they reached Pisa and pressed on to Florence. Paul was in his element because they were making good time and he could see that Liz had relaxed visibly in the last twenty four hours. He'd been concerned recently to see her change from the carefree young woman he'd married into someone who frequently looked tired and in some way burdened and withdrawn, as if struggling with some problem she couldn't quite solve. At first he thought the children were proving too much for her and hoped that after Maria arrived she'd find life a bit easier. But as the weeks passed and she didn't lighten up he'd begun to think that there was something seriously wrong.

'Have you decided what you'd like to see in Florence?' he asked as they drew closer to the city.

This holiday was a new departure. Normally they went to visit Paul's mother in Vienna, taking in the surviving relatives at the same time. His mother's side of the family being non-Jewish had stayed in Austria after the Anschluss. Any sight-sightseeing was usually fitted in around visits to, and needs of, the many aunts, uncles and cousins. He'd never taken Liz to any of the usual tourist attractions like the Spanish Riding School or the opera, although on their first trip together they had visited Schönbrunn. The old Imperial Palace had saddened her; its vast, mostly empty rooms redolent of the last days of the Austro-Hungarian Empire giving her a tantalising glimpse of the splendour of a vanished era.

Usually they stopped off on the way over for a couple of days skiing and maybe another on the way home to explore if they felt like it. Even though the Anschluss and the Second World War were now well in the past, Paul insisted they spend as little time in Germany as possible. They'd always been on territory well known to him and Liz deferred to his knowledge and, to a certain extent, his wishes. But Paul's mother had died earlier in the year and for the first time they were free to go wherever they chose.

'I'd really like to visit San Lorenzo,' Liz said. 'I read up on Florence before we left and decided that if I saw nothing else it had to be the Medici Chapel. Michelangelo designed the new sacristy as well as sculpting the tombs of Lorenzo and Giuliano de' Medici. Kate tells me they're absolutely stunning. In the San Lorenzo Basilica, which is older, there are two bronze pulpits by Donatello and some more of his sculptures in the old sacristy.'

'Well that should keep us busy until lunch time,' Paul said, unconsciously following his Austrian heritage. Whenever they'd visited his Viennese relatives any sightseeing always revolved around the best places to eat and after protracted discussion it seemed to Liz that the chosen restaurant became the main point of the trip.

It was just after ten o'clock when they caught their first sight of Brunelleschi's magnificent dome which dominated the city whichever way they looked. The soft red tiles of the roof were silhouetted against a clear blue sky and, looking at its unique shape, they didn't need the guide book to tell them that it was a masterpiece of engineering. Paul manoeuvred the car into what seemed like an impossibly small parking space, heard Liz let out her breath in relief and at last they were free to wander.

They paused at the Ponte Vecchio to gaze across the Arno. 'I'm glad to find a piece of Europe that Hitler *actually* spared,' Paul said. He would never forgive the Germans for the atrocities committed against his family during the Second World War and the peremptory way in which he'd been uprooted from his home, his studies and the few possessions of his boyhood. He then fled to England and was forced to build his future in a country about which he knew virtually nothing, although deep inside he acknowledged that he was lucky to survive.

Liz had only begun to fully understand why his dislike had continued for so long when in 1960 Adolf Eichmann was captured and subsequently tried in Israel for his war crimes. It was the first time that such an occasion had been seen on television. Looking at his impassive face inside the glass box in which he sat throughout the trial, ironically to protect him from potential assassins, she at last realised that if another leader like Hitler should emerge, Eichmann and his fellow criminals would be more than willing to follow him and repeat their crimes against humanity. She saw no regret in that face, no shame, no remorse; in fact no feeling of any kind.

'This bridge has been here since Roman times.' Liz decided to make an effort to distract him from his wartime reminiscences. 'All the shops you see belonged originally to butchers and tanners until the Medici kicked them out in the 1500's and replaced them with goldsmiths and diamond carvers. I think the smell of meat must have offended the refined Medici nostrils. This bridge was a covered way leading from the Pitti Palace to the Medici offices, now the Uffizi Art Gallery. The German commander in charge of the army's retreat across the river during the Second World War couldn't bear to blow it up so he disobeyed orders and left it for us to enjoy. So you see they aren't *all* bad.' Liz tucked her arm through Paul's.

'Well *good* for him.' Paul couldn't keep the sarcasm out of his voice.

They strolled across five hundred years of history pausing every now and then to window shop. Paul enjoyed shopping, but then he did it so rarely it was a positive treat. Inevitably there was a lot of stuff for sale to try to tempt the tourist, most of it, resistible, but suddenly Liz stopped.

'Look at that lovely necklace!' She stood in front of a jewellery shop displaying a long string of amber beads in the centre of the window. He knew she loved the warmth of amber and the occasional bits of natural history one sometimes found entombed inside. There weren't any petrified bugs in this particular piece, but there was something about the oval shape of the beads and the colour; neither the palest yellow or the darkest brown but somewhere in between.

Paul dragged her into the shop before she knew what was happening and, spotting the owner, pointed first to the necklace and then to Liz. 'Ah! Inglese?' The owner said. 'You like to try on?' He addressed his remark to Liz. 'Si, per fa'vore,' she replied, not wishing to be outdone.

The necklace looked stunning with the cream top she was wearing. The beads were warm to the touch, their weight negligible and the length perfect, reaching halfway to her waist. He watched her take it off reluctantly, after she looked at the price tag, and hand it back to the owner. 'Grazie tanto,' she said.

'You like?' he asked.

'Moltissimo,' she assured him.

He rubbed the beads vigorously against the front of his jacket and then held a piece of tissue paper against the amber. It stuck to the surface of the beads. 'Real amber, you see?' He had now turned his attention to Paul. Liz smiled a reluctant farewell and was turning to leave the shop when Paul asked if she really would like the necklace.

'An early wedding anniversary present, perhaps?' he suggested and watched as the expression on her face turned to pure delight.

'Well, that would be fantastic!' He guessed she hadn't expected him to remember that their fourth wedding anniversary was coming up at the beginning of November. To his surprise she kissed him full on the mouth as they left the shop and he knew she didn't care who saw her. It was worth the expense to see a flash of the old Liz.

They continued their walk across the bridge and, although they stopped every now and then to look, they managed to get to the other side without buying anything except for another postcard to send to Marcus.

'Just a brief diversion,' Liz said. 'If we take a right turn now we can walk to the Piazza della Signoria and take a quick look at Michelangelo's David.'

'Right! Let's do it!' Paul quickened his pace and took Liz's arm, forcing her to walk faster in order to keep up.

'I'm so glad I'm married to you and not Yorkshire Joe.'

'He'd probably smother you in diamonds. Did you notice

his wife was wearing a huge solitaire ring?'

'I was too busy trying not to laugh to take in her jewellery. All I can say is it's wasted on her and if I owned it I'd be terrified of losing it.'

'Just as well. I don't think I'm in a position to match it at the moment. I only hope the business isn't falling apart whilst we're away. Antonia isn't really up to running the show on her own now that we've expanded so much. It's a very different operation from the one she started thirty years ago when she turned their old house into a hotel.'

He saw the happiness leave Liz's face the moment he mentioned Antonia and wondered what had actually happened between the two of them and when. He had seen Antonia's role in the hotel, over the few years in which Liz had been involved, change slowly from an active participant in its success to that of a hawk-eyed observer. She appeared to do little work herself, but was always prowling round looking for faults. He knew also that Antonia would never retire. Away from the hotel she would have nothing to occupy either her mind or her days and attempting to run the business gave her a certain hold over both of them, which she was unwilling to sacrifice.

They continued walking and finally stood in front of Michelangelo's magnificent statue, or at least the replica which replaced the original, and contemplating David took his mind away from the business and its problems. Liz was reading from her guidebook. 'Michelangelo worked on the original piece for three years. Whether he did anything else at the same time, I'm not quite sure. What I do know is that at least two other sculptors were defeated by such a huge block of marble. It must be all of sixteen feet high.'

Michelangelo had given David the large hands and feet of a gawky adolescent which, to Paul's mind, struck a jarring note with the marbled muscle of the rest of him. A pebble lay in the sling which rested in his relaxed hand indicating that he had yet to make his fatal shot. After gazing at the statue for several minutes, Liz turned her attention to an overweight and ageing male tourist who'd propped himself against David's plinth with total disregard for the celebration of male beauty above him. His belly overlapped his trousers and his balding head formed a stark contrast to David's luxuriant curls. Liz pointed her camera and managed to snap both statue and man before he moved. The contrast between the divine marble manhood depicted by Michelangelo and the manifestations of the worst excesses of modern living were obviously too much of a temptation for Liz and her camera. '*You* are absolutely wicked!' Paul laughed down at her. 'Now the poor guy's been immortalised.'

'Why don't you take his place and then I can guarantee your own immortality?' Liz invited. But Paul took her elbow and turned her away from the statue.

'San Lorenzo calls,' he said, 'or had you forgotten?'

They retraced their steps, turned smartly right into Via Roma and walked swiftly towards Piazza Santa Giovanni and the Duomo. Liz resisted the impulse to suggest yet another diversion and they pressed on to Borgo San Lorenzo. When finally they stood in front of the chapel commissioned by Cardinal Giulio de' Medici, Liz was obviously so excited to see the five hundred year old memorial to Medici money that she clutched Paul's arm and almost dragged him towards the entrance, trying at the same time to take in the soaring dramatic arches around the church, which formed a stark contrast to the unclad brick walls.

'Donatello's dramatic, rectangular, bronze and marble pulpits were his final works. In fact his pupils finished them.' Paul had taken over the guidebook and was skim-reading the information; cutting through the verbiage swifter than a lawnmower through grass. 'Donatello died before he finished these pulpits and he's buried in what's known as the Martelli Chapel. Before and After the Crucifixion,' he elaborated waving an arm towards the densely populated reliefs, first on the right pulpit and then on the left.

His haste had nothing to do with a lack of interest in art and everything to do with the hundred and fifty miles they had to cover after lunch and they moved swiftly on to the chapel.

It was octagonal, surmounted by a cupola and Paul found

its walls, which were covered in precious marbles, finely worked stones and gilded bronzes: a touch oppressive. On the lower section of the walls were the sixteen coats of arms of the Medici dukes worked in marble and precious stones. 'Mmm. A bit over the top don't you think?'

'Absolutely right,' Liz agreed.

Finally they reached Michelangelo's new sacristy. The simplicity of the interior was a welcome contrast. Light flooded in from the windows which had been placed high in the walls. The chapel was a perfect cube surmounted by a dome, at the centre of which a glazed lantern allowed yet more light to pour in. Each of the two tombs bore a seated statue of a Medici duke. Giuliano was depicted as a military man, obviously a man of activity; Lorenzo was portrayed as poetic, philosophical, his pose more that of a thinker. The reclining figures lying at the feet of the two men were more memorable than either. On Lorenzo's tomb was a male, representing evening and a female signifying dawn, whilst on Giuliano's the male depicted day and the female night. The male faces were quite rough as if the sculptor had insufficient time to finish them, but, in spite of that, there was both power and beauty immortalised in blue-grey marble.

Paul was particularly attracted by the female figure on Lorenzo's tomb. She was beautiful and slender, reclining on one elbow, her left arm raised and her index finger resting against her neck. Her legs were bent, the left one slightly raised, her hair streaming down her back. 'Lucky old Lorenzo,' he said to Liz, 'to lie in such splendour.'

'And with a beautiful woman to keep him company,' Liz added.

'Ah! But cold and immovable,' Paul reminded her.

He thought of Michelangelo chipping away day after day, employed by the most powerful of all the Renaissance families and knew that he would never be immortalised, certainly not commemorated in such a glorious setting. The knowledge made him feel unusually humble: almost a nobody.

They left the chapel at last and Paul, with his hotelier's instinct for good food, found a charming restaurant close to

San Lorenzo. The information on the menu told them it had been created in what had been a sixteenth century gallery. Behind the service counter a dazzling display of hams and Italian sausages hung from meat hooks, interspersed with strings of garlic and tomatoes on the vine. At the bottom of the display several cheeses had been piled as carefully as if they'd been placed for a still life picture. On the opposite wall racks of wine bottles, all full, left the visitor in no doubt that this was a place that knew its craft. The walls were painted pale terracotta and Liz fell in love with it at once.

'We'd better not stuff ourselves too much as we'll be eating dinner with your friend later,' Paul said, beginning to study the menu. 'A pity though, I think I could work my way through the *carte* given enough time.'

In the end they settled for a wild mushroom risotto and a salad; much to the disappointment of the waiter whose attempts to sell them various specialities of the restaurant failed dismally. They chose a light, dry white wine to wash it down and every time a waiter passed delivering dishes to another table Liz scrutinised the food and sniffed the aromas that wafted in their direction wanting to taste them all.

At the end of their meal they sipped fragrant Italian coffee, savouring every last mouthful in a way they never did at home. 'There's been so much conflict here and yet so much beauty still survives,' Liz said. 'Odd isn't it that a lot of what we've seen this morning depended on the Medici bankers.'

'You can't have art without commerce,' Paul said. 'How can you create anything unless someone is going to pay for the paint or the marble at the end of the day? At least you can, but even artists have to live. I doubt if starving in a garret is guaranteed to inspire the creative force for long, certainly not nowadays.'

Liz wished that Paul could take his eye off the money every once in a while and enjoy whatever pleasures crossed his path. But then she thought of Yorkshire Joe, reached across the table, took Paul's hand and squeezed it. 'I love a man who has such positive opinions,' she said.

They carefully wrote a postcard for Marcus over lunch, taking advantage of the restaurant table and the time spent waiting for food to tell him how much they missed him. 'I hope this reaches home before we do,' Paul said as they posted it on the way back to the car.

Later, as they were driving towards Perugia, Paul began to talk about an idea that he'd been turning around in his head for some time. He'd been meaning to discuss it with Liz for months, but had been so involved in the refurbishment of the banqueting rooms that the time for airing plans had been limited. Whenever he'd had a spare half hour, Liz was either preoccupied with the children or out of the hotel on some errand or other.

'How would you feel about looking for a house to buy when we get home? I'm tired of being at the beck and call of the hotel every waking moment and now that there are four of us, to say nothing of Maria, the flat seems to grow smaller every day. What do you think?'

He felt rather than saw Liz's surprise. He was concentrating hard on the driving, his eyes firmly on the road ahead.

'I think you've just given me the nicest present I'm ever likely to get,' Liz said, sliding her arm along the back of his seat.

He glanced at her quickly and saw that her eyes were suspiciously bright. 'That makes two in one day.' Paul laughed, but knew he was on the way to easing whatever worry Liz had been carrying around for the past few months. He moved on to practicalities. 'Do you think you could contact a few estate agents when we get back? The banqueting season will be starting any minute and I don't think I'll have too much spare time. But now I know you're in agreement I don't see any point in hanging around.'

'What sort of price range do you think I should aim for?' Liz asked, thinking, *good old Paul! Once he's made his mind up he can't wait to get started.* It had been exactly the same when he'd asked her to marry him. 'No point in hanging about,' he'd said and within two months of their engagement they were married.

'We should be able to find something fairly decent for

around £5000-£6000. If it has a bit of character, so much the better, but I think we'd better draw the line at anywhere that needs extensive redecoration or repair. Not really on with a couple of small children is it? Once we find somewhere I'd like us to move in as quickly as possible.'

'Would you like me to sell Ivy House?' Liz asked.

'Not for the moment. It's great as a bolt-hole, don't you think? You don't want to offload it do you?'

'Not really. It's the only thing I've got left that reminds me I once had a family. But if I sold it we could buy somewhere bigger. That would give us more scope when we start looking.'

Paul took his hand from the steering wheel, reached over and squeezed Liz's own as he heard the sadness in her voice. 'You hang on to it for the time being. If we can't find anywhere suitable we might have to think again.'

Ivy House was a legacy from Liz's grandmother. Little more than a cottage, tucked away in a small Wiltshire village, it was reachable in about two hours from the hotel, a big plus for both of them when time off was at a premium. Liz's grandmother and her parents had been sheltering in the cellar of her parents' home when the house took a direct hit. Her grandmother with great presence of mind had snatched Liz from her makeshift cot and made a dash for the stairs. Both Liz's parents had been crushed beneath the collapsed outer wall. Granny inherited the cottage from her second husband.

A lovely old couple, Sid and Evie Perkins, lived next door and acted as caretakers, keeping an eye on the place and lighting the Rayburn in cold weather to keep the water pipes from freezing and the kitchen warm. In return they had a large patch of Ivy House garden to grow vegetables, most of which they used themselves, but if they knew Liz and Paul were coming down they usually left a selection on the kitchen table.

The landscape was suddenly becoming more built up and he guessed they were approaching Perugia. Kate had warned them that the suburbs were ugly and, looking out of the window, Paul agreed with her. She'd also advised them not to attempt to drive into the town centre with its medieval buildings and narrow streets, many ending in flights of stone steps. They were looking for a particular car park which was close enough to Kate's flat to allow them to walk the final bit of their journey if they left their heavy luggage in the car and just took their overnight bags. She'd explained that her apartment was just behind the cathedral and relatively easy to find.

Paul slowed down because of the volume of traffic, which gave Liz time to study her town centre map and find some kind of orientation. He'd been driving for the best part of three days and looked forward to a relaxing evening.

'Slow right down,' Liz said. 'If my map reading is up to scratch you should see a signpost fairly soon.'

'Am I looking to left or right?' Paul asked.

'Now you're just being ridiculous!'

Two minutes later he felt her restraining hand on his knee. 'Try the next turning right,' she said. 'Now tell me I'm wonderful!' It was impossible to miss the triumph in her voice as they turned into the car park.

'Oh great! I actually have a wife who can read a map! Well that's my job done, now it's over to you.' He took their bags out of the boot before locking the car.

'If we cross the car park and go down a flight of steps we should come to the Corso Vannucci. From there it's a straight walk to the duomo.'

Twenty minutes later they were in front of the cathedral. 'Kate's flat should be behind there,' Liz said, pointing. 'We're looking for colonnaded balconies built around a courtyard.'

'It sounds very grand.'

'It's only rented.'

'Let's try over there.' Paul pointed to the fountain which lay between the duomo and the town hall. 'Round the back perhaps?' he suggested. They crossed the square and found a courtyard, surrounded on three sides by what looked like flats. The walls of the flats were painted a pleasing shade of burnt sienna. A walled walkway ran in front of them. Slender pillars surmounted the wall and these were linked by arches, which were joined to the wall above so the walkway was covered against the weather. Several of the walls had terracotta troughs which had been planted by the owners. They looked to be several centuries old.

'Kate's flat is on the second floor,' Liz said, making for the staircase in the corner of the courtyard. It was dark and steep and he was glad they weren't burdened by heavy luggage and that the evening was still light enough to allow them to see where they were going. They found Kate's flat almost halfway along the walkway and within seconds they were caught up in a flurry of hugs and kisses as Liz's old friend welcomed them to her apartment.

Like many Italian buildings, the interior was dark; the small windows were better at protecting the occupants from strong sunlight than providing illumination. The covered walkway made the rooms even darker, but it was both cool and quiet now that they were away from the traffic. Kate's living room was simply furnished with a large damask-covered sofa that had seen better days, a folding table with barley sugar legs and a couple of upright chairs. There were several lamps dotted about and these were lit, although it was barely six o'clock. They projected a soft glow into the dark interior. Kate poured wine for them. Paul walked about restlessly, explaining to Kate that as he'd been driving all day his backside needed a rest.

'I only got back from the university an hour ago,' Kate said. 'Do you mind if we go out to eat?'

'We were going to suggest it anyway,' Paul replied quickly, 'and it's our treat. You've been good enough to offer us a bed for the night so it's the least we can do.'

They told Kate about the Yorkshire couple they'd met in Viareggio, embellishing the story and doing the Yorkshire accent, laughing again at the thought of anyone frying Parma Ham. Later Liz and Paul tidied up in Kate's tiny bathroom and by eight o'clock they were sitting in a nearby trattoria.

CHAPTER THREE

'Can you give us directions to the Campidoglio?' Liz asked Kate once they'd ordered their food. 'Believe it or not that's where Paul's esteemed friend wants us to meet.'

'I'll lend you my Rome guidebook,' Kate offered. 'I'll pick it up when I come across to see you on Sunday. It has a good map and I'll show you the place before you leave. Why the Campidoglio particularly?'

'Bruno's coming to the end of his sabbatical,' Paul explained. 'As usual he's behind with his research and doesn't want to waste an opportunity. He's asked us to meet him under the equestrian statue of Marcus Aurelius, which will give him the opportunity to take a last look.'

'The only thing I can tell you about it,' Kate volunteered, 'is that the bronze was originally gilded. Personally I think it must have looked a bit brash. I remember one of my father's American friends buying a small eighteenth century replica of a brass cannon in some West End antique shop and immediately asking if she could have it gold plated. Can you imagine?'

Liz could imagine only too well. Kate's father seemed to rub shoulders with many people who "Had more money than sense" as Liz's granny would have put it. Kate often complained that her father was always very full of himself, but none-the-less never refused his money. Liz knew that he was supporting her current Italian studies and couldn't help reminding Kate that she was lucky to have a father at all, even if he did annoy her from time to time.

Their food arrived and Liz's mouth began to water at the prospect of another Italian meal. Their affection for food had been obvious on every plate since the beginning of the trip. Each meal she'd eaten tasted as if it had been cooked with love.

Everything looked deceptively simple, but was presented with great care and the quality of the ingredients was flawless. She looked down at her salad of mixed peppers, which were strewn with capers and sprinkled with olive oil. The peppers had been chargrilled and the skins removed so that they were soft and slightly warm; they tasted delicious.

For their second course they had tiny lamb cutlets coated in crumbs, fried and accompanied by a huge mixed salad, which they shared with one guilty portion of chips between the three of them. They drank a wonderful soft red wine, which tasted so good they ordered a second bottle. There was a part of Liz that envied Kate for living in Italy long term, at least for the duration of her studies; but then she looked at Paul and reminded herself how lucky she was to be married to the man she loved and prayed that their marriage would last. Paul had exactly the right combination of qualities for her: attractive, with a great sense of humour, he worked hard, loved his children and was never boring. As if that wasn't enough, he was an accomplished lover and the moment he touched her she could feel herself melting into him, wishing that time would stop and that the rest of the world would forget them altogether.

As the evening progressed, Kate told them about her latest boyfriend: an Italian doctor, Luigi, who was living and working in Rome. Kate had always been choosy in their college days, so Liz guessed he must be someone special. His father was a senior consultant, Kate told them, which meant that he would be well-heeled enough to pass muster with her father. They'd met at a party given by one of Kate's new university friends and had been seeing each other regularly ever since. Luigi was specialising in orthopaedic surgery and hoped to become a consultant himself in a couple of years, Kate explained. She pulled out her diary and showed them a picture of him, which she'd tucked between the pages. Liz saw a man who looked quite tall for an Italian, but whose dark hair, brown eyes, olive skin and casual elegance were typical of his nationality.

'You'll find Rome very crowded at the moment,' Kate warned them. 'Because of the Vatican Council just about every hotel in

Rome is fully booked. Luckily I reserved a room for you in good time. You'll find the Grand Hotel a bit of a gin palace but at least it's fairly central and you should be comfortable.'

The council convened by Pope John XXIII was an attempt to create unity between all Christian sects. He'd been trying to revitalise the church and bring it up to date since his election in 1958 and this, the culmination of his efforts, was the most momentous event in the Roman Catholic calendar for many years. They speculated about the likely success or otherwise of the project.

'At least the hotels will do well out of it,' Paul said. 'We could do with a similar boost to trade in our neck of the woods.'

'You'd never guess he was a hotelier would you?' said Liz, rolling her eyes wildly and taking a long drink from her wine glass.

'I think Pope John is aiming for closer cooperation between East and West, so at least he's making an attempt,' Kate said. 'There are representatives from all over the world attending, including some protestant observers.

'He'll have his work cut out,' Paul added, 'when you think of the amount of prejudice he's up against.'

Liz looked at him long and hard across the table wondering if he was aware of his own prejudices, but didn't want to ruin a good evening by pursuing *that* particular argument.

They were all reluctant to leave. It had been one of those rare occasions when the company, the food and the wine merged into one of those special times, which each of them would remember with affection for many years to come. They linked arms as they walked back to Kate's flat, making sure that Paul was in the middle. They talked about nothing and laughed a good deal. Liz secretly hugged herself, knowing the evening wasn't quite over for her and she could relax knowing that, for the fourth night in a row, they wouldn't be interrupted.

On Thursday morning Kate suggested taking them to the Palazzo dei Priori, which housed the Umbrian National Gallery. She had no lectures before eleven o'clock and, if they felt like it, the palazzo was only a stone's throw from her flat. Liz looked at Paul for confirmation thinking he might be raring to leave soon after breakfast. To her surprise he acquiesced. 'It's only just over a hundred miles to Rome and we might as well take it slowly. After all, if I know anything about Bruno, it'll be all systems go once we arrive, so we might as well take this opportunity for a leisurely morning.' *Or as near to leisurely as we're ever likely to get,* Liz thought.

'Like most buildings in Italy,' Kate explained as they walked towards the palazzo, 'this one took ages to finish. Construction began way back in the thirteenth century and ended half way through the fourteenth; started again early in the fifteenth century and finished towards the end of the sixteenth. The semi-circular flight of steps opposite the fountain wasn't added until 1902.'

'Well the result is certainly impressive, so perhaps the delay was worthwhile.' Liz admired the blonde stone as she spoke, which was highlighted by the early morning sun. They stopped walking briefly to admire the imposing three storey building inset with rows of delicately arched windows leading up to the crenellated edge of the roof.

'It has the largest collection of Umbrian art in the world and takes you through the entire history of Umbrian painting,' Kate elaborated as they walked up the steps. 'The gallery begins on the second floor and I'm not going to have time to show you everything, so I hope you'll trust my judgement. I'd better start with Piero della Francesca. It's a pity you didn't take time to stop off in Arezzo, you could have seen some of the best examples of his work.'

'The next trip perhaps?' Paul said with a meaningful look at Liz.

By this time they'd reached a large altarpiece painted originally for Sant' Antonio portraying the Madonna enthroned sitting in a classical niche. But the most arresting part of the painting was the Annunciation scene on the pinnacle worked with a delicacy and sense of proportion which was way ahead of its time. Piero della Francesca's other life as a mathematician may have influenced his attitude towards composition and his attention to proportion and scale. His Madonna, however, was pale, with a pointed chin and heavy eyelids, which made Liz wonder on whom she was modelled. She certainly didn't appear to be Italian or Jewish either come to that.

Kate showed them a tiny gem-like Madonna painted by Gentile da Fabriano which, she explained, was reckoned to be an international Gothic masterpiece. The artist had used layers of near-transparent paints and a good deal of gold, but they'd been applied with a very delicate hand.

Liz found Pinturicchio's Madonna and Child more to her liking. The Madonna was wearing a dark blue robe with gold embroidered borders to the sleeves and had been painted against the background of a hillside surmounted by two delicate trees, one on either side of her head. The infant Christ had dark hair, which made him more convincing to Liz's way of thinking and she wondered why so many paintings of the Madonna and child depicted a Jewish baby as an improbable blonde.

They just had time to admire some of Perugino's work before Kate had to leave and they returned briefly to the flat to pick up their bags and say their goodbyes.

On the way back to the car, Paul suggested they buy food for a picnic lunch. 'All this culture has given me an appetite.' He sniffed the air as they approached a bakery and their nostrils were teased by the smell of freshly baked bread. They bought some pane el formaggio, a local speciality, and a little further on discovered a small shop bursting with every conceivable kind of sausage. They rounded off their purchases with a bunch of grapes from a market stall and a bottle of wine.

'Shopping's never this much fun at home,' Liz said. 'Maybe it has something to do with being on holiday or the novelty of the produce or perhaps because everyone who serves you is good humoured and patient.'

'I hope your leg muscles are in good shape,' Paul said as they reached the bottom of the steps, which had been so easy yesterday when they'd been travelling from the other direction, but which looked daunting when viewed from the bottom. They stopped talking to conserve their breath for the climb and, although they managed to get to the top without pausing, they were both pleased when at last they reached the car.

They drove for a couple of hours through the beautiful Umbrian landscape, silvered with olive groves, interspersed with pines, cypresses and poplars. Ochre-washed farm buildings with faded pink triangular rooftops broke up the lines of vineyards. The landscape looked as if it had simply grown into a mellow perfection for everyone to enjoy without the benefit of human intervention.

It was just after one o'clock when Paul pulled off the road onto a small track and stopped the car without any prompting from Liz. They climbed out, stretching legs which had stiffened up after the long climb up the steps out of Perugia followed by a couple of hours of inactivity. Within minutes they were eating the cheese-flavoured bread with slices of mortadella, which tasted wonderful in the softly scented afternoon air. An occasional bee droned by and the birds sounded as if they were auditioning to sing in some sublime oratorio.

Liz looked across at her adored husband, sitting with his back against a tree, face lifted to the sun. It was a long time since she'd seen him so carefree and happy. Eighteen months ago he'd had a routine medical check prior to taking out additional life insurance. 'Now that the family's increasing,' he'd joked at the time, 'and as I've nothing else to leave you, I might as well find an insurance company who'll be able to support you all after I've gone!'

The very thought that he might no longer be with them, however far into the future Liz looked, made her feel as if the world might end altogether. How many couples think about being separated after a mere two and a half years of marriage? In the course of the examination, the insurance company doctor discovered that Paul's blood pressure was so high that not only had he recommended that Paul see his own GP as soon as possible, but also refused to authorise additional life cover.

Eventually their doctor had diagnosed essential hypertension. 'Just a fancy name for high blood pressure,' Paul said, at the same time dismissing the doctor as, 'an old quack spreading gloom and despondency to keep himself in business.' After a few false starts they'd managed to find a drug which brought Paul's blood pressure closer to normal. But Liz worried that he continually ignored medical advice to take life a little more easily and slow down. It was then she'd seen for the first time exactly how ruthless his business partner could be.

Antonia had knocked on the door of their flat early one evening and then burst in without waiting to be invited. 'I've been looking all over the hotel for Paul,' she said. The eyes that met Liz's were cold and accusing making Liz feel as if she were harbouring some underling slacker.

'He had a doctor's appointment, just a routine check, you know he has to have them every month now.' Normally she managed a surface politeness when speaking to Antonia knowing that a declaration of open warfare would make Paul's life untenable. But on this occasion she didn't bother to hide her dislike. Considering the hours that Paul put into the business she felt that Antonia had no reason to chase after him if he disappeared for half an hour. He normally told her if he was going out, but this time he'd either forgotten or chosen not to let Antonia know.

'Tell him I want to see him the minute he comes back,' Antonia snapped and then added as a parting shot, 'I've no time in my business for people who can't pull their weight.' Before Liz could think of a suitably cutting reply, Antonia had turned on her heel and left.

Liz felt hot, angry tears sting the back of her eyes. She'd always thought that Antonia had been a good friend to Paul as well as being his business partner. In her self-appointed role as surrogate mother, she was always recommending some film he might like to see, lending him books that she had read and enjoyed, asking him if he'd remembered to organise a dental check-up. Later Liz had played that single sentence over and over in her mind, each time wanting it not to be true, but knowing only too well that it was.

When Paul came back to the flat she'd passed on the first part of Antonia's message, modifying it to try to take the sting out of it. 'Antonia would like a word, when you have a minute.'

'I ran into her in reception.' His reply was curt and tight-lipped. Liz never revealed the final sentence.

⁓

Paul packed away the remnants of the picnic thinking he'd give them to Bruno when they reached Rome. He and Anna had a small apartment for the duration of their stay and he suspected that shopping for food was low on their list of priorities. He pulled Liz to her feet and then on an impulse wrapped his arms around her, held her close and kissed her. Watching her eating lunch he'd realised what a crucial part of his life she was and he wanted to prolong the perfection of the afternoon. Because of the demands of the business and Antonia's increasing inactivity in it, he had no idea when they might be able to escape like this again.

'I suppose a quickie's out of the question?' Liz tilted her head away from him, smiling.

'My God, woman, you're insatiable! And for your information I'm absolutely knackered! Come on!' He opened the car door and slapped her playfully on the bottom as he unceremoniously bundled her inside.

As he drove towards Rome he thought about seeing Bruno again, remembering again their last days in Vienna and the fear their exit visas would be revoked at the last minute and they'd be unable to escape the horror the city had become.

Both he and Bruno had been working hard for their matura, the final examination which would enable them to go to university if they passed it successfully. Except that now there was no university that would accept Jews. It was just after the Germans took over Vienna that Bruno met Anna. He was on his way to school, hurrying along the street with his books under his arm, when he spotted a young woman standing in a doorway. She signalled frantically to him to come over and he imagined he saw fear in her eyes. It had been a while since a non-Jewish woman had either looked at or spoken to him and, after hesitating for a fraction of a second, he walked over to the doorway. She immediately opened the door to the house and pulled him into the hallway, at the same time putting two fingers to her lips and beseeching him with her eyes to keep quiet.

Only then did he hear the tramp of the storm troopers' boots as they walked in step across the width of the street. He must have been lost in his own thoughts not to have realised he was in danger of making up the daily quota of Jews to be caught and interrogated before being sent to the labour camps. As the sound of the marching died away they both relaxed and Anna smiled at him for the first time.

'I owe you my life.' Tears of gratitude spilled down his cheeks. He brushed them away with his coat sleeve and, with a presence of mind which would never again desert him, he pulled a pen from his jacket pocket and opened an exercise book. 'Please write your name and address. When this nightmare's over I'll find you and thank you properly. Until then this will have to do.' He kissed her swiftly on the mouth to show his appreciation for what she'd just done for him. If she'd been caught she would have been shot for harbouring a Jew and he never forgot that single act of courage which fuelled his determination to survive in a city which had been turned on its head.

He served in the US Army from 1942-46 and was involved in many of the bloodiest campaigns, including Anzio. It took his division eleven months to battle their way from Sicily to Rome, the first European capital to be liberated on June 4th 1944. By the time the Germans surrendered, fifteen million military personnel and thirty five million civilians had been killed.

When his regiment was disbanded at the end of 1945 he volunteered for additional duties in the American sector in Vienna wanting to begin his search for Anna. He'd kept her address. He knew the district could have been bombed and he may not be able to find his way amongst the post-war chaos of the city now divided into British, American and Russian sectors. Fortunately the house had survived and he went on many occasions, but there was never a reply no matter how hard he knocked or for how long he rang the bell. As time went by he grew more and more despondent and began to think that Anna must have been one of the millions of casualties.

One day he was making a routine inspection of a soup kitchen, one of several initiatives started under the United Nations Relief and Rehabilitation Administration. The place was teeming with Displaced Persons liberated either from the concentration camps, forced labour or prisoner of war camps. They looked dispirited and lost, not knowing what was going to happen to them next. They'd spent so long being ordered about and forced into one activity or another that all the spontaneity and joy had been knocked out of them and he was certain that, for some of them, it would be a long time before they trusted themselves enough to make a rational decision.

Suddenly he spotted a familiar face ladling out soup to a shuffling queue and, although he hesitated at first, he knew the moment he saw her smile that his search was over. Later he joked that he'd refined his kissing technique after their first unpromising encounter eight years ago and went on to woo her with as much food and chocolate as he could legitimately liberate. Paul had never met anyone who valued his wife more than Bruno.

It was nearly six o'clock when he finally reached the outskirts of Rome and Paul forced his concentration back to his driving. 'How's my master navigator?' he asked, turning briefly towards Liz.

'Well don't hold your breath, but I'm on the case.' She laughed. Half an hour later, after a couple of mistakes, they finally reached their destination.

CHAPTER FOUR

Antonia drank half a cup of coffee then pushed away her breakfast tray. The coffee could have been hotter, the toast was lukewarm and rubbery. If this was the kind of breakfast their guests were eating, the hotel would be out of business before Christmas. Tomorrow she would eat in the dining room then she'd be in a better position to judge.

She picked up her jacket from the chair on which it had been carefully placed ten minutes ago and inspected it for possible marks or stray hairs, even though she'd brushed it after she'd taken it from her cupboard, and shrugged irritably into it. She walked into the small hallway outside her sitting room and checked her appearance in the mirror one last time.

The image that stared back at her looked distinctly out of sorts; hardly surprising. She'd been working relentlessly for almost a week now and was feeling the strain. For the first time ever she wondered if perhaps she wasn't expecting a little too much of herself. After all, at sixty five most people had retired, or were at least thinking about doing so, before infirmity, senility, or both, put paid to any post retirement activities.

She was a small woman, no more than five feet two inches in her stocking feet, although she managed to add a couple more inches once she had her shoes on. Her bones were correspondingly tiny and she was particularly proud of her hands and her ankles, which she'd once heard someone describe as being like spun glass, although that was a long time ago. She hadn't heard anyone describe her as anything for some time now. Whenever any of the staff saw her coming they usually clammed up and she'd long ago abandoned her regular tours of the dining room to see if the guests were happy, after Paul explained that checking was the head waiter's job.

She walked slowly down the stairs to reception, her eyes

moving rapidly around the area checking to see that the flowers were fresh, there were no dirty ash trays on any of the low tables, no newspapers lying around on either of the sofas. She stopped briefly to stroke the two Persian cats who sat either side of the reception desk. Omar, the white one, nuzzled his head against her hand and purred with pleasure; Khayyam, his black partner, closed his green eyes disdainfully and then began systematically to wash himself with complete absorption and total disregard for anybody but himself. Antonia knew that the receptionists hated both of them, but it amused her to think that over the years they'd become quite a talking point amongst their guests.

The day ahead neither interested nor excited her. When Paul was around he filled the office they shared with joie de vivre and a consistently lively and amusing commentary, either about the business or the guests, or sometimes just life in general. Without him the hours stretched drearily in front of her, monotonous and boring. A time to be got through rather than enjoyed. She forced herself to go through the mail, a job she always insisted on doing even though the hotel secretary was perfectly capable of sorting it and sending it to the appropriate person for attention. But this was her domain and she liked to keep a finger on the pulse.

One eyebrow lifted a fraction when she saw the butcher's bill and wondered if perhaps the chef was on the fiddle. She'd heard her fellow hoteliers talk about 'chef's perks' at Hotel and Catering Association meetings; the general consensus being that it was OK providing they didn't get too greedy. This was a conclusion with which Antonia wholeheartedly disagreed. She must remember to have a word with Paul about it when he returned from cavorting around Italy with that wife of his.

Her own trips to Europe with Paul seemed aeons away now and she'd long ago accepted they were a thing of the past. In 1950 when petrol was finally de-rationed she'd tempted Paul to try out her father's MG Tourer and then casually suggested that if he wanted to make the trip to Vienna to see his mother that it would be OK for him to borrow it. Although hoping at the time he would invite her to join him it had been a gamble and she'd been euphoric when it paid off.

Between stopovers they'd shared some simple but, to her, magical roadside picnics when they'd bought rolls or bread and slices of sausage. After the austere wartime diet even slices of salami tasted like the food of the gods. Of course once they reached Vienna Paul's mother and her relations had taken him over and, as Antonia didn't speak German, time had hung rather heavily. She'd bought a small piece of petit point and some embroidery silk and picked away at it to keep herself occupied during the many hours of family reunion and reminiscence.

But going over old memories would only make her more depressed, so there was really no point. Action was needed. If she couldn't have Paul she would do the next best thing and take his son out somewhere for a treat.

As someone who'd neither married nor had children, Antonia wasn't naturally maternal. But now that Marcus had begun to talk he'd suddenly become much more interesting to her and he looked so much like Paul it was easy to warm towards him. She'd developed the habit of popping into the flat, usually when Liz was out somewhere at the hairdresser or shopping or whatever else it was that she did to occupy her time, collecting Marcus and taking him out. Now that they had a baby, the au pair found plenty to do when Marcus wasn't around and Antonia convinced herself that she was doing everyone a favour. 'I'll be out for the rest of the morning,' she told the secretary before making her way up to Paul's flat as she still called it.

A wide smile almost split Marcus' face in two when he saw Antonia come into the sitting room. He left the building blocks which he'd piled into a teetering tower and hurled himself across the room grabbing her round both knees. 'Toni! Toni!,' he cried jumping up and down with excitement, and then, 'Let's go out! Let's go out!' It hadn't taken him long to appreciate that going out with Toni usually meant ice cream or chocolate, sometimes both, and on really special days they might visit the toy shop where he would be allowed to choose something to take home.

'Ask Maria to get your jacket,' Antonia said without bothering to check whether or not Maria had alternative plans for him. She would have brushed them aside anyway as being unimportant or less important than a trip out with his favourite auntie. Within minutes they were walking down the stairs together hand in hand. The feel of his small fingers next to her own was comforting and, for the first time that morning, Antonia smiled.

It was almost ten o'clock on Friday morning when Paul and Liz walked up Michelangelo's gently escalating staircase towards the Piazza del Campidoglio and the equestrian statue of Marcus Aurelius. When they'd arrived the previous evening, the concierge had spirited their car away to the hotel garage and Liz suggested they leave it there. 'It will be good to walk for a change after all the time we've spent sitting during the last few days,' she told Paul, and as they walked swiftly down the Via del Corso breathed a sigh of relief knowing that Paul would be taking a much-needed break from driving and her navigational skills were temporarily off the hook.

Everywhere they looked they were reminded of the Vatican Council. Rome was awash with clergy and they saw countless men in red or black soutanes and the distinctive flat black hats with turned up brims sported by the younger clerics when not in church.

It was easy to spot Bruno and Anna once they reached the piazza, even though both had their backs to the staircase. They were standing by Marcus Aurelius' impressive plinth in deep discussion.

'Brace yourself for a potted history,' Paul said as they walked towards their friends

'Potted I can take,' Liz replied, 'but if he gets too convoluted I'm afraid he's going to lose me completely.'

Paul walked up behind Bruno and clapped him on the back. 'How are you doing, you old rogue?' he asked and Bruno immediately turned round and embraced his old friend with genuine affection. Once they'd all greeted each other and the kissing had stopped, Bruno lost no time in living up to Paul's prediction and launched into his favourite subject. 'Michelangelo persuaded Pope Paul III to allow him to make this statue the focal point of his plan when he was commissioned to restore the Campidoglio,' he said. 'It was transferred all the way from the Vatican, quite a feat five hundred years ago when you come to think about it.'

'I see a lot of the gilding has disappeared.' Liz dredged up the only piece of information she had on the statue and trotted it out not wanting to let Paul down.

'Ah well, there's a legend that the world will end once all the gilding flakes off the horse, so depending on how superstitious you are it may be as well if what little there is left is preserved for as long as possible.'

Liz caught Paul's "What did I tell you?" expression and quickly resumed her study of the statue. 'Have you noticed he's riding without stirrups?' Bruno asked coming to stand behind her, leaving Anna and Paul to talk to each other. Liz had got as far as wondering what it was about this equestrian statue that was different from others she'd seen, but hadn't quite worked out what it was. 'Stirrups hadn't been introduced to the West in the 1500's,' Bruno continued, warming to his theme.

'He's not wearing armour either, or carrying a weapon. In fact he looks positively benevolent.' Liz had the feeling that Bruno would be deeply disappointed if one of them didn't take an interest and said the first thing that came into her head.

'Some historians think that there might originally have been a fallen enemy resting under the uplifted hoof of the horse's right leg and that Marcus Aurelius raised his right arm in a gesture of clemency. But the absence of armour tells us that he was the bringer of peace rather than a military hero. It's the only surviving bronze statue of a pre-Christian Roman emperor. The others were all melted down for coin.'

'How did Marcus Aurelius manage to survive, when others didn't?' Liz asked, aware that she was being drawn by Bruno's scholarship.

'Would you believe it - mistaken identity,' Bruno answered, with more than a hint of triumph in his voice. 'There were those who mistook him for the first Christian Emperor, Constantine and as such worthy of preservation, so he survives for all of us to admire. It's really refreshing to talk to someone who shows even a spark of interest,' he added, smiling at her. 'For most of the year I'm trying to enthuse a bunch of students who vary both in scholarship and their degree of attention. Sometimes I think they're only studying art history as a soft and pleasant option to other branches of academe which might require more consistent hard work and study.'

They walked across to the balustraded perimeter of the piazza to rejoin Anna and Paul who were deep in conversation and looking towards the Forum. 'I might as well take you on a quick circuit as we're so close,' Bruno said. 'As none of us has much time we'd better not waste it by doubling back on ourselves.'

Here we go again, racing against time, Liz thought before joining Anna for the short walk. On the few occasions the two had met she had been slightly in awe of her. For one thing she seemed to devote herself completely to supporting Bruno, frequently doing some quite detailed research for him. Many of the footnotes for his books had been written by Anna, who neither wanted credit nor was given any. The budget and the domestic details and planning were her domain, leaving Bruno free to pursue his career with a single-mindedness in which he revelled. Liz felt that Anna's devotion to Bruno was almost saintly.

'Bits of this area look like the equivalent of a Roman building site. Don't you think?' Bruno waved an arm around the ruins of the Forum. 'In fact it *has* been looted for building materials over the years. You're walking along the Via Sacra, the oldest street in Rome. It runs right through the site,' he elaborated, before going on to show them the Temple of Julius Caesar, supposedly erected on the spot where Julius Caesar was cremated. He pointed out the Palatine Hill where Romulus allegedly founded Rome. They saw the Temple of Jupiter, the House of the Vestal Virgins and the Arch of Septimus Severus. After that Liz's mind failed and, as her empty stomach began to complain, the cultural indigestion also kicked in and she hoped it wouldn't be long before someone suggested lunch.

'The site is still being excavated as you can see,' Bruno told them before showing them the remains of a villa which had recently been unearthed. It was difficult to see from the fragments exactly what the villa had been like, but it was a reminder that the site had been residential until Julius Caesar had it cleared and substituted buildings more useful to public life, together with temples celebrating the glory of Roman emperors. *It was early civic development on a grand scale*, Liz thought as she took in the remaining fragmented columns, arches and buildings, which had survived for more than two thousand years. Even the reliefs on some of the arches had been preserved, remains of exquisite sculpture beautifully softened by time.

She glanced at her watch and to her surprise discovered that it was already one thirty. The morning had evaporated as they'd become absorbed in Roman history. If only her stomach would stop protesting. She walked over to Paul and, trying to speak as quietly as possible, said, 'I don't know about you, but I'm starving. Do you think we might plead for a lunch break?'

Either Bruno overheard or he too was feeling peckish and he came over to join them, suggesting they might walk towards the Spanish Steps, grab a quick bite to eat and then go off to the Villa Borghese. Liz didn't argue, but fell into step with Anna and they began to retrace their steps along the Via del Corso.

They ate lunch in a restaurant at the top of the Spanish Steps from which they had a panoramic view of the city. Liz was enchanted by it and the way the buildings had been shoehorned in to make the most of the available space, but in some indefinable way managing to avoid obvious overcrowding. Directly opposite was a church, adjacent to which someone had built a block of flats, but they were no more than four storeys high and boasted a roof garden, which gave them an aura of expensive elegance.

Anna told them they were desperately trying to finish all their work so they could leave Rome by the middle of next week at the absolute latest. Their two children had been living with Anna's mother during their absence and they felt it was time she was liberated. Paul said they were hoping to leave by Monday. 'I promised Liz we'd have a quick look at Venice on the way home, so we shouldn't hang around or it may just be grounds for divorce.' He smiled across the table at Liz as he spoke hoping that nothing on earth would persuade his wife to leave him.

After lunch they turned away from the restaurant and walked towards the entrance to the park surrounding the Villa Borghese. 'This was a vineyard before Cardinal Scipio Borghese turned it into a park in about 1600,' Anna told them. 'Rome acquired it from the Borghese family in 1903 and now everyone can use it. It's about a hundred and fifty acres; the largest park in Rome.'

It was certainly impressive, although perhaps a little wilder than its London counterparts. Liz's eye was drawn to a large lake, in the centre of which was an island and a small Ionic temple, which she thought invited moonlight trysts. There were other temples in the park as well as fountains and statues.

The Villa Borghese dominated everything, its white walls gleaming in the late autumn sunshine. A twin staircase led up to a balustraded terrace, behind which were tall windows simply but elegantly arched. 'Napoleon's favourite sister Pauline lived here for a while,' Bruno said. 'She married Camillo Borghese eight months after her first husband died. By all accounts she was quite a goer and had strings of lovers even after she married. She scandalised Roman society when she commissioned Canova to do a couple of sculptures of her and posed for him almost completely nude. I'll show you one of the pieces when we go inside.'

Ten minutes later they stood in front of Canova's statue. 'Well she was certainly a looker!' Paul said, grinning at Bruno and doing his best not to focus on Pauline Borghese's beautiful breasts.

'Not only that, but by discarding the usual drapery and having herself sculpted in neo-Classical style, she succeeded in transforming herself into a goddess!' Bruno added. 'I hope you've noticed the apple in her right hand; I'd say she looks like the archetypal temptress. Now -' Bruno paused for effect, 'I want to show you the masterwork of a master sculptor.'

He led the way into an adjoining room and they were soon admiring Bernini's Apollo and Daphne. 'It's wonderful!' Liz exclaimed as she gazed at what she could only describe as moving marble. Compared with this the Canova looked much too static. The sculptor had portrayed Apollo at the moment he caught up with Daphne after chasing her through the forest. But the moment he touched her she began to turn into a tree. Daphne was holding up in horror the hands that were already metamorphosing into leaves and the bark of the tree was rapidly imprisoning her legs. Soon she would lose her human identity and Bernini had managed to convey accurately the shock of the moment. 'I think that is one of the most moving pieces I've ever seen,' Liz said and then added, 'in every sense of the word. Look at the way Apollo's draperies stream out behind him. He looks as if he were still running!'

'There's one more piece you must see before we leave,' Bruno said and they all moved into the next gallery to look at another Bernini; Pluto Abducting Proserpina.

'He seems to have had a thing about capturing women,' Paul said. 'Did he have an unsatisfactory love life and was this his way of getting his own back?'

'I don't think there was a shortage of women in his life, but if I'm honest it's his work that interests me rather than who he slept with,' Bruno said, before pointing out the imprints of Pluto's fingers in Proserpina's flesh.

'She didn't want to be captured, did she?' Liz added. 'See how she has her hands up in an attempt to ward him off? I can't say I blame her, Pluto looks terrifying, and the way he's grabbed her! You can see she's not going to get away, can't you?'

'Tomorrow I'll take you to the church of Santa Maria della Vittoria and show you perhaps Bernini's finest work, but I won't spoil it by telling you too much in advance.' Bruno was in heaven, indulging his love of sculpture and sharing it with sympathetic friends.

'Well I don't know about anybody else, but I'm ready for a drink and a bath,' Paul said, glancing round quickly at everybody as if to gauge the likely response. 'Will it be possible to get a taxi back, do you think? I don't fancy that long walk across the park, if I'm honest.'

'Sure. We'll go out by the other exit,' Anna said. 'I'm afraid Bruno gets carried away when he's looking at works of art.'

Liz reached for Paul's hand as they walked away from the Villa and squeezed it. 'Thanks for the intervention,' she said. 'I'll join you in that bath.'

'Don't expect miracles, I'm low on energy right now.'

Liz glanced quickly up at his face and saw lines of tiredness etched around his mouth. She reminded herself that he'd driven halfway across Europe and she'd forgotten how tiring sightseeing could be. Various strategies for an easy evening began to turn over in her mind. There'd be no point in suggesting that they all eat at the hotel. Anna wouldn't enjoy a single mouthful, but would worry her way through the meal thinking about what it was costing. Perhaps at least she should invite them up to their room to use whatever facilities they needed and then they could simply walk to the nearest restaurant and, with any luck, have an early night.

Anna spared her from making a decision. 'We have one or two things we really must do, could you give us a couple of hours do you think? We'll stop by your hotel sometime between seven thirty and eight and find a place to eat that won't cost a fortune.' Liz sent up a silent thank you to anyone who might be listening. Anna had just offered them a priceless gift - a whole two hours of free time!

'God I'm bushed!' Paul said as soon as they were in the privacy of their room. 'I keep telling myself how lucky I am to have someone like Bruno to show me around Rome. If we were here on our own we'd be walking around like everyone else, poring over a map. Just think of it, I might have missed Napoleon's sister!'

Liz stuck her tongue out at him and poured them both a gin and tonic. 'I'm glad you bought this on the ferry,' she said, tapping the side of the gin bottle. 'It's at times like this that I really know why I married you.'

'Surely not for the gin?'

'Absolutely not. For your foresight. I'll go and run a bath.'

'Now I know why I married *you*.' Paul raised his glass in a brief salute as Liz disappeared into the bathroom.

They climbed gratefully into the bath, complete with drinks which Paul had topped up. 'Now I know what Heaven feels like.' Liz leaned back, closed her eyes and sighed deeply, thankful that the tub was big enough for two.

'I still think the other place might be more fun.' Paul put his glass on the floor and began to soap himself.

'It couldn't be more fun than this.' Liz opened one eye.

'All I can say is you're very easy to please.'

Normally Liz would have issued a challenge - "Try me" or "Let me show you!" - But there was something in his face that stopped her. He seemed to be making heavy weather of the simple task of washing himself and Liz thought that he was probably a good deal more tired than he was admitting. 'We could forget about dinner and go straight to bed,' she said. 'I'll get dressed and make an excuse to Anna and Bruno.'

'No. After all we're only here for a long weekend and God knows when we'll all manage to meet up again. I'll be fine in a few minutes.'

Liz jumped out of the bath, wrapped herself in a towel and began to massage his shoulders, trying to transmit some of her own energy into him. More than anything she wanted to curl up in bed with him so that they could recover from all the sightseeing, but she knew that if they did recovery would be the last thing on the agenda. 'Why don't you have a nap for half an hour,' she suggested. 'I promise I won't let you sleep on.'

'I think I might just do that,' Paul said, pulling out the plug and climbing slowly out of the tub. 'Sorry. I'm behaving like an old man.'

'I'll switch the bedroom light out and do my face in the bathroom. You'll find it easier to sleep in the dark.' Liz turned back the bedcover and grabbed her make-up bag before killing the lights. As soon as Paul was settled she retreated to the bathroom, wondering how on earth she was going to spend half an hour putting on her face. Then she immediately cursed herself for worrying about such an unimportant thing when what really mattered was Paul's tiredness and his survival of the evening ahead. She pushed her previous concerns about their future together to the back of her mind. It had been a tiring day and coming so soon after their journey perhaps it had been too much for Paul. She hoped the rest would revive him so he'd be able to get through the evening ahead without falling asleep.

CHAPTER FIVE

Bruno and Anna were waiting in the foyer when Liz and Paul came down. Anna looked uncomfortable, as if she were there under false pretences. Bruno on the other hand appeared completely at home. He was wearing a dark corduroy jacket, his concession to dressing up, which although of fine quality had definitely seen better days. His silvery hair was freshly brushed. He wore it rather longer than was fashionable and it curled slightly just above his collar. Anna had changed the thick wool skirt she'd worn earlier in the day for a thinner one which looked as if it had been lying at the bottom of her wardrobe for several weeks, the creases all too visible. Liz, in her plain black dress and her new amber necklace, felt a touch overdressed and wished she could think of an excuse to run back to their room and change.

Bruno jumped to his feet the moment they appeared and began to walk towards the exit. 'I hope you don't mind, but we ran into some friends earlier and asked them to join us at the restaurant,' he said. 'Hans is a Lutheran pastor, currently working in Augsburg and he's at the Ecumenical Council as a protestant observer.' He offered no further explanation and Liz's spirits sank as her hopes for a quiet evening with two close friends receded. She glanced quickly at Paul who was making noises of assent and silently agreed with him that there really wasn't another way to respond.

The restaurant was tucked away in a side street and exuded an old world charm with dark oak tables, panelled walls and crimson velvet upholstery. An appetising smell of cooking made their nostrils twitch. Bruno called for a carafe of wine and they sipped appreciatively whilst studying the menu. Hans and his wife arrived ten minutes later and Bruno introduced everyone before calling for more wine.

Hans Lebermann apologised for their lateness and for still wearing his clerical collar. He'd been at a special briefing which had gone on far longer than he'd expected. On closer inspection he looked a little weary as anyone might who'd been concentrating for most of the day on Church doctrine. His wife, Ruth, was English and well-upholstered, but the spare flesh looked as if it was kept in place by a firm corset. Her face was innocent of make-up, her grey hair had been permed into curls the size of chipolata sausages. She was wearing a grey pleated skirt, a white silk shirt and a hand knitted Fair Isle cardigan.

Paul immediately began talking to her, asking what she found to do with herself whilst her husband was in session, if this was her first trip to Rome and if she worked full time in Hans' diocese. As Liz watched she saw Ruth visibly warming towards him. He was holding her gaze and appeared to be listening to every word she said as if his future happiness depended on her responses to his questions. She'd noticed before that he had this facility and had teased him about it many times, calling him an old smoothie. It wasn't as if he deliberately set out to win people over, but just that he had a natural and effortless way of communicating so that perfect strangers meeting him at a party would remember him as: "That charming man with the slightly foreign accent."

Liz's knowledge of ecumenism was absolute zero, added to which she was not and never had been a regular churchgoer, so doubted her ability to maintain a conversation with Hans for very long if she pursued religious lines. The only thing she knew about Luther was that he'd successfully challenged the supremacy of the Roman Catholic Church and that his ninety five theses had subsequently caused outrage in Rome. This made her wonder why the Pope had invited protestant observers, Lutheran in particular, to the Council and she asked Hans how he saw his role. He explained that historically there was conflict between established Catholic teaching and religious freedom and one of his tasks and that of his fellow observers would be to decide what model of religious freedom should be put before the Council. Lutherans, he elaborated, did not regard ecumenical councils and their canons as binding on the conscience except when Council decisions followed scripture; then they were considered authoritative. He told her there was presently a good buzz within the Vatican and the feeling that in an updated Church there would be new opportunities for evangelisation, for dispelling bigotry and for stimulating missionary activity as well as a new emphasis on charity and social justice.

To Liz it all sounded a bit too good to be true given the diversity of opinions and backgrounds that had to be accommodated and she confided this to Hans who shrugged and said, 'If we don't try we don't achieve. It's as simple as that.'

She was spared from further exploration of the subject when their food arrived. She'd ordered Fritto Misto and was pleased to see several different kinds of seafood on her plate as well as a selection of vegetables, all of them coated with a light batter. The tails of the fish curled upwards so they looked almost flippant. Bruno had ordered Trippa Romano, but she saw him look longingly at her plate.

'Would you like to try some?' she invited, knowing from past experience of eating with Bruno that he liked to pick and mix. He didn't need persuading and swiftly speared a piece of red mullet and a small courgette before offering her some of his tripe. Fortunately her Yorkshire grandmother had introduced her to tripe and onions during the war, one of the few foods not rationed and relatively easy to obtain. It was so rarely available in England nowadays that she'd almost forgotten it was still considered a delicacy in some parts of Europe. It was one of the few foods that Paul disliked and she saw him look away as Bruno spooned some onto her plate.

'Has anyone heard the news this evening?' Hans asked the table at large. Four days earlier John F Kennedy had announced the discovery of Russian missile installations in Cuba, which had been picked up by routine reconnaissance photographs. He'd made a statement to the effect that if any nuclear missile was launched from Cuba it would be regarded as an attack on the US by Russia and demanded that the Soviets remove all of their offensive weapons immediately. Tension had been building on both sides ever since and Kennedy had ordered low level reconnaissance missions every two hours. Only yesterday he'd indicated that the US was preparing for military action.

Ruth said she understood that Krushchev had written to Kennedy. She wasn't sure about the contents of the letter but knew that, if an agreement was not reached fairly soon, there was a real chance of nuclear war breaking out between the two countries.

Liz thought of their two children back home without their parents. Would Maria know what to do, or anyone else in the hotel for that matter? She caught Paul's eye. 'I think if a nuclear war were imminent we'd have some kind of warning,' he said, trying to sound as cheerful as possible. 'I would think the aftermath of Hiroshima would be enough to deter anyone from following that route, don't you?'

There were murmurs of agreement from around the table. The three men remembered only too well the reasons for their exit from Austria and each had their own horror story. One of Paul's friends had smuggled out a large diamond brooch when she left Vienna. Her mother had stitched it into the hem of her coat as an insurance against future privations of whatever sort. If it had been discovered Paul was quite certain that she would have been shot and the diamonds looted. His own mother as the wife of a Jew had been forced to live in the ghetto in Vienna and, although she had never spoken about that time, subsequent post-war newsreel footage had shown the world just what terrible places the ghettoes were and to survive at all showed him just how resilient she was.

Liz, desperate to lighten what was rapidly turning into a gloomy evening, turned to Bruno. 'Are we anywhere near the Trevi fountain?' she asked. 'If so, I'd love to take a quick look on the way back to the hotel.' Her hectic life with Paul had taught her to make the most of opportunities as they presented.

'It's about a five minute walk just around the next corner; it will be easy to take a look on the way back.' His face lit up at the prospect of showing off not just another work of art but a truly memorable piece of sculpture and he immediately emptied his coffee cup and called for the bill.

The Lebermanns pleaded an early start the following morning and said goodbye as soon as they reached the restaurant exit. Bruno tucked his arm through Liz's and walked her briskly towards Via Fontane. She heard the sound of water long before they turned the final corner and saw one of the most visited and famous fountains in the world in all its rococo splendour. The area was still crowded although it was late evening and Liz's mouth gaped as she looked at the most stunning fountain she'd ever seen.

'The original was built at the end of an aqueduct, the Aqua Virgo, in 19BC.' Bruno was off again, enthusing about his favourite subject. 'This model wasn't built until 1762. Of course you'll recognise Neptune.' He pointed to the central figure, riding in a shell-shaped chariot pulled by two magnificently prancing horses, each one guided by a Triton. 'The horses symbolise the moods of the sea,' he went on. 'You can see that one is calm and restrained whilst the other is restive.'

'They're just like the two cats in the hotel,' Liz said. 'Omar is docile, but Khayyam doesn't give a toss about anybody and never comes when he's called.'

'Ridiculous names for cats,' Bruno said. 'Whom do they have to thank for their christening?'

'Antonia I imagine, they are after all *her* cats.' Liz shrugged her shoulders dismissively, not wanting to think about Antonia.

Bruno and Anna had stayed at the hotel on their first visit to England after the war. From what she'd heard from Anna, the visit hadn't been an unqualified success. Returning at the end of one afternoon, tired from sightseeing and with two small and fractious children in tow, Anna had overheard Antonia complaining to one of the staff about giving free accommodation to "those Jews". Although Paul had invited them to stay on future trips, they'd always declined.

Paul. Where was he? Liz noticed suddenly that he wasn't standing next to Anna and felt panic begin to rise. She looked around trying to find him. The area was well lit, including the fountain which was floodlit, but there were a lot of people standing around and it took Liz a little time to find some kind of orientation. Eventually she spotted him, sitting on a low wall, a little way back from the fountain's basin. She left Bruno and walked across to him.

'Are you all right darling?' She sat down beside him on the wall and took his hand. It felt cold and clammy.

'I don't feel all that brilliant to be honest. In fact right this minute I doubt if I could summon enough energy to get up.' He had beads of sweat on his upper lip and his face was the colour of putty.

'Was it something you ate?' Paul never drank too much, so that line of questioning was unnecessary.

'I don't think it's an upset tummy, but I feel really wretched. Can you ask Bruno to call a cab? I'm sure I'll feel better once I get to bed.'

Liz waved to Bruno to attract his attention, but he was still gazing at the fountain and it was Anna who finally spotted her and came over. 'Do you think you can call a cab?' Liz asked, trying to keep the panic out of her voice for Paul's sake. 'Paul isn't feeling too well and I think we should try to get him home as soon as possible.'

'Our best bet is the Via Barbarini.' Anna waved her arm around the pedestrian area to enforce the futility of trying to get a cab to come to them. 'I'll get Bruno to give you a hand with Paul.' She walked back to where Bruno was still standing gazing at the fountain and spoke quickly to him, at the same time pointing towards Paul. Bruno immediately came over, put his arm around his old friend and helped him to stand. Liz went around to the other side and together they began to walk away from the fountain.

'I'll go on ahead,' Anna said. 'Take your time and I'll try to have a taxi waiting for you.'

The three of them began to walk slowly. What had seemed like a few steps moments ago now seemed like a route march. Step by painful step they crawled towards the Via Barbarini. Liz had Paul's arm around her neck and felt his weight bearing down on her shoulder. Her terror was all inside and she cursed herself for not noticing earlier that Paul was feeling rough. If she hadn't asked Bruno to show her the Trevi Fountain Paul could be tucked up in bed by now. If she'd insisted on driving some of the time instead of letting Paul take the wheel the whole way from England he could have slept in the car, although she knew from past experience that this was unlikely. Thank goodness for Bruno and Anna, she daren't think about how she would have managed on her own.

Somehow they made it to the Via Barbarini and miraculously Anna was waiting with a taxi. Between them they half lifted, half dragged Paul into the back seat.

'I've got pins and needles in my right side,' he said, as soon as he was settled. Liz felt her heart contract in anguish and began to rub his right arm to try to get the circulation going even as she did so feeling it was a futile gesture. She heard Anna ask the driver to take them to the nearest 'ospedale' and didn't argue with the decision, but marvelled at the calm and decisive way in which Anna had taken control.

'Listen! I want to tell you something!' Paul's voice sounded urgent against her ear.

'Try not to talk darling,' Liz said. 'Whatever you want to say will keep until you're feeling better.' She kissed his mouth closed, wishing she could wave a magic wand and take them back to yesterday when Paul had been fit and happy.

'Listen!' Paul said again, this time more impatiently. A split second later his head slumped onto her shoulder and he lost consciousness.

Anna was urging the driver to go 'a rapido'. It seemed to Liz as if he were on a deliberate go-slow, unlike just about every other motorist in Rome. This had to be some kind of nightmare she was living through. Any minute now she would wake up in a cold sweat, thankful it had all been some awful dream. But the street lights weren't part of any flight of fancy, nor the muted sound of traffic filtering into the taxi and she wasn't imagining the weight of Paul's body slumped against her. She recognised the Via del Corso and knew they would soon be passing their hotel and reluctantly accepted that this was the present, a grim reality which even in her darkest moments she'd never imagined.

Within ten minutes the driver stopped in front of the hospital. It was nearly midnight and there wasn't a soul in sight. Paul was still unconscious and there was no way that Bruno, even with help from the taxi driver, could get him inside the hospital. 'I'll try and find someone to help us,' Anna said and disappeared into the building. The minutes stretched and, although Liz wanted to scream, she waited in total silence holding Paul's hand until Anna reappeared with two porters and a wheel chair.

They were taken into a small room just off the reception area and waited again whilst one of the porters disappeared. 'He's gone to find a doctor,' Anna explained.

Liz stared silently at Paul's inert body and felt cold fingers shredding her heart. She willed Paul to open his eyes, to rally in some way, to grin at her and tell her not to worry, that everything was going to be all right. He remained slumped in the wheel chair, breathing stertorously in a way that was so unlike him that she felt fresh waves of terror.

The door opened and the porter returned with a man she assumed was a doctor judging by the stethoscope hanging from his pocket. It looked so casual it was almost as if he'd shoved it there as an afterthought. He was wearing pyjamas under his white coat and was smoking a cigarette, which he extinguished by squeezing the end between his thumb and index finger. 'Buona sera,' he said to the room at large, before walking over to Paul and feeling his pulse.

'Parla Inglese?' Anna asked. It seemed to Liz that she was the only one who'd retained not only the power of speech but the presence of mind to ask the right questions. The doctor looked at each of them in turn before shrugging his shoulders. 'Non.' His reply reminded Liz that she wasn't dreaming but in the middle of a real life nightmare. It didn't take them long to reach the conclusion that their combined knowledge of Italian was totally inadequate to describe Paul's medical history.

With a quick flash of inspiration she felt in Paul's pockets and retrieved, from the top one inside his jacket, a strip of tablets wrapped in tinfoil: his current medication. She handed them to the doctor at the same time thinking, *how many hundreds of different kinds of pills are there on the planet and what are the chances that this doctor will recognise them and be able to diagnose what's happening to Paul?*

Tears of frustration stung the back of her eyes. 'What the hell am I going to do?' she said to Anna. 'How can I tell this man about Paul's medical history when my knowledge of Italian would just about stretch to buying aspirin if I had a headache?'

'I'll ring the British Consul,' Anna said with a determination which left Liz staring at her open-mouthed.

'But it's after midnight, Anna. We can't expect anyone to answer the telephone at this time of night.'

'Crises don't always happen conveniently between the hours of nine and five o'clock!' Anna said. At that precise moment Paul vomited violently. The porters produced cloths to clean him up and somehow in the ensuing disruption Anna negotiated the use of the telephone with the doctor. Liz, partly occupied by wiping around Paul's mouth, heard Anna speaking into the instrument and realised thankfully that she'd been wrong to assume that no one would bother to answer. Anna held out the receiver, 'I've got a vice-consul on the line,' she said, 'would you like to explain Paul's symptoms to him?' Liz crossed the room to continue the call.

'I'm really sorry to disturb you so late,' she began, 'but my husband is very sick and I need someone who can explain his symptoms to the doctor.' She was reassured by the English voice at the other end of the line telling her that they were there to help at any hour of the day or night. She explained Paul's high blood pressure, the drug he was taking to control it, that he not only lived a very busy life back home but had driven the best part of a thousand miles in the last five days. Almost as an afterthought she mentioned that his mother had died earlier in the year after her third stroke so, she suggested, perhaps there was a hereditary factor to be considered as well as the frantic lifestyle her husband insisted on living.

The voice promised to relay all this information to the doctor and to call at the hospital in the morning in case he could be of further service. 'Which hospital is it by the way?' he asked. 'I haven't the faintest idea,' she said. She turned to Anna. 'Do you know which hospital we're in?'

'San Giacomo.' The doctor answered the question almost before she'd finished asking it. Liz handed him the telephone. 'Perhaps you'd be kind enough to tell the vice-consul,' she said, even though he'd already told her he didn't speak English. She watched as he listened for a few minutes to the voice at the other end. With relief she saw comprehension slowly spread across his face, like the rays of the sun illuminating a previously dark space. He replaced the receiver and said a few words to Anna, slowly in Italian, miming to accompany his words in case she hadn't understood. Finally he pointed upwards and Liz assumed that he was proposing to admit Paul.

'I'd better stay with him,' she said to Anna. 'Thank you both for all your help. I honestly don't know what I'd have done without you.' She put her arms around Anna and kissed her goodnight feeling a choking sensation in her throat. Bruno kissed her on both cheeks. 'Try to get some sleep,' she said to both of them and watched as they walked away into the Roman night where there was still action and bustle and normality.

Two men in uniform led the way towards the lift and then into a large ward which was in near darkness but punctuated by dim lights over the separate beds so that it was still possible to see. She helped them remove Paul's jacket and trousers and watched as they put him into bed. One of them indicated a chair by the bedside and she sat down gratefully, suddenly feeling an overwhelming tiredness. The two men had a brief conversation before the elder of the two disappeared. The younger man took a chair from beside the next bed before sitting down on the same side as Liz. She found his company reassuring, afraid of not knowing what to do if Paul's condition should suddenly change.

She took Paul's hand and squeezed it, trying to communicate

some kind of comfort, hoping he could still recognise her touch. The only movement came from the bed opposite as the occupant got out, retrieved a urine bottle from his bedside locker and peed into it. Seeing him made her realise she was sitting in a ward full of sick men and she wondered how many of them had noticed her presence and, if so, if they minded. In an attempt to escape from her surroundings and the nightmare of the evening she leaned forward, put her head against Paul's hand and tried to sleep.

An hour later she woke, disturbed by the sound of Paul vomiting again. She helped the attendant clean him up and then slept briefly until dawn. She opened her eyes but her head remained on the bed. Was it her imagination or could she feel something rubbing against her knee? She stayed quite still. Yes, there it was again, a slow backwards and forwards movement. After the nightmare of the last few hours she should have been ready for anything. Except that the anything she was now feeling was somehow out of context and belonged to another scenario altogether. Slowly she lifted her head and, as she did so, the attendant moved back in his chair, smiling uncertainly at her.

Liz pushed her chair away from him. Her cheeks burned with embarrassment as she tried not to think about which bit of him had been rubbing against her. She leaned forward and stroked Paul's forehead, which felt hot and sticky, then fished in her bag for a hanky, dipped it into a flask of water on the bedside locker and wiped him slowly and carefully as if there were nothing else in the world she'd rather be doing at that precise moment.

To Liz's relief the ward sister appeared. A short, stout, brisk woman who looked around the ward, came across to Paul's bed, took in the scenario, and addressed herself directly to the man. Liz caught the words 'partire' and 'adesso' and gathered they were being asked to leave. She needed no second bidding. After the night she'd just spent, the last thing she wanted was the sight of a dozen men performing their early morning ablutions and she followed the attendant out of the ward.

Once they reached the corridor he turned towards her, lifted an imaginary cup to his lips and spoke the magic word 'Caffe' before beckoning her to follow him. Liz reckoned he'd be ready to go off duty as soon as he'd downed a coffee and, anticipating some kind of staff canteen, she smiled tentatively and trailed after him. The small room in which she found herself a couple of minutes later was a long way from a canteen. The word sluice sprang to mind, but she noticed that there was a kettle in one corner and assumed he knew what he was doing. There were no chairs, so presumably their stay would be fairly short.

The coffee, when he finally presented it in an espresso-sized cup, was lukewarm and tasted terrible. After the first sip Liz downed it in one gulp as if she were drinking medicine. 'Grazie,' she said, handing back the cup, wanting more than anything to escape the confines of this windowless little room. She eyed him warily, half afraid of what he might do next, at the same time reasoning that his instinct for self-preservation would surely prevent him from doing anything he might later regret. To her relief he beckoned her once again and this time took her to an office, spoke briefly to an assistant and promptly disappeared.

CHAPTER SIX

An assistant pulled back a chair in front of a small table and then gave Liz a form and a pen with which to complete it. The form, written in three languages, French, German and English, covered three sides of foolscap paper. Liz quickly wrote in Paul's name, age, address and their telephone number and then tried to answer the questions about his medical history. It wasn't long before she realised how little she knew of his childhood ailments. Had he ever had measles, chicken pox, mumps? She'd been married to this man for four years and had no idea if he'd had measles. She chewed the end of the pen, wondering what to do. Should she make an educated guess or tell the truth? She opted for the latter and simply wrote "don't know."

The form then moved on to details of both his parents and their medical history. His mother was easy, at least Liz knew how she had died, but what to say about his father? She was tempted to write "Murdered in Dachau, possibly as a result of poisoning by Cyclon B gas." But after thinking for a moment she put "Killed during World War Two."

She ploughed on through the other questions realising what heavy weather she was making of a fairly routine form. After half an hour of thinking, chewing the end of the pen and mentally beating herself up for not knowing more about Paul's medical history, she answered the last question and braced herself for whatever she would have to deal with next.

She handed the form back to the assistant and then waited, feeling scruffy and inappropriately dressed, longing for a bath and the chance to put on a new face and more casual clothes. She fingered the amber necklace finding much-needed comfort in the warmth and smoothness of the beads. There were things to do today, like finding out how much money they had with them and if Paul had taken out any insurance. In the future she would play a more active part in their business affairs. How could she have been so feeble and feminine to sit back and leave Paul to make all the decisions?

Would he be capable of making decisions when he recovered? Would his speech be affected? Would he remember he had a wife and two children? Would he know his name? He was fluent in both English and German, would he forget the English and speak only German? The thoughts went round and round and were both a blessing, because they kept her mind occupied, and a curse because she could only guess at the answers.

She was assuming the worst. That Paul had suffered a stroke which might leave some kind of permanent disability. But if she expected the most awful outcome anything less would be a bonus. He was too young to be disabled. She daren't think about what Antonia might do or say once she knew the truth. What if he couldn't work? What would they do then? Where would they live? Their flat went with the job. Thank goodness she still had Ivy House. That was a real bonus. She began to feel better and mentally squared her shoulders. *Don't worry Paul,* she said to herself, *somehow or another we're going to get through this.*

Her thoughts were interrupted by the arrival of the vice-consul. He was tall and slim with greying hair which, although thinning, still waved slightly on the right side of his parting. His moustache echoed the colour of his hair and he was dressed in a well cut grey suit of Prince of Wales check.

'Mrs Hirsch? I'm Michael Shand, British Consular Service.' He came towards her hand outstretched and grasped hers with both his own. His voice was a credit to whichever English public school had been responsible for his education.

'I can't tell you how glad I am to see you.' He looked so reassuringly English that Liz wanted to embrace him on the spot.

'I'm so sorry to hear about your husband. How is he this morning?'

'Still unconscious I'm afraid. I think he must have had a stroke. I told you last night that his mother had similar problems.'

'Indeed. The doctors normally do their rounds at about ten o'clock. I suggest we make our way to his ward beforehand then I can have a word and put them in the picture.'

He handed her his card as they walked towards Paul's ward and told her to ring him any time she needed help. He invited her to use the embassy address as a poste restante. 'Hotels don't always pass on the mail as efficiently as we would like.' He smiled apologetically before asking her, 'Are you all right for money?'

If I'd had a father, Liz thought, *I would have liked him to be just like this!*

'There are some traveller's cheques back at the hotel and whatever cash Paul has in his notecase. I'm not sure how much. I have a little money of my own, just pocket money really, nothing very substantial.'

'I'm assuming your husband signed your traveller's cheques? If you need to cash any I'll come with you to the bank on Monday and we can sort it all out then.'

By this time they'd reached Paul's ward. Liz's first instinct was to walk straight in to see if there'd been any change in his condition, but remembering her earlier encounter with the sister she hung back. 'It's all systems go at this time in the morning to get everything ready for doctor's rounds,' Michael Shand said, showing a knowledge of hospital procedure, which surprised Liz. The corridor was conveniently lined with benches and they both sat down to wait.

Ten minutes later a group of doctors appeared. There must have been at least six of them and Liz wondered idly why it took so many at one time to make a daily survey of the patients. They looked amazingly well turned out, wearing smartly cut suits under their white coats, and she couldn't help but contrast them with the doctor they'd seen the previous evening.

Michael Shand rose to his feet, walked purposefully over to the group and then beckoned Liz to join him. A man, who Liz assumed was the senior consultant, shook her hand and murmured 'Signora,' in a way which, under any other circumstances, would have made her go weak at the knees. The vice-consul passed on all he knew about Paul's illness. Occasionally the consultant interrupted to ask a question, which Michael Shand then referred to Liz. He switched between English and Italian with rapid fluency and Liz found herself warming towards him as the conversation progressed.

When the consultant was satisfied that he had all the information he needed, he disappeared into the ward with his fellow doctors. Liz and the vice-consul resumed their seats and waited for them to reappear. After twenty minutes or so they emerged and, to Liz's amazement, paused at the entrance to the ward and, as if obeying a hidden signal, they all lit cigarettes. It was then she noticed the large ashtray standing on the floor at the entrance to the ward and realised its significance.

They stood in a group and talked for a few minutes before the consultant came over and spoke briefly to the vice-consul, glancing at Liz from time-to-time to include her in their conversation. When he'd finished he rejoined the group, they extinguished their cigarettes and went on to the next ward. Liz wondered how many packs they managed to get through in a day.

'They're going to give your husband a lumbar puncture.' Michael Shand's face now wore a sympathetic expression. 'They think that in all probability your husband had a brain haemorrhage, but the lumbar puncture will confirm it.'

It sounded so blatant. Liz didn't want to put a name to whatever was wrong with Paul. Deep inside her head she still nurtured the faint hope that there had been some dreadful mistake. That Paul was merely recovering after the stresses and strains of the journey and would wake up at any moment and demand to know what all the fuss was about. But, now that a member of the medical profession had actually put a name to what might be wrong, the last vestiges of hope were extinguished as easily as a guttering candle.

Suddenly Liz remembered a phrase from her conversation

with Michael Shand. She'd told him that Paul had some cash in his notecase. They'd been out to dinner last night and Paul would have taken his notecase with him. She remembered helping the porters to take off his jacket and trousers. At the time she'd been so distressed she hadn't thought to go through the pockets. So where were his clothes now? She must find them.

She turned to the vice-consul and voiced her concerns. 'Do you think you could have a word with the sister for me?' she asked him. 'I suppose it would make sense to take his clothes back to the hotel, rather than leave them lying around here,' she added feeling almost disloyal to Paul as she spoke. Suppose he regained consciousness and wanted to get dressed. How would he feel? The rational side of her brain dismissed the thought as nonsense. If he did come round there would have to be a period of recuperation and further assessment before the hospital discharged him and she would be able to bring his clothes when the time was right.

Michael Shand returned with the sister. 'Your husband's clothes are in his bedside locker,' he said. 'If you go with Sister now she'll show you where. In the meantime,' he paused briefly and looked at his watch, 'I think I've done just about all I can for the moment, so I'll be on my way. Don't forget you have my number if I or one of my colleagues can be of further help.'

Liz thanked him, they shook hands briefly and she turned and followed the sister into the ward. She kept her eyes on the floor, remembering the previous evening and not wishing to see any bits of male anatomy that were normally off-limits. As she bent to open the door of Paul's locker a couple of porters arrived to take him down to theatre. She stood up guiltily, as if caught in the act of pinching her own husband's property, and watched as they transferred Paul from his bed to a trolley. His eyes remained closed. His face had neither colour nor expression. She watched them take him away before returning reluctantly to his locker.

Bruno and Anna were waiting in the corridor as she left the ward. Liz gave them an up-to-date bulletin. 'I'm going to wait until I know the result of the test,' she said, 'and then I think I'll take these clothes back to the hotel and tidy myself up a bit.' She knew they were short of time, remembering they had a deadline for leaving the city. 'If you have things you want to do,' she said, taking Anna's hand and squeezing it, 'I promise you I'll be all right.' She looked from one to the other desperately wanting them to stay, but at the same time realising they had their own agenda.

Bruno put his arm around her shoulder. 'There's nothing pressing we have to do. We'll wait with you for the result of the test and then we'll go back to the hotel with you. By then you'll probably be ready for some lunch.'

Suddenly the tears which Liz had been holding back all night flowed freely down her face. She felt in the pocket of Paul's jacket and pulled out his handkerchief. She could smell him as she blew her nose and his scent made her tears flow more copiously. 'I'm sorry, I'm so sorry,' she sobbed. A chasm had opened separating the happiness of the last few days from the utter desolation of now. She felt she was letting Paul down in some way by giving way to her emotions and was relieved that he couldn't see her.

A trolley was wheeled past them in the corridor and she realised that Paul had returned from theatre. She blew her nose and mopped her eyes one last time before shoving the sodden handkerchief into her bag. The senior consultant was speaking to Anna. His face looked grave and, as he spoke, Anna flipped through the pages of her dictionary, but Liz caught the word "emorragia" and needed no further definition. She wished it didn't sound like another nail in Paul's coffin.

Anna disappeared briefly into the ward. 'I've left the number of our flat,' she told Liz when she returned. 'There's nothing more we can do for the moment. I've told them we'll be back later this afternoon.' She tucked her arm through Liz's and together they left the hospital. Liz felt guilty for leaving Paul behind, but knew that if their situations were reversed he would do the same. She inhaled the smell of him from his clothes as they walked down the Via del Corso trying to draw some of his strength from the fabric and wondering how on earth she was going to break the news to Antonia.

'I'll have to telephone Antonia.' She looked first at Anna and then at Bruno as they sat around the table in the Grand Hotel restaurant. She'd been surprised when they'd suggested lunching there, but saw no point in arguing. It was by far the smartest place she'd eaten in since they'd left home and Liz didn't want to think about the cost.

'You must try to keep your spirits up,' Bruno advised. 'I can't think it's going to be an easy conversation, however sensitively you try to break the news.'

Liz knew that neither Anna nor Bruno had much time for Antonia and it was a comfort to know that all three of them were on the same side. 'I'm not really very hungry.' She looked briefly at the menu, watched the words swim into each other and felt incapable of making any decision even about a simple thing like what to have for lunch.

'Some soup would be good. Yes?' Anna smiled across the table, her face radiating concern.

'Soup will be fine. Will you choose for me?' Liz felt that, whatever the choice, the odds on her tasting the food were remote.

'Tre Zuppa La Ferdinando,' Bruno spoke briefly to the waiter before turning back to Liz. 'This soup is a classical Italian dish associated with the Grand Duke of Tuscany,' he explained and Liz smiled in spite of herself thinking, *good old Bruno, bringing history into the choosing of food*! If she asked him to tell her more about the Grand Duke and exactly why he'd had a soup named after him, he'd be sure to know and would be wasting his time utterly. Her brain was so worn out she couldn't take in any more information.

The waiter reappeared and placed a very large, very deep plate in front of each of them. The flavour wafted upwards on a delicate spiral of steam and Liz's hand moved instinctively towards her spoon, but stopped abruptly as she gazed into the depths of the plate. A single, perfectly spherical, poached egg floated plum in the middle of a generous pool of clear soup. At the very bottom she could see a few morsels of chopped chicken. Some shreds of torn basil leaves kept the egg company. *Oh my God! It's the Cyclops!* She wanted to laugh aloud and guessed she must be verging on hysteria. She was tempted to shout "Odysseus, where are you?" but the thought of upsetting Bruno and Anna when they were being so kind to her triumphed over her first instinct. She filed the image away thinking to tell Paul when he regained consciousness.

'Do eat a little, it will be good for you.' Anna's voice urged her to reach for her spoon again. *I'm being force-fed,* Liz thought. Not in the violent way of a goose in Perigord or a suffragette in Holloway, but in the gentle way that parents try to persuade their children and, although it still boiled down to force-feeding, Liz knew that whatever it took she would eat every last mouthful of the damned soup.

How could she eat when Paul was fighting for his life a few kilometres away? Was she going to continue feeling guilty for trying to carry on normal patterns of living for the duration of his illness? She dipped her spoon into her plate, taking care not to disturb the poached egg, and at last tasted Ferdinando's speciality. It was quite delicious. Tears came into her eyes and she put down her spoon and took each of their hands in her own. 'Thank you for being so kind. I know you'd much rather be poking round one of your old churches.' She looked at Bruno.

He shrugged, 'The churches will still be here when we come back next year.' But Liz knew that for Bruno every minute spent away from gazing at a Bernini sculpture or a significant Roman monument was wasted time; an unforgiving minute which he'd been unable to fill. She remembered Paul's notecase in her handbag. 'I want you both to know how grateful I am,' she said, 'and I'm sure Paul feels the same and just to prove it he's going to buy us lunch!'

The colour drained from Antonia's face as she listened to Liz's voice and the words began to shape themselves into sentences whose meaning she understood only too clearly. 'So, tell me again. What kind of haemorrhage?' Her voice asked the question to which she didn't want the answer unless it was significantly different from the information she'd just received.

'A *brain* haemorrhage. I'm afraid Paul's had a stroke.'

'How is he?'

'Unconscious I'm afraid.'

'Is he in hospital?'

'Where else would you expect him to be?' Liz spoke through gritted teeth.

Antonia ignored the sarcasm in the last sentence. 'So would you like me to send you the money to fly him home?'

'It's kind of you to offer, but I'm afraid he's too ill to be moved at the moment.'

'You're absolutely sure about that?'

'I only wish I wasn't.'

'Well, if you change your mind my sister knows a very good man in Harley Street.'

'Thank you. I'll bear that in mind and keep you informed.'

Antonia sensed that the conversation was effectively at an end as far as Liz was concerned, but felt no inclination to let her down lightly. 'Marcus is here,' she continued, changing her voice to one of false brightness. 'We've just been out. Would you like to speak to him?' She turned her attention to Marcus. 'It's Mummy. She's calling all the way from Rome. Isn't that nice?'

She picked up Marcus and sat him on her knee and, keeping one hand on the telephone receiver, she put Marcus' hand just above her own. 'Say hello to Mummy,' she urged taking care to keep her own head close to his so that she could hear what Liz was going to say.

'Hello Mummy.'

'Hello darling. Are you having a lovely time?'
'I've been shopping with Auntie Toni.'
'Aren't you a lucky boy?'
'I miss you. Is Papa there?'
'Not at the moment, darling, but we'll be home soon.'
'Promise?'
'I promise. Love you.'
'Love you too. Bye.'

Liz dropped the phone as if it were red hot and burst into tears. Anna sitting next to her had overheard Liz's end of the conversation and put a tentative arm around her shoulders, waiting for the sobs to subside. 'We always knew it wasn't going to be easy,' she said once Liz had cried herself out. 'Perhaps we should be charitable and remind ourselves that your phone call must have been a terrible shock for Antonia.'

'I'm not feeling in the least bit charitable. I swear I'll swing for that bloody woman one of these days. Of all the insensitive, insufferable . . .' Liz ran out of adjectives and shook her fist wildly in the air as an alternative way to let off steam.

'She didn't say she was coming over?' Anna looked across at her.

'No, thank goodness.'

'Well then, at least you've got the best part of a thousand miles between you.'

'Not nearly enough!'

'I was talking to Bruno this morning on the way over to the hospital and we thought perhaps it might be a good idea for you to move into a more modest hotel. This place is fine for a couple of nights, but if you're going to be here for any length of time it could be a bit expensive. What do you think?'

It was so typical of Anna to look at the practicalities, Liz thought. She'd searched through the briefcase in which Paul carried all their maps and paperwork and the only reference to insurance she could find referred to the car, so what Anna had just said made perfect sense.

'I'd ask you to stay at the flat, but it's impossibly small and full of Bruno's papers and all the other clutter we've accumulated whilst we've been here,' Anna apologised. 'There's a small place near the Piazza di Spagna, where you would be comfortable. It's not nearly as grand as this,' she waved her arm indicating Liz's bedroom, 'but it's a fraction of the price.'

'Do you think they'll have a room?' Liz asked. 'My friend in Perugia mentioned that Rome is bursting at the seams at the moment with the Ecumenical Council in full swing.'

'They could take you from tomorrow,' Anna said, confirming what Liz already suspected, that Anna had made the decision for her.

Tomorrow. Sunday. Kate had said she would come over on Sunday and Liz had forgotten all about her until a few minutes ago. 'I need to make another phone call,' she said to Anna. 'I think it would be sensible to ask my friend not to come over as we planned.'

Liz made the phone call to Kate, promising to ring her again later in the week once she knew more about the likely outcome of Paul's illness; then she and Anna rejoined Bruno who was waiting for them in the hotel lounge. 'I've just been catching up on the international news,' he said, putting down the newspaper. 'It seems a U-2 has been shot down over Cuba and Kennedy's advisers who are handling the crisis have just received a second letter from Kruschev. This time he's asking that all US missiles are removed from Turkey in exchange for the Soviet missiles in Cuba. It looks as if the next twenty four hours will be critical.'

The thought of the possibility of a nuclear war paled into insignificance against the despair that Liz was feeling. Surely neither Kruschev nor Kennedy would be insane enough to let it happen? In any event there was nothing that any of them could do to avert the crisis and to sit and worry at this stage wouldn't do any good to anyone. 'If we're all going to be blown to bits at any minute,' she said, 'I think I'd like to be as close to Paul as possible. I'll be perfectly OK on my own and I can find my way to the hospital, so if the two of you would like to go off and do something . . .' She let her voice tail away.

'Wouldn't you like some moral support?' Anna asked, not looking at Bruno.

'You've already done more than enough and I know you're at the stage in your sabbatical when every minute counts.' Liz knew that in a similar situation she would be torn between duty and necessity and felt it only fair to offer them the choice, and in any case desperately wanted some time alone with Paul just to be next to him, hold his hand, talk to him maybe. 'I'll meet you both later, perhaps for a quick bite to eat.' Now that her mind was made up she willed them both to get going.

'Well, if you're absolutely sure,' Anna said.

Liz left them outside the hotel and walked towards the hospital and Paul.

CHAPTER SEVEN

Paul's left side was itching and he longed to reach over and scratch it, but couldn't move his right hand however hard he tried. *That'll teach you to ignore doctor's advice*, he thought, and although that didn't make his present situation any easier at least he *could* still think, so that was a plus.

Keep your pecker up, this is just a temporary setback, he told himself. *A timely warning*. Wasn't that what the medics said when they were trying to convince you that you weren't facing the Grim Reaper after all? He would have to do some strict negotiating with Antonia when they arrived home and convince her once and for all that in future he would need to spend more time outside the hotel, i.e. not working.

It would be a help not to be living over the shop, so finding a house should be a priority and Liz would be onto that in a flash now that they'd both had a fright. Of the two of them, she would probably be the more scared, and he knew would do everything she could to make life easier for both of them in future.

It looked as if he'd have to ease back on his love life for a bit. A pity that. They'd had the best sex ever on this holiday and no wonder with neither the kids nor the intercom to interrupt! Perhaps he'd overdone things, trying to prove he was twenty one again. Fat lot of good it had done him. His mother had always told him never to show off and if she was still alive he would be delighted to tell her how right she was.

And why had he shown off? Not just once, but time after time since the beginning of their holiday, consistently trying to prove to Liz what a formidable combination age and experience was! If only Antonia hadn't told him that worrying story about Liz he wouldn't have tried quite so hard, but there was no point in regretting that now.

Antonia said she'd seen Liz walking into a rival hotel at two thirty in the afternoon holding hands with a perfect stranger - male of course. At first he'd thought that Antonia's indignation was more to do with Liz and her friend patronising one of their competitors, but on reflection he knew that this was just another ploy of Antonia's to try to create a rift between himself and Liz. Why? In God's name why?

Surely she realised that Liz was a permanent part of his life, the mother of his children as well as his chosen partner and best friend? No, now he came to think about it, it wasn't just Liz that Antonia had tried to discredit over the years. She'd always been highly critical of any woman he'd brought back to the hotel. And her criticisms had always been so clever, never direct, but more oblique. 'Are you sure she'll fit in with your circle of friends?' she would ask or, 'Don't you find her voice just a little strident?' 'Do you think she'd make a good mother?' She'd never really enjoyed sharing him with anyone; Bruno and Anna, for instance, and even, on occasions, his own mother.

Perhaps now was a good time to get out from under her, start another business with Liz perhaps? But if they were going to become home owners he would be hard pressed to find enough capital to buy even a modest restaurant. No. Antonia would just have to learn that he needed time for his other responsibilities

Supposing the worst was to happen and he didn't come out of this; what then? How would Liz manage? He'd put by a little money, but it wouldn't take them very far. Thank goodness Liz had her hotel management diploma; at least she would be able to get a job, although it wouldn't be easy with two small children even if they did have an au pair to share the day-to-day routine. He shouldn't really be thinking along these lines, but concentrate instead on mustering every last ounce of his energy and getting better as soon as possible.

Someone took hold of his left hand. He could tell from the feel of the fingers that it was Liz. He wished he had some way of asking her to scratch the maddening itch that refused to go away. But he'd gladly put up with the itch if only he could hold her in his arms again, feel her body relaxing against him, tell her what she meant to him, pay her the compliments that he so seldom had in the past. Come to think of it, the thought of holding her and the feel of her hand should be having a more physical effect. He turned away mentally from the useless organ that now lay between his legs, lolling helplessly inside the bottle that some efficient nurse had placed there to stop him from committing the ultimate degradation for a grown man, that of peeing on the immaculately laundered sheets.

When Liz arrived at the hospital, Paul had been moved into a different, smaller ward. There were only six beds in all and a uniformed porter had been brought in to keep vigil at Paul's bedside. Liz wondered what Paul was thinking about and hoped it wasn't the forthcoming banqueting season. Time enough for that when they arrived home. She assumed the vital part of his brain which controlled thought was still intact. If only she knew a bit more about the effects of a cerebral haemorrhage she would be in a better position to judge.

Nobody in Liz's immediate circle had ever had a stroke, so she knew nothing about the likely post-operative effects. How had his mother been affected by her three strokes? She'd become slower, put on weight, but, more importantly, she hadn't lost her speech and her memory seemed to be intact. At least she'd remembered birthdays and appeared to function in the same way as everyone else. The knowledge provided the first grain of comfort for Liz since Paul first became ill.

She bent forward and whispered in his ear. 'Don't think about a thing except getting better. I've told Antonia and she's accepted that you'll be over here for however long it takes. I also spoke to Marcus who sends his love and to tell you how much he misses you. I said we'd be home soon. Just so you don't worry, I'm still sending a postcard every day to let him know we're fine.'

What she didn't add was that the postcards now had an additional message for Maria on the current state of Paul's health. They read like a contradiction in terms. A printed message for Marcus telling him where they were and what a lovely time they were having and a written footnote for Maria letting her know how ill Paul was.

She continued whispering in Paul's ear. 'The doctors here are doing all they can. They have a male orderly posted by your bed to monitor your condition. I don't think that would happen back home, do you? You're not going to believe this, but he's reading a comic! I can't see the title; it could be a children's comic for all I know.

'I want you to know how much I've enjoyed this week. I don't think it could have been better, do you? I loved our lunch sitting by the lake in Geneva, although it was a bit rushed, and I'll always remember the fantastic rose window in the cathedral in Rheims. It will be great to see the pictures when we get home; an opportunity to remind ourselves of the memories we've created.'

Liz straightened up and, with her free hand, began to rub the crick in her neck. She'd be able to talk to Paul much more easily if she could climb into bed and lie beside him and she wondered how the rest of the occupants of the ward would react if she did. She looked around. All the other patients seemed much older than Paul. Her lack of Italian precluded any kind of sensible conversation. There was an old boy in the corner being visited by his wife and, judging by the tragic expressions on both their faces, they were milking his illness for all it was worth. Liz felt instinctively that once he was home and convalescent his wife's life would become a nightmare of routine fetching and carrying. To quote her granny, "She would be rushed off her feet!"

When Paul was better she'd try and be as good a nurse as possible. It wasn't a skill at which she excelled, but for him nothing was too much trouble. The main problem would be keeping Antonia out of his hair, but somehow or other she would manage it. She bent down again and put her mouth close to Paul's ear. 'I'm going to leave you now, darling,' she whispered. 'I think you need some peace and quiet, but please remember I'm crazy about you and while I'm about it thanks for the great sex!' She brushed the lobe of his ear with her mouth and left.

Antonia paced back and forth in the privacy of her own sitting room, inwardly raging that so many miles separated her from Paul. How could she help him from this distance? If Liz was at all sensible he'd be flown home tomorrow where he'd be cared for properly by people who knew what they were doing. He'd been crazy to take off on a madcap trip halfway across Europe. She knew from past experience that he would drive like a maniac just to show Liz how competent he was.

Thinking back over the past twenty years there had been very few phases of Paul's life in which she hadn't been involved. It had been such a pleasure to help him become the man he now was. He'd only been a boy of seventeen when he arrived in this country and when she'd invited those refugees over for tea on Sundays she'd taken on the role that normally a mother would fulfil. It was a bonus for her that Paul had kept on coming back. Even after he joined the British Army after war was declared he'd spent every leave with her and started to help in the business. Over the years she'd guided him on what to wear, where to shop and what to read. She'd introduced him to her father's tailor and supervised the choosing and making of his first real suit after the war, persuading him to give that dreadful demob number to the gardener, telling him that no self-respecting man would be seen dead in it.

They'd been to the theatre together more times than she could remember and, at Paul's insistence, some concerts, although the latter weren't really to her taste. They'd visited art galleries, trade exhibitions and regularly sneaked into hotels being run by their competitors to compare prices and the type of food being served in their respective restaurants. And now, just when he needed her the most, she couldn't even talk to him! It was so unfair..

❦

On Sunday morning, Anna helped Liz to move from her hotel. It wasn't until she started to pack that Liz came across the cardboard tube containing the Klimt. Paul had intended to give it to Bruno as soon as they arrived, but had forgotten to take it on their first morning. Since then it had stayed in the bottom of the wardrobe. Liz saw the unshed tears in Bruno's eyes as he removed the print from its protective tube and wished with all her heart that Paul could have seen how much pleasure his gift had given.

They'd heard an announcement that Kruschev had agreed to dismantle all missile installations in Cuba and return them to the Soviet Union. In response he'd expressed the hope that the United States would not be invading Cuba in the foreseeable future. The world breathed a collective sigh of relief that the crisis had been averted and life could continue much as it had done before.

Paul was still unconscious and Liz sat by his bed for a while holding his hand. She hoped he couldn't feel her distress through the tips of her fingers and wondered for the umpteenth time what else could be done to help him. The orderly sat on by his bedside. He was still reading a comic. Liz wondered idly if it was a different one from the day before or if he was just a very slow reader.

After a while a Roman Catholic priest appeared and began walking around the ward, pausing at each bedside to have a few words with the occupant before pronouncing a blessing, making the sign of the cross and moving on. When he reached Liz he asked her in English if she was Roman Catholic. She shook her head negatively and he moved on. No few words. No blessing. Surely he'd heard about the Ecumenical Council and what it hoped to achieve?

She couldn't let Anna and Bruno sit here all day when their carefully mapped-out life had been so disrupted and they had who knows what else to do before they left for home on Wednesday. Liz felt it would be selfish to ask them to change their travel plans, admitting to herself reluctantly that Paul could remain in a coma for several weeks. After half an hour she whispered into Paul's ear that she was going to leave him to rest.

'I really don't think we can do anything useful to help Paul,' she said to Anna. 'I'm going to leave him in peace. Shall we walk or something and I'll come back later?'

Bruno seized the moment. 'Let me take you to Santa Maria della Vittoria and then you can see Bernini's Ecstasy of Santa Teresa.'

'I'd really like that,' Liz said, trying hard to sound sincere. If she went along with Bruno's suggestion, at least for a short time, the activity might stop her endless "If only . . ." internal dialogue.

They caught a bus to Via XX Settembre and walked the short distance to the church. Her first impression as they entered was of florid marble columns and ornately carved cornices, which seemed like a fussy and elaborate setting in which to worship a simple carpenter, even if he did turn out to be the son of God. The scent of myrrh reminded her that Mass had recently been celebrated, but the damp chilly air wrapped itself around her, clinging to her clothes, deepening her gloomy mood and reminding her that she was here as one half of the couple she had been only two days earlier.

Santa Teresa hit her like a thunderbolt. She was rising up to meet the seraph whose spear was pointing towards her genitalia rather than her heart which, if Liz's memory served her correctly, was its intended target. Her head was thrown back, her mouth half open, her eyes partly closed, her face bore an expression so ecstatic it was as if Bernini had sculpted her at a moment of orgasmic release.

'She's finally about to achieve the mystical union with God which she'd worked towards all her adult life,' Bruno said. 'The seraph is a reminder of an earlier vision she had when he drove his spear repeatedly into her heart through her entrails, causing her considerable physical as well as spiritual pain.'

Liz could hear Paul's voice in her head, *'Surely even a nun couldn't hope for an orgasm with God! And if that was her goal should she have been rewarded with sanctification.'*

She tried hard not to smile. It would be too cruel to spoil Bruno's moment.

'Look at the folds of her habit.' Bruno was speaking again. Liz looked. They were considerably more voluminous than any she'd ever seen on any nun and were swirling about her like demented waves in a stormy ocean, the fabric moving around her with a liquidity seldom seen in marble. 'They represent her inner turmoil,' Bruno went on and Liz found it easy to believe him.

It was a work of art like no other Liz had ever seen. It asked, no demanded, to be looked at and became more disturbing the longer she stood in front of it. She was looking at the most intensive emotional experience between birth and death; that of complete sexual surrender. Viewing this in any other context but in church she would have felt like a voyeur, except that the saint had been placed so as not to escape attention and any feelings of guilt were inappropriate.

If only Paul could be here to see it with her instead of lying supine and alone in his hospital bed. Would they ever make love again? Would she cry out as Santa Teresa was surely doing in her immortalised image? Cry real tears again as she occasionally did when she and Paul shared the moment that Santa Teresa was experiencing on her own? Her throat constricted and she told herself sternly not to be pessimistic. Acting totally out of character she fished out a few lire, selected a candle, lit it from one of the others burning in front of a nearby altar and said a prayer for Paul's safe recovery.

Later the same day when they returned to the hospital, Liz was surprised to find Hans Lebermann and his wife sitting by Paul's bedside. 'We're so sorry,' they said in unison, rising to their feet, each of them taking one of her hands and squeezing them as a gesture of comfort. 'We've been praying for you,' Ruth added. 'What a terrible end to your holiday. Such a tragedy.'

Liz, although moved by their kindness, was dismayed to be viewed as the victim of a tragedy. Then she counter-argued they'd only met two days ago and the two of them could have chosen to do nothing. She told herself sternly to be charitable. Surely this was the way in which all committed Christians behaved - with scant regard for their own inclinations and a desire to show kindness to others? Not living in an environment where Christianity featured very strongly, people like the Lebermanns were not part of her immediate circle. She knew that Paul too would be touched by their genuine concern and hoped that if they'd talked to him as she had earlier in the day he'd been able to hear and understand what they were saying, knowing that it would be appropriate and concerned and that he would be comforted by their words.

'It's really kind of you to take the trouble to come and see Paul,' she began, wondering at the same time how they'd got to know of his illness. Anna or Bruno must have told them and she felt an inner disquiet that she and Paul were being discussed, even though certain that any talk would have been merely informative and stemming from genuine concern on Bruno and Anna's part. It always surprised her if she learned, usually inadvertently, that either of them had been the subject of a conversation between third parties.

'This has all been a dreadful shock as you can imagine,' she went on. 'I only wish we weren't quite so far away from home.'

'But wherever you are, God is by your side.' Hans Lebermann was first and foremost a priest and never lost an opportunity to remind those with whom he came into contact that God was omnipresent.

'I'm afraid I'm not aware of Him being here,' Liz replied, wishing that if God were around he'd pass on to her the ability to speak more fluent Italian enabling her to have a more meaningful, to say nothing of more frequent, dialogue with the medical staff about Paul's condition. Her Italian phrase book was fine providing that all that was wrong with you was a hangover or an upset tummy, but it was sadly lacking in more complex medical details.

'You must have faith,' Hans persisted. 'God will never let you down.'

Liz hoped fervently that he was right, although her innate scepticism made her reluctant to believe him.

༄

Once they'd said goodbye to the Lebermanns and left the hospital, Liz began to focus on the practicalities of the forthcoming week. She suggested to Anna and Bruno that they all find somewhere to eat and, once they'd ordered and were waiting for their food, raised the question of their departure. 'I want you both to know how grateful I am for your help and concern, but let's face it, Paul could still be in a coma a month from now. It's pointless for the pair of you to hang on, particularly as you have other things that you must do back home.'

Bruno's expression told her she'd struck the right chord and, before Anna could remonstrate with her, went on. 'I promised I'd phone Kate later this week once I knew more about Paul's illness. You may remember she'd originally planned to come over today. I'm sure she'll be happy to keep me company for a few days. I'll ask her to join me later in the week. She can share my hotel room, as I've got a double, or stay with her employer if that's what she would prefer.'

'What you're saying makes good sense,' Bruno said. 'I feel a bit ghoulish sitting by Paul's bed wondering what's going to happen next.'

'I can't expect you to put your life on hold because of Paul's illness. We both have families to think of and you have a job to go back to. I'm sure that I'll manage with Kate and our friend from the British Consulate. That was an inspired idea of yours to call them.' She turned to Anna and squeezed her hand in gratitude.

'Talking of the British Consulate reminds me that I must look in tomorrow and ask Michael Shand if he can help me to change some of our traveller's cheques. The next holiday we take I'll know better than to leave all the financial arrangements to Paul.' She saw the briefest of eye contact between Anna and Bruno and thought bleakly - *they don't think there's going to be another holiday. They don't think Paul's going to survive.*

It was a heart-stopping moment for her. She'd pushed the thought to the back of her mind, not wanting to admit that Paul just might not make it. Paul *always* made it. He always solved the problem, whatever it was. He was strong, indestructible, her rock, her husband, for God's sake, and she needed him. The children needed him. The hotel needed him. None of them could manage without him. She couldn't bear to think about it. She sent up a silent prayer for Paul's recovery. That made two today; an all-time record. Hans Lebermann must be getting to her. She smiled inside her head, half afraid that a smile on her face might be misinterpreted, and then almost immediately pasted on another for Anna and Bruno.

When, on Monday morning, she sought out Michael Shand, she was surprised when he handed her a telegram. 'This arrived for you early this morning,' he said. 'How's your husband?'

'Much the same as when you saw him on Saturday, I'm afraid. Perhaps you can imagine how difficult it is just the day-on-day waiting? In the meantime, may I take you up on your offer to help me change some of our traveller's cheques? I seem to have come to the end of my ready money.' Her fingers closed around the telegram and, although longing to open it, stowed it away in her bag. It was concrete evidence that someone in the outside world had bothered to send a message and it would keep for a treat to read when she and Michael Shand finished their negotiations with the bank.

'Take more money out than you think you'll need,' he advised. 'It will be easier in the long run.'

Liz didn't want to think about the long run. More than anything she wanted to be home, talking to her children again and to anyone who would understand what she was trying to say. In the bank she stood mutely, leaving all the negotiating to Michael Shand, feeling like someone who was too stupid to conduct her own affairs. When she'd finished signing for her money she pushed the lire into her notecase and, after thanking Michael Shand for his help, turned towards the now familiar route to the hospital.

She opened and read the telegram as she walked and was surprised to find a message from Paul's cousin Oscar. SHOCKED TO HEAR NEWS. WHAT CAN I DO TO HELP? ANTONIA A BIT SHORT ON DETAILS. SARAH SENDS LOVE. OSCAR. Liz pressed her lips tightly together and continued walking. Oscar and Sarah must have called into the hotel, perhaps for dinner. She'd mentioned that she could be contacted at the British Consulate and given Antonia the address. Later she would call Oscar and fill him in with the details.

She began to think seriously about the impact the news of Paul's illness was having on Antonia, acknowledging she must be worried sick about the future of her beloved hotel. Paul had mentioned she was no longer up to running things on her own. So what would she do until Paul could take up the reins again and continue to run the business? Would she get in an agency manager or lose patience altogether and appoint a replacement? Whatever she decided, Paul was a shareholder and couldn't just be sacked. Or could he? Liz, uncharacteristically, began to worry about their future.

Walking through the door she smiled at the other occupants of the ward feeling more in need of a friend than at any time in her life. Paul still lay with closed eyes and every part of her willed him to recover. There was a hollow inside her, a huge emptiness which came from despair and uncertainty about what might or might not lie ahead. At twenty seven, married for four years, knowing Paul for only six, she felt this was a cataclysm she was unable to face.

Sitting down by the bed she took Paul's left hand in her

own. His fingers curled round hers and transported her briefly back to the night in Viareggio when they'd walked hand-in-hand through the early evening. She laid her cheek against his hand, closed her eyes and felt her heart begin to crack open.

CHAPTER EIGHT

On Tuesday morning Liz arrived at the hospital just in time to see Paul's eyes fluttering open. Her spirits soared and a huge wave of relief swept over her. He was coming out of his coma! She knew he could do it! Deep down she'd always believed that it would be all right. 'Hello darling,' she said, taking his hand. 'What a fright you've given us! Squeeze my hand if you're feeling better.' She scanned his face anxiously, waiting for some sign of recognition. A wink, the merest smile, anything, anything would do just to reassure her that he was beginning to make a recovery.

After a few seconds his eyes closed again. She couldn't believe that he would do it deliberately and told herself his reaction had been involuntary. The euphoria that she'd been feeling a few seconds ago disappeared and tears of disappointment ran down her face. She bent over him and whispered close to his ear, 'Paul. Paul. Can you hear me?' There was no response. She turned away from his bed and went to stand in the corridor, needing to be alone with her distress.

How long would this go on? It was like walking down a never-ending tunnel, plunging on and on through eternal blackness, seeing no proverbial light towards which she could move with any degree of optimism. How long before her strength gave way? That mustn't happen. The children were at home waiting and she had to keep her spirits up for them. Did Paul have any idea what he was putting her through? How could he be so careless of his health with so many people depending on him? At that moment she hated him with a deep corrosive passion and for a few moments felt like hitting anyone who crossed her path – particularly Paul. But then she admitted to feeling sorry only for herself and shrugged away her irritation, knowing it had no place in the current drama.

※

Anna and Bruno left Rome early on Wednesday. Liz choked back her tears when they said their goodbyes, not wanting them to feel guilty about leaving her. 'Kate will be arriving soon,' she told them, forcing a smile and deliberately omitting to mention that Kate wouldn't be in Rome until Thursday.

Michael Shand stopped by the hotel to deliver an airmail which had arrived at the consulate for her. Liz pushed it into her bag to read later. When he enquired if there was anything he could do she took advantage of the moment and asked him what her options would be if the worst was to happen and Paul didn't recover, knowing she would want to leave Rome as quickly as possible. She couldn't frame the sentence 'What if Paul dies.' But he was astute enough to interpret her meaning.

He told her it would be easy to arrange to have Paul's body flown home which would cost in the region of two hundred pounds. Liz would then have to make arrangements for transporting him from the airport to wherever she wanted him to go. Alternatively he could organise a funeral service in Rome and, if Liz had no objections, Paul could be cremated and his ashes flown home. To fly a small urn would be considerably cheaper, he pointed out, and although in a Roman Catholic city cremation wasn't usual, it was certainly possible.

Liz wondered how she could be thinking about Paul's funeral whilst he was still alive, let alone weighing up the cost of the different options and talking about transporting him as if he were a parcel. But she'd been away from home for almost two weeks, was chafing at the bit to return and forgave herself by arguing that Paul would be doing exactly the same if their situation was reversed. The only difference being that Paul would have a much better idea of exactly how much money he could spend, whereas Liz hadn't a clue about the state of their finances. Would Michael Shand think her hard hearted or would he understand her desire to be practical? She thanked him for his help and the moment he disappeared tore open her airmail before going to the hospital. It was a brief note from Oscar's wife Sarah.

Liz dear,

We were both so shocked to hear about Paul. We looked into the hotel on Saturday evening and Antonia told us the sad news when we asked if she'd heard from either of you. She was rather short and didn't give us many details, but mentioned that Paul was too ill to be moved.

We went up to the flat to see how Maria was coping and everything seemed fine. Both the children were perfectly all right. I just want you to know that we'll do anything we possibly can to help you, so please don't hesitate to contact us - whatever it is you need.

We are thinking about you constantly. You must be out of your mind with worry, but we are hoping that we shall hear some good news soon.

Love from both of us,
Sarah

Liz folded the letter and slipped it into her bag. It was hard to remember a time when so many people had shown her so much kindness whilst she, on the other hand, had been cold-bloodedly planning Paul's funeral. Her own callousness surprised her when others were expressing so much concern. But the thought of Paul's body going home in the hold of an aeroplane, shoved in with a whole lot of cargo, filled her with horror. So perhaps she wasn't totally without feeling? She knew the route to the hospital so well by now that there was no need to concentrate. The porter on duty at the entrance recognised her, smiled and called 'Buon Giorno!' to her as she walked in.

Some of the occupants of Paul's ward greeted her in Italian whilst others merely smiled. Paul lay unmoving, connected to the drips which provided him with nutrition and fluids. His face was pale, verging on grey, and she imagined she could see the shape of his skull underneath the putty-coloured skin. Self-pity was just beginning to overwhelm her again when Ruth Lebermann arrived. 'I had to come into town to do some shopping,' she told Liz, 'and I thought you might like to come over to the flat for some lunch. You must be feeling lonely now that Anna and Bruno have left.'

All this kindness from a comparative stranger was almost unbearable. It was less than a week since they'd met and already Ruth had visited the hospital twice. 'Why don't you let me take us both out to lunch?' she suggested, thinking to save Ruth the trouble of preparing food, let alone entertaining someone she scarcely knew. Ruth swiftly brushed aside her offer. 'I won't hear of it. It's difficult for me to find enough to occupy my time with Hans away at the Vatican all day and I never was very good at embroidery! So you see you'll be doing me a great favour.' She glanced across at Paul. 'I suppose there's been no change since I last saw him?'

Liz told her that Paul had opened his eyes briefly on Tuesday morning and admitted with a new sadness in her voice that he'd failed to recognise her. She shrugged helplessly and confessed, 'It's the endless waiting I find so difficult. If only he could tell me how he's feeling, I'd find it a bit easier to keep coming in to see him. As it is . . .' Her voice tailed away and Ruth took her arm. 'You mustn't lose hope. Miracles can still happen,' she said. 'Come and I'll show you the flat.' Liz, after a last reluctant look at Paul, allowed herself to be led out of the hospital.

'We're close to the Castel Sant'Angelo,' Ruth explained as they walked briskly towards the bus stop. 'It's so handy for the Vatican. Hans makes a point of walking there every day to help him counteract the long hours of sitting down. It's fine now because the weather is good, but if it turns really cold he says it would be helpful if he could use the private pathway that still connects the Castel Sant'Angelo with the Vatican. I don't think it's likely that the Pope will grant him special dispensation, do you! Have you been to St Peter's yet or the Sistine Chapel?' she asked as they climbed on board the bus.

'Unfortunately not,' Liz replied. 'We only managed one real

day of sightseeing before Paul was taken ill.'

'It would be a pity to miss it now that you're here,' Ruth added. 'Perhaps when your friend arrives you'll find time for a quick visit.'

'Maybe,' Liz said absently, thinking *how can I think about sightseeing when Paul is fighting for his life?*

The flat was in a small block and had a prime view of the huge circular fortress of the Castel Sant'Angelo. This was Liz's first time across the Tiber since her arrival and she looked about her with interest as they walked the short distance from the bus. At any other time she would have been longing to explore a building which had first been constructed by the Emperor Hadrian as long ago as 123 AD, but under the present circumstances had to be content to admire it from the outside.

Ruth took her on a brief tour of the flat which struck Liz as functional rather than decorative. She was amused to see that the bidet in the bathroom was full of woollen socks which were soaking in cold soapy water and wondered how long they'd been there. Perhaps no one had bothered to tell Ruth that if you soaked wool it was likely to shrink?

They ate a selection of cold antipasti for lunch, which Ruth had bought that morning on her brief excursion into Rome. She told Liz how difficult it was to fill her days constructively. As most of the clergy attending the Ecumenical Council were Roman Catholic there were few clergy wives to whom she could relate and she admitted to not enjoying sightseeing on her own. She also missed her family, a son and a daughter, who were back home in the States. They were both at university and, although they would have jumped at the chance to take some time out, both she and Hans had been reluctant to separate them from their studies.

Liz, to her own surprise, began to talk about her fears for the future and explained her situation briefly to Ruth. 'Our flat is linked to Paul's job and if he can't work I can see that we may have to move out of the hotel,' she said. 'I could take over at a pinch because of my qualifications, but I'm not sure that Paul's partner will wear it.'

Ruth's face assumed a sympathetic expression. 'Surely he would want to be as helpful as possible under the circumstances,' she said, making the same assumption as everyone else on first being told of Paul's business partnership.

'His partner's a woman,' Liz explained, but decided not to elaborate, ignoring the look of polite enquiry that came over Ruth's face. She moved the conversation onto safer ground expressing surprise at the number of male clergy walking around the city every day and confessing that she'd never before seen shops that sold only religious vestments of one kind or another. 'A bit like boutiques for the clergy,' she added.

'As you've probably gathered, Rome has a tremendous number of churches and religious establishments of one kind or another,' Ruth said, 'and of course the place is packed with visiting clergy. I should think the hotels are having a field day.'

'Do you enjoy being married to a man of the church?' Liz asked, not sure whether or not a Lutheran would be classified as a priest, a clergyman or simply a pastor.

'I enjoy being married to Hans,' Ruth smiled as she poured coffee for both of them. 'But being married to the job is something else and at times I feel like Hans' unpaid deputy. If someone comes knocking at the door and Hans is out I feel duty-bound to entertain them until he returns. On other occasions I have to show up at events in the parish simply because I'm Hans' wife. I used to be a teacher and when things aren't going well for Hans I feel I'd love to be back at work but,' she paused and Liz saw an expression of regret flit across her face, 'I didn't really know what I was taking on when I agreed to marry him and now I feel I owe it to him to be as supportive as possible. I really don't know how he'd react if I decided to return to my old career.'

Her frankness surprised Liz who had filed her away as the dutiful partner of a deeply religious man and wondered if there were other regrets which had been put to one side for the sake of supporting his career. There were parallels with her own life. She too had married the job and tailored her private life to fit around Paul's commitments to the hotel. Did she regret it? Not the marriage, how could that be? There was no question of her love for Paul, but it was difficult to carry on a normal day-to-day life with an almost total lack of privacy. Recently she'd found herself wondering several times each day why she didn't feel happier. Over the past four years she'd felt her own personality slowly eclipsed by the demands of the children and the hotel. Perhaps when they bought a house and moved out of Antonia's orbit their life would be easier. It was a comforting thought.

Glancing at her watch she saw that it was almost three o'clock. 'I really must be going,' she said. 'I'd like to look in at the hospital again and then perhaps I'll grab something to eat and have an early night.' Most of her nights had been disturbed since Paul had been taken ill and an opportunity to catch up on lost sleep was too good to miss. With Kate arriving tomorrow this was perhaps her last chance for the next few days.

'You've been so kind to me,' she told Ruth. 'I can't tell you what it means to me to have a friend to talk to.' The word friend slipped out before she realised it. Surely friends were people you'd known and cultivated for some time, not someone you'd met only a week ago? Ruth just smiled with pleasure and patted her arm reassuringly as if to signal that she felt OK about it.

'I'll walk with you to the bus stop,' she said. 'It can be confusing finding your way round a strange city when you don't know the system and everything travels on the other side of the road!' Liz immediately regressed to childhood, remembering how her grandmother had given her similar instructions on her first day at grammar school. But, unlike her grandmother, Ruth didn't tell her to refrain from talking to strange men! Once on board she was grateful for the information Ruth had given her. The light was beginning to fade and she listened carefully as the driver called out the names of the stops, afraid that a lapse of concentration might take her to a part of the city which was alien and would leave her miles away from the hospital.

The hospital! The hospital! Who'd have thought she could travel all the way to Rome and spend so much of her time walking to and from a hospital? She hadn't been inside a hospital since her grandmother's death and she hoped it would be a long time before she saw the inside of another.

Paul still lay unmoving, still as an effigy on a tomb. He looked so different from the active man who'd shared her life for four years and who had always been such a dynamo. There had been times when she'd complained about his restlessness. Now if only he could move she would fall on her knees and thank all the saints in Christendom. She sat for perhaps an hour holding his hand, stroking it gently from time to time and hoping that he knew it was her. She couldn't look at the other occupants of his ward, afraid of the pity or, worse still, hopelessness that might show in their eyes.

Occasionally she smiled across at the orderly who still sat by Paul's bed, thinking how boring it must be for him. He'd exchanged his comic for a paperback, which looked like a Western judging by the lurid cover featuring a man on horseback with a busty blonde thrown across his saddle. Liz wondered why Paul was the only patient to have the benefit of an orderly. Was it that Paul was more sick than everyone else? Or that he might have a sudden relapse? Or yet again that the hospital was simply taking precautions in case she decided to sue them when she finally returned home? Her inability to speak Italian precluded her from asking and added to her feeling of frustration, which grew worse as each day passed.

It was five o'clock when she left, realising that, for the first time since her arrival, she had time to kill before dinner. She could go back to the hotel, perhaps try to take a quick nap. But if she dozed now, sleep might elude her later and yet another night would be spent tossing and turning and weighing up the pros and cons of her present situation. Her hair needed washing, she could go back to the hotel and do it, but the last time she'd been in Austria it had been possible to get a shampoo and set without booking in advance and it could be they had the same system in Italy. *If I pass anywhere that looks halfway possible before I reach the hotel I'll treat myself*, she thought and immediately began looking on both sides of the Via del Corso.

Suddenly she remembered passing a hairdressing salon in the Piazza di Spagna when she'd called in to see Michael Shand. Perhaps they wouldn't want a customer to arrive so late? Maybe they had an appointment system after all? Oh Liz, *shape up for goodness sake*, she told herself. *Do you want to have your hair done or what? You can only ask. Let them decide whether or not they want to take you!* Why was she dithering when normally it would be the decision of a moment?

When she found the shop she hesitated again, loitering on the pavement and peering in through the window. There were several women inside, some being shampooed, others sitting in front of mirrors having their hair rolled up, snipped or combed out. The salon must still be open for business. Squaring her shoulders, almost as if she were about to visit the dentist, she walked purposefully inside.

'Inglese.' The receptionist inquired.

'Si,' Liz replied, wondering what it was about her that signalled her nationality so positively.

'You like haircut, washed, set?' the girl asked.

'Oh, washed and set please,' Liz said, mentally castigating herself at the same time for taking so long to make up her mind.

'Follow me please,' the girl invited, leading Liz into a small cloakroom, taking her jacket and handing her a pale blue gown before seating her at a wash basin. Her heels clicked on the tiled floor. Liz glanced down and wondered how it was possible to spend a whole day teetering about on such high, spiky heels. The shoes were black patent and had an elegant simplicity which Liz envied. A week in Rome and she hadn't once looked into a shoe shop! The realisation came like a bolt from the blue and was another reminder of the degree to which Paul's illness had absorbed her.

The warmth of the hairdryer lulled her into a brief sleep and she woke only when the stylist, who had previously rolled up her hair with a speed and efficiency which left Liz lost in admiration, shook her gently by the arm.

'Madame is tired, yes?'

'Just a little,' Liz admitted. 'I've been having a trying time recently.'

'I shall make you look very beautiful. Your husband will want to take you somewhere special.'

Liz felt the unshed tears which lurked permanently at the back of her eyes and wondered if Paul would ever take her out again - anywhere. She managed a shaky smile. 'He isn't very well at the moment I'm afraid.'

The girl's cheeks grew pink with embarrassment and Liz immediately regretted speaking the truth. It would be easy to pretend that she was about to go out 'somewhere special.' Trying to brush over the momentary embarrassment, she said, 'I'd still like to look beautiful, so please do your best,' and was relieved when the girl smiled back at her.

The transformation was amazing. No hairdresser in England had ever succeeded in making her look better. The girl worked with the confidence of someone who has been well trained and with a good eye for what suited whom. 'Bella!' she said, smiling with pleasure once the girl had finished and wishing for the umpteenth time that she had a more fluent knowledge of the language so that she could do more justice to the effort the stylist had put in.

Paul can't see me, he doesn't know how beautiful my hair is, Liz thought bleakly as she left the shop. Would he ever see her again? Would he recognise her if he did? It had been so hard on Tuesday when he'd opened his eyes and failed to connect with her. Did he remember who he was, where he was, what he was doing here? After the brief respite in the hairdressing salon her mind buzzed again with unanswered questions that whirled like a vortex around her head.

Head down, thoughts miles away, she turned instinctively towards her hotel and bumped into none other than Michael Shand who was just on his way out of the consulate. 'Mrs Hirsch! What a surprise!' he said, removing his hat briefly as only an Englishman would. 'How's your husband?' he asked, almost before Liz had time to take in exactly with whom she'd collided. She shrugged. 'Oh I honestly don't know. On Tuesday

I thought he was coming out of his coma, but since then it seems as if he's sinking more deeply into it, if that's possible.' Her hand went up to brush away the tears before they could run down her face.

'Come and have a drink,' he said quickly and Liz realised forlornly that he hadn't been fooled about the way she was feeling. 'There's a place just around the corner where they actually provide seats. You've probably gathered that the Italians have a predilection for drinking on the hoof.' Liz *had* noticed. Every time she'd passed a bar there had been a crush of people standing at the counter either drinking coffee or something stronger. 'It's kind of you to offer,' she said, 'I'm between friends at the moment and in a city which I don't know very well so I'm at a bit of a loose end.'

He placed a hand under her elbow and weaved his way expertly through the evening commuters. A few moments later they were seated in a small restaurant with a bar out front where several couples were already gathered. 'Is wine all right for you?' She nodded and he ordered a couple of glasses of white. Liz leaned back in her chair, contented to let someone make decisions for her.

'I'm sorry, would you have preferred red?' Michael Shand asked when the waiter delivered two large goblets to their table.

'White's just fine. Cheers!' Liz raised her glass in a brief salute. 'Is it normal for Italian men to stop off and have a drink on their way home?' She'd noticed several times a tired commuter dive into a bar for a quick espresso or grappa before diving out again. 'Yes, although they don't sit around chewing the fat for an hour or two hoping that the children will be in bed by the time they arrive home as they would in England!' He smiled at her across the small marble-topped table, but his smile didn't really make him look happy, Liz thought. There was sadness behind his eyes where the smile didn't quite reach.

'At the moment there's nobody waiting for me at home,' he volunteered. 'My wife is currently in England. She left at the beginning of July when the weather became unbearably hot; said she couldn't stand another scorching summer in Rome.

I'm still waiting for her to return. She was terribly disappointed when I didn't get the job of consul; felt that at my age I'd served my time and should be suitably rewarded.' He smiled again, rather ruefully and Liz wondered what it had cost him to make such an admission.

'And how do *you* feel? Would you have liked the job?'

'Frankly, no. I'm more than happy doing what I do. Of course it will make a difference to my final pension and I think Margaret would have preferred a larger sum. Well what wife wouldn't?'

Liz couldn't help thinking that if his wife wanted more money for her old age there was nothing to stop her from going out to earn it. Perhaps that was the reason she'd gone back to England? Perhaps it wasn't the done thing for consular wives to work? She began to feel sorry for Michael Shand and wondered how he spent his lone evenings in a city like Rome. 'Do you have many official functions to attend?' She imagined him in a dinner jacket hobnobbing with the beautiful people of Rome in a variety of elegant venues.

'Some. Of course there would be rather more if I had the top job. Margaret enjoys socialising, but then she doesn't really appreciate the amount of business networking that goes on at most of these affairs. On the surface it looks as if everyone is out celebrating, but underneath we're working away like mad, rather like ducks paddling under water.'

Liz hoped he might find himself a mistress if he hadn't already. She conjured up for him a slinky, Latin lover; all dark hair, scarlet lips, chic clothes and jangling gold bracelets! She was just about to fantasise about the romantic evenings the two of them might spend together when he leaned towards her and asked, 'Do you have any plans for dinner?' Liz came sharply back to reality and wondered if by the remotest chance he'd guessed her thoughts and then dismissed the idea. Michael Shand might be intuitive, but she was quite certain he wasn't a mind reader.

'No,' she said carefully, 'I have no plans.'

'Then please stay and eat with me. I promise you'll be giving pleasure to a lonely old man!' His eyes had lost their look of sadness and Liz didn't want to be the one to bring it back. 'I don't really feel capable of giving pleasure to anyone at the moment,' she admitted, feeling that perhaps his confession deserved to be reciprocated and at the same time wanting to warn him that he wasn't about to embark on an evening of unbridled passion! 'I'm so steeped in misery and worry I feel I must depress anyone with whom I come into contact. But if you feel strong enough then thank you very much, it will be a pleasure to have dinner with you.'

❦

Did he feel strong enough? When was the last time an attractive young woman, a virtual stranger had agreed to have dinner with him? What a question! For the first time in years he felt free from the straightjacket of his marriage and he didn't need to wonder what Margaret's reaction would be if she could see him now. Under the social exterior she adopted for party occasions her jealousy seethed perennially just waiting for an opportunity to erupt. If he so much as looked at another woman, accusations of infidelity would be hurled at him at the earliest opportunity.

Their life together had been punctuated by a series of melodramatic outbursts and it seemed to him that however hard he tried she would find fault with something, anything to propel them both into a pitched battle. He remembered vividly the morning he'd driven her to the airport. 'I suppose you can't wait to get rid of me,' she'd accused as they approached the terminal.

'Margaret, it's your decision to leave,' he'd replied wearily.

'And why do you think I'm going?' she'd demanded.

'Well, you said that the heat of this city was insupportable.' He'd mentally cringed at the derisive snort with which she'd greeted his remark and wondered why he lacked the courage to tell her not to bother coming back until she learned to trust him.

But that was what was wrong with their relationship. He

could never succeed in convincing her that her suspicions were unfounded; that he'd never seriously looked at another woman since the day they'd married and that he might, just might, be lonely all by himself in Rome after her departure.

He'd reached the stage of believing she was on a crash course to self-destruction and would end up either clinically depressed or mentally unhinged in some way. If only someone would have the courage to advise her to see a therapist, perhaps she might be encouraged to confront whatever demons were gnawing away and consistently making her unhappy. If he was to make such a suggestion himself she would go off the deep end and accuse him of wanting to lock her up forever.

On balance he thought it more than likely that he would be able to get through dinner with an attractive stranger very nicely thank you.

CHAPTER NINE

When the waiter came over to see if they would like more drinks, Michael Shand asked him to reserve a table in the restaurant. 'The food here is excellent,' he told Liz. 'I've eaten here many times,' he paused briefly, 'particularly since my wife left.' Liz flashed him an encouraging smile, picking up on the wistfulness in his voice. 'I've been forcing myself to eat for the last few days,' she said, 'as you can imagine what with worrying about Paul and everything . . . But suddenly I feel quite hungry. I had an early lunch today and it was rather frugal, by Italian standards anyway.'

He looked across at her, remembering the first morning he'd met her at the hospital. She'd looked tearful and dishevelled on that occasion, scarcely surprising after spending a night at the bedside of a sick husband. *Then* he wouldn't have given her a second glance, but now she'd been transformed in some indefinable way. What was it about her that was so different suddenly? Ah! Got it! She'd had her hair done! What a difference it made and what a lucky husband to have such a concerned and attractive wife. He couldn't visualise Margaret being quite so distressed if by any chance he should find himself with a life-threatening illness.

He sipped his wine wondering how on earth he'd managed to find the courage to invite Liz Hirsch to join him for dinner. In his younger days he hadn't been quite so timid, but years of being married to Margaret had sapped both his energy and his confidence and he'd learned to look the other way if anyone tried to flirt with him at a party or an official dinner. Funny how quickly you got out of the habit of making small talk with people you scarcely knew socially, although he did it all the time in his official capacity. Somehow this totally unexpected and delightful meeting couldn't be dismissed as mere business. Would he have asked an unattractive older woman or a fellow Englishman to share dinner with him? The latter maybe, the former probably not.

The waiter reappeared to let them know their table was ready. Michael Shand got to his feet and stood to one side to allow Liz to precede him. What on earth were they going to talk about for the rest of the evening? He must tread carefully in any case; she'd had a tough week one way and another and to add to her distress now would be letting the side down.

He'd enjoyed helping her in practical ways, but then that was one of the aspects of the job; to provide assistance to British citizens who found themselves in some kind of trouble when they were abroad. Was he now going beyond the call of duty? However far he stretched his imagination, inviting her to dinner had nothing to do with duty. He was being uncharacteristically selfish and taking advantage of the moment.

'The escalopes with calvados are really good,' he said, 'and if you like courgettes they have some stuffed with mozzarella, coated in batter and deep fried; they make an excellent starter. Liz listened carefully and then without bothering to look at the menu said, 'I'm happy to take your advice, I haven't tried either since I arrived, so it will be a new experience for me. I really enjoy good food. Did I mention that Paul is a partner in a hotel and we're always trying to build up the restaurant side of the business?'

'And do you work in the hotel as well?' he asked, grateful that she'd opened up a line of conversation and seeking to prolong it.

'I fill in from time-to-time as occasion demands. I sometimes help in reception or housekeeping if we're short of staff or extra busy. As you can imagine hotels are rather labour intensive and even the most carefully controlled rotas fall apart if someone gets sick or wants a holiday.'

'We have similar problems,' he said, relieved they'd found common ground so easily. He was spared from further comment for the moment as their food arrived and the waiter began to fuss around, opening napkins and shaking them before placing them on the laps of his two customers, checking to see that they had bread and finally topping up their glasses from the carafe of wine that Michael Shand had ordered with the food. After a last look around the table he wished them, 'Buon appetito!' and left them to enjoy their meal.

'These are delicious,' Liz said as she tasted the courgettes. 'I wish we were more adventurous with vegetables at home.'

'When the courgette flowers are available they're treated in the same way and I enjoy them enormously.' Michael Shand couldn't remember the last time he'd had a conversation about food and began to relax for the first time since Liz had walked into him.

'Thank you for coming to my rescue,' Liz said. 'Somehow or another food never tastes quite so good when you're eating alone, does it?'

Well he'd certainly had plenty of practice since his wife had gone back to England. 'I'm inclined to agree with you. But then sharing anything is usually more enjoyable, isn't it?'

'Almost everything,' Liz agreed, 'the one exception being shopping.'

Michael Shand stopped eating and looked at her in surprise. 'But I thought . . .'

'You're quite wrong!' Liz was emphatic. 'Very occasionally perhaps shopping for furniture or something like that which will be shared, then it's fine to have one's husband along; otherwise forget it! ' He watched her fingers twine around the lovely amber necklace and guessed her husband had probably helped her to choose it. He tried to visualise when and where they'd bought it and wondered if it had been to commemorate a special event, the birth of a child perhaps? An anniversary? A birthday? Well, food and shopping! What next?

As they waited for the next course, Liz leaned towards him across the table looking, he thought, quite conspiratorial. 'I really *must* tell you something, but I warn you it may come as something of a surprise,' she said. Her blue eyes had a mischievous light in them, which he hadn't seen before, and he braced himself for whatever was coming. 'When I first met you in the hospital, the day after Paul . . .' Her voice tailed away and she took a long drink from her glass of wine as if she suddenly needed some Dutch courage. 'You were so kind - and then I never knew my father - but I felt that if I had I would have wanted him to be exactly like you!'

Her statement caught him unawares. So she saw him as a father figure. Oh dear! For her sake he tried to assume an expression which would tell her that he was flattered. 'I'm not sure that either of my children would agree with you,' he began, 'but it's kind of you to say so. Was your father killed in the war?' *It would be much more comfortable to talk about her family than his own*, he admitted, trying to wipe memories of the more spectacular family arguments from his mind.

Liz told him about the bomb that had destroyed both her home and her parents and of her grandmother who had first rescued and then brought her up. He listened attentively, dimly aware of the noise of their fellow customers in the background. The clatter of cutlery and muted voices all around made it seem as if the two of them were isolated from the crowd, almost as if they were on an island. He cut off a piece of his veal escalope, found it quite perfect and congratulated himself on his choice.

Much to his own surprise, he began to tell Liz about his own part in the war. His unit had been part of the Allied invasion of Sicily in 1943 and he painted a vivid picture of running ashore from a landing craft against the relentless shellfire which bombarded them; of men all around being blown to pieces; of the ear-splitting noise of gunfire and exploding shells; of running on adrenalin for the three days it took them to gain control of the island as the Italian army retreated. 'It was an absolute nightmare and I was very lucky to survive,' he finished.

'Was that your introduction to Italy?' Liz asked, trying to visualise this gentle, courteous man, who had been so kind and helpful to her, being involved in armed combat.

'Yes. I came as a foe and returned as a friend. I suppose when you think about it that's the best way round.' His faint smile showed her that the comparison pleased him. He hadn't remained a foe for long of course. During the long march northwards towards Rome they'd come across many grateful Italian families who'd seen them as liberators and treated them accordingly, sharing their own limited supplies of food and, more often than not, wine.

And then there was Catarina. How could he forget her? Although highly improbable considering they were in the middle of a war, an impromptu concert had been arranged for the liberating Allies in the courtyard of a Roman church and, for a couple of hours, it seemed as if the war and all its bloody horror was a million miles away. Catarina was about twenty and still studying music. She had played Bach's double violin concerto together with a fellow pupil from the Accademia Nazionale di Santa Cecilia. The haunting notes of the two violins had floated out onto the evening air before disappearing upwards towards the stars and, by the end of the performance, his weren't the only eyes that were moist. To this day he'd never heard a more moving interpretation of that particular work and was reminded of Catarina whenever he listened to it.

After the concert there'd been an informal party and he'd made a beeline for Catarina who had, through a combination of music and looks, cast a spell over him. He was in the mood to be seduced. Having survived Sicily, Anzio, and the long march up through Italy to Rome he, as a consequence, felt heady, fit and victorious. Later that same evening he'd buried his face in her lustrous chestnut hair and felt he would die of happiness.

For the short time he was in Rome he'd seen her every day when they'd been free. She'd made the whole war seem almost worthwhile. How they'd talked! His Italian quickly improved and she'd shown him as many of the historical sites that could be fitted into their limited time together.

Given the circumstances, it was inevitable that he would fall completely in love with her and he was as certain as could be that his feelings were reciprocated. But, at twenty years old, not only was she below the age of consent, but still had her music studies to complete. Having seen many of his fellow officers and men blown to smithereens, his own future was, not to put too fine a point on it, uncertain and he felt that it would be unfair to tie her down via a formal engagement. He'd promised to return at the end of the war and they'd kept in touch initially by letter. But as the war progressed, her letters became fewer and by the time peace was declared she'd met a brilliant French pianist and they'd become engaged at the end of 1946. He could still remember feeling that the world had ended when he read the story of their engagement in the newspaper.

Although the performances of her French husband featured regularly in the press, Catarina was rarely mentioned and he assumed she'd given up her career to give birth to what would inevitably turn out to be musically-gifted children. He'd seen her only once since his arrival in Rome as vice-consul. He'd spotted her shopping in the Via Condotti, but Margaret had been with him and he'd chickened out of introducing the one to the other. The possible reprisal, he felt at the time, could have been considerably worse than any part of the war.

'Would you like some coffee?' Liz's voice jerked him sharply away from his reveries and back into the real world. 'I'm sorry,' he said, 'I was miles away. Talking about the war evokes certain memories.' She smiled at him across the table. 'I can imagine! I'd love a quick coffee. Will you keep me company? After that I simply must go. I only hope that the coffee doesn't keep me awake. I'm rather short on sleep right now.'

'Perhaps a brandy would help?' He said.

'I'm sure it would, but I'm not going to risk it. We've already had several glasses of wine and I'm not really used to drinking quite so much.'

Michael Shand felt himself reproached and ordered coffee for both of them. He wouldn't sleep, but felt it would be churlish to leave her to drink coffee alone. 'You said earlier this evening that you were "between friends" at the moment. Does that mean you have a friend arriving soon?' He asked.

'Oh yes, Kate, she'll be here tomorrow. We were at college together. She didn't like working in the hotel industry and is now learning Italian in Perugia and has been teaching English to the children of one of your Roman judges. She's going to stay with them while she's in Rome. Speaks Italian fluently of course. It will be good to have someone around who can ask questions at the right time. It's so frustrating visiting Paul and not being able to find out exactly what's happening.'

Michael Shand hid his disappointment that she wouldn't be looking for a dinner companion tomorrow and began to feel redundant. 'Well, don't forget I'm still at your disposal whenever you need help,' he said, signalling to the waiter to bring the bill. Five minutes later he said goodbye at the entrance to her hotel and continued his lonely journey home. It had been an unremarkable evening in many ways, but so enjoyable to be eating and sharing a conversation with a woman without the terrible feeling of walking on eggshells.

Liz unlocked her bedroom door, stared at the huge double bed without enthusiasm and resigned herself to another night of broken sleep. She'd underestimated how difficult it could be to sleep alone when you were accustomed to the company and warmth of another human being. For the last four years she'd been so used to curling her own body into Paul's that she'd taken his closeness for granted and now found sleeping alone insupportable. The routine of getting ready for bed was wearying, but Kate would be arriving tomorrow and that was a consolation.

Kate went straight to the hospital when she got off the train from Perugia. She'd brought a small overnight bag, not wanting the burden of heavy luggage. Walking from the bus to the hospital she thought back to the night Liz and Paul had stayed with her in Perugia. None of them had realised then that the light-hearted evening they spent together might be the last for some time. How could they have known? Life was unbelievably cruel sometimes. Liz and Paul were two of the nicest people she knew. Paul's good humour was infectious. Not only that, but when he talked to you he made you feel as if you were the one person he wanted to have a conversation with. And now this.

The porter at the hospital directed her to Paul's ward and she arrived to find Liz sitting in the corridor outside just staring into space. Kate touched her arm and tried not to show surprise at the ravaged face that turned towards her. 'Kate! Oh Kate!' Liz said and burst into tears.

Kate wasn't accustomed to comforting her friends and thanked her lucky stars it wasn't a role she was called upon to fulfil very often. Nonetheless she did her best, putting her arms around Liz and patting her back hoping to reassure her in some small way. 'The doctors are doing their rounds at the moment,' Liz said between sobs. 'When they've finished will you ask them how they think Paul is progressing and how long they think it might be before he recovers?'

Kate waited for the clutch of doctors to appear at the entrance to the ward and took advantage of their cigarette break to put forward Liz's question. The response wasn't encouraging. Signor Hirsch had been in a coma for almost a week now, they told her. If he'd been going to recover they would have expected him to do so sooner. They thought he might be developing pneumonia, she must understand that he'd been lying in bed for the past seven days and all the inactivity wasn't helping. They were sorry they couldn't have more positive news. It was just a matter of waiting. Perhaps she would tell the signora that they were doing everything possible, but miracles were beyond them and they had to rely on medicine alone. Then, with expressions of regret on their faces, they put out their half-smoked cigarettes and moved on to the next ward, leaving Kate to pass on their cheerless message.

She watched their retreating backs wondering what exactly to say to Liz before walking into the ward to take a look at Paul, hoping to find some inspiration in the few minutes that the inspection would take. He wasn't hard to spot. All the other patients were sitting up and talking and there was an orderly sitting next to Paul's bed reading a paperback with a lurid cover. She stroked Paul's forehead with a tentative hand; it felt cold and clammy. He was breathing quite heavily and Kate felt her heart sink. After a few seconds, she turned away reluctantly to go back to Liz.

'I can't pretend it's good news. You wouldn't want me to lie to you, would you?' She scanned Liz's face anxiously wondering how she would react.

'I saw him before you did. Every day he looks worse than he did the day before. I suppose deep down I was hoping for some kind of miracle.'

'The doctors seem to think the next few days will be critical.' Kate didn't want to spell out the scant details they'd given her, wishing she had a packet of magic dust that she could sprinkle over Paul to make him better.

'For God's sake, let's get out of here!'

Kate was surprised by Liz's tone of voice, which sounded harsh and strident. 'Liz, you're sure . . .' Her own voice was tentative.

'Absolutely. What's more, I've just remembered something.' Her face lit up and Kate saw the beginnings of a smile. 'I've been so involved one way and another I'd quite forgotten, but the car is sitting in the garage at the Grand Hotel and I haven't used it for a week. Let's get it out and go somewhere, anywhere out of this damned hospital.'

'Where would you like to go?' Kate asked as they left and began to walk down the Via del Corso.

'I haven't seen the Sistine Chapel yet,' Liz replied, 'and goodness knows if I'll ever come back here. What do you think? Does it sound like a good idea to you?' Afraid that her friend might think her hard-hearted, she added, 'Let's face it, Kate, we can't do anything if we stay in the hospital and I'm so tired of sitting in that corridor, trying not to notice the pitying looks from the other patients in the ward.'

They walked into the foyer of the hotel, had a quick word with the concierge and then waited for the car to be brought round to the main entrance. Kate suggested that they sign it out permanently to avoid paying more garage fees and Liz agreed before settling the account.

'Will you drive?' She asked Kate as they walked towards the car. 'You're much more familiar with Italian traffic than I am and to be absolutely honest the thought of driving through Rome terrifies me.'

Kate knew better than to argue and held out her hand for the keys, settled herself behind the steering wheel, adjusted the seat position slightly and eased her way expertly into the line of traffic on the Via del Corso. Within minutes they were cruising round the Piazza del Popolo at a speed which made Liz bite her bottom lip and, as they swept across the Tiber, she had to stop herself from pushing her right foot hard down on the floor. She'd completely forgotten what a reckless driver Kate was.

Within a few minutes Kate was parking expertly in a street close to St Peter's Basilica. 'Let's have a quick coffee,' she said to Liz, 'and then I'll give you the guided tour.'

As they stood at the counter of a small pasticceria, the smell of vanilla and coffee wafted towards them and they each chose a small pastry from the selection displayed behind the counter.

'Funny, isn't it,' Liz said, nibbling and closing her eyes for a moment in mock ecstasy, 'I find our English cakes completely resistible, but these smell absolutely wonderful and taste delicious.' Kate smiled indulgently at her friend, but couldn't help wondering how Liz could separate herself from the drama back at the hospital and behave, well, as if she were on holiday.

'I'll take you into St Peter's first,' Kate said as they finished their coffee and walked back into the open air. 'It will be a pity to miss it as we're so close. It was built on the place where Peter the apostle was crucified,' she explained as they walked across the elliptical piazza outlined by Bernini's beautiful colonnade.

They stopped briefly in front of the huge bronze doors at the entrance to the basilica, lost in awe at their sheer size and magnificence, before walking slowly into the huge space that was the largest church in the world.

Liz stopped again to look around at the monumental

splendour. 'It's unbelievable!' Kate smiled and led the way towards Michelangelo's masterpiece, the Pietà just to the right of the entrance. She saw her friend look at the sculpture of the dead Christ lying across the lap of his mother and watched her hand move to her mouth. It was beautiful in its simplicity, but Liz expressed surprise at the youthfulness of the Virgin Mary, who appeared to be the same age as her son, younger if anything. 'This is the only piece of sculpture that Michelangelo signed,' Kate explained, pointing to Michelangelo's carved signature on the sash running across Mary's breast. 'I think a fellow sculptor was trying to claim ownership and so Michelangelo put his mark where it would be seen. He never did it again.'

Liz pulled out her guidebook which hadn't been used since she and Paul had left Florence and found the entry for St Peter's Basilica. 'I guess I should have a look at Bernini's Baldacchino.' She began walking towards the enormous bronze edifice which sheltered the holy relics of St Peter and enclosed the papal altar. 'It says here that they used nine hundred and twenty seven tons of bronze to construct it. Isn't it amazing that they had the technology five hundred years ago to calculate the likely strength of the floor they would need to support it?' The guidebook told them that the baldacchino had been constructed under the direction of the Barberini pope, Urban VIII, and the monument was decorated here and there with bees, a symbol of his family, which appeared again in the family crest.

They walked around the huge space, absorbing the magnificence and spare-no-expense splendour of the decorations. 'I think it would take several visits to be able to absorb everything,' Liz said. 'The piece I shall remember is the Pietà. I love its simplicity and gentleness and I think in some indefinable way it reaches deep into your soul and moves you in a way that few other works do.'

On the way out they paused long enough for Liz to take a last, lingering look at the work and feel the tears sting the back of her eyes yet again. Paul would have loved it. Her tears were really for him and the things he wouldn't see on this trip.

Briefly she allowed herself to hope that perhaps one day in the future they would come back together.

Finally they left, walked across the piazza and turned left towards the Vatican Museums and the Sistine Chapel. 'I'm going to whisk you through the museum,' Kate said. 'The Sistine Chapel is at the very end and I don't think we should linger or we won't have time to see it properly.' They went through the first museum at a brisk trot, pausing only when Kate suggested a brief detour to visit the Raphael Rooms. 'These rooms were painted by Raphael at the beginning of his career in Rome early in the sixteenth century,' she explained to Liz. 'They're historic rather than religious,' she went on, before pointing out that in a depiction of the School of Athens Raphael had taken artistic license and meshed features of his contemporary artists with those of the great philosophers. Plato resembled Leonardo da Vinci whilst Euclid had been painted to look like Bramante.

'Right! Now you've had the build-up, let me show you the grand finale!' Kate led the way into the Sistine Chapel. Wisely she stayed silent as her friend took in the interior of one of the most famous churches in the world. She watched Liz's mouth open in surprise and a few moments later saw the tears begin to flow down her cheeks. She remembered feeling much the same the first time she came here and tucked her arm into Liz's giving it a quick empathetic squeeze.

Liz brushed away her tears with the back of her hand before opening her guidebook for a more detailed explanation of the stupendous works of art which were all around and above her. The sheer majesty and complexity of the structure, even without the paintings, was mind-blowing, and the addition of the murals and the exquisitely painted ceiling made it almost too much of a good thing.

'I'd advise you just to concentrate on the ceiling,' Kate said. 'As you can see it represents different episodes in the Creation, beginning with Adam and ending with the Last Judgement.'

Liz stared up at the powerful representation of God touching his finger to Adam's, which was the most dominant feature of the Creation. She'd seen pictures of it so many times, but felt that no picture could do justice to the reality. The Last Judgement covered the entire wall above the altar. It seemed inconceivable that one man could have created such a monumental work. Was Michelangelo so exhausted by the labour that had gone into it that he'd portrayed his own face on the flayed skin of St Bartholomew, which the saint was holding up at Jesus' feet, she wondered?

They stood for perhaps fifteen minutes admiring the lifelike poses of the many figures in the masterpiece. 'I think I read somewhere that Michelangelo really changed the way in which figures were depicted,' said Liz. 'It's amazing that many of them twist in a completely realistic way, a long way from the more formal poses which many of his contemporaries favoured. However hard you look it's impossible to find a single human sitting straight up and facing forwards.'

Kate agreed. 'Think what it must have been like to model for Michelangelo. I bet there were some stiff necks and aching limbs at the end of his sessions. I wonder if they had osteopaths in Renaissance Rome!'

Liz smiled at her friend. 'Looking at some of the figures up there,' she gestured towards the ceiling, 'they may not have had osteopaths, but I wouldn't mind betting that there was no shortage of volunteer masseuses!' They laughed together as they walked towards the exit leaving behind five hundred years of art history.

'Would you like some lunch?' Liz asked Kate. 'My treat.'

Kate looked at her friend and felt herself struggle between a genuine feeling of hunger and a niggling guilt at staying away from the hospital longer than was absolutely necessary. 'Shouldn't we be getting back to Paul?' she asked, remembering the real reason for her visit.

Liz shrugged and held out both hands in a gesture of complete helplessness. 'Kate, I've been watching over him for the best part of a week. If I thought sitting by his bedside would make him better believe me I'd be there, but I've reached the stage now where I realise that I've absolutely no power to make Paul well. I don't even know if he realises that it's me holding his hand or recognises that the voice whispering into his ear belongs to his wife, or even remembers he has a wife.'

Kate prayed silently that she would never be in the same position. She'd been so envious when Liz married and even more so when the children arrived. Now she counted herself lucky not to be fretting over a seriously ill husband and wondered how soon she could phone Luigi. In the meantime they must find somewhere pleasant for lunch. She tucked her arm through Liz's. 'Come on, let's get back to the car and I'll drive us to Trastevere.'

CHAPTER TEN

Paul's arm ached from the drip, which he assumed was pumping some kind of nourishment or medication into him, possibly both. He thought longingly of tasting real food; the texture of it on your tongue, the slow release of the flavour as you chewed, the gradual easing of hunger as you progressed through the meal. He remembered some of the more memorable meals he'd eaten. His first schnitzel in Austria, where he'd gone as soon as foreign travel was allowed after the war, crisp and golden on the outside, juicy and succulent within. It had tasted like the food of the gods after the horrible stuff he'd been forced to eat in the army and immediately post-war in England. After his demobilisation he'd told everyone that eating British army food had been considerably worse than fighting the war.

The antipasti he'd shared with Liz in Portofino had been perfect and he'd thought at the time that England still had a long way to go before they learned to produce a luncheon that could be so simple and needed no improvement.

Some of his own culinary attempts were worth remembering. He'd jugged a hare when he and Liz had been at Ivy House one weekend. He tasted it again and saw the pieces of meat bathed in fragrant gravy, which he'd enriched with port and redcurrant jelly and garnished with succulent, fat prunes and crisp bacon rolls.

His mouth was dry. He'd give his eye teeth for a mouthful of decent claret, which would do far more for him than whatever it was they'd pumped into him since he came into . . . Where was he? He couldn't remember. How did he get here? Why was he alone? How long before he could get up? Oh God! He was confused, tired and weary and suddenly finding it hard to breathe. The next time his doctor told him to take things easily he'd be inclined to listen with more care. Until then . . .

🦋

Liz looked around with renewed interest as Kate drove them into Trastevere. The picturesque medieval area and narrow lanes could have been a million miles from Rome instead of a mere stone's throw away across the Tiber.

They walked across the piazza in front of Santa Maria in Trastevere, which Kate described as most likely the oldest church in Rome. A fountain tinkled temptingly in the centre of the square, but Kate was making her way with some determination towards a narrow lane, one of several which led out of the piazza. The lane was lined with restaurants and bars and, glancing upwards, Liz saw plants scrambling down the walls from carefully tended garden terraces and assumed that there were people like herself who were 'living over the shop'.

'Do you think it's warm enough to eat outside?' Kate asked as she stopped in front of an unprepossessing looking trattoria.

Liz held out her hand as if trying to feel the temperature. 'It should be OK,' she said, 'but if we choose hot food it might not stay that way for very long. What do you think?'

'I think you've just given us a very good reason to eat inside.'

The room they entered had uneven cream-washed walls, which looked as if they'd been standing for centuries. The floor was tiled in mellow terracotta and there were no more than half a dozen bare wooden tables, each bearing a stem of brilliant yellow single chrysanthemums.

A smiling middle-aged woman materialised and pulled out chairs for each of them in turn. She was the archetypal Italian mama with dark curls, brown eyes and a body which bore testament to a couple of decades of good eating. Liz began to look forward to lunch.

'Buon giourno!' They greeted each other simultaneously. The woman produced menus. 'You like wine,' she said, making it a statement rather than a question. Kate affirmed that they would indeed like wine and ordered a carafe of house white.

They were halfway through their meal when Liz glanced sideways at her watch and discovered it was nearly three o'clock. Oh my God, poor Paul! She'd put him to the back of her mind since they left the hospital and her conscience told her it was time to be getting back to him. 'Would you mind if we skipped coffee?' she said. 'I think I should try to look in on Paul before everyone settles down for the night.'

Kate had been wondering for some time if Liz intended to return to Paul, but hadn't liked to mention it. For a few hours her friend had seemed to relax, on the surface anyway, and she felt it would be unkind to drag her back to the awful reality of what was happening to her before it was absolutely necessary. 'Il conto, per favore,' she said, catching the eye of the signora and reaching for her handbag.

'Lunch is on me,' Liz said firmly. 'I can't tell you how good it's been just to get away from that awful hospital for a few hours, but more than anything to be with someone with whom I can relax for the first time since Paul was taken ill. Not everyone would have made the effort to come all the way from Perugia and I really appreciate it.

Kate shrugged away Liz's thanks. 'Remember when you and Paul took me under your wings when I was working at that ghastly hotel in London. And that other time when I split up with Justin and you poured wine and sympathy into me! A few days in Rome are nothing and it will give me an opportunity to see Luigi some time. So you don't owe me anything. I hope you'll get a chance to meet Luigi, perhaps some time this weekend.'

Liz smiled, recalling the number of times that Kate's heart had been broken in the past and hoped that this Luigi character wasn't about to break it again. 'I'd like that.' She rose reluctantly, not wanting to quit the comfort and homeliness of the trattoria, which represented a brief escape from the nightmare that her life had become. She walked slowly back across the piazza, relishing the late afternoon sun and trying to memorise the layout, the architecture, the atmosphere; only too aware that Rome was waiting on the other side of the Tiber, hating herself for not wanting to be there.

Normally when she went into the hospital the porter on duty would look up, smile and wish her 'buona sera.' This afternoon was different. He failed to meet her eyes as she approached and Liz had a sickening feeling as they made their way to Paul's ward that they were walking towards bad news. She saw the nurse compose her features into a suitable expression of sympathy before telling her that Paul had died at three o'clock without regaining consciousness and that they'd moved him into a side ward. All the other occupants of Paul's ward who were able to get out of bed were sitting outside in the corridor, smoking and not speaking to each other. They too failed to make eye contact with Liz as they saw the nurse breaking the news to her.

She looked at the lifeless body that had once been her wonderful, vital husband and longed to be back at home with their children - the only tangible piece of Paul that was left. She couldn't cry, but sat staring at him, trying to commit his face to memory. Half of her was relieved that he was now at peace. The other half was violently angry at the injustice of it all. At forty two he was too young to die. His children needed him. The business needed him. She needed him. She stared at his empty shell trying to absorb the reality that they would never share another joke, another meal, or a new and exciting experience. They'd just had their last holiday together and the future, normally so full of hope, promise and excitement because Paul was part of it, now looked like a dangerous place; unbearably bleak, lonely and uncertain. How on earth was she going to survive and how could she ever have contemplated a future without him when he was still alive?

The guilt she felt overtook her sadness and she vowed never again to be discontented with her life. She turned reluctantly away from Paul when the sound of voices drifted through the dark mists of her thoughts. First the slightly foreign accent of Hans Lebermann and then, in more subdued tones, the voice of his wife. Kate had walked towards the entrance to the ward and was introducing herself. Liz forced herself to meet their eyes and then to walk towards them, take their outstretched hands and listen to their expressions of sympathy. Their compassionate words and unstinting kindness gave her absolutely no comfort.

Hans Lebermann walked over to the bed and made the sign of the cross over Paul before turning his attention to Liz. There was a cheap reproduction of Holman Hunt's *Light of the World* hanging on the wall. He gestured towards the picture with his right hand. 'Remember that He was in this room,' he said quietly.

'I'm sorry, but right this minute God seems a million miles away,' Liz replied, 'and what's more, if He dares to come anywhere near me in the foreseeable future I shall tell Him exactly where to go.' She knew it was a horrible thing to say to any priest let alone one who'd shown her nothing but humanity since they'd first met. But although her own words filled her with self-loathing it was impossible for her to apologise. If he was a true Christian he would understand the pain she was feeling. If he wasn't then he would take umbrage and leave. Either way she didn't care.

༉

Hans Lebermann smiled a sad smile and, from the inside pocket of his jacket, pulled out a small, worn, leather bound copy of the Bible. He turned the pages swiftly until he came to Matthew chapter eleven. '"Come unto me, all ye that labour and are heavy laden, and I will give you rest. Take my yoke upon you, and learn of me; for I am meek and lowly in heart: and ye shall find rest unto your souls. For my yoke is easy and my burden is light."' He spoke the words with the confidence of someone who had read them many, many times before.

On the evening when he'd first met Liz and Paul he'd guessed that if the pair of them had ever succeeded in finding God they'd probably never followed Him and thus it was highly unlikely they'd ever encountered His peace of mind, His strength in temptation and His courage in difficulties.

He felt intuitively that now would not be the time to quote from the Anglican Catechism, particularly after what Liz had just said to him. How could he then show her that her attitude was condemning her, if not to outer darkness, then to some Godless place where her soul would find neither peace nor comfort? If he was to suggest to her that she confess her sins, turn her back on them and thus take a crucially important step which would bring her nearer to God, in her present mood she would probably slap his face or tell him to go to hell!

He looked across to where she sat. Her drooping shoulders and the anguish in her eyes told him the desolation she was feeling; looking at Paul, almost devouring him as she tried to fix every last detail of him in her memory. How could he get across to her that Jesus Christ had died for her when the perimeter of her life had shrunk to an area the size of a single bed containing her dead husband? He wished that there were fewer times, like now, when he felt his own inadequacy as a priest.

He leaned forward and took Liz's hand. 'Believe me I can understand your anger. But if there are times in the future when you need strength I can only advise you to turn to God and He will be there for you. Now I should like to say a prayer for the repose of Paul's soul, but only if you agree.' A few seconds passed before he felt a slight pressure as her fingers squeezed his own briefly and he saw a single tear appear in the corner of her right eye before he closed his own and began to recite, '"O Almighty God, with whom do live the spirits of just men . . ."'

＄

When Hans Lebermann had finished, Liz was silent for a moment, and then, 'Thank you,' she said, 'that was very kind of you.'

'I'm only sorry that I was unable to administer Holy Communion to Paul before he died. Will you be flying him home to be buried?' he asked, thinking that to move on to practicalities might be the most sensible next step.

'No,' Liz said decisively. 'I've already discussed it with Michael Shand, the vice-consul. He's going to arrange for Paul to be cremated and will have his ashes flown home to me later.'

'And has he offered to find an English speaking priest for

you?' Hans tried not to let the concern show on his face, but he'd heard that funerals arranged for foreigners were sometimes done on the cheap and felt that, after all her suffering, this poor woman deserved better. He also knew that in a predominantly Roman Catholic country like Italy the arrangements for cremation could be primitive to say the least.

'We didn't go into details,' Liz said, 'but he's been so helpful since we met I'm sure I can count on him one last time.'

'Well,' Hans Lebermann pulled a card from yet another inside pocket, scribbled the phone number of their flat on it and handed it across to Liz. 'Here's my number and if you need any help please do get in touch. If you let me know the date and time Ruth and I will be there to support you.'

Liz shook his hand. 'You've both been more than kind,' she said. 'It's hard to believe that you've only known us for a week.' The plural slipped out without her realising what she'd said. She turned to Ruth and kissed her briefly on the cheek thinking that the poor woman probably had to endure occasions like this every week of her life and thanked her lucky stars that she'd terminated her relationship with the Cambridge theology student with whom she'd had a brief fling in the days before she'd known Paul.

'Right, I need to get to a telephone,' Liz said to Kate as soon as she could be certain that Hans and his wife were out of earshot. 'If we get a move on we should be able to catch Michael Shand before he leaves his office and if he's already gone then I'll make sure that one of his staff gets in touch with him as soon as possible. I know that his wife's in England at the moment so unless he's found himself some gorgeous Italian girlfriend it's unlikely that he'll be dashing off home early.'

The vehemence with which Liz spoke surprised Kate, who'd been quietly watching the scene playing out in front of her for the past half hour and wondering how she managed to be so self-contained. She hated to think what her own reactions might be if ever she found herself in a similar situation, knowing that in Liz's place she'd probably go completely to pieces. 'Right lets go,' she said. 'If you like I'll let the nurse know that we'll be making arrangements . . .' She let her voice die away not wanting to say the words funeral, burial or any of the other hideous words normally associated with occasions like this.

Fifteen minutes later they were back in the hotel. When Kate explained to the manager what had happened he not only invited them to use his office but, after making the sign of the cross and giving Liz his condolences, sent in a tray of coffee to keep them going whilst they made their phone calls.

Michael Shand replaced the receiver and sighed deeply, wondering how he could feel so much sadness for someone he scarcely knew. At times like this he hated his job, but also realised it was within his power to do everything he could to smooth the paths of troubled tourists. He wondered if Liz knew that it was All Souls Day, when every responsible Roman Catholic in the city would be saying prayers for the souls of their dear departed. Liz had told him she wanted Paul to be cremated as soon as possible so that she could get home to her children and who could blame her? He'd offered to go to her hotel at eleven o'clock the next morning, by which time he had to find a suitable church, a priest and an undertaker. Fortunately his contacts book was comprehensive and he didn't doubt for one moment his ability to deliver.

Antonia replaced the receiver with shaking hands and cursed herself for not flying out to Rome to be with Paul at a time when he surely needed her most. And now it was too late. A friend, a business partner and confidante had disappeared in an instant. The time she'd spent with Paul in the years he'd been helping her run the business had been some of the happiest of her life, the closest she would ever get to a man that she could call her own.

Her fiance David had been killed towards the end of the First World War. Another couple of months and he would have been safe and her own life would have been very different. They would have married, had children and she would have had someone to love and comfort her at times, like now, when she needed a friend.

How on earth was she going to pay off the substantial bank loan they'd taken out to finance the improvements to the public rooms if Paul wasn't here to help them through the banqueting season? Even if she managed to find a replacement manager he couldn't, correction, wouldn't be half as good as Paul.

She'd only bought the hotel in the first place to find her father something to do after he lost his job in the City and, though it pained her to admit it, he'd been more of a liability than an asset. For one thing his heart hadn't been in it. He'd seen it as working in 'trade', something a gentleman never did. Somehow he'd missed the point that gentlemen, if they were clever, didn't get themselves fired from their firm for embezzlement. Over the years it had needed all her ingenuity to keep him as far away from the money, and thus temptation, as she possibly could.

Paul had given her something she'd never received from her father, hands on support and, perhaps more importantly, encouragement. He'd dedicated himself heart and soul to making the hotel a success. His energy had flagged a bit since he married Liz, but she knew he would regain his former enthusiasm once the novelty of his marriage wore off. In the meantime she'd kept up a steady barrage of projects to make sure that he didn't go soft on her and run away with the idea that just because he was a partner he could start to put his feet up and leave others to do the running around. She'd worked like a dog all her life and saw no reason why everyone else shouldn't do the same. But there was no point in feeling sorry for herself; there was a great deal to be done during the next few days, so the sooner she got down to making plans the better.

CHAPTER ELEVEN

Signor Damiano seized Liz's hand and then bent over to kiss it. The expression on his face showed a delicate blend of tenderness and sympathy which he'd developed over his years as an undertaker and, after much practice, had now honed to perfection. 'La povera signora,' he murmured, lifting his head at last and giving Liz a soulful look which allowed her the full benefit of his lustrous dark brown eyes. Her smile of gratitude was rather faint. If her present situation wasn't so tragic she would have laughed aloud. The Italian undertaker looked as if he'd stepped straight out of a local amateur dramatic production. He was shorter than any of them. Thick, dark hair slicked back with some highly perfumed oil which wafted towards her in nauseous waves. She hoped Michael Shand, who was standing by in his role as vice-consul, would be able to draw the meeting to a close as quickly as possible.

To her surprise he'd told her that he'd managed to arrange Paul's funeral and cremation service for Monday morning and offered to book her a seat on the first available plane the same afternoon. To Liz this seemed like amazing efficiency and, when she'd said as much, he'd merely shrugged. 'Well you did tell me that you wanted to return home as quickly as possible.' He managed to sound as if to carry out her slightest wish would make him the happiest man on earth.

Liz, uncharacteristically, was happy to leave any practical arrangements to anyone willing to take them on. Normally competent, she felt lost and totally unable to grapple with the realities of funeral and flight arrangements in what was, after all, a foreign country. To her relief Signor Damiano left them at last with a final bow in Liz's direction, his right hand resting lightly in the region of his heart. Liz felt he looked more like a *commedia dell'arte* character than ever and wouldn't have been surprised if he'd pulled a lace hanky from his sleeve and waved it towards her with a flowery flourish.

'I wonder if you could let me have your husband's passport,' Michael Shand said once the undertaker had left. Seeing her questioning look he added, 'I'll need it in order to get a death certificate.' He looked almost apologetic as he spoke and Liz immediately felt sorry for him. It was, after all, the weekend and whether or not he was supposed to be on duty she could think of many other things that he would probably rather be doing than arranging a funeral for a British tourist.

'It's in my room, I'll get it for you straight away.' She spoke with relief that at last she'd been faced with a request with which she could comply easily. Even so, she was apprehensive about handing over Paul's passport to a consular official and felt as if in so doing she was condemning him to eternal incarceration in some appalling prison.

Kate hadn't been present at their discussion. Liz had waved away her offer of moral support, feeling that she deserved a break after all the drama they'd been through together. They were due to meet at noon and Kate had promised to try and bring Luigi along so that at long last Liz would be able to meet him. She hoped one way or another that some of Kate's happiness might rub off on her. The finality of Paul's death had left her not only numb with shock at the unexpectedness of it all, but also with a deep and underlying sadness. At the moment she felt as if she were wrapped in a dense, grey blanket through which she could neither see nor feel, and found herself wondering if this was what a depressive illness was like and if, in time, she might fall victim to a full blown clinical depression.

'My employer has invited us all to lunch tomorrow,' Kate said later as they sat in the restaurant waiting for their food to arrive. Earlier, Kate and Luigi had collected Liz from her hotel and they'd walked for a good half hour to the Piazza Navona.

Although Liz had accepted their invitation to join them for lunch, her appetite was non-existent. 'I'm not really very hungry,' she said when the waiter produced the menu. But Kate had persuaded her to have a little fish, urging her of the need to 'keep her strength up'.

'You sound a bit like my old granny,' Liz said, managing a faint smile and, at the same time, allowing herself to be persuaded; it was, after all, much easier than arguing. She sat watching Luigi talking to Kate. They were speaking to each other in Italian, so it was easy for Liz to take a back seat. His eyes never left Kate's face and it was obvious that he was delighted to see her again. Liz wondered if the pair of them would eventually decide to spend the rest of their lives together and, if so, would Luigi persuade Kate to relocate to Rome? She was the sort of sophisticated woman who is happiest in a city and Liz guessed that it wouldn't much matter to Kate where that city was.

She watched Luigi's hands, which were resting lightly on the table, as he talked to Kate. His long, delicate fingers looked as if they belonged to an artist or a musician. But then putting together broken bones was a profession which demanded both precision and, from time-to-time, difficult manipulation, so his delicate fingers could be a considerable asset.

'Luigi's just told me he's decided to specialise in sports injuries,' Kate said as their food arrived. 'He's been agonising for ages not only about which branch of orthopaedics to concentrate on, but also which part of the human body.'

'What made up his mind?' Liz asked, feeling slightly uneasy talking about Luigi as if he weren't sitting directly beside her. Kate rolled her eyes and her face wore an expression of amused tolerance. 'Apparently some mega football star was admitted to the hospital a couple of weeks ago with a broken foot and Luigi helped the surgeon realign a couple of fractured metatarsals. Once he realised that the man's future career was at stake his mind was made up.' She picked up her glass before raising it in a mock salute in Luigi's direction. 'To Signor Luigi Franchetti, sports surgeon *extraordinaire*!' Liz raised her own glass. 'Here's to your future success,' she said, 'and to many more mended metatarsals.'

After lunch, Luigi left them and went back to his hospital, but promised to meet them the following day for their lunch with Kate's employer. It was only then that Liz realised that in all the turmoil of the last week she'd completely forgotten to buy presents for the children and persuaded Kate to take her shopping. Kate, only too pleased to have an excuse, took Liz first to an enchanting toy shop tucked away in a corner of the Piazza Navona and then suggested that they take the car and go to Upim and Standa where they'd be able to buy a wide range of children's clothing without breaking the bank. On the way, Liz asked Kate to stop by a post office to allow her to post what would probably be the last card she would send to Marcus from Rome. She'd chosen a picture of the Spanish Steps and written that she and papa were having a lovely time. Some time soon she would have to break the news to Marcus that he no longer had a father, but for the moment . . .

'I don't know if I should even be spending money,' she confided as they sat in a small bar drinking coffee and recovering from their shopping trip at the end of the afternoon. 'Do you know, I have no idea how much we have or rather how much money *I* have,' she corrected herself hastily. 'I've always left the financial planning to Paul and we don't even have a joint account. Somehow it was easy for me to carry on using my own bank account after we married. Paul paid me an allowance and I have a small legacy from my grandmother that I mostly use for the maintenance of Ivy House but, to be honest, that's about it.'

'Well, you'll have plenty of time to sort out your finances when you get home,' Kate said. 'Paul's solicitor and possibly his accountant will soon put you in the picture. Does Paul have a pension fund?' she queried.

Kate spoke with the assurance of someone who has an accountant for a father. 'Well, I think he has, but I don't really know the details. What I do know is that he tried to increase his life assurance policy a short while ago and that's when we discovered he was hypertensive. It's not something we've ever discussed in depth.' The expression on Kate's face told her that she'd been more than remiss to be so vague about her future, but then she'd never contemplated life without Paul. 'Don't forget we've only been married for four years,' she said, aware that she sounded defensive. 'I'll worry about money once I'm home.' There was a good deal more to worry about before she even got there, but she'd just survived what was possibly the worst week of her life and, by some miracle, would find the strength to deal with other emergencies as and when they happened.

Antonia waited until nearly midnight before going downstairs and letting herself into the office she shared with Paul. Both the public rooms and the reception area were quiet. Most of the guests had disappeared, either to bed or home; only the faint murmur of voices coming from the bar reminded her that there were either residents or diners still drinking. Well, they were hardly likely to bother her and if the night porter chose to put his head round the door he would be easy to deal with.

She'd collected the spare set of keys from behind the reception desk, knowing that there were certain drawers in Paul's desk which were locked. Thank goodness he kept all his papers in the office; it would have been impossible for her to access them in the flat. Her fingers shook with suppressed excitement as she began to pull out the drawers that weren't locked. They contained the usual predictable office paraphernalia: supplies of paper, envelopes, paper clips, a stapler, an assortment of catering and hotel catalogues of one kind or another. Nothing of any great interest to anyone, let alone Antonia.

Slowly and methodically she moved down the stack of drawers until she came to one at the bottom left hand side that was locked. She riffled through the bunch of keys until she found one she thought would fit. The lock resisted. She tried another. Ah! That was better, the lock turned and she opened the drawer. She pulled out a small collection of cards that were lying on top of a pile of files and papers and opened them one at a time. She'd never thought of Paul as the sentimental type, but it soon became clear that he'd saved every card - Christmas, birthday, postcards even, that Liz had ever sent him. Her mouth tightened and the expression in her eyes hardened as she read the brief expressions of love that they contained: "To darling Paul. Thank you for three marvellous years." "For my favourite old man on his fortieth birthday." "Kate and I are having a wonderful skiing holiday. It would be perfect if you were here." Antonia read them all, her misery increasing as she worked slowly and deliberately through the pile.

She removed the files next. They were all meticulously labelled: LEGAL; ARMY; RECEIPTS; FAMILY. She opened the legal file and immediately spotted the long, narrow envelope labelled Last Will and Testament, which was the one she sought. She'd take them up to her flat and read them in peace. In any case, the envelope containing Paul's will was sealed and would have to be steamed open before she could read the contents, and that was impossible in the office.

At the very bottom of the drawer she found a small black leather box lying on top of a square, white envelope with Liz's name on it in Paul's bold handwriting. She opened the box and found a pair of diamond earrings, which she recognised as a pair that had belonged to Paul's mother. He'd shown them to her after his mother's funeral. They'd belonged initially to his Jewish grandmother and his father had given them to his mother as a wedding present. She was looking at an extremely handsome pair of pendant earrings. The diamonds set in platinum looked cool and icy. A single, slender line of tiny stones supported a fan-shaped cascade of larger gems, which flashed a rainbow spectrum as Antonia held them up to the light. She'd never owned such impressive jewellery and felt her throat constrict with envy as she turned them this way and that before finally replacing them in their box.

Surprisingly, the white envelope wasn't sealed. Unable to

contain her curiosity, she drew out the letter, which was just a single page written on the hotel writing paper.

My darling Liz, she read, *I've just come back from seeing the quack who tells me that if I don't take more care of myself I'll be facing a very short future. Would you believe it? I'm writing this on the spur of the moment in case I don't make it through the night!*

I'd hoped to give you Mother's diamond earrings on our tenth wedding anniversary, and with care I might still do that. However, if the worst happens, you'll get them anyway. Their sparkle reminds me of the glint in your eyes at certain moments - I'll leave you to decide which moments I mean!

I know you'll take great care of the children. I want you to know how special you all are to me and I hate to think that we might not all grow old together. Believe me I couldn't have had a better wife and I couldn't have loved anyone more than I love you.

Thank you for all the happiness.

My love,

Paul.

A single choking sob escaped from Antonia and hot tears begin to roll down her face. She reached up to the shelf above Paul's desk, pulled down a box file, opened it and emptied the contents onto a nearby table. She hastily stuffed everything she'd removed from the drawer into the box file, relocked the drawer and, pausing only to replace the bunch of keys in reception, she stumbled back up the stairs to the sanctuary of her flat.

Liz woke early on Monday morning to the unmistakeable sound of rain beating against the hotel window. It was the first rain she'd seen since they'd left home two weeks ago. Forcing herself to get out of bed she crossed the floor, opened the shutters and stared out at the desolate, grey landscape, which couldn't have mirrored her own internal feelings more accurately if the weather had been ordered specifically. She leaned her forehead against the cool glass. 'Oh Paul! Paul! The world is crying for you!' How on earth was she going to get through the next few hours?

It was November 5th and back home later on, images of Guy Fawkes would be burning on bonfires all over the country, or at least they would if it wasn't raining in England. Today she and Paul should have returned after their holiday and be letting off their own fireworks for the children, but Paul would never again be back at home. Today, like a Guy Fawkes effigy, his body would be turned into a heap of ashes and, in a day or two, what was left of him would be flown home in the cold hold of an aircraft along with other pieces of luggage or, worse still, freight.

She ordered a pot of coffee via the hotel's room service. It would be sensible to try and eat something, but there wasn't the remotest chance she'd be able to force it down, so she stuck to coffee and drank it whilst packing her suitcase. Only then did she get ready for Paul's funeral. She owed it to him to look her best and applied her make-up carefully and put on the black dress that she'd worn to dinner on their first night in Rome.

Earlier she'd rescued Paul's raincoat from the boot of the car and, on a whim, she tried it on for size. The sleeves were a bit long, but if she turned them up and did up the belt there was a good chance she could get away with it. The raincoat still smelt of Paul and it was a comfort to be able to inhale such a tangible memory of him.

Finally she was ready. She took a quick look around the room, gave the bathroom the final once-over and lugged her suitcase into the lift. By the time she'd settled her bill Kate had arrived with the car and, after stowing Liz's luggage in the boot, drove towards the cemetery.

They were both uncharacteristically silent throughout the journey. There seemed to be absolutely nothing to say. Liz gazed out of the window at the sodden Roman citizens, but felt detached, almost as if the scene in front of her was a movie.

'Friday was All Souls Day and they make a big thing of it

over here,' Kate said as they finally drove into the churchyard. 'Just look at the graves.'

Liz looked. Most of them were decorated with huge wreaths and bore a picture of the occupant. In some cases the photographs were flanked by a small lantern. Liz had never seen anything like it.

'Some of the families will be on short rations for the next few weeks,' Kate said. 'Mother Church exerts a high price for fidelity in countries like this. A lot of those families,' she paused and waved a hand in the direction of the graves. 'Many of those families will also have half a dozen children or more as they're not supposed to practice contraception. So you see how tough it can be for the faithful.'

The car drew up in front of a small church and Liz saw, to her surprise, a clutch of people waiting in front of it, sheltering under a motley collection of umbrellas. Michael Shand detached himself from the group and came towards them with his hand outstretched.

'It's really kind of you to come,' Liz said, forcing the words past the catch in her throat. She was surprised that he was there, but then she hadn't expected anyone to turn up, although she'd remembered to phone the Lebermanns, mostly because she'd felt that they'd be hurt if she forgot them.

'Let me introduce the Right Reverend Canon Forwood,' Michael Shand extended his right hand in the general direction of the priest who came towards Liz on cue, shaking her hand and offering his condolences. Liz thought how amused Paul would be if he knew that a member of a cathedral chapter had been detailed to preside at his funeral. She introduced Kate and then walked towards the Lebermanns who were standing just outside the church porch. Hans Lebermann looked a little disconcerted; either as if he were in the wrong place or in the right place but at the wrong time. It came to her in a blinding flash that she should have suggested to Michael Shand that he be invited to take the service and cursed herself for not becoming more involved in the arrangements. Oh well, too late now. She would have a word with them afterwards when the whole ghastly business was over. Signor Damiano materialised from the depths of the porch where he'd been sheltering from the rain and went through his hand-kissing ritual, taking care to include Kate.

Canon Forwood led the way into the church, which smelt damp and dusty, as if it hadn't been used recently. It was small, bare and dingy. The pews bore a light coating of dust and it had obviously been a long time since anyone had sat in them. As they assembled awkwardly in the front rows, two men, who looked to Liz like gravediggers, walked into the church from a front entrance bearing Paul's coffin between them. "Alas! Poor Yorrick!" Liz thought and wondered irreverently if by any chance they'd chucked his skull in with Paul. Bleakly she remembered snippets of Hamlet's speech.

"I knew him Horatio; a fellow of infinite jest, of most excellent fancy . . . Here hung those lips that I have kissed I know not how oft . . ." She daren't continue and felt mortified that she'd not thought more deeply about this funeral. There was no music; no flight of angels to sing Paul to his rest. She glanced quickly at Hans Lebermann whose eyes were closed as if he were offering up a prayer. As well he might. What was he thinking as he surveyed this travesty? The tears began to flow down her cheeks as she realised that there were no flowers. Not a single bloom. And outside, the graves of the dead were adorned and embellished in honour of All Souls Day. She felt a deep, burning shame. How could she have allowed this? She clutched Kate's hand as Canon Forwood's voice began. '"I am the resurrection and the life, saith the Lord; he that believeth in me, though he were dead, yet shall he live: and whosoever liveth and believeth in me shall never die."'

'Can you ever forgive me?' Kate spoke silently to Paul as the voice of the priest continued to recite the service. What a wonderful seven days they'd spent together before this awful tragedy had put such a cruel end to it. She fingered the amber necklace that she'd hung around her neck on impulse before leaving the hotel and remembered the sunny morning in Florence when Paul had bought it for her. She didn't deserve it.

Paul should have married someone who would have taken better care of him, not allowed him to die so young and when he finally quit his life in old age would have taken rather more care over his funeral service. What a blessing that Antonia was far away in England. At least she would never know how badly Liz had let him down.

Canon Forwood was standing at the end of the pew waiting for her to leave. Was it all over? The service seemed cruelly truncated without hymns or loving friends to speak a final tribute. She turned and walked towards the canon who took her arm and led her towards the church door. Once in the open air, he raised a protective umbrella and held it over her against the pouring rain.

'I'm afraid cremation in Italy isn't quite the same as it is in England. I suggest you wait in the car. I'll do the rest of the service and join you shortly. Liz didn't argue. After the horrors of the church she daren't think what the crematorium would be like. An open fire? A concentration camp gas oven? A blazing pit complete with screaming corpses? 'I'm happy to wait,' she said, feeling more like a traitor than ever as she watched the canon, the vice-consul and the undertaker disappear towards the crematorium.

'I can't tell you how sick I feel.' Ruth Lebermann came towards Liz and put her arms around her. 'This is the most terrible excuse for a funeral I've ever witnessed. I'm going to persuade Hans to complain to the consul. It's an absolute disgrace. I think you've been completely ripped off. When I'm back in England I shall suggest to our MP that he raise the matter of tourist exploitation in the House.'

Liz smiled and patted her hand. 'It's good of you to be concerned, but please don't blame Michael Shand. He's been doing his best to make my life easier and I'm afraid I'm as much to blame as anyone for what went on in there.' She jerked her head towards the church. 'It would have been nice if someone had cared enough to dust the pews, but nothing we do or say will bring Paul back.' She turned towards Hans. 'Forgive me for not asking you to take the service. I'm not firing on all cylinders at the moment. I hope you understand. You've both been so helpful and I really appreciate your concern. I'd ask you to join us for lunch, but we're leaving for the airport just as soon as the cremation is over. I doubt that we'll have time to eat.'

Just then the men rejoined them. Goodbyes were said. Thanks reiterated. At last the ghastly fiasco was over. Liz climbed into the car as Kate started the engine and stared through the rain-spattered window hating Rome, the weather and, most of all, herself.

CHAPTER TWELVE

She sat alone, plumb in the centre of a puddle of misery, in the departure lounge at Leonardo da Vinci Airport. The runway was flooded, her flight had been delayed for an hour and there was no choice but to wait out the time as patiently as possible. In spite of trying hard not to think about Paul, her mind refused to stop drifting back to the day in Portofino when the sun had been shining and she'd been sitting opposite him with nothing more important to do than eat a delicious lunch and look forward to getting him into bed. It had been such a happy day with her lovely holiday stretching out in front of her and now it was all over. Her life with Paul ended.

The concerns she'd felt then seemed pointless and empty. To think she'd been unhappy because she didn't see more of him when every night she'd had the luxury of curling up next to him and stealing his warmth. With hindsight she'd been spoiled and selfish; too absorbed with her own concerns, not nearly enough with Paul's. She would have to live with the guilt for the rest of her life and she deserved any criticism that might conceivably come her way in the future.

Don't keep on thinking about him, she told herself. *It's pure self-indulgence. If you continue you'll probably end up crying in the middle of the airport. Instead you must think about home and the children and make a mental list of all the things you'll have to do tomorrow.* At least she could look forward to seeing Oscar again. He'd promised to meet her at Heathrow and drive her back to the hotel or he would if she ever got out of this place.

She pulled a book out of her bag knowing the chances of her being able to concentrate on it were remote. If her life was a novel, some divine stranger would pick up on her sadness and make it his mission to comfort her. Alternatively, some long lost friend would chance by and they'd be able to catch up on the missing years until the plane took off. This being reality, she sat and looked at the print on the page without seeing any of it.

After twenty minutes she gave up, closed the book and thought instead about the lunch they'd had the previous day with Kate's employer, the formality of which had taken her completely by surprise. The family lived on the second floor of a small medieval palazzo, which had been converted into apartments. Tucked away in an unprepossessing street about five minutes away from the Campo de' Fiori, it had been transformed with considerable flair into an elegant residence. Long floor-to-ceiling windows were curtained in pale gold brocade and the old parquet floors were strewn with a variety of mellow oriental rugs. The furniture was large, old and well cared for in keeping with the surroundings.

The lunch party included the elderly parents of the judge and his two grown up children who did their best to converse in English, mostly for Kate's benefit, but also as a courtesy to their English guest. The food was served by a woman whom Liz took to be a maid, although a bit on the elderly side to answer to that description.

The lunch was equally splendid. They began with mezzelune, half moon pasta parcels which were bathed in a creamy sauce and, as if that wasn't enough, served in a drum of pastry. The thought that anyone would go to so much trouble over a starter for Sunday lunch was a revelation to Liz. This was followed by quail, which had been cooked with white grapes in a delicate chicken broth until they were exquisitely tender and the meat fell off their tiny bones. They finished with fruit, which was served on beautiful hand-painted porcelain and which they ate with silver knives and forks with mother-of-pearl handles. By the end of the meal, Liz felt as if she had been transported to a previous century and wondered how many Roman citizens routinely ate food of this standard and in such refined splendour.

Her enjoyment of Sunday lunch was interrupted when her flight was called and she was able at last to cut herself loose from the city in which she'd lived through so much drama and personal sadness. Once on board she found herself sitting next to a Roman Catholic priest and felt an overwhelming desire to grab him by the lapels of his jacket and shake him until his belief rattled in his throat. *I'm slowly becoming unhinged*, she thought bleakly, fastening her seat belt and wondering how long it might be before she went stark raving crazy. As the plane taxied down the runway, the priest crossed himself fervently and, even though steeped in misery and with her spirits at zero, the action brought a faint smile to her face.

About half an hour after take-off, a stewardess came round with plastic mugs of tea and leathery-looking fruit pies. Liz waved both away, although she'd eaten nothing all day. Her mood deepened and darkened. After all the deliciously tempting food she'd eaten during the last two weeks, British mass catering seemed awful and she thought longingly of the delicious smell of vanilla in the pasticceria on the way to the Sistine Chapel. She closed her eyes in desperation and to her surprise slept until the pilot's voice announced that they would be landing in about twenty minutes and that it was raining in London.

Nearly an hour later she pushed her luggage trolley into the arrivals hall and scanned the crowd anxiously, searching for Oscar. She must have been looking in the wrong direction and failed to see him until suddenly he materialised in front of her trolley. Oscar. Tall, blonde Oscar with the same intense blue eyes as Paul, which crinkled deeply at the corners when he smiled. He was wearing a battered tweed jacket which made him look like an English schoolmaster, which belied his Austrian background.

'Liz. Welcome home!' he said, putting an arm around her and kissing her briefly on the cheek.

'Oh, Oscar!' He looked so reassuringly wonderful that her voice broke and she burst into tears.

'I don't normally have that effect on women!' He took control of her trolley and draped an arm casually around her shoulder, at the same time steering her firmly towards the car park.

Liz smiled through the tears. It was so like him to try to be cheerful.

'We looked in at the hotel yesterday,' he went on. 'Thought I'd better let the old dragon know I was picking you up just in case she decided to send a reception committee or something. Where's Paul's car by the way?'

'In Rome with my friend Kate. She's going to contact the Automobile Club Italiano and I'll contact the RAC over here. Hopefully between the two of them they'll be able to make arrangements to ship it home. I didn't really feel up to driving back by myself and Kate has to stay in Italy until her course finishes, so I couldn't really ask her to drive home with me. She's already done so much. Now, tell me how things were at the hotel. Were the children OK or didn't you see them?'

'Sarah went up to see them whilst I was talking to Antonia. They were having tea and Sarah said they seemed fine, although since Marcus heard you were on your way home he's never stopped asking when you'll be back. I'm sure you'll both be relieved to see each other again.'

'Poor little thing, he doesn't know he has no father anymore and I'm going to be the one to break it to him some time over the next few days. How on earth am I going to tell him? How will he react? Will he hate me for not bringing Paul home with me? Do you think Paul and I were wrong to go on holiday without the two of them?' She knew that some of their friends had been critical.

'Who am I to say what's wrong and what's right?' Oscar hedged, not wanting to spoil her homecoming. She'd had a rough enough time over the past week to last most people for several lifetimes. 'As things turned out, it's a blessing they weren't with you, isn't it? Actually, I think it took a great deal of courage to leave them at home,' he went on. 'I'm sure with hindsight you'll think it was exactly the right thing for you and Paul to have done and, let's face it, few of us are in a situation where we're able to leave the children. I mean organising the help and everything would be too much effort for most of us. Do you want to talk about Paul?' he went on. 'Antonia's been a bit sparing with the details.'

'Well, I didn't talk to her at any length, long distance phone calls from hotels being expensive, and I really only gave her the bare facts to warn her not to expect Paul back at work. Whatever any of us think about her, she's still his employer; or *was*,' she corrected herself quickly. 'And I thought she might want to get in a temporary replacement as we're in the middle of the banqueting season.'

'Brace yourself for an ace smoothie!' Oscar said. 'Antonia introduced me to a French character she'd acquired from one of the agencies. He's acting manager at the moment. If I tell you that he overdoes the French accent, oozes charm and that I wouldn't trust him as far as I could chuck him, you might begin to get the picture.'

Liz tried to visualise the man already filling Paul's shoes, or attempting to, and felt a moment of bleakness. She'd been trying to come to terms with the reality that she may no longer be involved in the day-to-day running of the hotel. The emotional part of her didn't want to face it, the other more rational side, knew she must.

'I have to accept that whatever kind of replacement Antonia finds for Paul it isn't any of my business any more. That part of my life is over and I have to start to look ahead and think about what I'm going to do next.' It was a painful admission and the tears started to flow, unchecked, and she found herself crying in a way that she hadn't cried at any time during the past week.

Oscar took his left hand off the steering wheel, reached over, took one of hers and squeezed it briefly, trying to convey sympathy in a way that he couldn't put into words. 'Whatever you need, just ask,' he said. 'Sarah and I will do anything we can to help you get over this. It must have been an absolute nightmare for you. Ah! At last!' He put his foot hard down on the accelerator as they left the traffic on the A41 and moved onto the A1 and into the outside lane. In what seemed like no time at all the built up area was behind them and they'd moved into open country. From time to time they saw the glow of a bonfire sending sparks up into the cold night air in celebration of the foiled plot to blow up the Houses of Parliament all those years ago. The bonfires reminded her of the horrors of Paul's funeral and the crematorium she hadn't been allowed to see. 'I expect Paul's ashes will be arriving either tomorrow or the day after,' she said. 'The vice-consul said he would put them on the first possible flight.'

'Just let me know the details when you get them and I'll collect them for you.'

'Oh, Oscar, will you really do that for me? That would be wonderful. I suppose Antonia will be fed up with me for having Paul cremated in Rome. It was a fairly chastening experience, I have to say.'

'I can imagine.'

Liz felt a knot tightening in her stomach as Oscar kept his foot on the accelerator and they rapidly ate up the miles. She'd been removed from the reality of their old existence for two weeks and dreaded her return more as each mile passed. 'You were asking for details about Paul earlier.' She turned towards Oscar in an attempt to divert her attention from whatever lay ahead and briefly told him what had happened. 'I feel so guilty,' she confessed. 'First for letting him drive all that way, second for not having the sense to notice how stressed he was before we left home.'

'Forget it!' Oscar said. 'Paul was his own man. If he made up his mind on a course of action, nothing that you, I or anyone else said could dissuade him. You must know *that*, Liz, you were closer to him than most of us.'

'I suppose you're right. But if only I'd known …'

'Believe me, you couldn't have made any difference. Paul knew the score. He told me only the other week that he was living on borrowed time. Ah! It looks as if we've arrived.' He slowed down and turned the car into the driveway past the sign that announced: Bishop's Hall Hotel, Bishop's Wood, Hertfordshire. Liz could already see the Georgian manor house through the rain-sodden trees, its pale washed walls looking ghostly in the early evening darkness. It seemed as if months had passed since she'd last been here instead of a mere two weeks.

Oscar stopped the car in front of the imposing, pillared entrance and, as Liz climbed out, went to retrieve her luggage from the boot. 'Ready?' He asked. She smiled at him and shrugged her shoulders, not trusting herself to speak. *How would I have managed without him*, she thought. Simply to have him standing next to her gave her so much comfort. They walked together into the reception area.

'Evening Mrs Hirsch.' George, the hall porter came forward from behind his desk. 'Here, let me take that,' he nodded towards her luggage, then, 'I'm ever so sorry to hear the news,' he added, his eyes not quite meeting hers.

'Thank you, George. It's very kind of you.' How many times would she have to go through this same dialogue in the next few days?

'Perhaps it's best if I leave you here,' Oscar said as George disappeared towards the stairs with the luggage.

'Oh! Yes! I suppose you're right.' Liz stood on tiptoe and kissed him goodbye. 'Thank you for meeting me. You'll never know what a help you've been. Give Sarah my love and I'll be in touch during the next few days.'

'Anything we can do, you only have to ask.' He raised his hand in a brief salute and turned towards the door. Liz watched him leave with a lump in her throat and then turned away and walked swiftly towards the staircase to catch up with George. She noticed Khayyam sitting in the out tray in reception as she went past. The supercilious expression on his aristocratic black face was less than welcoming. 'You get to look more like your owner every day,' she muttered to him as she passed. He took not the slightest notice and went on washing himself in his usual detached and unconcerned fashion.

Once they were upstairs, Liz took out her key and opened the door into their small hallway. 'I think I'll be able to manage from here,' she said to George. 'Thanks for your help.'

'Pleasure, Mrs Hirsch.' He brought two fingers to a spot just above his right eyebrow, a legacy from his days in the army. Liz knew he did it with all the customers.

She opened the door into the sitting room. It was empty and eerily quiet. She felt a moment of panic. Where was everyone? More particularly, where were Maria and the children? She walked over to Marcus' bedroom, opened the door and looked inside. Empty. She'd spent the last few hours anticipating seeing the children again and they'd both disappeared! Her heart began to beat faster. Don't panic! There's a simple explanation. They were here yesterday. Oscar said so! She looked at her watch. It was six thirty and Emma should be in bed.

Just at that moment the door to the smallest room in the flat opened and Maria came out. She held a warning finger to her lips which told Liz that Emma at least was in her bedroom and asleep. 'Hello, Mrs Hirsch, I'm so glad you're home again,' she said. 'I think Emma must be teething. She's been so fretful, it's taken me a long time to get her to sleep.'

'I'll have a quick peep in a minute,' Liz said, 'but first I must say hello to Marcus. Where is he by the way?'

'Oh, there's a bonfire in the village. Miss Harvey took him down about half an hour ago. I *did* put his warm clothes on.'

Maria looked so apologetic that Liz felt any kind of remonstration would be unfair. She knew how determined Antonia could be and fumed inwardly at the tactlessness of the woman. Surely she realised that Liz would be desperate to see him after two weeks away? But, of course, that was the reason she'd taken him. If it hadn't been the village bonfire it would have been something else.

'Would you like me to go to the village and pick him up?' Maria asked.

'No, no. I'll wait for them to come back.' Liz said. 'After all, you could miss each other in the dark. I hope they won't be too late or that young man will be exhausted in the morning. Now I'll just go and take a quick look at Emma. I promise I won't wake her up.' Liz smiled at Maria. It can't have been easy for her looking after two small children with someone like Antonia constantly breathing down her neck, as well as being surrounded by well-meaning members of the hotel staff who were only too ready to chip in with their two pennyworth of good advice on the bringing up of children.

She opened the door to Emma's room and tiptoed over to her cot, even though her shoes made no sound on the thick carpet. She looked down at her sleeping daughter and thanked God she was too young to know what had happened to her father. Her face was hot and flushed and the blonde down on her head, which was all that she had in the way of hair, was damp. Her hands were raised in an attitude of total surrender and Liz left them alone, not wanting to disturb her. She continued to stand there for perhaps five minutes before she turned away, wanting Paul, not daring to think about what this homecoming would have been like if he'd been with her.

The knock on the door came just as she was leaving Emma's room. She braced herself, sensing that Antonia had returned with Marcus, and opened the door.

'Marcus!'

'Mummy!'

He took a flying leap and Liz staggered back as he made contact, winding his legs around her waist and his arms about her neck. He planted a sticky kiss on her cheek and Liz held him away from her, looking first at his mouth and then at the partly eaten toffee apple, which he still clutched in his left hand.

'I see you've been enjoying the bonfire.'

'Would you like a lick?' He held the apple out towards her and she took a quick lick at the toffee, thinking how much like Paul he looked. How was she going to bear it? Watching him every day, growing more like his father as time went by, until perhaps the inevitable happened and he metamorphosed into a complete replica.

Antonia still stood by the door waiting. Waiting for what? A complete post-mortem? A blow-by-blow account of everything that she and Paul had done since leaving the country? *Don't let her see how much you mind that Marcus wasn't here when you arrived. Just don't give her the satisfaction of knowing you're annoyed.*

Keep calm she told herself. With difficulty she found her voice at last.

'It was kind of you to take Marcus to the bonfire. I hope he wasn't any trouble.'

'He's *never* any trouble and it was good to get out of this place for a while.'

'Would you mind if we didn't talk tonight? It's been a long and traumatic day. My flight was delayed and as I haven't seen Marcus for two weeks I'd like to put him to bed myself. Perhaps we can make time tomorrow?'

Antonia inclined her head. 'I'll be in my office at ten thirty. Come and have some coffee.' She made it sound more like a summons than an invitation. 'Goodnight Marcus.'

'Night night Toni.' Marcus waved his toffee apple in a farewell greeting as Liz closed the door and sighed with relief. The encounter she'd been dreading was over.

'Where's Papa?' Marcus asked, wriggling free and taking a bite out of his toffee apple. It was the question she'd hoped he wouldn't ask. She couldn't tell him. Not tonight, not before he went to bed. She needed time to work out exactly what she was going to say and how best to put it across so that he felt as little pain as possible. 'Papa's not here at the moment,' she said, 'but he sent you a present. Would you like to see it?'

'Yes! Yes! What is it?' He jumped up and down, his eyes shining with excitement.

'Come and unwrap it and then you'll find out. But, first, let's wash your sticky fingers; I think you've got nearly as much toffee on them as there is round the apple.'

She took hold of the less sticky hand, led him to the bathroom and gave him the once over with a wet flannel. He screwed his face up as she wiped his mouth and her heart hurt with pity for him. His presents were in her hand luggage and she carried the bag into the sitting room and pulled out an oblong box which had been the last thing she'd packed.

'It's a car! It's a car!' His face lit up. Thank goodness, he seemed to have forgotten that Paul wasn't around to see him open it.

'That's not just any old car. It's a Ferrari.'

'What's a Ferrari?'

'It's one of the best cars in Italy. It goes too. Let me show you.' She fished around in the box, found the key, inserted it into the shiny red metal bodywork, wound up the clockwork motor and let the car zip across the carpet.

'Again! Again!' Marcus said, his voice fizzing with excitement. 'Look, Maria! I've got a Ferrari! It's the best car in Italy! Mummy says!'

'Who's a lucky boy then?' Maria appeared in the doorway. 'Is it all right if I go out later?' she asked. 'The family of a friend is having a firework party and I'd like to go. I'll put Marcus to bed first.'

'That's all right, I'll do it. You deserve a night off and thank you for looking after the children so well. I'm sure it hasn't been easy.'

A look passed between the two of them. Liz made a point of not criticising any of the hotel staff in Maria's presence, but the girl was no fool and must have picked up on the tension from time-to-time. 'I put a cold supper in the fridge for you,' she said. 'I'll be eating later with my friend.' She'd met up with several au pairs at her English class at the local college and they got together when days off coincided or when one family arranged a special event like tonight's firework party. 'Have a good time,' Liz said. 'I'll see you in the morning.'

She turned to Marcus who was trying to turn the key in the side of the Ferrari and making heavy weather of it judging by the expression on his face and the muscle-power he was exerting. 'Here, let me help you.' Liz put her hand over his so that she could turn the key without crushing his fingers. 'You'll soon get the hang of it. Once you've wound it a few times it won't be quite so stiff. Remember, not to wind it too hard or the motor will break and it won't go at all.' She took the key out and watched him as he let the car go again. How on earth was she going to tell him about Paul and when?

CHAPTER THIRTEEN

Antonia was in her office by eight o'clock the next morning, carrying under one arm the files she'd previously removed from Paul's desk. In the interim she'd been through them all, removed several letters, some photographs and all Liz's correspondence to Paul, including the cards. The diamond earrings and the accompanying note from Paul were now hidden underneath her underwear in the chest of drawers in her bedroom.

Once the files were back in place she went into the hotel dining room for breakfast and, after that, made a quick tour of inspection, taking in all the public rooms. There was a dirty ashtray in the lounge. She took it out to reception and asked the young woman on duty to change it for a clean one. The hotel grapevine worked extremely efficiently and it was important that Monsieur Legrange got the message that she'd been on the warpath. The sooner he knew he was on trial the better.

Antonia was a competent needlewoman and was dressed in a tailored grey wool frock, which she'd made herself from a Vogue pattern of a Hardy Amies design. Wearing it always made her feel good and it was easier to dominate when she looked her best. By the time Liz knocked on the door at ten thirty she'd opened all the mail, dealt with some, passed on others and made several phone calls. So far her day was going extremely well.

'Sit down,' she said, noting with some satisfaction that Liz looked tired and a bit frayed around the edges. In front of her was a list of questions, previously prepared and tucked into the corner of her leather-bound blotter. Whether Liz would be able to answer them all to her satisfaction remained to be seen. A waiter arrived with a tray of coffee. Antonia glanced ostentatiously at her watch. The coffee was five minutes late. She made no comment, but knew by the expression on his face that the gesture had registered.

She poured coffee for both of them and pushed the milk jug towards Liz then sat back in her chair and waited. Liz, sensing Antonia was expecting her to begin, said the first thing that came into her head. 'I was surprised to get a phone call from Peter Kilby earlier this morning. I can't imagine how he got to know of Paul's death, but he told me that Paul made a will.' Peter Kilby was the solicitor for both the hotel and Paul.

'Paul was very efficient. I would have been surprised if he hadn't.'

'It's just that he never discussed it with me.'

'Perhaps he thought it would distress you.'

'Why should he think that, do you suppose?'

'Oh *Liz*, I don't know! Some people are superstitious about these things, as if the very act of making a will might hasten their death.'

'It seems to have worked in Paul's case, doesn't it?'

Antonia shrugged off the sarcasm. 'Do you have any idea where he put it?' Liz asked, feeling it was bad enough that Paul had died so unexpectedly without having told her he'd made a will and then forcing her to embark on a treasure hunt to locate it.

'He kept most of his papers in his desk, unless they were too personal and then I'd expect them to be *somewhere* in the flat.' Antonia chose her words carefully. The flat always seemed to her to be absolutely chaotic with bits and pieces strewn all over the place. It was a wonder Paul ever found anything. Of course when *she'd* been growing up, children and their numerous possessions were always kept well out of sight, but in today's world things were different. Space in the flat was irrelevant as far as she was concerned.

'Well,' Liz said, 'I had a quick look through the desk in the sitting room before I came down and I couldn't see it anywhere.' She didn't tell Antonia she'd spent several hours last night ransacking the flat looking for a letter, a note, a slip of paper, anything addressed to her. Subconsciously she was looking for his farewell. Even though she argued to herself that it was unreasonable to expect him to say goodbye when he hadn't been certain he wasn't coming back. She'd looked through the small desk that they shared, his briefcase, his coat and trouser pockets and cried herself to sleep with a combination of disappointment and frustration when she'd found nothing. She ran her fingers through her hair, crossed and uncrossed her legs and took a quick sip of coffee.

'Well, you're welcome to look through his office desk.' Antonia gestured towards Paul's desk with her right hand. 'When we've finished our conversation I'll leave you in peace and you can examine it at your leisure. Now, perhaps you'd like to fill me in with a few details. How Paul *died*, for instance.' Now that Liz was home she wanted to know *everything*. She'd spent the best part of a week trying to imagine exactly what was going on in Rome and wondered time and again how someone as strong as Paul could succumb so quickly to an illness from which many recovered.

Liz did her best to take Antonia through the key events. 'You'll appreciate that because of the language barrier it was quite difficult to track the progress of his illness, but Anna had the bright idea of contacting the British consul and one of the vice-consuls came to the hospital to translate, so at least they knew Paul's medical history. Then my friend Kate came over from Perugia and was able to speak Italian to the doctors. In the end I'm afraid Paul died from pneumonia.'

'Such a pity you couldn't fly him home. Pneumonia is, after all, curable with penicillin or some such.'

'Oh Antonia! It's not as if we were in the back of beyond! I'm sure Italian medicine is on a par with English. Anyway, Paul was much too ill to move. You know how hard he worked, particularly *before* he went away.' Liz's voice was defensive and slightly raised to make her point.

Antonia shrugged. 'Well it's too late now for recriminations, we'd better move on. You will be holding a memorial service?'

'I'm sorry?' Liz's eyebrows shot up in twin question marks.

Antonia could see that she'd wrong-footed her and began to elaborate. 'Well, you must see that Paul's friends and business contacts will want to pay their last respects and, of course, the hotel staff would like to say goodbye to him.' She noted with some satisfaction that Liz's cheeks had grown pink with embarrassment and sat back again to wait.

'Yes, yes, I'm sure you're right. It's just I hadn't really thought too much about it. I'll ring the vicar later and see when he can fit us in.' Liz emptied her coffee cup and Antonia immediately refilled it without bothering to ask if Liz would like more.

'A Friday afternoon would be the best time,' she began. 'The business visitors check out after breakfast and our weekend guests don't normally arrive until Friday evening. We have no function booked on Friday week. Perhaps that would be a good day?'

Liz knew she was being backed into a corner. To hell with Antonia! It had been bad enough going through that awful funeral service in Rome without opening all those wounds again. A voice in her head told her she was being selfish and that Paul's friends and colleagues deserved the opportunity to say goodbye. 'I'll see what I can do and let you know,' she said and braced herself for what might be coming next.

'What's happening to the car?' Antonia asked. 'You do realise, don't you, that it's a *company* car?'

Liz didn't miss the emphasis. She knew only too well and lost no time in telling Antonia the plans that had been put in place for its safe return. 'Luckily Kate's looking after it for us,' she said, 'otherwise we should have to pay garage expenses or leave it sitting on the street. I phoned the RAC this morning. They'll be in touch.'

Liz knew this was the time to raise the question of her future. Technically she no longer had the right to be living in the flat which, like the car, went with Paul's job. Suddenly it seemed that everything she'd taken for granted belonged to the hotel and she wondered what else Antonia might want to reclaim. There was a faint hope that Antonia might say something, offer to give her a trial as manager or housekeeper perhaps, either role was well within her capability, but she knew that working with Antonia would be a nightmare for both of them. However hard she tried, she couldn't turn herself into Paul, and that was what Antonia really wanted. Not for the first time she longed to change places with him. If it was her corpse that had recently been turned to ashes, life for Antonia and the children could have continued as before.

'Had you thought about putting an announcement in the newspaper?' Antonia's voice stopped any further speculation. Once again Liz admitted she hadn't and Antonia had succeeded in catching her out for the second time in ten minutes. Her retaliation was swift, aware even as she spoke that she sounded petulant and defensive. 'Antonia, I got back just last night. I know that Paul's death has been a great shock to everyone, but my first consideration was the children. I haven't seen them for two weeks, remember.' Oh blast the woman! She was superb at finding all Liz's weak points; like a dentist with a probe, poking about looking for the source of pain and then twisting the instrument to make it hurt more.

Antonia ignored the outburst. 'I drafted an obituary notice. I thought it might save you the trouble. The Times and the Daily Telegraph should be enough.' There was an expression of triumph in her eyes as the typewritten notice was pushed across the desk. Liz tried to read it, but the words blurred as the tears came into her eyes. Antonia mustn't see how much she was hurting. 'Perhaps I can look at this later,' she said. 'I'll let you know if I think it needs altering. Now, if that's all . . .'

She rose to her feet, preparing to leave the office and suddenly remembered her need to go through Paul's desk. 'Perhaps I can come back when you're at lunch and sort out the desk,' she said. Antonia had promised to leave her in peace, but showed no signs of moving and she couldn't bear the thought of opening drawers and sorting through papers under her watchful eye.

'As you please.' Antonia's voice was icy and her eyes matched. She picked up an envelope from her desk and thrust it towards Liz. 'You'd better take that with you.'

It's my notice to quit the flat, Liz thought bleakly. I wonder how long I've got before I have to move out and make room for M. Legrange or whoever is going to take over from Paul. How on earth am I going to find the time with all the other stuff I have to organise?

'It's Paul's salary cheque for October. You'll have to add it to his estate.'

'Oh! Thank you.' It hadn't occurred to Liz that the hotel might owe Paul money. It was a small crumb of comfort. Perhaps she wouldn't have to quit the flat too quickly after all? She walked slowly up the stairs back to the comparative refuge of her own quarters feeling, as always after an encounter with Antonia, incompetent and useless and wondering which task to do first. The draft obituary notice was still in her hand. Perhaps that would be a good a place to start.

HIRSCH on November 2 1962 in Rome, Paul Johann aged 42 of Vienna, Austria. Managing Director of Bishop's Hall Hotel. Father of Marcus and Emma, husband of Elizabeth. Paul was cremated in Rome, but a memorial service will be held at All Saints Church, Bishop's Wood on ???, at ???.

Liz inserted dearly loved in front of husband and then, after some consideration, put adored in front of father and finally put both in front of Managing Director. Fortunately the vicar was at home when she called and half an hour later she left the obituary notice on Antonia's desk having arranged for Paul's memorial service to be held on Friday November 16th at two thirty p.m.

She searched through Paul's desk with frenzied fingers. Her heart was pounding as she riffled through papers, most of them connected to work. Finally she came to the bottom left-hand drawer and found the files that Antonia had replaced earlier. The one marked LEGAL was on top. Liz pulled them out, wondering as she did so how it could be that this particular drawer seemed much tidier than the rest. Perhaps Paul didn't look at the contents very much? Maybe the very fact that the drawer contained files made it easier to keep tidy? She removed the files and, with her heart still thumping, took them up to the flat.

The phone was ringing as she walked into the sitting room. Maria had taken both the children out for a walk, so Liz had no alternative but to answer it.

'Hello Liz, it's Sarah.'

'Oh, hello Sarah,' Liz said after the smallest pause during which she tried to pull herself together, not wanting to sound tearful.

'Oh my dear, we're *so* sorry. Oscar told me when he got back last night how upset you were. Come and have some supper with us one night this week when you've got yourself sorted out a bit. In the meantime is there anything I can do to help?'

Liz smiled into the phone. 'I've just had a session with Antonia, I can't tell you how good it is to hear a friendly voice. I really appreciated Oscar being at Heathrow to collect me.'

'He told me you burst into tears when you saw him.'

'Nothing personal. I was just so pleased to be home again, as you can imagine.'

Oscar and Sarah had become close friends after Liz and Paul married. They ran a restaurant nearby and when work permitted shared meals, occasional visits to the theatre and children's outings. Liz valued the friendship, which was all the more precious as Oscar and Sarah weren't connected with the hotel. She and Sarah got on like a house on fire and had shared confidences and gossip on many occasions over snatched cups of coffee or tea.

'Oh, Sarah, I'd love to come over. I've just spent the best part of an hour answering Antonia's questions. It felt like the Spanish Inquisition. I have to go and see Paul's solicitor later this afternoon and tomorrow morning the vicar's coming over to talk about a memorial service. Would tomorrow evening be OK? Maria went out last night, so I don't mind asking her to babysit. We could make it later in the week if you like, I'm not exactly inundated with invitations to dinner at the moment.'

'Just you wait! Attractive young widows aren't that thick on the ground. I'd say you'll be much in demand once the word gets around. Let's say seven thirty, shall we? Give me a chance to get the kids to bed.'

'Perfect. And thanks for thinking of me.'

'It's nothing. The least we can do. See you tomorrow,' Sarah said and hung up.

Noises in the hallway told her that Maria had returned with the children and Liz knew that for the moment any attempt to try and read Paul's will was out of the question. She needed to be quiet in order to take in the details and felt reluctant to open the envelope. The fact that Paul hadn't discussed it gave her an unnatural fear of what might be inside.

Normally Maria collected lunch for the family from the hotel kitchen. They had an understanding with the chef that their food would be picked up before twelve thirty. After that the restaurant filled up and, on a good day, service became frantic. The flat had a tiny kitchen with a refrigerator, a sink and a small stove, which was adequate for re-heating hotel food or for simple cooking. Liz assumed it would be all right to carry on as before until such time as someone told her it wasn't and she took Marcus into the bathroom to go to the lavatory and wash his hands while Maria went to the kitchen.

'Would you like to help me lay the table?' She watched as he put knives and forks on the wrong side of the table mats and decided to let everyone change them around later. Somehow or another having the knives on the right seemed unimportant at the moment. She tried not to think about telling him that Paul wasn't coming back.

As things turned out there was no time to read Paul's will before her visit to Peter Kilby. Emma woke up just as they were finishing lunch and Liz decided to feed her while Maria played with Marcus. Emma's gums were sore at the front where her first tooth would soon appear and, as Liz put the spoon of sieved food into her mouth, she turned her head this way and that trying to avoid contact with the hard metal. Liz persevered for about half a dozen spoonfuls before giving in and reaching for the bottle of milk, which had been warming in a saucepan. Emma fastened on eagerly and drank as if milk would soon be out of fashion. 'Better try and give her some boiled water later, perhaps with some rosehip syrup,' Liz threw instructions to

Maria over her shoulder as she grabbed her handbag and made for the car.

Peter Kilby's office was on the High Street in the old part of Bishop's Wood. Parking anywhere on the street was forbidden to allow easy access for through traffic and Liz had to put the car in a nearby car park. As she locked the door she spotted June, a friend she'd met at ante natal classes when she'd been pregnant with Emma. She lifted her arm and waved, but June turned abruptly away from her and almost ran out of the car park. Liz could swear June had seen her, but supposed she could have been mistaken.

Looking at her watch, she realised she just had time to drop the holiday films into the chemist to be developed. There were only two reels, but at least she would have some memories of the first week of their holiday. It wasn't much of a consolation, but it was something.

She ran up the slight incline to reach Peter Kilby's office in time for her appointment. She was panting by the time she arrived in reception and still breathless when shown into his office within seconds of her arrival.

Peter Kilby rose to greet her with some difficulty. His high colour and generous waistline indicated a lifestyle dedicated to self-indulgence. His middle shirt button was straining at the leash and Liz caught a glimpse of a white cotton vest stretched across his convex stomach. For some reason she disliked vests on men and had often joked about it with Paul. 'I like my men cold but sexy,' she'd told him, sliding her arms around him to emphasise the point. She brought her attention back with difficulty to Peter Kilby. *Get a grip, Liz, you're not supposed to be thinking about sexy men, this is serious stuff. Any minute Peter K is going to ask you if you've read the will and you'll have to admit you haven't.*

She sat on the edge of her chair, facing the solicitor across his vast desk. The mahogany surface was shining and completely uncluttered. He offered tea and seemed disconcerted when she asked for coffee. Leaving the flat in such a hurry she hadn't had her usual after-lunch cup and, having just come back from Italy where they drank it all the time, hadn't realised that to ask for it might prove problematic for the office of a country solicitor. When it arrived it was instant and there were splodges of powder floating on top which had failed to dissolve.

Peter Kilby opened a drawer in his desk and pulled out a coaster, which he placed with great care underneath her saucer. Liz stirred the cup vigorously whilst waving away the offer of both sugar and biscuits, praying she wouldn't spill hot liquid onto the antique surface of the desk. She watched him take a large bite from a wholemeal digestive and warned herself silently not to think about his straining shirt button.

He cleared his throat, opened Paul's file and took out a document which Liz recognised as Paul's will. She raked around in her handbag and produced her own copy. The envelope was creased where she'd pushed it hastily into her bag and it looked shabby beside the pristine document that sat in front of the solicitor. Before he could ask the question, Liz leaned forward with what she hoped was a winning smile. 'I know you'll think it strange, but I haven't read Paul's will yet. I didn't find it until a couple of hours ago and since then I've been busy with the children. I had no idea he'd made one until you rang me this morning. Could you give me the key points? I'm sure you don't want to sit watching me whilst I wade through it.'

If Peter Kilby was surprised by her admission he didn't show it. In his line of business you never knew what surprising revelations would come sailing across the desk and he was a past master at keeping his face expressionless. He'd been a solicitor for long enough to know that if you mentioned the good news first it made the not-so good a little more palatable. He unfolded Paul's will slowly, smoothing out the pages on top of his blotter, and at last began. 'Any assets that Paul has when all debts are settled have been bequeathed to you as the surviving spouse. Although Paul gave me a rough idea of money he has on deposit I have no way of knowing what his total liabilities are and, before you leave, I'll go through a list with you to help me get an idea of where things stand. You will of course be charged Estate Duty on any assets over £4000.' He paused briefly to give her time to absorb the information and thought how much easier his life would be if his clients took the trouble to confide in their families before they died.

'I'd always understood that Estate Duty was a tax only wealthy people paid,' Liz said, meeting the eyes that were looking at her over the top of horn-rimmed spectacles. 'Well, Harold Macmillan is always telling us we've never had it so good, so I suppose we must expect to give the government a small contribution when we finally ...' He let his voice tail off and permitted himself a faint smile at his own joke.

'So you're telling me that even though Paul paid income tax all his life and has left two very young children who will need care and education for the best part of twenty years, Her Majesty's Government is still going to relieve us of what they no doubt think of as our ill-gotten gains?'

'I'm afraid so.'

'Well I hope you haven't got any more nasty surprises tucked up your sleeve.' Liz picked up her coffee cup and downed the remaining liquid. It was quite cold and tasted horrible.

Peter Kilby resisted the temptation to help himself to a third digestive biscuit, not wanting to hamper the rest of his delivery. He sensed correctly that his client was becoming edgy and feared she might be even more so before their interview finally came to an end. 'As to his shares in Bishop's Hall Hotel.' He paused again, completely unaware that it was his hesitant speech that was setting his clients' teeth on edge. 'His shares in Bishop's Hall Hotel have been left in trust for the benefit of your two children, that is to say, for Marcus and Emma.'

He saw the look of surprise on Liz's face and pressed on quickly. 'There are, you will understand, tax benefits. The hotel shares will be entirely free of Estate Duty.'

'Any minute now you'll be telling me that the Chancellor of the Exchequer is really Father Christmas in disguise,' Liz put in quickly and then, 'I'm sorry,' she said. 'That was a cheap point to make. You don't make the legislation yourself, after all.'

'But I always try to advise my clients as to the best course of action to take, even though they don't always listen.' He smiled again at his ability to make jokes at his own expense. 'Perhaps this might be a good time to mention that I am one of two trustees, the other one being Oscar Hirsch, who is, I believe, a cousin of your husband. No doubt Paul made these arrangements with your best interests in mind, thinking perhaps to spare you any undue worries about any legal procedures that may be involved.'

Liz resisted a strong desire to scream at the suggestion that her frail female brain might somehow crack under the strain if she had to make a decision. 'Could you explain to me exactly what the effects of that last bequest are likely to be?' she asked. 'What if, for example, Miss Harvey decides at some stage in the future to sell the hotel? After all. she isn't a young woman and our children are both very small. I honestly can't see her running the place for the next twenty years unless she finds an exceptional manager who can continue to build up the business as Paul has for the past fifteen years.' She badly wanted to add, 'And kill themselves in the process,' but in view of her previous jibe thought better of it.

'In that case the trustees will have the power to deal with the shares and use their discretion to do whatever is best for the children. We could sell the children's shares at the same time if we consider the offer to be of future benefit to them,' Peter Kilby replied. 'Incidentally, as we are now acting for Paul, we have written to Miss Harvey telling her that we cannot continue to act for the hotel. In legal terms, you understand, there would be a conflict of interest.' He saw Liz's eyebrows shoot up in surprise and, for perhaps the first time since she'd walked into his office, began to feel sorry for her. He could still hear Antonia Harvey ranting over the telephone when she'd called to tell him that Paul had died, telling him firmly that Paul's marriage to Liz had been a terrible mistake and that he should never have embarked on this latest madcap holiday. What had chilled him most were her final words. 'Such a waste of an investment.' The coldness in her voice convinced him that she really meant it. He assumed she was referring to the years she'd spent teaching Paul the business and once he'd put the phone down told himself that, however long he remained a solicitor, he would never get used to the vindictiveness of some human beings. It was bad enough that such a young woman had lost her husband, without having to deal with a frustrated old spinster like Antonia Harvey. Additionally, she was grappling with a whole lot of legal details which were quite alien to her. He wished he didn't have to tell her the details of Paul's final legacy.

'There's just one last thing I have to mention,' he began. 'Paul left a very small bequest to Miss Harvey as a token of their long friendship. He noticed Liz's eyes flick away sharply from his own and watched her stare with apparent deep concentration at her hands. 'He left her his collection of Austrian ceramic figures. You're probably aware of the pieces?'

'Hard not to be when I see them every day of my life,' Liz said. They weren't hugely valuable as it happened, but had been picked up by Paul on various trips to Vienna. The pieces in question were a series of small figures made by a particular ceramics factory. On their own they were relatively inexpensive, but they had a certain charm and to Liz, because Paul had collected them, they were priceless.

Peter Kilby heard Liz sigh. The sound was the most gentle exhalation and yet so poignant that he felt a lump in his own throat. He cleared it loudly. 'Would you prefer to continue another time? A little more coffee perhaps?' He was a member of that breed of Englishmen who are completely incapable of dealing with weeping women and hoped with all his heart that she wasn't going to cry.

'No, I'm fine thanks.' Liz tried to sound confident. 'I'm sure you have other business to get on with, so if you let me know what information you need I'll try to supply you with the details as quickly as possible. It may take a few days, but I'll try not to keep you waiting too long.'

Peter Kilby relaxed visibly now that he felt they were on the home straight. 'Let's do the assets first,' he said. 'First I'll need his bank statements and details of any investments he had, building society deposits, stocks and shares, that sort of thing. I think he mentioned a life insurance policy. You've just come back from Italy, I believe. Perhaps any un-cashed travellers cheques or unused currency could be paid into his bank account. If there's any money lying around at home perhaps you can pay that in as well? Tell me, did you take the car?'

'Yes, we took the car, and since I flew back from Rome I'm afraid the car's still there, although one of my friends is looking after it until the RAC can bring it back home. I suppose you already know that it's a company car, so you won't need to add that to your list of assets.' Liz spoke quickly and decisively, wanting this whole interview to be at an end as soon as possible.

'Yes, I did know. However, if you have any petrol coupons that you didn't use, I will cash them in for you and, as you flew home, I shall be reclaiming a portion of your cross channel ferry fare and, if you let me have details of your air fare, I'll put it in as a legitimate expense.' Liz silently acknowledged his efficiency and began to cheer up slightly. Left to her own devices, she would never have dreamed of trying to reclaim money that she'd already spent. She made a mental note to be careful in the future before writing off liabilities that could be turned into assets. Peter Kilby started speaking again.

'As Paul wasn't born in this country, I'll need sight of his naturalisation papers and he should have some certificates of post-war credit. Perhaps you could drop them in when you're passing.'

'Certificates of post-war credit?' Liz queried.

'Yes, let me explain. When the war began, the rate of income tax was increased and allowances reduced in order to raise sufficient revenue to pay for the war. The additional tax paid was recorded and credited to the taxpayer. If you're able to find Paul's certificates I will be able to reclaim it for the benefit of the estate.'

The estate sounds so impersonal, Liz thought, *as if it belongs to nobody.* 'Right. Thank you for explaining,' she said. 'I'll do my best to find them.'

'I'll also claim a death grant,' Peter Kilby went on, 'and you do realise, don't you, that you will be entitled to a widow's pension?'

'I really hadn't given it a thought.'

'The local income tax office will be able to help you. Do you have a death certificate?'

'I believe the vice-consul in Rome was applying for one. I have his card if you need to get in touch. Paul only died on Friday, as you know, and what with the funeral arrangements and everything there hasn't been a great deal of time.' She rummaged around in her bag, found the card and handed it across the desk.

'Right, that's just about all, I think.' Peter Kilby levered himself to his feet. 'You will send me any outstanding bills, won't you, funeral expenses and the like and any of Paul's personal property you may have in the flat will have to be assessed and added to the estate.'

He came round to Liz's side of the desk and shook her hand. Liz thanked him and made her escape thinking what a grizzly business the law must be.

CHAPTER FOURTEEN

Liz sprinted down the stairs desperate to shake off the stuffy legal atmosphere of Peter Kilby's office. Once in the fresh air, she stood breathing deeply, trying to fill her lungs. It felt so much colder than Rome and she surprised herself by wishing herself back there. After the vibrancy and beauty of the old buildings interspersed with Roman ruins and even the frenzied Roman traffic, Bishop's Wood seemed dull and middle-aged.

'What brings *you* into Bishop's Wood in the middle of the afternoon?' The voice interrupted her thoughts and she frowned briefly, partly at being disturbed and partly because it took her a moment or two to recognise the speaker.

'Oh! Hello! I've just been to see my solicitor.' She racked her brains trying hard to remember the name of the man standing in front of her. He was a frequent guest at the hotel and against her better judgement she'd agreed to have tea with him one afternoon a few months ago when they'd bumped into each other.

'Nothing serious, I hope.'

'I only wish it wasn't.'

'Come and have some tea and tell me all about it. If you have time, that is.'

Liz looked at her watch as a formality, at the same time thinking, to have tea once with a virtual stranger is just about acceptable, but to make a habit of it . . .well. Suppose we're seen by someone who knows me. What will they think? Although it's perfectly innocent. What else could it be? But after the interview she'd just had it would be a relief to talk to someone who wasn't connected with Paul. She smiled inwardly remembering a similar conversation she'd had with herself the first time he'd asked her to have tea with him. *Then* she'd been seething after a heated exchange with Antonia and was bursting to let off steam to anyone who would listen.

'Well, I mustn't be too long,' she said, 'but I reckon I'll be safe for half an hour or so.' They walked across the road to the George, which Antonia always described as a pub with rooms which was, in reality, a pleasant country hotel. His name came back to her as she followed him into the lounge, Tom Merton, ex-army. Before that he was at some public school, Stowe if she recalled correctly. She always seemed to be on duty in reception at Bishop's Hall when he stayed with them. He was an area manager for a financial group and sometimes held team meetings there.

'Funny how we keep on running into each other.' He settled himself into an easy chair, crossed one leg over the other and smiled at her across the low table, which separated their two chairs.

Liz shrugged. 'Bishop's Wood is a small enough place and I don't leave it very often, just occasionally for holidays.' He was waiting for her to tell him why she'd been seeing her solicitor and suddenly, perversely, she felt annoyed with herself for allowing him to persuade her into having tea with him. Exactly the same emotions had gone through her mind on the previous occasion; only then Paul had still been alive and she'd felt guilty as well and a touch deceitful talking about Antonia to a perfect stranger.

'I've only just come back from holiday. I was in Rome for a couple of weeks,' she began.

'Not a city I know. The nearest I've been to Italy was during the war when I fought alongside the partisans in Yugoslavia.'

Looking at him across the table it was difficult to imagine him fighting anything. He was immaculately dressed in a grey worsted suit, his nondescript brown hair carefully parted and brushed and he was wearing suede shoes. She tried to imagine him in battle fatigues, his face smeared with mud.

Their tea arrived. She hadn't heard him order it, but supposed he must have. 'Shall I be mother?' he said, reaching forward towards the teapot and pouring the tea as he got no response from her. She was thinking what a stupid cliche and was irritated all over again remembering previous conversations with him which had been littered with similarly trite remarks. She stared at her cup without enthusiasm and as the silence stretched knew he was waiting for her explanation.

She stirred her tea vigorously although it contained no sugar and then took her time over the first sip. The longer he waited the more irritated she became and swore not to accept invitations so easily in future. Finally she set down her cup. 'There isn't an easy way to say this, so I might as well come straight out with it. Paul, my husband, was taken ill in Rome and died a few days ago.'

His face registered concern. 'Oh, I'm sorry. How awful for you. Was it a heart attack?'

'No. A stroke. It happened quite suddenly the day after we arrived and he died without regaining consciousness.'

'That's tough. What will you do now?'

'Do?' What a damn silly question. 'I suppose I'll *do* what everybody else does in a similar situation: I'll carry on with my life.' What a bleak prospect. Life without Paul. Not so much a life but a sentence where every day she had to face the same dilemma of what to do with the rest of it.

'I'm sure the children will be a great consolation to you.'

Yet another cliche. Did he never have an original thought? Or had he learned a series of stock replies and observations in the army or at school? Was that what institutionalisation did for you?

'*My* children,' she said with some emphasis, 'have just lost their father. If anybody needs consolation *they* do.' She watched the colour rise in his cheeks and realised she'd gone too far. It wasn't *his* fault that Paul had died and her life had just fallen apart and it was unfair of her to project her anger at herself onto him. 'I'm sorry,' she said stiffly. 'As you can imagine, I'm still in shock. I went away a wife and came back a widow; not a role I ever contemplated. I guess it will take some time before I get used to it.' *Like never,* she thought bleakly.

He leaned forward and took her hand awkwardly. 'Please let

me know if there's anything I can do.'

His hand felt soft and on the moist side of warm. Liz slid her own from under it as gently as she could, not wanting to offend him any more. 'It's kind of you to offer, but I suppose I'll learn to cope in time. Fortunately Emma is too young to even know what's happened. I haven't told Marcus yet. I guess that's going to be difficult when I finally get around to it.' She looked at her watch, quite deliberately, thinking, *I have to get out of here.* Aloud, she said. 'I'm afraid I must go, Maria's been coping with the children single-handed whilst we've been away and I don't want to push my luck or she may leave and then I really will be in a mess.'

He felt in his inside pocket for his notecase and pulled out a couple of pound notes to pay for their tea. Then, to her surprise, he took a card from another section and handed it across the table. 'I meant what I said earlier. Here's my office number. Don't hesitate to call me if you need any help.'

Liz took the card, which was still warm from his hand. 'Thank you,' she said, rising to her feet, 'and thank you for the tea.'

'Oh, it's all part of the service.' He smiled and stood up. Liz wondered how often he trotted out that particular phrase in the course of a day's work and if his staff steeled themselves waiting for it or was it so much a part of their day-to-day business-speak that none of them noticed? The next time she saw Tom Merton coming she'd take care to have an urgent appointment. What was he doing inviting her out for tea anyway? Surely he couldn't have some ulterior motive. Or could he? She shivered in the cold air as she realised there was no longer anybody to shield her against the rest of the world; solicitors, businessmen or indeed any chancer that she might encounter some time in the future.

It had grown dark while they were having tea and the darkness accentuated her feeling of gloom. She walked swiftly to the car park realising that, although relieved to be putting a distance between Tom Merton and herself, she didn't want to go back to the hotel either. But the children would be waiting and she'd left in such a hurry at lunchtime she owed it to them to be home as soon as possible. She'd already been away far too long. *How hard it is to be a good parent,* she thought, and wished that it was Paul shouldering the responsibility, feeling that he would make a much better job of it.

On the drive back to Bishop's Hall she realised that almost without thinking she'd been storing up snippets of conversation to share with Paul later that evening. But then the reality hit her yet again. Such evenings were a thing of the past. The tears began to run down her face. She neither wanted to nor knew how to stop them. It had been a dreadful afternoon. An afternoon without Paul. An afternoon when she couldn't even look forward to spending even a tiny part of the evening with him. How could she have felt so deprived of his company before when every day she'd seen him, spent time talking to him, laughed with him? Her future stretched out like the dark road in front of her only, unlike the road, there was no ending in sight; nothing but an endless avenue of unrelieved black misery.

On Wednesday morning she received a telegram from Michael Shand. URN ARRIVING LONDON AIRPORT MONDAY 1600 HOURS FLIGHT BEA 267 WAYBILL 0601842055. Liz stared at it for several seconds thinking *that's all that's left of Paul.* His charred bones had been crushed and pushed unceremoniously into an urn, reduced to a couple of handfuls of ash, before being loaded into an aircraft hold with who knows what else. It seemed a dreadful way to end a life and she wondered, not for the first time, if she'd really done him a disservice by having him cremated in Rome. Would it all have been more dignified if his body had been flown home? Pointless to speculate. She couldn't undo what was already done. She put the telegram in her bag to give to Oscar later when she went over for dinner and thanked her lucky stars for good friends.

The rest of the week seemed to last forever. It was as if time had slowed, making the hours extend. Even though she was fully occupied, the days were endless and she grew to dread the time, usually around eleven, when she felt justified in going to bed, knowing that the minute her head touched the pillow Paul would dominate her thoughts. He climbed into her mind and stayed there demanding her attention. It was useless trying to read. She couldn't concentrate on the printed page and in the end gave up. Then, when at last she fell asleep and longed to meet him in her dreams he remained stubbornly absent as if he'd never been part of her life.

Promptly at eight o'clock every morning the intercom rang and Liz clenched her teeth knowing that it would be Antonia asking when the car was coming home. She repeated the same information daily knowing Antonia would be back on the phone tomorrow asking the same question. Antonia's memory had never been in doubt and Liz knew the calls were a deliberate strategy to remind Liz who held the purse strings or, in this case, the car keys.

And then there were the letters. She hadn't anticipated quite how many there would be and forced herself to read them, steeling herself against the kind words which so many people had taken time to put together. Some of the business letters were addressed to Antonia with requests to "pass on our deepest sympathies/condolences to Mrs Hirsch." These had been annotated by Antonia as "acknowledged/thanked by telephone/invited to memorial service."

A surprising number of letters came from old school or college friends, even in some cases their parents, who'd seen the notice in the newspaper and written impulsive letters of condolence. Most were unanimous in praising Paul's kindness, charm and wonderful sense of humour and expressed themselves as shocked, dismayed, sad or shattered to hear the news. Some contained brief passages of scripture: "Be strong and of good courage." Others simply said that God would be of help and to put her trust in Him. One of his old friends wrote: "What a blessing he didn't survive to become disabled, he would have found that impossible." Some expressed opposing views: "Your children will be a great consolation." "You will need to be strong for your children." Some hoped that she might find happiness again. One from an old school friend urged her: "Don't give in! Life isn't always like this!" She hoped with all her heart she was right.

On Thursday, the day before Paul's memorial service, she was reading through the latest batch, working as if on automatic pilot; slitting envelopes, scanning the contents and putting them to one side to be read in detail and answered later. Sometimes the combination of words or their sincerity would succeed in penetrating the careful carapace that she was growing to try and stave off some of the pain. Then, before long, she would once again be brushing away the tears that never seemed to be far away.

At the bottom of the pile a stiff, white envelope with large, regular writing penned in thick black ink. There was something about it that made her pause. She picked it up, sniffed it and smelt nothing but ink and paper. She slit the envelope open slowly, opened the single sheet and read one sentence: *I could tell you things about Paul that would surprise you.*

She dropped it as quickly as if it had been on fire and wrapped both arms around herself as an involuntary protection. What on earth . . .? The telephone rang. She jumped up in shock letting it ring, half expecting the perpetrator of the letter to be at the other end of the line. The instrument continued to ring. Her mind cleared. There was only one person who never gave up on a phone call if she had an idea you were anywhere near. Liz picked up the receiver. 'Hello Antonia,' she said wearily.

'I just wanted to check that all the plans are in place for Paul's memorial service.' 'Plans?' Liz tried to keep the shake out of her voice. Her mind still numb after what she'd just read.

'I take it you've chosen hymns, ordered flowers, had leaflets printed.' Antonia's voice went on. Liz smiled with relief and mentally patted herself on the back. All three tasks had been accomplished and, just for once, she was ahead of Antonia.

'Of course the hotel will provide refreshments after the

service,' Antonia paused for a fraction of a second, '*naturally* there will be no charge.' Liz wanted to slam the receiver down, better still shove it down Antonia's hateful throat. Instead she forced herself as she had so many times in the past to curb her natural instincts. 'Thank you, Antonia, that's very kind of you.' She brushed the tears away from her eyes, replaced the receiver and burst into loud, ugly sobs.

When she'd calmed down she called Sarah. 'Will you do me the most tremendous favour?' she said before Sarah could even ask her how she was feeling.

'Fire away. I can always exercise my power and say no.'

Liz smiled, hearing the warmth in Sarah's voice, knowing deep down that she'd be unlikely to say no. 'Do you think you and Oscar could come to lunch on Friday and then hold my hand and get me through Paul's memorial service, only I honestly don't think I'll be able to survive it on my own. The funeral in Rome was bad enough and this will just open old wounds. I know I'm being selfish . . .'

'Oh, Liz, of course we will.' Sarah's voice was affectionate, reassuring; exactly what Liz needed. 'Why don't I get Oscar to pick up Maria and the children and bring them over here for the afternoon? Unless of course you want them to be at the service.'

'Oh goodness me, no. They're far too young. I'm still trying to pluck up the courage to tell Marcus that he no longer has a father, but somehow the right moment hasn't come along yet.' Liz felt like a supreme coward, but every time Marcus asked when Papa was coming home she backed off from telling him the truth.

'Plenty of time for that,' Sarah said. 'You'll know when the time is right and then it will probably be a whole lot easier than you imagined.'

'I only hope you're right.'

'Well, I'll get Oscar to pick the children up about twelve and then we'll come back together when he's dropped them off. How does that sound?'

'Absolutely perfect and thank you for being so kind.'

'Well, we are family after all,' Sarah said cheerfully.

The only family I have close by and where would I be without them, Liz thought as she put the phone down.

Somehow, in spite of all the activities, she managed to find time to search for the information that Peter Kilby had requested. Unpaid bills were easy since Paul had always kept them in an outsize paperclip in his desk. Others proved elusive and, having searched both the flat and Paul's desk in the hotel, she could find no trace of his naturalisation papers or his certificates of post-war credit. In desperation she asked the secretary that Paul and Antonia had shared, but she had no idea where Liz might find them. Finally Liz was left with no alternative but to ask Antonia. The following morning there was a blue file on Paul's desk with all the missing pieces of paper inside. She wondered idly what other bits of information Antonia might be hiding, but even as she framed the question knew that the odds of finding an answer were a million to one. How could you accuse someone of hiding information when you didn't know what you were looking for?

It was a relief when Friday morning dawned. She'd been waking early ever since her return and jumping out of bed the moment she heard Emma cry; her daughter's signal that she was awake and needing attention. For Liz it seemed important that she should provide whatever it was that Emma needed as quickly as possible and swiftly developed a routine beginning with nappy changing and moving forward to breakfast. By the time Emma had finished, Maria was up and dressed and she took over Emma while Liz spent time with Marcus.

Acting on impulse she'd decided not to depend on the hotel for lunch for herself, Sarah and Oscar and dashed into Bishop's Wood to buy a selection of delicatessen and salads knowing that none of them would be really hungry. Oscar and Sarah were also grieving for Paul. Oscar was losing yet another relative when he'd lost so many already. The day after Oscar left Vienna with the kindertransport en route to England, his parents had been picked up and deported to Theresienstadt in Czechoslovakia. He never saw them again. They perished like so many other friends and relatives who paid the ultimate penalty for being born Jewish.

It had taken both he and Paul a long time to adjust to British food and she wanted to give him a treat in return for his and Sarah's kindness to her. It was a relief to be doing something practical at which she excelled. She always enjoyed preparing food, even when, as now, it was a simple meal and was always gratified if guests asked for second helpings. She decided to serve lunch on some old family china inherited from her grandmother, which gave her comfort because of its association.

The memory of the letter still mocked her. That bold black, uncompromising writing which stared at her every time she opened the top left-hand drawer of her desk. She took it out several times, turning it over and over in her hands, trying to divine who the writer could be. Was it perhaps a practical joker or some enemy who was taking the opportunity to make her suffer, to increase her torment in some way? If so, why? Try as she might, she couldn't understand what was behind it. Perhaps the question would never be answered and the mystery would remain unsolved until one day it slipped into the dim recesses of her memory to be buried in the deep hole marked 'forgotten' like other periods of pain she'd experienced in the past.

But there were things to do. First of all, Paul needed a decent send-off after that travesty of a funeral in Rome and she went through a mental check-list hoping and praying that there was no vital detail she'd overlooked. *Tomorrow it will all be over* she told herself, *and then I'll be able to concentrate on the future.* Marcus must be told and, as she waited for Sarah and Oscar to arrive, she began to make a rough plan of what she might say to him. Perhaps she'd take him for a walk and tell him then; his attention would be diverted sooner or later by whatever they encountered. They would spot a disappearing rabbit or pick up fir cones or fallen leaves and he would quickly re-focus his attention away from the painful truth.

The sound of the doorbell cheered her up. For the next few hours, anyway, there would be diversions and she'd be spared the repetitive question which kept on spinning round in her mind. Why, oh why, did this awful tragedy have to happen to Paul? She pushed a welcoming smile onto her aching face and opened the door to Sarah and Oscar.

'Hello there. Don't you look elegant?' Sarah wrapped her in a smothering, scented embrace and thrust a bunch of red roses into her hand which she'd mixed with scarlet berries. 'These were the most cheerful thing I could find. I thought they'd help to lift your spirits when we've all gone home.'

'They're lovely. Thank you.' She managed somehow to hold back the tears which lurked permanently just waiting to spill over at the slightest opportunity. 'I'm not going to take up valuable time by giving you pre-lunch drinks.' She pulled out chairs for both of them. 'I thought we'd wade straight in if that's OK by you.' She looked at each of them in turn and they both agreed. She'd previously uncorked a bottle of Austrian wine, one of several they'd picked up in the Wachau on last year's holiday, and handed it to Oscar. 'Will you be an angel and pour this while I help everyone to food?' she asked.

Oscar stretched out a hand and took the bottle, pouring a little into his own glass and tasting it before giving some to Liz and his wife. 'Looking at the label I'm sure it's excellent, but just as well to make sure,' he said. Liz was serving out a selection of cold meats and fish. 'I only wish Bishop's Wood had a better selection of continental foods, but I did the best I could. Please help yourselves to salads,' she invited, waving a hand in the direction of some shallow entree dishes which she'd filled with a variety of colourful leaves and vegetables.

'This looks wonderful,' Sarah said. 'It's such a treat to be sitting down and eating lunch at a civilised time instead of fitting food in around the punters. Isn't it darling?' She looked across the table at Oscar, willing him to share in her appreciation of Liz's efforts. 'Absolutely!' Oscar came in bang on cue. 'I've got to hand it to Paul, if he chose this wine, it's excellent. Make's me feel quite homesick to be drinking it.' He raised his glass. 'To Paul.' The women echoed his toast and the air resounded with the tinkle of clinking glasses.

'Oh I *do* wish he was still with us,' Liz said, gulping a large mouthful of wine and handing round chunks of crusty brown bread.

'What's the betting the old rascal's watching!' Oscar squeezed her hand and Liz was comforted by the strength he transmitted. 'Have you ever known Paul to miss out on a good meal?' he added, forcing Liz to smile. She daren't indulge in the luxury of remembering all the intimate dinners they'd shared and the more riotous ones they'd eaten with friends. This last holiday alone had so many memories which were particularly poignant, as almost all their dinners had been a prelude to great sex. She'd save them up for a treat and think about them later when the service was over and everyone had gone home.

'That was a really lovely meal,' Sarah said when they'd finished and were drinking coffee, still sitting around the table with the remnants of cheese and the last of the wine.

'I'm glad you enjoyed it. Believe me, I'm so grateful to the pair of you. Antonia's laying on some kind of refreshments after the service. I do hope you'll stay for those as well.'

'We're here for as long as necessary. It's Saturday tomorrow, so it won't matter if the children are late to bed for once. Now I suppose we'd better get a move on or we shall have to answer to Antonia.' She looked across at Liz, 'Ready?'

'Just let me get my coat and tidy my face. French dressing usually plays havoc with my lipstick and I want to be a credit to Paul.'

They walked up the path to the church. Liz tried hard not to look at the tombstones as they approached the fifteenth century timbered porch. The sun came out briefly over the squat, square tower and shone over the moss-coated, tiled roof. The strains of a Bach chorale drifted towards them and the vicar, who'd been waiting for them under the porch, walked forward and welcomed them. Liz began to feel calmer as Oscar put his hand under her elbow and led the way towards a front pew. The church was more than three quarters full, but Liz took in the congregation as a whole rather than individual members. She'd asked a local florist for a single pedestal which stood slightly to the right of the pulpit. The scent of lilies helped to dispel the normal musty smell of the church and they were perfectly complemented by long stemmed roses and carnations all in white against a background of copper beech leaves.

Liz bit her lip hard and clenched both hands into tight fists as she heard the vicar's voice. 'Dearly beloved, we are gathered together to remember Paul Hirsch, whose life ended so tragically in Rome.' Seconds later there was a rustle from the congregation as they reached for their orders of service and began to sing "The King of love my Shepherd is." Liz tried to join in, but the words stuck in her throat. They'd sung it when she and Paul were married; her reason for choosing it now. She hadn't been able to sing it then either because she'd been so happy she was afraid of crying and ruining her careful bridal make-up.

The vicar recited a psalm and then read the lesson before Oscar walked to the lectern to pay a brief tribute to Paul. Liz had asked him, knowing that he would speak from his heart, and she listened intently as he talked about the time he'd spent with Paul when they were both boys together in Vienna; of the skiing trips; their membership of the boy scouts; their escape to England and their sadness at leaving Austria. He then looked straight at Liz and said how pleased and proud they were to have her as a family member, what a good wife she'd been to Paul and how happy she'd made him. Finally he paid tribute to Paul's sense of humour and said how much he'd valued his friendship. He opened his arms in conclusion to embrace everyone. 'I'm sure you would all like to join with me in offering your affection, support and sympathy to Liz and her two children.'

That did it for Liz. The tears spilled over and she hastily pulled out the handkerchief she'd remembered to put in her pocket just before they'd left for the church. When Oscar stood once again beside her, she reached out impulsively and took his hand, squeezing it in gratitude, then looked across the aisle to where Antonia sat, swathed in Persian lamb, her face expressionless. It was then, she noticed for the first time that Antonia was not alone. Beside her sat a woman dressed in a simple black trench coat, her hair hidden under an elegant matching turban. Liz assumed she must be a friend of Antonia, but couldn't remember ever seeing her before in the hotel. And then, as the final hymn was announced, the woman turned slightly as she rose to her feet and Liz caught sight of an immaculately made-up face and the glint of pearls in her ears. Cold fingers of fear squeezed her heart and she knew instinctively that she was looking at the author of the letter that lay in the top drawer of her desk.

CHAPTER FIFTEEN

Liz was shaking as she left the church, smiling automatically at friends in the congregation, but not stopping to talk to any of them, needing time to calm down. She waited for Oscar to unlock the car before climbing into the back seat and settling well into the corner. It would be really marvellous if she could disappear for the next hour, or render herself completely invisible, become an apparition at whatever it was that Antonia had planned. But she owed it to Paul's supporters and friends to circulate, thank them all for coming and above all to listen to whatever they were about to say to her about him.

Who *was* that woman and why was she here? If she was an ex-girlfriend, why couldn't she just call it a day and vanish? What was she hoping to achieve? What did she want from Liz if indeed she wanted anything? Could it be that she and Paul had some kind of secret relationship? Why hadn't he mentioned her?

Her mind went back to the night in Rome when Paul was taken ill. He'd been trying to tell her something before the stroke had robbed him of his speech. Had he been about to make a confession? Was the amber necklace a gift to ease his conscience? How could he have been so deceitful? Had she done something really dreadful to him to make him find a soul mate elsewhere? Was she useless in bed? The thoughts went on and on.

'You're very quiet.' Oscar's voice reminded her where she was.

'Sorry, Oscar. Just thinking.'

'You held up brilliantly.' Sarah had a gift for saying the right thing at the best time.

'It wasn't easy,' Liz said. 'Thank you, Oscar, for your lovely words. I hope Paul was listening.'

'You can bet your life he was!' Oscar chuckled. 'Ah, here we are. Only another hour or so and it will all be over.'

'I can't say I'll be sorry. Although I feel so churlish saying that; everyone has been so kind.'

'Paul was a great guy.' Oscar's voice held real warmth. 'I shall miss the old so and so. We were good mates. Let's go in and give him a good send off.'

Liz wondered if he knew the mysterious woman who'd been standing next to Antonia and, if so, why didn't he mention her? She thought of asking him and then decided perhaps not. She would wait and see if she turned up at the hotel and then try and find out some more.

Two of the hotel waiting staff stood in the foyer with trays bearing glasses of champagne, which they offered to the arriving guests before directing them to the hotel lounge. Gaston Legrange hovered in the background, impeccably groomed and smooth as silk. Liz disliked him more every time she saw him without really knowing why. She stopped to talk to friends and acquaintances en route to the lounge, thanking them for coming, trying to listen to their words of sympathy.

Two long tables bore plates of delectable finger food. A couple of waiters circulated offering canapes, tiny sandwiches and other tempting savouries. The whole set up was a testament to Antonia's impeccable taste. Liz said 'Hello' to a couple of men who supplied the hotel with wine and whom she'd come to know well. Paul had always trusted their recommendations of good wine to buy for laying down, bargains for drinking now and the occasional rare vintage for special occasions. He'd bought several cases for their own use which were stored in the cellar at Ivy House.

Suddenly she caught the whiff of a Turkish cigarette, turned around and then stiffened as she saw who was smoking it. The woman she'd seen in church had detached herself from Antonia and was now standing alone surveying the room.

'I don't think we've met, I'm Liz Hirsch.'

'Eloise Moncton.'

The cool grey eyes surveyed Liz, but their owner made no

attempt to smile and Liz felt like an unwelcome intruder.

'Are you a business contact of Paul's?' Liz *had* to know.

'You could put it like that. I own a small hotel in Knightsbridge, a legacy from my father. Paul helped me a lot in the early days when I was a bit wet behind the ears.'

Liz found it hard to believe that this self-assured, worldly creature could ever be anything of the sort. She sipped her champagne, partly for Dutch courage, mainly to give herself time to frame her next question. 'Am I right in thinking that you wrote to me and either forgot to sign the letter or deliberately chose to remain anonymous?'

Eloise allowed herself the faintest of smiles before bending down and stubbing out her cigarette in a convenient ash tray. 'I didn't know if Paul had mentioned me,' she said.

Liz's heart began to pound uncomfortably. 'Why would he do that?' she asked.

'Ah!' Her voice was low, scarcely audible. 'The fact is we were planning to be married.'

The thumping heart was now being pulled out of Liz's chest. The hand not holding a glass clutched at the back of a chair and for a moment she thought she might fall over. 'I simply don't believe it,' she said at last.

Eloise Moncton shrugged. 'That's entirely up to you. But take a look around. Would you choose to stay in a place like this if the alternative was a half share in a more exclusive establishment, what's more one that has considerable potential? In short a hotel that is much more Paul's scene.'

Keep cool, Liz told herself, resisting a strong temptation to smack Eloise Moncton hard across her sneering, carefully made-up face. How dare she suggest that a hotel into which Paul had put nearly twenty years of his working life wasn't his scene?

'I suggest you leave right now,' she said. 'It can't have escaped your notice, but we've all been trying to give thanks for Paul's life and to come here trying to make trouble suggests not only complete insensitivity, but also an extreme lack of good taste.'

She stretched out a hand and removed the half-drunk glass of champagne from Eloise. 'We can play this either way. I can ask one of the staff to escort you from the premises or you can go of your own free will.' She took a step backward and waited. Eloise Moncton's eyes swept over her in one cold, disdainful stare and then, without another word, she picked up her handbag - glossy black patent - and left.

Oscar had been watching the two women from the other side of the room. As Eloise left he saw Liz drain her glass and take another from a passing waiter. Her face was white as chalk and he guessed her mind must be in turmoil imagining who-knows-what nastiness. He made his way slowly across to her, guessing she was probably more in need of a shoulder to cry on now than at any time since Paul's death. On the way over he picked up a plate of sandwiches, which he held out towards Liz as he reached her side.

'That stuff's lethal if you drink too much without eating.'

'Oh Oscar!' She took a sandwich and nibbled at a corner of it as if it were poison. 'Did you see that dreadful woman who just left?'

'You mean Eloise Moncton?'

'You know her?'

'Sure, I know her. Daddy left her Moncton's Hotel in Knightsbridge.'

'You must tell me everything you know about her.' The blue eyes pleaded and he knew she wouldn't be fobbed off easily.

'Forget her Liz, she's history.' Oscar sipped half-heartedly at his champagne, wishing it were whisky, hoping to deflect any further questions.

'How can I forget her? She sent me a letter. Not threatening exactly, but hinting that she could tell me things about Paul that might surprise me.'

'The last ditch attempt of a disappointed woman!' Oscar smiled and helped himself to a sandwich.

'Please, Oscar, don't tease! She told me that she and Paul were going to be married.'

Oscar laughed. 'She must be joking! Can you really see Paul married to that iceberg?'

'You *must* tell me the story.' He'd never seen her look so agonised.

'OK,' he said, 'but do you think we can go somewhere a little more private?'

'Come up to the flat,' Liz said. 'There's nobody there at the moment.'

Oscar followed her out of the lounge, signalling wordlessly to Sarah as they left and putting the sandwiches on the buffet table before following Liz up to the flat. He waited while she switched on lamps and drew curtains. 'Before we talk, let me give you a proper drink.' She crossed to a side table.

'Scotch would be nice. I'm not really a champagne fan.' He stood waiting while Liz poured a generous two fingers of whisky and held out the glass. 'Help yourself to either water or soda. I'd hate to drown it for you.' She crossed to her desk, opened the top drawer, took out the letter and handed it to Oscar who, after squirting a splash of soda into his glass, settled himself on the sofa.

He glanced at the contents. 'She was always a drama queen! Whenever they were together she was always clinging to his arm and if Paul did manage to escape for a chat with an old chum you can bet your sweet life it wouldn't be long before the dreaded Eloise joined them to muscle in on the conversation.'

'So tell me how they met, how long they knew each other. Why did he marry me if *she* was so important to him?' Liz came and sat beside him on the sofa and Oscar thought how vulnerable she looked; as if the poor thing hadn't had enough to cope with during the past two weeks. He squeezed her hand in a clumsy attempt at comfort.

'Paul married you because he loved you and Eloise wasn't important to him. She's a friend of Antonia's sister Celia. They met at a party she gave to celebrate something or another. Paul made a big hit with Eloise. He wasn't trying, you understand, but looking back I can't remember there was much competition.

One of the reasons Paul and I were invited I guess. Celia must have been a bit short of men.'

Celia was a modestly gifted artist, specialising in painting the pets of anyone keen enough on immortalising their favourite animal to pay her fee. Although she worked from photographs, the final portraits were very lifelike and caught the imagination of a well known art critic a few years ago and she'd enjoyed a brief period of media attention. She'd painted both Omar and Khayyam as a birthday present for Antonia. Liz remembered only too well that Paul had spent several hours with his camera trying to get exactly the right pose. The portraits now hung one either side of the chimney breast in Antonia's sitting room. Liz always imagined their eyes watching her whenever she was in Antonia's flat. Just thinking about them gave her the creeps.

'How long ago was this?' Liz asked, putting down the glass, now empty, which she'd been twisting around and around in her hands.

'Five, no six years ago I think.' Oscar did his maths carefully trying to remember how long Liz and Paul had been together. He knew there'd been an overlap, but wild horses wouldn't make him tell Liz and so add to her distress. He hoped she wasn't about to go digging too deeply into Paul's past and prayed he could convince her that Eloise had been no more than a brief and relatively unimportant interlude in his life.

He knew Eloise had tried to get Paul back after his marriage to Liz. She'd manufactured some problem with the hotel, convincing Paul that he was exactly the right person to deal with it. Paul had later confided to Oscar that it was the first time he'd ever encountered such a blatant attempt at seduction and described how brutal he'd had to be with Eloise to stop her making fools of both of them. He'd told her as bluntly as he could that he was now married, that Liz was expecting their first child and that the two of them were now the centre of his life and likely to remain so. 'She threw my photograph at me!' Paul had laughed. 'Frame and all! When I ducked, she stamped on it. I wouldn't mind betting the glass ruined those stiletto heels of hers!'

Later on she'd phoned Oscar pleading with him to try to get Paul to see sense, as she'd put it. 'I know it's me he really loves! I've so much to offer him!' she'd wept down the telephone. 'He'll listen to you, I know he will.'

Oscar had played what he thought was a trump card at the time. 'We're not just talking about three adults here, but an unborn, innocent baby. Like it or not, Eloise, Paul's decided where his future lies and I'm sorry to say it isn't with you.' He could still hear the crack in his right ear as she'd slammed down the phone.

'So why did she write to me? Why did she turn up at the funeral?' Liz persisted. 'Surely it would be more dignified to stay in the background? And don't forget, she told me they were going to be married. Do you think that Paul was planning to leave me sometime soon?' Her tears spilled over and ran unchecked down her cheeks. Oscar pulled a handkerchief from the breast pocket of his jacket and offered it. He slipped an arm around her shoulders and patted her back awkwardly with his free hand as her sobs grew louder.

'Don't cry, Liz, she isn't worth it,' he said, wishing that Sarah had followed them up to the flat. When it came to mothering, he'd put his money on her any day.

After a few minutes, Liz calmed down, pulled away from Oscar and blew her nose. 'I'm really sorry. I didn't mean to weep all over you; but it's been such a traumatic day, one way and another, and now this hateful woman.'

'As I said earlier, Liz, she's past history and a good five years older than Paul, maybe more. I'm sure you have nothing to worry about. After all, there's very little she can do now that Paul . . .' He paused, not wanting to spell out Paul's death. He hoped to God he was right and that they'd heard the last of Eloise.

'I must let you go. Sarah will be wondering what's happened to you.' Liz tried hard to smile. 'I don't know what I would have done without the pair of you. I'm sorry but the tears never seem to be very far away and it doesn't take much to start me off.'

'It will get better, I promise. Don't be too hard on yourself and you know where we are if you run into trouble. By the way, I almost forgot to tell you. I went to Heathrow yesterday and picked up Paul's ashes. I'm afraid I left them at home. You didn't say you wanted to have them for the service, so I just hung on to them. I hope that's OK?'

'Thanks, Oscar. Would you mind keeping them for a little while longer? My mind's in such turmoil I honestly don't think I could bear to see them at the moment. I'll let you know as soon as I've decided what to do with them. Now, shall we go and find Sarah? I'm sure she'll be longing to get away.'

'One of us will drive Maria and the children back; or would you like us to keep them for the night?'

'No, the company will be good for me. Left to myself I'll just sit and brood.'

'If you're sure then.' Oscar stood up and they went to find Sarah.

Eloise tapped a varnished fingernail impatiently on the steering wheel as she was forced to stop the car yet again. The Friday night traffic seemed to be more gridlocked than usual. It was her own fault for allowing that hysterical little wife of Paul's to get rid of her so easily. She'd planned to hang around until most of the crowd left, hoping Antonia would invite her for dinner, so that she could put her proposition to the test. Driving back later would have been a doddle; instead of which, she was stuck in a jam and who knows what time she was going to get home.

She felt her stomach rumble, reminding her that she'd skipped lunch to be in time for that God awful memorial service. Paul would have hated it. Mawkish twaddle, most of it, and the rest downright lies. She lit a cigarette wondering how she was going to survive for the next few months. Useless to blame herself that the hotel refurbishment had gone way over budget. How could she know that most of their old clients would choose to sleep and eat elsewhere after such a complete change to the comfortable environment they'd known for so long? She'd heard via reception that some of their regular punters had complained they didn't recognise the place after the improvements. Well, she wasn't providing a home-from-home, but a state of the art hotel, if only they knew it.

She badly needed a major investor; failing that she'd have to do something drastic. In the past she'd always managed to come up with some brilliant idea when a crisis loomed. It was just a question of putting her mind to it. Correction, her not inconsiderable mind. She tossed her cigarette end out of the window and smiled lazily as the traffic began to move at last. She let in the clutch and put the car into gear as the beginning of a plan began to form.

Liz slept badly thinking of Eloise Moncton and wondering over and over again just how important she'd been to Paul. She'd seemed so confident speaking to Liz as if her future life with Paul had been all mapped out before he died. Perhaps it had? But Paul had been talking about buying a house the night they'd driven into Perugia and one which was within easy commuting distance of the hotel. If he'd been planning to ditch her and the children, he'd surely have suggested that she move out of the flat and into Ivy House, then he'd have been free to pursue whatever he was planning with Eloise. Perhaps Oscar was right and she was just trying to dramatise the situation for her own satisfaction. After all, if she'd once been in love with Paul and hadn't replaced him, she was possibly feeling as bereft as Liz herself; if she was capable of feeling anything which Liz doubted.

She riffled through the post and spotted an airmail letter with an Italian postmark. The name of the sender was on the back: Hans and Ruth Lebermann. She slit round the edges and opened the letter, which was written in tiny type by Hans with a handwritten message at the end from Ruth.

My dear Mrs Hirsch,

Our thoughts are with you and we have just written to the Reverend Ward in the hope that he will be able to offer you all the spiritual support that you will need now that you are home again.

I feel that I let you down by not speaking to the British Consul and persuading him to let me conduct the funeral service for Paul. To watch that dreadful hard breathing through that night and then to have your hopes raised and dashed in the following few days is more than most of us could have taken. Naturally we had prayed for his recovery throughout his illness and yet one had to add "Whatever happens not as I will but as Thou wilt," especially when the prolonged unconsciousness indicated the likelihood of permanent brain damage. We have no explanation for it, no rational answer at all to the question why this should have happened to you. All we can do is put our faith blindly in the One who some day will answer our questions and reunite us in another life. That is why I asked you (and why one has to ask oneself every day) do you believe in God? Do you believe in Christ? Do you believe that nothing, neither life nor death, can separate us from His love? This is the only way to go on living and to become, as St Paul says in that Romans 8 passage, "More than conquerors through Him that loved us."

It is easy to type such words, quite another to carry them out in practice; and it takes more than our own will power. I have always loved the collect in the Prayer Book for the 4th Sunday after Epiphany: "O God who knowest us to be set in the midst of so many and great dangers, that by reason of the frailty of our nature we cannot always stand upright: Grant to us such strength and protection, as may support us in all dangers, and carry us through all temptations, through Jesus Christ Our Lord." In future when I pray this collect you will be very much included in it.

Ruth joins me in kind remembrances and warmest good wishes for you and the children. We look forward to meeting them before long. We shall be in London early December, so it will be easy to make a date then before we fly home to the States for Christmas.

God bless and keep you always,

    Your friend,
    Hans Lebermann

Ruth had written at the bottom. *We have protested to the Consul not the Vice-Consul about the appalling funeral service that they inflicted on you and have suggested in the strongest terms that they charge you the lowest possible fee. I still feel angry when I think of the exploitation of your grief. We'll see you soon and think and pray for you until then.*

Yours very sincerely,

Ruth Lebermann

Liz folded the letter carefully and placed it on her desk. It had never crossed her mind that the British Consulate might be exploiting her. She'd simply assumed that the funeral service they'd arranged had been a standard deal offered to any stranded tourist. In any case it was too late to change it and she had no way of comparing the fee with that of other Roman funeral directors. She must write back to the Lebermanns as soon as possible, thank them for their concern and try to reassure them that she was coping. Whether the Reverend Ward, her local vicar, would be in touch again, who could say? Then she told herself firmly that she must try to be strong and that now, today, was absolutely the right time to tell Marcus that he no longer had a father.

'Would you like to go for a walk?' she asked. He was busy freewheeling his precious Ferrari up and down the small hallway of the flat.

'Are we going to buy sweeties?' Marcus looked up briefly. The expression on his face made him look so much like Paul that her heart flipped over.

'I thought today we'd just walk,' Liz said. She didn't want Marcus to think that every time he went for a walk he should buy sweets. 'If we walk across the park and into the woods who knows what we might find? We'd better take a bag so that you can bring back any treasures.'

'OK,' he said. It was unusual for him to be so acquiescent and Liz wondered briefly if he might be coming down with some childish ailment. She rumpled his hair. 'Let's find your warm clothes and welly boots, it looks a bit blowy outside.' She went into the kitchen where Maria was washing some of the children's jerseys. 'I thought I'd take Marcus for a walk before lunch. Will you be OK to look after Emma until we get back? I promise we won't be late.'

Maria had the rest of the day off and Liz knew she'd made plans to go and meet some friends. 'I'll take Emma as well if you'd like to get off early,' she added, anxious to make life as easy for Maria as possible. The last three weeks hadn't exactly been a bed of roses for her.

'No we'll be fine,' Maria said, squeezing soapsuds through a collection of woollens. 'Once I've finished these it will be time for Emma's sleep.'

'Right then, come on young man,' she said to Marcus, 'I'll help you with your boots.' She bent down and straightened his socks, which were wrinkled under the soles of his feet, and then sat him on her lap while she pulled on his boots before handing him a pair of mittens she'd bought for him in Rome. 'There, now you'll be as warm as toast,' she said pulling on her anorak and putting a folded plastic carrier bag into her pocket. "Bye Maria,' she called out taking Marcus' hand in her own as they left the flat.

They crossed the park at the back of the hotel, pausing briefly by the lake so that Marcus could look at the fish and search for frogs, his most recent wildlife interest, then continued until they reached the small wood that bordered the property. 'Look Marcus! Conkers!' Liz said, bending down and picking up a handful of the shiny, copper nuts. 'Shall I put them in the bag?' She pulled out the folded carrier from her pocket. Marcus didn't look at her but stood scuffing the leaves with his right foot, both hands plunged deeply into his coat pockets. Liz doubted if he had even seen the conkers. 'Is everything OK?' she asked picking up on the body language and his complete lack of enthusiasm for their walk.

He continued to look down at the ground and Liz suddenly had a sickening feeling that something was really wrong. Normally he'd be running around all over the place in the way that puppies run when they've been let off the lead. She squatted down so they were eyeball to eyeball and put an arm around his shoulder. He didn't respond, didn't snuggle up, didn't lean against her, didn't look at her. 'Marcus,' she urged, 'if there's something wrong, please tell me and then I can help you make it all better.'

Marcus stayed quiet, kicking moodily at the leaves. Liz shook him gently. 'Come on sweetheart. If you don't tell me, how can I help?' A couple of minutes went by before Marcus lifted his head slowly and looked at her steadily. To her dismay she saw a large tear form in the corner of one eye and roll slowly down his cheek. She drew him close and hugged him, feeling his body shake as the tears started to flow. 'Oh darling,' she said, 'I suppose you've guessed Papa isn't coming back.' Perhaps he'd overheard one of the staff talking or just put two and two together as time went by and his father didn't return. To her surprise he pulled away from her and through his tears he shouted, 'Why did you have to send Papa away?'

His accusation was so unexpected she felt as if he'd kicked her. 'But darling, I didn't send Papa away. Why would I want to do that when we all love him so much?' Liz found a crumpled handkerchief in her pocket and mopped his brimming eyes. 'You know I wouldn't want Papa to be anywhere but with us,' she continued, desperately wishing for the umpteenth time she hadn't delayed telling him for so long. When at last his tears subsided she asked, 'Whatever gave you the idea that I might send Papa away?'

'Aunty Toni told me.' He shifted awkwardly from one foot to another looking so dejected that Liz felt ready to commit murder on his behalf. How could anyone be so heartless as to tell a child such a blatant lie? Didn't Antonia realise it could have future and severe implications? For all she knew Marcus could grow up hating his mother forever more; never believing or wanting to believe the real story. Then Liz realised with a sudden clarity the real reason for Antonia's mischief. What would she do next to ruin all their lives? Almost immediately she urged herself not to jump to all sorts of rash conclusions. Looking around she spotted a fallen log. 'Let's go and sit down and then you can tell me all about it,' she said, taking his mittened hand in her own and walking across to the log.

'Now Marcus,' she said when they were both settled. 'Think very carefully because we must get this absolutely right. Are you sure it was Toni who told you I'd sent Papa away?' Marcus nodded solemnly. 'You wouldn't make it up would you?' Marcus shook his head from side to side. 'Would you like me to tell you the real story?' Marcus nodded, lifting his tear-washed blue eyes to meet hers. Liz drew a deep breath. 'The truth is that Papa got sick when we were away. A lot of doctors tried very hard to make him better, but they just weren't clever enough. Papa's gone to a place called Heaven and he's probably playing with the angels right this minute.'

'Why can he play with the angels and not with me?' His face was a picture of disappointment and Liz fought hard to control her own emotions. Would her tears never dry up? Her reply must be convincing and she took a moment or two to fix in her mind what to say. She held both his hands in her own.

'We can't go to Heaven unless we're really sick and don't get better. You wouldn't want to be *that* sick, would you?' She scanned his face anxiously, thinking what a lot for a small boy of two and a half to deal with. His next question made her smile in spite of the desperate half hour they'd just spent together. 'Shall we get a new daddy one day?' His face began to take on a more hopeful expression as he asked his question. Liz gave him a quick hug. 'I really don't know, Marcus. Some time in the future perhaps. Would you like to have some lunch now?' Marcus stood up and they walked slowly back to the hotel. Normally he would have begged for a few more minutes or would have run away and hidden behind a tree to try and prolong their time together outdoors, but then this was very far from a normal day. The terrible reality that their lives had now become hit her forcibly and the thought preoccupied her as they walked. She must never allow anything like this to happen again. The time had come to make plans for the future; all their futures.

CHAPTER SIXTEEN

Liz tried every diversionary tactic to keep Marcus occupied for the rest of the weekend, desperate for him not to brood over what Antonia had said. She kept him close to her side in case he should run into Antonia and give her the opportunity to pour more poison. She read him endless stories and wished she had a proper kitchen so they could do something practical together like making cookies. The best she could come up with was a makeshift children's tea and she let him stand on a stool and stir baked beans while she poached eggs and made toast. They played endlessly with his Ferrari, sending it from one side of the room to the other until she was afraid the motor would conk out. Finally she taught him how to play snakes and ladders and was delighted when, after she'd tucked him up in bed, he fell asleep almost immediately.

When both the children were settled she poured herself a glass of wine and sat down to think about her future; all their futures. The obvious course of action, for her own peace of mind if for nothing else, would be to confront Antonia and warn her not to tell Marcus any more lies. But what would that achieve? Antonia could turf them all out tomorrow and, although Liz knew that sooner or later they would have to leave, she would prefer to do it when there was time to pack their belongings properly and clear up the most pressing business she still had to deal with.

It was obvious that a move to Ivy House was her best, short term option. Then she'd get a job, preferably within easy commuting distance. There were several hotels in Salisbury. Surely one of them would employ her in one capacity or another? Her qualifications and her limited experience at Bishop's Hall should work in her favour. Would Maria come with them? If she didn't, work wouldn't even be in the equation. Once they'd moved she would find a nursery school for Marcus. Living in a hotel was far from an ideal life for him and gave him no opportunity to meet children of his own age. Finding friends or even a single friend would help him perhaps to forget that he no longer had a father or at least push the memory to the back of his mind. She must give strict instructions to Maria not to allow any more outings with Antonia. She was no fool and perhaps would get the message if all her outings with Marcus were to stop.

It was a relief to have a plan, even the most vague was better than nothing.

She was just about to sit down at her desk and reply to some more of the letters of condolence when the phone rang. It was George from reception. 'I have a Mr Richardson here. Says he's a friend. Shall I bring him up to the flat?'

'Oh!' Liz said in surprise. She hadn't been expecting anyone. Martin Richardson and his wife were both friends. They'd been at Paul's memorial service, so she was surprised that one of them should stop by so soon. 'Thanks, George, but I'll come down,' Liz said, wondering what on earth Martin Richardson could want at eight thirty on a Saturday evening.

'Hello there! What a surprise!' she said, walking across the foyer to where he was standing in front of George's desk. He looked a trifle shifty and mindful that George was standing within earshot, and of the comings and goings around them, she suggested they go up to the flat.

'As you can see I've been consoling myself,' she offered by way of explanation, once they reached the flat. Pointing to the half empty bottle of wine she asked, 'Would you like a drink or are you in a hurry?' To her surprise he accepted a glass of wine and settled himself in an armchair.

'How are you feeling after yesterday? It must have been quite an ordeal.'

'To be honest I feel a bit wrung out one way or another. A couple of surprises I hadn't bargained for.'

'The hotel did you proud I thought. Anne and I thought the refreshments were delicious.'

He hasn't come here to talk about the standard of catering at Bishop's Wood, Liz thought, reaching for the bottle to top up his glass. At least he hadn't asked her to elaborate on her two surprises, so that was something. She watched him shift in his seat as if he were uncomfortable and then listened as he cleared his throat, bracing herself for whatever was coming.

'Anne asked me to have a word about the christening,' he said at last, taking a long pull from his wine glass and looking as if he wanted to be anywhere but sitting in Liz's flat.

'Oh yes! It's coming up quite soon isn't it?' They had a three month old daughter and had asked Liz and Paul to be godparents before they went away on holiday. Liz had forgotten all about it in the flurry of activities since her return.

'Well the thing is,' he hesitated, drank some more wine, crossed and uncrossed his legs. 'The thing is it seems we've been a bit careless and we appear to have too many godparents. After Paul died Anne asked another couple to take your place and as she'd already asked an old school friend to be the other godmother we're left with one too many godmothers.'

'And you'd like me to stand down?' Liz put in quickly thinking to spare him further embarrassment.

'Would you mind?' Martin drained his glass, put it on a side table and ran a finger around the inside of his shirt collar.

Liz wondered idly if the Anglican Church would fall apart if one little girl had three godmothers instead of only two and if Anne had given a second thought about the possible effect that a rejection might have on her so soon after Paul's death. 'Of course I don't mind!' she said with false brightness, jumping to her feet and preparing to show Martin out. The sooner she released him from his obvious misery the better. She watched him rise slowly to his feet but was totally unprepared for the kiss he planted full on her mouth.

'I knew you'd understand,' he said. 'But I thought it would be kinder to tell you face-to-face than over the phone.' He took both her hands in his own. 'I want you to know that if you ever need,' he paused, searching for the right word, 'if you ever need any *consolation*, you only have to let me know.'

Liz was completely lost for words. Consolation my foot! First time she'd heard it called that before! She didn't know whether to laugh in his face or spit in it. But she knew the sensible, and admittedly more ladylike, response would be to draw a firm line under the last few minutes, just in case he got any wrong ideas. 'Thanks for the offer, Martin, but I think it will be a very long time before I'm able to seek *consolation*, as you put it, from anybody. Say hello to Anne for me and tell her not to worry any more about her surplus godmother.'

She walked over to the door, opened it and turned towards him. 'Thanks for coming. It can't have been easy for you. Do you mind if I don't come down with you? Only one way and another it's been quite a day.'

Well! Whatever next I wonder? Old friends or friend to be precise cutting her dead in the car park. Representations from Paul's ex- girlfriend. Overtures from at least two men. Rejected as a potential godmother. It was useless to pretend that none of it hurt. It all hurt, particularly the overtures. What in God's name did they think she was? Liz felt angry, dirty and useless by turns. She scrubbed at her mouth with a tissue trying to wipe off Martin Richardson's hateful unwanted kiss. Her plan to spend the rest of the evening writing thank you letters evaporated into thin air.

On Monday morning there was a telephone call from the RAC to tell her that Paul's car had now been returned and was awaiting collection in Dover. She scribbled down all the information and then called Oscar and Sarah. 'I'm about to throw myself on your mercy yet again,' she said as Sarah's voice came over the wire. 'I promise you this won't go on indefinitely, but right now I could really use some help.' She passed on the news about Paul's car. 'I'd appreciate a co-driver if it could be arranged. Obviously I'll need to take my car down and someone will have to drive Paul's car back. Any day will do, but I'd rather not leave it too long. For one thing Antonia calls nearly every morning to ask me when the car's coming back and once it's here I can tick it off my list.'

'I think I'm going to pass this one over to Oscar,' Sarah said. 'Fact is I'm nervous about driving other people's cars. It would be just like me to misjudge my distance and put a scrape down the side and I'd never forgive myself if I hurt that sleek monster of Paul's.'

The sleek monster was a gleaming black TR4. Liz had been dropping hints to Paul for some time that they should change it and buy something more suitable for a growing family. Her much loved Morris Traveller was great as an everyday runaround but wasn't up to doing the kind of speed that Paul preferred. He'd prevaricated and she'd refrained from pushing him, knowing how much he enjoyed driving the TR and that he would get around to choosing a replacement one day; probably the first time they discovered that two children and their miscellaneous clutter wouldn't fit in. She smiled now thinking about how good he was at wriggling off the hook. He'd loved that car and had no intention of giving it up without a struggle. Now it had given him up.

'Oscar's not here at the moment, but I'll get him to call you later. In the meantime, how are things?' Sarah's voice put a stop to her thoughts, forcing her back to reality.

'Oh pretty grim. I told Marcus yesterday that his father wasn't coming back.'

'That must have been tough. How did he take it?'

'It's difficult to say. Antonia apparently already told him that I'd sent Paul away.'

'Surely not even *she* would be so wicked.' Sarah's voice was incredulous.

'Well I had a serious talk with Marcus and he stuck to his story and then when I thought about it I realised that it would be a pretty outlandish thing for him to make up. In the final analysis who would you believe, your own child or Antonia?'

'Well if you put it like that . . . but he's such a little mite and that miserable old hag must have known how upset he would be.'

'Oh Sarah, I know. I've done my best to make it OK with Marcus, but with children you never know how deep the harm might be. They're so good at keeping things to themselves aren't they? I'm just trying to occupy him as best I can.'

'Let's hope he forgets soon and if you need any help you know where to come.'

'Thanks Sarah, but I've got to learn to stand on my own feet sometime. However, I don't think I'm up to driving two cars back from Dover, so if Oscar can help that would be fantastic.'

'I'll make sure he calls you as soon as he gets back and, in the meantime, please take care. You've had a major life crisis and you mustn't ask too much of yourself.' The concern in Sarah's voice, although comforting, made her feel more like a lame duck than ever.

Two days later she collected Oscar at half past nine in the morning for their drive to Dover. 'If I were really bloody minded I'd be telling Antonia to pick her own damned car up, but the fact is I'm trying to keep her as sweet as possible until I've fixed a date for all of us to leave,' Liz said, trying at the same time to concentrate on the traffic as they left Bishop's Wood.

'You're leaving! How come? When?' Oscar hadn't been expecting to hear such decisive news so soon after Paul's death and looked at her in surprise.

'I haven't fixed a date yet, but I've known ever since I got back from Rome I'm in a very precarious position and I don't want to leave it until Antonia gives me notice to quit or even worse pitches me out on my ear the first stormy night we get! The flat goes with the job and as Paul isn't here to do the job it's only a matter of time . . .' She let the sentence die away on a long sigh.

'If Antonia had any sense she'd appoint you in Paul's place. I'm sure you'd do a fantastic job; a whole lot better than that oily individual who's currently masquerading as manager.' Oscar pulled a face. 'Funny, isn't it, how you take a dislike to people?

The moment I saw him I smelled trouble. What do the staff think of him?'

'It's difficult to say. I've tried to keep out of everyone's way since the memorial service. It would be so easy to be drawn into hotel gossip and I think perhaps it's better if I don't know what's happening, and honestly I find their sympathy a bit hard to take. Most of them miss Paul as much as I do. I agree with you though, there's something about that Frenchman that makes me feel uneasy. Maybe he's just too good looking and smooth for his own good or he's used to getting his own way. Maybe his mother spoiled him. Who knows?'

'Sarah told me about Antonia's little fabrication. How does Marcus seem?'

'I kept him busy all weekend. I aim to send him to nursery school in the New Year. It isn't good for him to be hanging around with grown-ups all day and I hope he'll make some new friends of his own age.'

'I'll never understand that awful woman. What kind of a kick does she get from spreading wickedness around, I wonder.'

'She's missing Paul. I'm sure she blames me for his death. After all, if we hadn't gone away together when we did he may still be alive.'

Paul looked at her with real concern. 'I hope you don't really believe *that* Liz. Paul was old enough to take responsibility for his own health. You have enough to worry about without beating yourself up any more. And let's not forget that dear Antonia didn't exactly give him an easy ride, did she? There was always some task that had to be done whatever hour of the day or night or however inconvenient for either of you.'

Liz let out a deep sigh. 'I think I read somewhere that it's part of the grieving process to blame yourself for not doing more for the person you've lost. I can't help thinking I should have insisted on a holiday that didn't involve quite so much driving. We could have gone to Ivy House with the children and have taken them to the beach every day like normal families.'

Oscar laughed mirthlessly. 'Do you really see Paul spending two weeks building sandcastles? I *don't* think so. And if you *had* gone to Ivy House, what's the betting that you'd have been getting telephone calls from Antonia every day? Let's face it, Liz, you were married to someone who liked to be on the move all the time. Even when he was relaxing you could feel the energy coiled tightly like a spring just waiting to be released.'

Liz had forgotten just how long Paul and Oscar had known each other and found herself wondering how much more Oscar knew about Paul than she did. But there was nothing to be gained by probing further into Paul's past. 'Do you mind if I put the radio on?' she asked and, without waiting for a reply, pressed the button which effectively put an end to the conversation.

She must have been tuned in to the Third Programme on her last journey and asked Oscar if he was happy to stay with it. 'That's fine by me unless the programme turns out to be too intellectual for a philistine, in which case I shall suggest we switch to something more suited to my pedestrian tastes.' He flashed a quick smile and settled himself comfortably back in his seat to listen.

They'd joined a programme celebrating the work of the pianist Artur Rubinstein and were in time to hear the finale of a nocturne by Frederic Chopin. 'I remember trying to master this when I was little,' Oscar said. 'I can still see my teacher beating time and trying not to wince when I played a wrong note.' He glanced sideways at Liz who appeared to be concentrating intently on the road ahead. He switched his concentration to the announcer who was introducing the next work, the first Ballade in G minor. He settled back in his seat, closed his eyes and prepared to indulge himself. He'd always felt a deep sadness at the opening, which was full of darkness, uncertainty and hesitation, but his mood lightened a little as the music moved into a prettier, more romantic melody and his thoughts began to wander as the music continued.

Paul, a favourite cousin and one of his best friends, was lost to him forever and now it seemed that Liz would soon be going as well. All their lives were about to change and he realised with a shock that he would miss their evenings together when laughter and the warmth of their companionship had been combined with good food and always excellent wine. He felt the grey chill of loss envelop him in a way it hadn't since Paul's death. Life could be a bugger at times and he wondered why it was always the nice people who had to suffer. It had been the same when, as a child during the war, he'd lost his friends one by one as they disappeared into the horrors of the concentration camps. When, after the war, they'd seen the film footage as the camps were liberated he'd been consumed with white-hot anger at the injustice of it all.

The car swerved suddenly as the final, dramatic notes of the ballade signalled the end of the piece. He opened his eyes in surprise as he heard the tyres scrunching on gravel and the car stopped, jolting him forward in his seat. 'What in God's name . . .?' he said, turning to look at Liz who sat motionless clutching the steering wheel, tears pouring down her cheeks, shoulders shaking, and he forgot his own sad reminiscences in an instant.

'Liz, Liz, what is it?' But he knew, even if she couldn't tell him, that the music had stirred memories for her as it had for him. Whether they were passionate or tender or a combination of both he couldn't be sure and it didn't matter. What did matter was her distress. He hated to see her so upset. He put an arm round her shoulder, felt for a handkerchief, switched off the radio and waited.

Several minutes passed before she could speak. 'Oh, Oscar, I'm sorry. One day soon I hope we'll be able to meet without me crying all over you! It's just that piece. It was the last record Paul bought and I was just remembering the night he played it on our last visit to Ivy House.'

Oscar pictured the scene. Paul was a past master at creating atmosphere, whether romantic or otherwise. He'd seen him in action many times when they'd been teenagers in Vienna. He visualised Paul leading up to playing the record; perhaps cooking dinner for both of them, making sure the children were both settled, pouring wine or brandy, switching off most of the lights; creating the perfect romantic ambiance. No wonder Liz was devastated to hear the music again, knowing that she and Paul wouldn't listen to it together, ever.

He wondered how many more tender and passionate memories Liz had collected during their time together in Europe. Paul would have treated his holiday like any schoolboy making the most of every last minute, all the more precious because it was such a rarity to be released from his responsibilities as Antonia's partner, as employer and father. His heart went quietly out to Liz and he hoped and prayed that she'd be strong enough to come through this crisis. She was so young to have to bear the burden of providing for and taking care of such small children. When he got home he must have a word with Sarah to see if there was anything the pair of them could do to ease the load.

In the meantime it hadn't escaped him that Liz had had the presence of mind to stop the car in front of a likely looking pub. 'Do you fancy a quick bite to eat as we've already left the road?' he asked, looking at his watch. 'It's a little after twelve and we're not too far away from Dover, so if we eat now we can crack on and do the business with the car. What do you think?'

'I think you've just had a brilliant idea,' Liz said. 'However, I think I'd better move away from the front door and put this baby somewhere more suitable.'

'Try the car park,' Oscar said and was relieved when he saw Liz smile.

It would have been easy to linger over lunch but, thinking of the afternoon ahead, they ate a quick sandwich and pressed on. When they reached Dover, Liz stayed in the car leaving Oscar to complete the formalities and the next time she saw him he was behind the wheel of Paul's car, which still bore traces of Roman dust on its normally gleaming bodywork. Liz wanted to burst into tears at the sight of it, but clamped her jaws firmly together, telling herself she'd cried so much over Oscar since her return that she owed it to him to stay in control until the moment which would come soon enough when they would separate. She watched as he pulled in beside her and only then climbed out of her own car. 'I take it you'll be happy for me to drive back to the hotel.' He jerked his head towards the Triumph.

'Yes please and don't hang about waiting for me. Following someone else is a nightmare and my poor old girl isn't quite up to your speed.'

'Is there anything you want to take out before I deliver it back to Antonia?' Oscar asked, thinking to spare Liz any possible confrontation at the end of a long journey.

'There's a picnic basket and Paul's suitcase in the boot,' Liz said. 'I packed most of Paul's stuff into it before I left. I was afraid I might have to pay excess baggage if I brought everything back on my own.'

Oscar opened the boot and shoved the basket and the suitcase into the back of Liz's car. 'What about inside?' he asked.

'There are some maps and a few odds and ends. I suppose I'd better take them.'

Oscar reached into the glove compartment and handed Liz a pile of maps and a tin of travel sweets. 'The children will love me for rescuing these,' he said, handing the tin to Liz. 'Is that the lot, do you think?'

'Yes I think so.' Liz tried hard not to look at the map they'd used for the journey, which was still open at the Florence Rome section and which Paul had stowed in the glove compartment. 'Thanks a million for giving up your day, drive home carefully and don't worry about me, I'll be absolutely fine.'

'You're quite sure?' The expression on Oscar's face showed Liz the level of his concern. He knew that to be reunited with the car must be opening old wounds for her. 'Be sure to call us when you get back and take your time,' he went on and, before Liz could reply, he started the engine and was off.

Oscar pressed the accelerator and his spirits lifted as the engine responded. It felt strange at first to be sitting with his legs stretched almost horizontally in front of him, but as he ate up the miles he gradually adjusted to his new position, even though at times he felt uncomfortably close to the road. He'd always teased Paul about this car whenever the two of them had driven together, telling his old friend that it would be nice to be able to see over the hedges occasionally and more recently asking when he was going to get a real grown up car.

He hoped that Liz would be all right. It must seem to her as if, one by one, the tangible remains of Paul were being removed from her. At least the children were a permanent fixture and, although they were hard work at the moment, he knew the day would come when the tables would be turned and they would be a consolation. He only hoped that at some time in the future they would care for her as she was now caring for them.

He turned on the radio, needing to blot out other thoughts before he became too steeped in melancholy, and drove as fast as he dare. He wanted the handover to be done with and then to be back home with Sarah and the calm and safe haven which she unfailingly provided. Fortunately the traffic was light and, if there were no hold ups on the way back to Bishop's Wood, with any luck he'd be home ahead of the rush hour traffic.

'Evening sir.' George had seen him park the car and came out from behind his desk to open the door.

'Good evening George. As you can see I've brought Mr Hirsch's car back from Dover. Is Miss Harvey around? I'd like to hand it over personally if that's possible.'

'I'll just ring her flat and find out for you.'

George went back behind his desk, called his employer on the intercom and turned his attention back to Oscar. 'Miss Harvey will be down in a minute. Is Mrs Hirsch with you?'

'No, she'll be along directly. I had the faster pair of wheels and she asked me not to hang around. Do you think you could call a cab for me? My wife will be getting tea for the children and I don't want to disturb her.'

At that moment Antonia appeared and George took advantage of the interruption to call the taxi firm the hotel used for guests. Oscar held out the car keys towards Antonia. 'I've brought Paul's car home. I thought I'd better hand it over personally. Liz and I have taken out all their possessions so it's ready for whatever you intend to do with it.'

Antonia took the keys wordlessly and then walked out of the hotel to where the car was standing and walked slowly round it. 'What's the betting she's counting the wheels?' Oscar said to George.

'I'll give you ten-to-one,' George replied with a conspiratorial wink as Antonia returned.

'I see the badges are missing from the front.' Antonia spoke coldly and looked towards Oscar, waiting for an explanation.

'Badges?' Oscar was mystified.

'There were two badges: the British Automobile Racing Club and the British Racing Drivers Club.'

Oscar held out both hands in a helpless gesture. 'I suppose they disappeared during the journey home. No doubt there are collector's who'd be glad to get their hands on a few free badges.' He was spared further interrogation by the arrival of his taxi. 'My cab's arrived and I'd hate to keep him waiting. Goodbye George,' he said and walked swiftly out to the waiting car. 'Thank you would have been nice,' he muttered under his breath as he climbed in the back and went gratefully home to Sarah.

Two days later Liz was driving into Bishop's Wood to see Peter Kilby who'd telephoned on the day she'd been picking up the car to request a meeting as early as possible. Driving out of the car park at the back of the hotel she heard the note of a familiar engine and braked instinctively as she recognised the sound of the TR. It couldn't be . . . it was. Paul's car was newly washed and polished to within an inch of its life. Sitting behind the wheel, looking smoother than ever and with a self-satisfied smile stretching from ear to ear, was Gaston Legrange.

Liz sat frozen in disbelief. She hadn't thought about what might happen to the car once it had been handed over to Antonia. Subconsciously she'd expected it simply to disappear, to be sold perhaps, but certainly not to be driven in and out of the hotel on a daily basis as a constant reminder of its previous owner. 'That's just like you, Antonia,' she muttered to herself. 'Inflict as much pain as you can while you still have the strength.'

She stayed motionless behind the wheel with the engine still running for several minutes and then slowly reason kicked in and she began to view the whole episode more dispassionately. It is a company car after all, driven by the previous manager. The hotel now has a new manager, so it stands to reason that he should have the company car. But, in spite of all her arguments, the reality of what she had to face left another shard of pain in her side. She put the car in gear and continued her journey to see her solicitor.

Peter Kilby rose to his feet as Liz walked into his office. 'Ah, Mrs Hirsch, how good of you to come in at such short notice. I do hope that you're well.'

'I'm fine, thank you, but rather mystified as to the reason for my visit. I had the message from Maria, our au pair. She's still learning English and didn't tell me why you wanted to see me.'

'With good reason, I didn't give her any details.' Peter Kilby shuffled papers and avoided meeting Liz's eye. 'The fact is there's been a rather unexpected development since we last spoke. I thought it better that we discuss it face-to-face rather than by letter.'

'If it's about the car, we picked it up yesterday and it's been handed over to the new manager,' Liz rushed in hoping to pre-empt any unnecessary delay. 'Oh. Thank you for telling me, I must get Miss Harvey to give me a receipt, but no, it isn't about the car. The fact is I've had a representation from a Miss Eloise Moncton.' He saw the colour drain from Liz's face and wished that his profession didn't compel him to pass on unpalatable pieces of information to his clients. Life would be much easier if he could simply 'lose' the letter and carry on as if nothing had happened, but the fact that Miss Moncton had legal representation made any other course of action impossible.

'I have met Miss Moncton. She came to Paul's memorial service. I understand she had some kind of relationship with Paul before he and I met.' Liz didn't want to sit and listen to a protracted explanation of exactly who Eloise Moncton was.

Peter Kilby appeared relieved that she knew so much, thus saving him the pain of breaking the news to her. He cleared his throat and began. 'It seems that Miss Moncton offered Paul a fifty per cent share in her hotel in return for a capital sum. Apparently that sum is now outstanding and she is claiming it from Paul's estate. Please understand that I have to ask you if you had any knowledge of such an arrangement.'

Liz told Peter Kilby the substance of her conversation with Oscar after Paul's memorial service and also that Eloise had intimated that she and Paul were planning to be married. 'It was all a complete surprise to me, as you may imagine,' she confessed, willing Peter Kilby to believe her. 'And if Paul *were* planning to go off and get married to someone else you'd think he might have mentioned it to me, wouldn't you? In fact, while we were on holiday he suggested that the time had come for us to buy a house so that we could all move out of the hotel. That doesn't seem to me like the action of a man who is planning divorce, does it?'

It crossed Peter Kilby's mind that if Paul had been planning to give up his job at Bishop's Hall and take up a new appointment with Eloise Moncton it would make sense for him to move his family out first, but he chose not to communicate this thought to his client.

'So how much is she asking for?' Liz's voice cut across his thoughts.

'Ten thousand pounds. However, I hasten to reassure you that there can be no question of payment unless there is a properly binding legal contract. Company Law requires that any such contract should be signed, sealed and delivered; even though Miss Moncton may persist in thinking that a verbal agreement between Paul and herself constituted such a contract.'

'Have you asked her solicitor if there is a written contract?'

Liz's heart was in her mouth as she asked the question.

'I have and there isn't, or at least if there is her solicitor was not a party to it. Do you know if, by any chance, Paul could have used another solicitor to have drawn up such an agreement? Remember that, until recently, we were solicitors for the hotel and Paul would probably have thought it wise not to involve us if he was contemplating this type of major undertaking.' He wished he didn't have to probe so deeply, but he couldn't file it and forget it until every conceivable avenue had been explored.

'When I came back from Rome I searched the flat looking for letters, documents, anything that Paul might have written. I found nothing. However, most of his legal stuff was in his desk in the office and that's where I eventually found his will. One thing that really puzzled me is that neither his certificates of post-war credit or his naturalisation papers were in his legal file. I had to ask Miss Harvey if she'd seen them anywhere and a couple of days later she handed them over. She could have other documents about which I know nothing.'

Peter Kilby felt his heart sink as he realised that he was facing an unexpected delay in settling this matter once and for all. 'I'll have to ask Miss Harvey,' he said. 'I'll telephone later and let you know the result as soon as I can.'

Liz realised that the interview was at an end, but went through the formalities anyway. 'Is there anything else we need to talk about?' she asked, resisting a strong temptation to look at her watch.

'No, I think we've covered the most pressing matter. I'm sorry to have troubled you, but it isn't unusual when money is at stake for all kinds of unforeseen claims to be made. Most turn out to be spurious as I am sure will be the case with this one. Please try not to worry and I'll be in touch as soon as I have any further news.'

'I only hope the next piece of news doesn't turn out to be quite such a nasty shock.' Liz shook his hand and left his office.

What next? She asked herself as she walked back to the car. Could there be more surprises to be uncovered in the days, weeks, months that lay ahead? Time she would spend without Paul, trying to rebuild a life that had been so happy until three weeks ago. Would she ever be without the knot of misery that seemed permanently tangled up somewhere deep inside? It *was* early days and things might get worse before they began to get better. She owed it to herself to cheer up for the sake of the people with whom she would come into contact over the coming weeks. After all, if she gained a reputation for looking on the black side she would soon find herself sidelined. Nobody enjoyed the company of someone who was permanently unhappy.

Suddenly she remembered the films she'd left at the chemist to be developed. This seemed a good time to collect them. She crossed the road and walked the short distance, her mood lightening as she looked forward to seeing the pictures, even though they would remind her of the last holiday she and Paul would ever spend together.

On impulse she decided to buy herself a lipstick at the same time. If she was going to try and cheer herself up a new lipstick, preferably an expensive one, would be as good a way as any. She chose quickly, a favourite deep coral, found the ticket for the pictures and went to the counter. The assistant found the pictures for her and then read a note which was pinned to the front of the envelope in which the prints had been packaged.

'It looks as if there was some problem with the film,' the assistant said handing Liz the envelope.

'Problem?' Liz echoed looking at the notice which read; *We regret that the enclosed pictures could not be developed due most likely to over-exposure. We suggest you have your camera checked before you take any more pictures.*

'There'll be no charge for the film,' the assistant assured her. 'Shall I take the money for the lipstick?'

Liz paid wordlessly. Useless to try and argue. She squared her shoulders and walked back to her car. Driving home she wondered again and again what could possibly have happened to spoil not just one but both films. Now she had nothing tangible as evidence of her last holiday with Paul. Would anything ever go right again? It seemed as if life had become one disappointment after another. No sooner had she dealt with one problem than another reared up in front of her like a venomous snake determined to do for her with the very next bite. *This time I'm not going to cry,* she told herself as she finally turned into the hotel drive, resolving to try and keep her memories of the holiday as fresh as possible. After all, they were the only thing she had left.

CHAPTER SEVENTEEN

Shopping for presents, planning decorations, buying treats and all the other activities which went with Christmas had always been a favourite time for Liz. Having spent so many years in solitary celebration with her grandmother she'd missed out on large family gatherings and, although many of her friends assured her that 'having the family for Christmas' could be something of a mixed blessing, she'd always imagined everyone else to be enjoying one party after another throughout the festive season, which had always added to her feeling of isolation and exacerbated her deep regret that she had no real family of her own.

For the last few years the hotel had offered an all inclusive Christmas break which began with dinner on Christmas Eve and ended with breakfast the day after Boxing Day. Since their marriage she'd mucked in and helped Paul whenever and wherever necessary and, although both of them were usually exhausted by the time the guests left, the appreciation they received made the effort more than worthwhile. This year a yawning gap had opened up and she hadn't the remotest idea how to fill it.

Last year had carried its own excitement. For the first time Marcus had been old enough to unwrap some of his smaller presents, although as his doting parents watched him gleefully rip off the paper they'd agreed that 'unwrap' wasn't perhaps the best word to use.

Liz went through the motions of making a list of presents and another for cards. It was good occupational therapy and made her think of other people for a while instead of being focussed on herself. But in spite of all her efforts her heart wasn't in it and she felt a fresh wave of mourning; this time for her own lack of enthusiasm.

How on earth was she going to get through one of the jolliest times of the year without Paul? If only she could hibernate until the whole holiday was at an end. But that was unthinkable. There was the family to consider and she couldn't deny them Christmas. One way or another she must get through it. What was it her granny used to say? 'Well dear, you'll just have to make the best of it.'

Unexpectedly, Sarah and Oscar came to the rescue, appearing out of the blue on a Sunday afternoon complete with children. 'We thought we'd invite ourselves for tea,' Sarah began. 'We brought a cake so if you can rustle up some sandwiches we won't need to feed the children when they get home.'

'Consider it done!' Liz said delighted for any diversion, however temporary, to take her away from her own gloomy thoughts. It felt almost like a return to old times as she chatted to Sarah in her tiny kitchen whilst they were making sandwiches, leaving Oscar to amuse the children. He was doing a great job if the sound of whoops and shrieks of laughter coming from the sitting room were anything to go by.

'We're not opening the restaurant on Christmas Day,' Sarah said. 'We think that Christmas with the children is more important than watching the world and his wife eat and drink too much. And to be honest, by the time we've paid the staff double time, there isn't that much profit in it. We'd love it if you and the children would join us, Maria too if she's around. Oscar and I discussed it at some length and thought that staying in the hotel over Christmas would be an unnecessary ordeal for you.' She stopped spreading Marmite and put an arm around Liz's shoulder. 'Please say yes,' she urged, 'at least that lot next door won't leave you any time to brood.' She waved her arm towards the sitting room.

For a few seconds Liz was lost for words and then, 'I'd half thought of going to Ivy House,' she admitted. 'Oscar probably told you that I'm thinking of moving down there anyway. I can't just go on living here without Paul and it would be a good opportunity to get the place ready so we can move in as soon as possible.'

'You can't spend Christmas moving house!' Sarah's voice rose to screeching point. To her relief, Liz smiled. 'Well I must confess I wasn't looking forward to the idea, but when I weighed it against the alternative of staying here there didn't seem to be much of a contest.' She reached into the cupboard for plates before pouring boiling water into the teapot. 'One day, perhaps when this nightmare is over, I may just be able to pay you back, but until then, thank you, it would be lovely to spend Christmas with you. There is a condition, however, you must let me make some contribution. You're doing all of us a big favour and it's the least I can do.'

'Well, we'll talk about that in a few days,' Sarah said comfortably. 'The important thing is that you won't be alone with your memories of last year.'

It was uncanny how Sarah knew how much she dreaded the looking back; the odious comparisons with 'this time last year' which she was trying hard to avoid but found impossible to escape. Just as she couldn't evade the cold, grey, misery that dogged her day after dreary day swirling around her, a never ending impenetrable fog. Now Sarah had given her the incentive she needed to make an effort to get through Christmas. She squared her shoulders, finished loading the tea trolley and they went back to join the others.

During the following week she spent every spare minute on Christmas preparations, knowing from past experience that unexpected events had an uncanny way of popping up and causing last minute delays and playing havoc with even the most carefully made plans. Peter Kilby rang on several occasions, either with queries or information, which forced her to set aside time to deal with one or the other. The weather suddenly turned colder and, when she looked out in the mornings, the lawns were sparkling with frost and the frozen gravel on the drive sounded sharper as it scrunched under the tyres of the visitors' cars.

Sitting at her desk writing cards on Sunday morning she

heard a key turn in the door to the flat. A quick glance at her watch told her that it was eleven o'clock. Maria had taken both the children for a walk and they weren't expected back until just before lunch. She swivelled round in her chair wondering who could be using a key to enter her flat, but before she could even get up to find out Maria burst into the room. Emma's pram was clearly visible in the hall, but there was no sign of Marcus.

'Oh, Mrs Hirsch! Please come into the garden quickly!' Maria's face was flushed and she was breathless from running.

'What on earth's the matter?' Liz asked, jumping to her feet, her heart beginning to thump as all kinds of possibilities flashed into her mind. Where was Marcus? Why hadn't he come back with Maria? For one wild ecstatic moment she thought, Paul's back! Marcus is with him! But then reality took over and her hopes just as quickly plummeted.

'We were walking by the lake,' Maria gasped, 'when Miss Harvey came along. The lake's frozen and she's taken Marcus for a walk on it. I'm so frightened.'

'Stay here and look after Emma, I'll go and sort it out.' Visions of Marcus sinking into the icy water helped to pump adrenalin into her system. She snatched a jacket from the peg in the hall and her feet moved as quickly as an athlete training for a hundred yard sprint as she tore down the stairs, through the hotel and out of the back door. She crossed the car park and as the lake came into view she spotted Marcus sliding across the frozen surface. 'Look Toni, I'm skating!' Liz heard him call as she ran across the lawn feeling the still frozen grass crunching under her feet.

Antonia was standing safely on the bank smiling encouragement at the small figure in front of her. When she saw Liz the smile faded quickly and she stood as if rooted to the spot. 'What on earth can you be thinking?' Liz yelled at her before turning her attention swiftly to Marcus. Silly of her to shout when she could scare him and trigger who knows what consequences.

'Come on Marcus, time for lunch. Walk carefully and try not to fall down.' He was some way from the bank and if he fell and broke the ice she mightn't be able to reach him in time. She reckoned he could freeze in seconds.

'But I'm skating!' Marcus called. 'Watch me!'

'I can see you, darling, and you're a very clever boy, but it's nearly lunchtime and I'd like you to come in now.' *Keep calm*, she told herself as she watched the expression on Marcus' face turn to one of protest.

'But mummy,' he began.

'But nothing, Marcus, it's time for your lunch and I'd like you to come indoors.' Her voice sounded harsh and strident in spite of her efforts to control it and for a few seconds she was afraid he might cry but, to her relief, he began to move slowly towards the bank, slipping and sliding on the frozen surface of the lake. Liz moved to a section where nothing grew, thinking that the ice might not be completely frozen around the reeds and water iris, which were still visible around parts of the edge. 'Come this way,' she called out to him and then, after opening her arms, 'I'm waiting to catch you.'

It took only a few minutes before she was able to reach out and pull him to safety, but to Liz it had been an eternity. She hugged him tightly, squeezing his slight frame hard against her. 'Please, Marcus, promise me you won't do that again unless I'm with you. The water is very deep and I'm not sure if it's frozen all the way across. Do you understand?' Marcus nodded his head slowly. He seemed to have picked up the tension in the way that small children do and when she took his hand firmly he didn't struggle to try and free himself.

Ignoring Antonia who was still standing as if she was frozen on the edge of the icy lake, Liz took Marcus back to the flat and handed him over to Maria. 'Here we are, all safe and sound,' she said with false cheerfulness. 'Will you be an angel and keep an eye on the two of them for a few minutes? There's something else I have to do.' Without waiting for a reply she retraced her steps and reached reception just as Antonia appeared, walking slowly from the rear of the hotel.

'I'd like a quick word, if it's all the same with you,' Liz said, taking care to look Antonia squarely in the eye. During all the time they'd known each other Liz had shied away from a direct confrontation, afraid that her temper might get the better of her and cause untold damage to Paul's career. Now there was no such fear and a white hot anger told her that the moment had come to face up to Antonia once and for all.

'I don't think this is a convenient time,' Antonia hedged.

'Convenient or not, I'm going to say what I have to say. I can do it right here or we can go somewhere more private.'

Antonia was aware that the receptionist on duty was already straining her ears to listen to their conversation. It would be all over the hotel by this evening and she had no wish to make it worse than it already was. 'You'd better come up to my flat,' she said, turning quickly towards the staircase, knowing without looking that Liz was following and also conscious that this time she'd overstepped the mark, although there was no way she was going to admit it.

When they reached her flat she sat down heavily in the nearest arm chair and gestured to Liz to do the same. 'I'd prefer to stand, thank you,' Liz said. 'What I have to say won't take long and I'm keen to get back to the children as soon as possible.'

'As you wish.' Antonia's tone was dismissive.

'I find what you did today quite unforgivable,' Liz began. 'Marcus is two and a half years old and to allow him to walk on the ice alone was foolhardy to say the least. I should also tell you that he's already confided in me that you told him that I sent his father away and that was an act of downright wickedness and mischief-making. Now you can say what you like, do what you like to me, but if ever you come near either of my children again I will not be answerable for my actions. Do you understand?'

Antonia said nothing. What could she say? Faced with such accusations, anything she said would simply sound defensive if she tried to deny the charges. 'I'd also like you to know,' Liz continued, 'I appreciate that you've given us all a home since Paul's death. It's a home to which I know we're no longer entitled now that Paul isn't employed here. I've been thinking about when we might move for some time now and I've reached the conclusion that we should go as soon after Christmas as possible. I'll let you have a date when I've made the arrangements. I'd hoped that perhaps we could have worked together in the hotel somehow, but I see now *that* would be impossible.'

Antonia knew that this was a last ditch stand, perhaps her only opportunity to let Liz know the full extent of her dislike. Her voice was cold and scornful and she rose to her feet so that her words would have greater impact. 'I doubt if *you* could survive on the wages I pay my *unskilled* staff.' The remark was designed to hurt and as Liz flinched she knew the barb had gone home. It was a small compensation.

❦

You will not cry, Liz told herself as she left Antonia's flat clutching the shredded tatters of her dignity around her as she walked back to her own. The showdown was long overdue. The two women had never liked each other and, although Liz consoled herself with the knowledge that Antonia wouldn't approve of anyone who succeeded in getting close to Paul, it irked her that she'd been unable, in the few years they'd been sharing the same roof, to win her over. To begin with she'd assumed that in time Antonia would accept her as Paul's wife and hoped that she might one day have an acknowledged role in the business, which could be to everyone's advantage. But as the years progressed Antonia had been less able to disguise her hostility, forcing Liz to accept that as long as Antonia continued to be the major shareholder in the business she would be sidelined.

❦

Two days later she had a phone call from Peter Kilby. 'I have good news and some that is, shall we say, less good,' he began when they had worked their way through the usual pleasantries. 'Firstly I've spoken to Miss Harvey and can confirm that she doesn't know of any solicitor that Paul might have consulted before his death. I've therefore written to Miss Moncton advising her that, unless she can provide written evidence of her arrangement with your late husband, then we cannot recompense her in any way.'

'Thank you for telling me,' Liz said. 'I'm assuming that's the good bit.' She heard the smile in his voice the next time he spoke. 'Indeed. When I was talking to Miss Harvey I made enquiries about the company pension fund. Were you aware that the hotel set up its own fund a few years ago?' Liz admitted she had no idea. 'Ah,' Peter Kilby continued. 'The fact is it doesn't appear as if Paul was a member of the scheme and I'm afraid therefore that he has no occupational pension,' he paused and Liz finished the sentence for him. 'Unless I know of any alternative fund that he joined.'

'Precisely.'

'Am I going to be broke?' Liz asked, thinking for the umpteenth time that things couldn't get any worse.

'Well, of course, if Paul *had* been in the fund the payments would have been quite small, but at least they would have been regular and payable in perpetuity. I've discovered that he'd made regular contributions to a building society, so the coffers aren't entirely empty.'

'Oh yes, I'd forgotten about those.' Liz was relieved that there was something about Paul's financial planning that she did know. He knew that if anything happened to Antonia he'd have to buy her shares if he were to take over the hotel and, for that reason, he put the money somewhere safe to which he'd have easy access. 'Is that all?' she asked. There was another pause at his end of the line, followed by a slight cough which set Liz's teeth on edge. She picked up a pencil and tapped it impatiently on her desk waiting for him to continue.

'I received an account from Bishop's Wood Hotel this morning.'

'Was it for food and drink for Paul's memorial service?'

'No it wasn't.' Peter Kilby hesitated again and Liz found herself wishing that he'd get on with whatever news he had to break and put her out of her misery. 'It's for food and accommodation for yourself and your children for the month of November. There was an accompanying letter which warned me to expect further bills to cover any additional time you choose to spend in the hotel.' He hesitated again and then, 'I'm really so very sorry. Sometimes I think I don't understand human beings at all,' he said.

'Don't worry,' Liz reassured him. 'I've always known that my position here was precarious. You know as well as I do that the flat goes with the job. I told Miss Harvey on Sunday that I'll be leaving the hotel as soon as possible after Christmas. I have a small cottage in Wiltshire and I intend to move the family down there until I can plan some kind of a future for us.'

'Of course, Paul's estate will pay the hotel account.' Peter Kilby, relieved at having dropped his bombshell, was quick to reassure her. 'I'm afraid Miss Harvey will have to wait until I can obtain probate and I shall of course write and inform her accordingly.'

'How long do you think that will take?' Liz asked.

'Oh, about six months if we're lucky. It might be a little longer.'

'Please take *all* the time you need,' Liz said. 'We must be sure that every 'i' is dotted, mustn't we?' It was the first cheerful thought she'd had for some time and she heard a chuckle from the other end of the line.

'Now, there's something *you* can do for *me*.' Liz told him about her confrontation with Antonia on Sunday and of the reasons for it. 'I'd be so pleased if you could write officially to Antonia and forbid her to have any access to the children. Make sure that she knows how worried I am.'

Peter Kilby assured her that he would write in the strongest possible terms and then made a comment which really surprised Liz. 'Bullies can't take it when you stand up to them,' he said, 'and it's just as well for Miss Harvey to know that she can't push you around.' When he replaced the receiver he congratulated himself on withholding a further piece of information which he felt she would find unnecessarily distressing.

In the course of his conversation with Antonia Harvey the question of Paul's shares in the business had arisen. She'd told him that Paul's shares from her had been a gift made at a time when he'd been single, in much the same way as a mother might bequeath part of her estate to one of her children, were the words she'd used, if he remembered correctly. She then went on to argue that she hadn't intended Paul to pass on the shares, which she expected would be returned to her in the near future.

He'd pointed out that no such caveat had been mentioned at the time the shares were transferred, but that if she had any written indication that a subsequent agreement had been reached then he would be happy to act accordingly. He hadn't heard from her since.

Liz was relieved to have a plan of action. It didn't matter that it was tenuous. However fragile, at least it was a plan as opposed to a vague idea, and the deadline meant that there were things to be done which occupied the yawning vacuum in her mind. So, on top of preparations for Christmas, she had to find a company to transport their few possessions to Ivy House. Most of the furniture in the flat belonged to the hotel but inevitably during their short time together they'd accumulated books, records and other household items in an attempt to put their own stamp on the place. And then there was the children's gear. She didn't even want to think about packing it. There was certainly more stuff than she could fit into the back of her car. Fortunately the envelopes of the Christmas cards she'd already written weren't sealed so it was easy to go through them all and insert her new address. She called Sid and Evie, told them her plans and asked them to light the Rayburn now that the weather had turned colder. Whenever she had a few minutes to spare she turned out drawers and cupboards, packing some of their possessions and turning out stuff they no longer wanted.

Finally she reached the cupboard in which Paul kept his

clothes and came to a grinding halt. What to do with them? The thought of anyone else wearing them was untenable and yet to transport the whole lot to Ivy House didn't make sense. They would have to be packed and unpacked again and then what? Leave them hanging for weeks, maybe months, in another cupboard where perhaps they might end up as a gourmet feast for the local moth population. A solution would have to be found, but she must be careful it was the right one.

In the end she went to talk to George. He'd been in the army and she thought perhaps he might know of some war veterans association to whom she could give Paul's entire wardrobe. 'I must be sure they're going to a good home,' she explained. 'I hate to think they won't be valued. Most of the stuff is excellent quality and there's quite a lot of it.'

George scratched his head. 'Can you leave this one with me, Mrs Hirsch?' he asked. 'Mr Hirsch always looked smart and we don't want his nice clothes to go to any old ne'er do well, do we?' Liz agreed, shuddering at the thought of Paul's suits ending up in a dreadful doss house. How she wished she had male relatives.

❦

A couple of days later, Ruth Lebermann telephoned. Liz had completely forgotten that the Lebermanns had mentioned they were coming to London early in December. 'Do you think you'll have time to see us whilst we're over here?' Ruth asked when they'd caught up on their respective bits of news. Liz thought briefly of all the hundred and one things that had to be done before Christmas and then remembered Rome again and the kindness the pair of them had shown her; fitting in trips to the hospital, coming to Paul's funeral, sparing their time for a man they scarcely knew.

When Ruth said casually that it would be lovely to meet the children, Liz invited them both to lunch the following Friday. Some time later she realised that she had no idea what kind of food they liked. Normally she would have checked when entertaining someone for the first time, but had forgotten to ask in the general upheaval that was going on inside her head. Perhaps she should phone them? Ruth had given her a number, 'in case anything turns up to change your plans.' Then she had a better idea. She would give them a drink in the flat and then buy them lunch in the hotel restaurant and they could choose exactly what they liked. A discreet word with the head waiter in advance and he could give her the bill when they'd left, which would avoid any embarrassment they might feel at having her pay for their lunch. It would be a tiny recompense for all the trouble they'd taken in Rome.

In spite of being muffled up in a heavy tweed coat, Ruth looked absolutely frozen when Liz picked her and Hans up at Bishop's Wood station. The day was bitterly cold and Liz was pleased the central heating in the hotel was so efficient. Her visitors would at least be warm. It was her first reconnection with people she'd met in Rome since her return and, although they'd shared an unhappy experience with her, she knew they were concerned for her welfare.

'I can't tell you how good it is to see both of you,' she said when they were both settled in her trusty Morris. 'As you can imagine, the last few weeks have been traumatic. I never realised that there was quite so much to do in the wake of someone's death. She surprised herself by saying the 'd' word and realised that until now she'd avoided using it. Was this a sign that she was moving forward? Beginning to heal? No, it was much too soon for that. In any case, this wasn't a good time for introspection. 'How long do you have before you fly back home?' she asked them.

'We have another week in London. Hans has a meeting with some other protestant clerics for which he needs time to prepare. He promised to give them a summary of the discussions that took place in Rome. I'm going to take advantage of some time to myself to do some Christmas shopping, although I shall have to be careful not to buy too much or we may end up paying excess baggage.'

Liz turned into the hotel drive, passing the illuminated Christmas tree which stood just by the entrance as a seductive invitation to customers both regular and potential. It made her acutely aware that her flat was piled high with cardboard boxes full of possessions she'd packed in readiness for their departure. She hadn't even put up a Christmas tree.

A moment later she had to swerve sharply to one side as Paul's TR came hurtling towards them, plumb in the middle of the drive. 'There goes a man in a hurry,' Hans said clutching the back of the passenger seat for support and turning to look out of the back window. 'Our new hotel manager,' Liz explained. 'That was Paul's car he was driving.' She looked into her rear view mirror just in time to see Ruth and Hans exchange meaningful glances.

'If he carries on like that he'll soon be your late hotel manager. Does he always drive as fast as that?' Ruth asked.

'Fortunately I don't see him all that often,' Liz explained. 'I think it's his day off today, so he may have a hot date lined up somewhere. Fancies himself a bit from what I've seen of him.'

She drove straight round to the car park and took them in by the rear entrance. 'Oh how lovely to feel warm again,' Ruth said, unbuttoning her coat as they followed Liz up to the flat.

'Please forgive all the boxes,' Liz apologised as they walked into her tiny hallway. 'I'm moving out after Christmas.' She saw the Lebermanns' eyes meet for the second time and the air was suddenly charged with unspoken questions.

'I see my daughter's still asleep.' Liz looked into the pram and then she asked Ruth if she'd like a quick peep. Ruth bent obediently over the edge of the pram. 'Such innocence!' she said. 'Don't you wish you could protect her forever?'

Before Liz could reply Marcus erupted from the sitting room. 'Come and see my Ferrari!' he invited. They all laughed and Liz was grateful that her son had successfully diverted their attention for the time being.

CHAPTER EIGHTEEN

Three quarters of an hour later, fortified by an excellent sherry that Liz unearthed from their drinks cupboard, they went into the hotel dining room, a place Liz rarely ate. When Paul had been alive they'd mostly shared meals in the flat and her presence caused some surprise amongst the few waiting staff on duty. Hans Lebermann was wearing his clerical collar and Liz wondered if the staff would think she was receiving some kind of religious ministration.

She'd explained to Ruth and Hans the reason for choosing not to entertain them in her flat and filled them in on her proposed move to Wiltshire. 'What a pity you can't carry on where your husband left off,' Ruth said. 'You would have been spared the upheaval of moving so soon after your husband's death.'

'Well in some ways, yes,' Liz replied, 'but a new beginning will help me to put all the horror behind me and I'm sure you'll agree that a hotel isn't exactly the best environment in which to bring up small children. Paul and I were about to start house-hunting anyway, so at least I'm spared that chore.'

Just then Antonia came into the dining room, stood for a couple of minutes looking around to see who was eating and waiting for the head waiter to show her to a table. Liz carried on talking, at the same time keeping one eye on Antonia. The head waiter moved to Antonia's side and talked to her for perhaps a minute; both glanced towards Liz from time to time. *How wonderful to have some kind of hearing device that would pick up the gist of the conversation,* Liz thought. Good job she'd made the situation clear to the head waiter beforehand; presumably once Antonia knew that she was paying, not only for herself but her guests, she'd be happy. To her great surprise, Antonia left the dining room as suddenly as she'd entered it.

It wasn't the most relaxed of lunches and Liz couldn't help but draw parallels with the first meal they'd eaten together in Rome. *Then* Paul had been with them as well as Bruno and Anna, so the combined effect of Ruth and Hans had been diluted. Liz began to wish she'd taken them to a restaurant instead of staying in the hotel, Oscar and Sarah's perhaps. But then she reasoned that whatever environment she'd chosen wouldn't have made that much difference.

Finally Hans Lebermann could contain himself no longer. He'd looked upon their lunch as an excuse for killing time during an interval which he'd set aside for spiritual guidance. 'Has David Ward been in touch with you?' he asked as they waited for coffee. He saw Liz grope in her memory trying to recall why the name rang a bell. 'Your vicar,' he prompted gently.

'Oh yes, I'd forgotten,' Liz replied. 'We were in touch when he organised Paul's memorial service, but that was fairly businesslike, just him doing his job really.'

'The priesthood is never *just* a job.' He hadn't meant to reproach her, but she sounded so defensive.

'He said a prayer with me when we discussed the form the service might take, but we haven't had any contact since.'

Useless to ask if she'd been to church, he'd only embarrass her when she replied in the negative. 'I'm sure you would find him a source of wise counsel,' Hans persisted, 'if, that is, you felt you needed spiritual help.'

He paused as the waiter brought their coffee and watched Liz stir her cup vigorously, although she'd put in no sugar, and guessed that she was deciding how many problems she was prepared to share with a virtual stranger. 'I'm sure you'll appreciate that I've had an awful lot to deal with since I came home,' she began. 'Some things I'd anticipated, others came out of the blue, and I've had to handle them in the most appropriate way possible. Mainly it's been legal stuff and, as far as I can tell, my solicitor is playing fair with me. There have been other things mainly to do with Paul's business partner. I don't want to go into details, but since Antonia is a stalwart supporter of David Ward's church I don't think it appropriate to discuss our personal difficulties with him.'

'God is normally impartial.' Hans Lebermann knew the moment he'd spoken that he'd just uttered a huge cliche.

'Ah, but are the people who speak His word?' Liz asked, thinking that she might have effectively put an end to the discussion. But she'd reckoned without the resourcefulness which had helped Hans throughout his religious life and fresh from the Ecumenical Council he was firing on all cylinders. '"He alone sees truly who sees the Lord the same in every creature"' he said. 'Not my words alas but spoken by Krishna according to the Mahabharata . . . the Hindu sacred text,' he elaborated for Liz's benefit.

Liz was momentarily lost for an answer, but found herself wondering if the Hindu nationalist who'd shot Mahatma Gandhi had read the work; either before or after he'd pulled the trigger. But she wasn't about to become embroiled in Indian history and the fights that had taken place between Hindus and Muslims since Partition. 'I'm sure you'll call me a cynic,' she began, 'but I'm really not convinced that every priest has the ability to be totally impartial in his judgement.'

Ruth had been listening quietly to their conversation and sensed that the pain Liz was feeling precluded any of Hans' arguments. She looked meaningfully at her watch. 'Didn't you say there was a train at three thirty, Hans? If we get a move on we could catch it.' Turning to Liz she added, 'Our hotel is quite a step from the station and I'm nervous about walking on frozen pavements, they can be horribly slippery when the temperature drops.'

'I'll drive you to the station,' Liz said as they rose to their feet. 'I really appreciate you taking the trouble to come down and it's been so good to see you both again.' It wasn't strictly true. On the one hand their kindness was overwhelming, on the other Hans' concern for her spiritual well-being left her feeling slightly uncomfortable. *If only they knew half the stuff that's come up since Paul's death* she thought *I wonder if their belief in God might not be just the tiniest bit shaken.* There! She'd used the 'd' word twice in the space of a few hours. Now that was progress!

'I wouldn't mind betting that young woman's been deeply wounded,' Ruth began when she and Hans were settled in their compartment.

'Her husband died a few weeks ago, she's bound to be feeling a tremendous loss.'

'I'm sure it isn't just the grieving. Remember she said she'd dealt with some unexpected problems since her return. I do wish she'd felt able to confide in us.'

'Remember that grief is one of the deepest pains that can be experienced and a supreme test for anyone, leave alone a young woman whose experience of life and the world is limited.'

'It must be so hard for her living in the place where her husband used to work; having to watch someone else driving his car. Her husband's business partner can't be the most tactful of women.'

'She's running a hotel. I don't suppose tact comes into it unless she's dealing with a complaining client.'

'A pity we didn't meet her, I would have liked the opportunity to see her in the flesh and then I could have summed her up.'

'You might even have liked her!' Hans couldn't resist teasing his wife.

Her loud sniff told him that she doubted it.

'Have another Martini!' Oscar refilled Liz's glass and placed a dish of olives on the table in front of her. Earlier they'd fed the children who were now tucked up after the usual warning that Father Christmas wouldn't come until they were asleep. Sarah knew that their five year old, Chris, would fight sleep until the bitter end, but Oscar had had a rough and tumble with him just before supper and she hoped it might just do the trick.

Liz looked a bit hassled when she arrived, having dropped Maria off to stay with a friend. It wasn't often she had the children all to herself and no doubt coping with them had taken its toll on top of everything else. Still, she'd made an effort to dress up for the evening and was wearing a black taffeta skirt and a plain cashmere sweater. Her hair was longer than usual and suited her; softened the face that still bore the ravages of her grieving. There were dark circles under her eyes and her cheeks looked a bit hollow as if she'd lost weight. *Maybe not eating properly*, he reckoned. He'd discussed with Sarah the possibility of having a party tonight, thinking that it might help Liz if she were forced to socialise. But Sarah pointed out that, as most of their friends had children, finding babysitters could be a problem on Christmas Eve, 'And Christmas Day will be hectic enough, so perhaps we'd better aim for a low key evening.'

'We decided to eat English,' Oscar said, once they were seated at the oval mahogany table, which had belonged to his parents and which he'd somehow managed to liberate from Vienna after the war. The table looked lovely. Long trails of ivy were resting on a wide strip of scarlet ribbon which ran the whole length. The colour of the ribbon was echoed in the scarlet candles, carefully placed in the silver candelabra - liberated at the same time as the table. Red crackers sat on dark green table napkins by each place. As soon as she saw it Liz felt a lump in her throat, appreciating the trouble Sarah had taken.

She'd eaten scarcely anything all day. In spite of her resolutions to have everything planned in plenty of time there had been interruptions and, at the last minute, she was scurrying round like a mad thing, packing the car, checking the presents, making sure the children had everything they might need over the short holiday.

Sarah placed a baked ham on the table. She'd studded it with cloves, smeared it with a mixture of mustard and brown sugar and basted it liberally with cider. 'You've really made a tremendous effort,' Liz said, 'and I want you both to know how grateful I am.' She drained the last of her Martini and started on the red wine that Oscar had poured for them all. He carved speedily and with the expertise that comes with years of practise. Sarah handed dishes of roasted potatoes and braised celery and urged Liz to try the Cumberland Sauce. 'Oscar brought it from the restaurant,' she explained, passing the sauceboat.

'Happy Christmas part one!' Oscar raised his glass and watched, slightly bemused, as Liz drained hers. 'I hope all was peaceful back at the ranch,' he said, after refilling her glass.

'I don't think there are quite as many people staying as usual. Mmm, delicious ham,' Liz spoke with her mouth half full. 'The weather forecast warns that we might have early snow and of course that will discourage some of the guests, particularly those who have to drive a long distance.'

'Oh! They warn us about potential snow every Christmas. If they'd grown up in Austria they'd soon realise it would be an unusual Christmas without it.'

'I had an unexpected day though,' Liz went on. 'The hotel staff had a whip-round to buy presents for all of us. A small delegation came up to the flat this morning, so I broke open the sherry and rustled up some mince pies. Wasn't it kind of them? It gave me the opportunity to tell them I'll be leaving after Christmas, just in case the word hasn't got around.'

'They probably knew shortly after you'd made your mind up,' Sarah put in, 'if I know anything about hotel grapevines.'

'Oh well, they know officially now. They told me how much they miss Paul and how the place just isn't the same without him. I gather Gaston Legrange isn't going down as well as Antonia hoped. I wonder if he'll stay and, if he does, will he have the ability to hold the place together? It's difficult enough with the staff onside, but if there's dissent there could be trouble.'

'I'll try to keep an eye on things. After all, as a trustee of Paul's estate, I feel I have a responsibility. I'd hate to see the children's inheritance disappear because of incompetent management.' Oscar looked hard at Liz trying to gauge her reaction, wondering if she felt sidelined by not being named as a trustee. But if she did feel any embarrassment she covered it successfully, tucking in to her dinner with every appearance of enjoyment and washing it down with the excellent wine he'd bought in the Neusiedlersee on their last trip to Austria.

He'd thought about inviting one of his single men friends as a companion for Liz, but there again Sarah had advised against it. 'She'll think we're trying to pair her off and it's much too soon after Paul's death. If you want to play Cupid I'd advise you to leave it for a while.' As usual he'd deferred to her judgement.

Antonia took herself up to her flat as soon as she decently could after standing in reception to welcome the guests as they arrived. How many times had she been asked if Mr Hirsch would be joining them later? She'd lost count and grown tired of telling them that Mr Hirsch was no longer with them. It was a kinder version of the truth she told herself, wanting to spare the guests a gloomy start to their Christmas. The disappointment on their faces on hearing the news had been palpable and, after a while, she could bear it no longer. It seemed as if every moment Paul was moving further away from her and at some point in the not-too-distant future would disappear completely and she'd be unable to remember the sound of his voice or even the way he looked.

They, by which she meant the staff, would get on much better without her anyway. As day succeeded day after Paul's death she felt more and more superfluous, whichever section of the hotel she was in. If she asked a question or gave an order to a member of staff they would listen deferentially, after all she was the boss. But there had been a subtle change in the atmosphere. The old informality had gone to be replaced by a creeping subservience which made her want to scream.

No argument would persuade her to join her guests in their

celebration of Christmas Eve, a festival which, in her childhood, had always been so much fun with her father home early for once and her two sisters and a brother all vying for his attention. There had always been a huge tree with real candles, which were lit as a special treat before they went to bed. The tears stung the back of her eyes as she recalled waking up on Christmas morning, feeling around the bottom of the bed with her feet until she encountered the stocking that her parents had lovingly filled for her. She would probe it with a big toe, trying to anticipate its contents from the weight of it.

There would be no more magical Christmases; no more unexpected and well-chosen presents from Paul; no opportunities to indulge Marcus. Her future looked bleak. What future? There was no future. Her only consolation was the past and the many treasured memories, which nobody could take away, like the Georgian silver tea caddy that Paul had given her only last Christmas. She took a sip from the glass of Tio Pepe which she'd poured in a forlorn attempt to cheer herself up and pulled a face as if she were being forced to drink vinegar. It tasted vile. It must have been opened months ago. She pushed it impatiently to one side.

The sound of the telephone interrupted her thoughts. Please God not a crisis. Not tonight. She lifted the receiver with reluctance.

'Antonia?' The unmistakeable voice of her sister sounded loud and shrill in her ear. 'Hello Celia,' she said wearily.

'Am I still expected for lunch tomorrow?' Antonia could hear a buzz of conversation in the background, punctuated by the occasional outburst of laughter: no doubt the reason why Celia felt the need to raise her voice. It sounded as if she were at some party, maybe with a bunch of her arty friends? Antonia couldn't resist a sarcastic reply. 'If you have a better offer, please don't refuse it on my account. There's always plenty going on here as you well know.' That was a big lie. The staff would have a field day if she took to her bed or stayed in her room until Christmas was well and truly over. Antonia hated herself for behaving in such a petulant way. Self-pity wasn't her style and it was unfair to Celia to offload her own distress.

There was a slight pause before Celia answered. 'I'm sure a working Christmas without Paul is very traumatic for you, but that's no reason to take it out on the rest of us. I'll see you at eleven thirty as planned.' Before Antonia could say goodbye Celia had rung off.

Later that evening at eleven o'clock Liz, Sarah and Oscar were still sitting round the table surrounded by the debris of their dinner. The ham had disappeared and had been replaced by a whole Stilton cheese, a bowl of fruit and another of nuts. A decanter of port had circulated several times and now stood, half empty, in front of Oscar. He glanced swiftly at Liz before replacing the stopper. Something told him that, the way things looked, it was the wisest thing he could do.

He'd known from the start it wouldn't be an easy evening for any of them and had deliberately kept the alcohol flowing in an attempt to soften the edges of their grief. They were trying in their separate ways to forget other evenings when the three of them had been four and their lives had been relatively untouched by the profound sadness which now they all felt. Somehow the evening had progressed without reminiscences of the past. The fact that Liz would soon be leaving gave them all room to speculate about her future which, to his mind anyway, was a more productive way to spend one of their last evenings together.

'I think if you don't mind I'll go to bed now,' Liz said, attempting not very successfully, to stifle a yawn and looking at her watch.

'Good idea!' Oscar said with some relief, 'I'm sure we're all in for a very early start tomorrow.' A flurry of office party lunches at the restaurant had kept him busy until nearly four o'clock. He was dog tired and longing for the moment when he could put his head on the pillow and say goodnight to Sarah.

In his childhood in Vienna they'd all followed the Austrian

custom of opening their presents on Christmas Eve and, what with the excitement and the correspondingly late night, they'd all been dead to the world on Christmas morning. At one stage he'd suggested to Sarah they might do the same, but with her usual common sense she'd pointed out that, since they were living in England they should follow English customs. 'We don't want the children to grow up thinking they're different from all their friends now, do we?' she'd asked. He'd agreed, although reluctantly.

He watched as Liz tried unsuccessfully to lever herself to her feet. Stupid, he hadn't realised how far gone she was. It took him a fraction of a second to move behind her chair, place a helping arm around her and try to help her to her feet. She was a dead weight and he signalled silently to Sarah who came around the table and took the other side of Liz.

'I'm so sorry,' Liz said. 'I started drinking this morning and ate very little until your wonderful dinner. At my age I should know better.'

'Don't worry,' Sarah's voice was soothing. 'We'll have you up to bed in no time and then you can sleep for as long as you need.'

The three of them climbed the stairs slowly, one step at a time. Liz had an arm around each of their necks and as Oscar was so much taller than either of them they made a bizarre threesome. It seemed like an eternity before they managed to get Liz to her bedroom and dump her unceremoniously on top of the bed.

'Can you manage on your own?' Oscar looked across at his wife.

'I think we've done the hard bit,' she said, 'the rest should be a doddle.'

Oscar backed out of the room and left them to it.

CHAPTER NINETEEN

Somehow Liz managed to survive Christmas, but the moment she was back at the hotel embarked on a frenzy of packing which lasted all of two days. She made careful calculations about the amount of stuff she could get into the car and arranged carriage for the remainder. That was the easy part. It was much harder to say goodbye to all the staff, but living in the hotel for four years she'd seen most of them on a daily basis and couldn't leave without making a proper farewell. She gave a forwarding address to one of the receptionists. 'I've told most people my new address,' she said, 'but there's bound to be someone I've forgotten.'

George had found an ex-army major living in reduced circumstances and Liz had carefully packed Paul's clothes, which George had promised to deliver in person. He was the last person to whom she said goodbye. 'I'll miss you all,' he said gruffly, his eyes looking suspiciously bright and not quite meeting hers as he took her keys for the very last time. On impulse she gave him a fleeting peck on the cheek before running out to join Maria and the family. The last she saw of him he was standing with two fingers raised to his brow in his usual salute.

It began snowing as they left Salisbury and soon the flakes were falling so thickly that Liz was forced to slow down as she turned onto the Blandford road. They'd had an early lunch before leaving and both the children were fast asleep in the back of the car. Liz hoped to arrive before it got really dark. The road leading up to the cottage was narrow and winding and even with good visibility could be hazardous if one met a careless driver coming in the opposite direction. She began to pray the car wouldn't let them down. Her mechanical skills were minimal and, although she could take care of the basic necessities, fixing a fan belt or changing a tyre were beyond her.

As they drove through Coombe Bissett she began to relax, knowing they were on the last leg of their journey. She leaned forward slightly, peering through the windscreen like a nervous old woman. 'Look for the sign to Broadstone,' she urged Maria, 'I'd hate to drive past the turning and have to double back in these conditions.'

As it turned out they both spotted the signpost at the same time. The snow had stuck to it and the name of the village was partly obscured, but Liz remembered Broadstone was the first turning after Coombe Bissett and, looking up the hill towards the village, spotted a well-loved clump of trees sitting on top of the first incline and knew she was almost home.

She was just about to accelerate up the hill when she spotted a single figure standing at the edge of the road. A man of indeterminate age stood clutching a faded blue tweed jacket and an apology for a raincoat around an emaciated frame. A cloth cap was pulled well down over his eyes. 'Oh look at that poor wretch,' she said to Maria. 'If we offered him a lift I suppose we could squeeze him in the back with the children, he must be nearly frozen to death, although of course he may not be going in our direction.' Maria wound her window down and Liz was able to look properly at the man who grinned inanely back at her. Saliva was dribbling down his chin through yellow, neglected teeth and within a couple of seconds Liz had the feeling that she'd be taking an incalculable risk if he were to get into the car. She trod hard on the accelerator and felt the wheels slip on the snow, spraying spumes of grey slush in all directions. Hastily she shoved the car into second gear and pressed the accelerator again, this time more gently and let out a long breath of relief as the tyres gripped. 'That was close,' she said, 'for a moment there I panicked. I've no idea who he can be, but I hope he finds some kind of shelter soon. I'm only sorry I couldn't be the one to help him.'

The closer they came to the top of the hill the more thankful Liz was for the extra weight they had on board, but was still relieved when finally they reached the top and turned right to drive the short distance down to the cottage. 'Glad I had the presence of mind to do a good big shop before we left,' she said to Maria. 'If we're snowed in we'll be able to survive for several days on what I've got in the back.'

'Do you have a pair of skis at the cottage?' Maria asked. 'If so, I can always ski down to the village for you.'

'Do you know, now I come to think of it, there is an old pair of Paul's in the cellar and you're welcome to use them, but I think you'd need a sledge to bring back any supplies or, failing that, the farmer and his tractor.'

A light was burning in the kitchen when Liz finally stopped the car. She guessed that Evie had been in to stoke up the Rayburn and left the light on as a welcome. 'Can you stay here with the children while I go and put on some more lights?' she asked Maria. 'Marcus could be frightened if he wakes up in a strange place.'

She unlocked the front door and was met by a welcome blast of warm air; Evie had not only stoked up the Rayburn but lit a fire in the sitting room and drawn the curtains to keep in the heat.

Liz switched on all the lights on the ground floor to make the place look as much like home as possible. Even as she carried out this small and mundane task she knew she was doing it as much for her own peace of mind as the well-being of her family. The enormity of the step she'd taken in moving them all so soon after Paul's death struck her forcibly the moment the front door was open. Thank goodness there was so much to do, she wouldn't have time to sit down and feel sorry for herself and all of them. Their lives now depended on her future actions and she knew if she was to dwell on the responsibility it would completely overwhelm her.

They carried the two sleeping children in from the car and put them on the sitting room sofa, returning to collect first the food and then their respective bits of luggage. 'Leave the cases in the hall,' Liz said to Maria, 'we'll move them later when we've fed the children.'

Two hours later Liz tiptoed down the stairs and went into the kitchen where Maria was making supper. Evie had left a dozen eggs, a pint of milk and a loaf of bread on the table. There was a note telling Liz that a couple of pork chops and some fresh vegetables were in the fridge. The smell of roasting meat told Liz that supper was well on its way and she sent up a silent prayer thanking anyone who might be listening for the twin benefits of Evie and Maria. She daren't think what this move would have been like without the two of them.

She'd used the bottom drawer from a chest in one of the bedrooms to improvise a cot for Emma until her own arrived from Bishop's Wood and read several stories to Marcus in an attempt to settle him down for the night. He'd told her in no uncertain terms that he didn't like his new house and wanted to go back to the old one. To console him Liz placed Emma in her drawer next to his bed to keep him company in his new surroundings. Until tonight they'd always slept in separate rooms.

Maria had turned on the radio in her absence and Liz guessed that she too was feeling the change and was seeking some kind of diversion. From force of habit she checked her watch as the seven o'clock pips sounded and then started to listen properly when the presenter issued a special announcement. A potentially dangerous man had escaped from a mental institution in the Salisbury area. He had been at large for almost twenty four hours and members of the public were advised not to approach him. Maria and Liz looked at each other in horror. Maria's mouth opened, but no sound came out. 'Oh my God,' Liz said. 'Do you think?' But she didn't need to finish the sentence; both knew what the other was thinking. 'I'll check the front door's locked and then I'm going to phone the police,' Liz said as Maria crossed the kitchen in two strides and locked and bolted the back door. 'I may be completely wrong but . . .' The sentence remained unfinished as she walked towards the phone.

When she came beck to the kitchen she suddenly remembered the wine that Paul had been buying for the last couple of years. A smile came over her face as she went down the few steps to the cellar and emerged after a few minutes with a bottle of Grüner Veltliner. 'Here's a taste of home for you,' she said to Maria, wiping the dust carefully from the bottle, 'and if anybody's earned it you have. It will go well with the pork chops. We can drink to our new home and I want you to know how much I appreciate your coming down with us. Without you this trip would have been downright impossible.' She drew the cork and poured large glasses for both of them.

CHAPTER TWENTY

February 1963

Most of the employees at Bishop's Hall were eating lunch in the staff dining room. The view from the window which, being staff quarters overlooked the car park, was even bleaker than usual and did nothing to lift their spirits. Britain was having one of the worst winters in living memory and the weather forecast promised more of the same. Outside the trees held up frozen fingers to the biting wind which whipped away the snow before it could coat and protect their branches. The hall porters had added snow clearing to their list of duties and started every morning by clearing the drive if it had snowed during the night. Most nights it had.

'This place feels more like a morgue every day.' Amy Jones, the housekeeper picked delicately at the meat on her plate. Stew had never been a favourite with her and, although she appreciated the chef's efforts to provide them all with warm and nourishing comfort food, knew that if she ate a morsel of fat her delicate digestion would be upset for days.

'What we all need is Mr Paul to cheer us up, put some optimism across our paths.' George was attacking his casserole with relish, wishing that Chef had thought to make some dumplings to go with it.

'My feet are like blocks of ice.' Aileen, the head receptionist, had settled for soup and a sandwich. 'Every time the door opens it's like the Arctic. For two pins I'll keep my boots on tomorrow whatever Madame has to say about it.'

'I'd like to see you stand up to her when she's in one of her moods,' Amy said. 'Bites your head off soon as look at you nowadays.'

'She's missing Mr Paul like the rest of us,' George put in, hoping to pour the proverbial oil before the conversation became any more depressing.

'Aren't you forgetting she's got Monsieur LeGrange to take his place?' Aileen spoke his name with an exaggerated French accent and braced herself as a chorus of groans issued from everyone around the table.

'She's welcome to him. French ponce.' Amy cut a miniscule sliver of fat from a cube of beef before putting the meat tentatively into her mouth.

'Now, Amy,' George remonstrated, 'he comes very highly recommended, according to Miss Antonia.'

Amy pulled a face at him, although it could have been her reaction to the beef for all he knew.

The weather had taken its toll on their visitor numbers and they were in the unusual situation of being under-employed. Normally they wouldn't have had time to moan, but would be eating their respective lunches with one eye on the clock and the other on the tasks to be completed before they went off duty. Business travel was down, weekend trade was non-existent and even though most of the pre-booked functions went ahead as planned they always ran with fewer numbers than originally expected.

'Talking of Monsieur LeGrange,' Richard the head waiter now joined the conversation, 'I did a stock check last week, before we had that dinner for Premium Petroleum, found I was down a dozen bottles. Our French friend and Miss Antonia are the only other people who have keys to the cellar.'

'So what have you done about it?' Aileen paused with a sandwich halfway to her mouth. The rest of the staff, sensing a juicy piece of gossip, listened avidly.

'I asked Monsieur LeGrange if he knew anything about it and he just shrugged his shoulders and told me that it was my responsibility to keep a check on the wine.'

'Which is exactly what you were doing,' said Amy.

'Well I hope you had a word with Miss Antonia,' George put in. 'Twelve bottles you said? That's a lot of wine.'

'Sure I told her,' Richard said. 'For one thing I needed to cover my own back, for another it's her money that's been lost.'

'What did she say?' asked Aileen, brushing crumbs from her lap and reaching for a copy of Caterer and Hotel Keeper. The place had changed so much in the last three months she was keeping an eye out for possible job vacancies.

'Promised to have a word with Monsieur LeGrange.' Richard shrugged. 'Fat lot of good that'll do.'

'I'll get one of the room maids to have a look round the flat next time she cleans it,' Amy said as she pushed her plate to one side.

'Stolen wine. It's sure to be displayed prominently, isn't it? Anyway, he's probably flogged it by now.' Richard's years in the industry had taught him most of the fiddles.

Amy ignored him. 'We'll keep tabs until he slips up. Sooner or later all criminals make a vital mistake.' She spoke with the certainty that years of reading detective novels had given her then looked at her watch and pushed back her chair. 'Best get a move on or there'll be trouble. One by one the rest of the staff followed suit.

Antonia replaced the telephone receiver carefully, let out a sigh that went to the depths of her soul and wondered if the hotel would ever run smoothly again. For perhaps the first time in her life she acknowledged the debt of gratitude she owed to Paul. Under his administration things had always run like clockwork or, if they hadn't, he'd taken good care that she wasn't troubled by problems. Now she would have to deal with this latest on her own and the thought of the forthcoming interview filled her with dread.

They'd recently done a small function for the local Rotary Club, a dinner-dance to mark their fortieth anniversary, and the treasurer had just rung to say that on checking the account he'd discovered they'd been charged for more wine than they'd consumed. Antonia had first apologised and then questioned him carefully to make absolutely certain that he was right. 'We had tables for eight,' he confirmed. 'Four bottles of wine had been pre-ordered for each table. When I came to check the account each table had been charged for five.' He went on to say that there was an understanding in the Club that any member ordering extra wine on the night would be expected to pay for it then and there and not put it on the bill.

Antonia knew all this to be true. The Rotary Club were old and valued customers and fairly predictable in their habits. 'Send the account back to me and I'll make sure you have a corrected amount by return,' she said, 'and please accept my apologies for the mistake.' They'd made the occasional error in the past, of course, but nothing quite so stupidly obvious as this one. Either someone was being very greedy or downright foolhardy. Intuitively she knew the identity of the 'someone'. They'd only had one new member of staff in the past six months and that person was Gaston LeGrange. Once she had the account in her hands as evidence she would tackle him, in the meantime she'd be keeping a close eye on him.

Two days later Gaston LeGrange walked out of Antonia's office. Even though he'd tried to explain away overcharging for wine as an 'administrative error,' his ears were still singing after the ticking off he'd just had. If Antonia could have seen his face as he closed the door she would have been amazed to see him smiling broadly. He was the kind of man who tried always to have an ace up his sleeve or alternatively a 'Plan B'. Right now he had the equivalent of both. Sitting in the top drawer of his desk, in Paul's flat, which he'd taken over when Liz and her family left, was the business card of Eloise Moncton. They'd had a long conversation just before she left the reception they'd laid on after Paul's memorial service and she'd told him that if he was ever looking for a job to give her a call.

He'd driven up to London on his last day off and given Moncton's Hotel the once over. What he saw was impressive. It had been newly refurbished and in excellent taste. The minimalist public rooms lent an air of refinement which distinguished it from some of its more florid counterparts in other areas of the city. He hadn't asked to speak to Miss Moncton, preferring to prowl around on his own, taking things in at his leisure. He'd bought a drink at the well-stocked bar and was gratified that his beer had been served correctly chilled, but not too cold, and there were bowls of olives on the counter as well as the ubiquitous peanuts. He hadn't seen the bedrooms, but if they were decorated to the same standard as the rest of the hotel he had no reason to worry.

Who'd stay in a dead and alive hole like Bishop's Wood when they could be working in London? The possibilities for leisure out here were extremely limited and the clientele in the one club he'd managed to find were unbelievably unsophisticated, particularly the women. Eloise Moncton, on the other hand, was the last word in chic, and the fact that she was a few years older than himself would make her all the more grateful if at some unspecified time in the future he were to pay her some attention. He'd lived pretty much on his wits for the past thirty five years and he guessed he could go on doing that for as long as he needed. His future suddenly seemed decidedly rosy.

When Tom Merton checked into Bishop's Wood for his quarterly meeting with his sales team he was disappointed not to find Liz on duty behind reception. When, after making a few discreet enquiries, he discovered she'd left, he felt unaccountably disappointed. Not that she'd ever given him the slightest encouragement, but he'd hoped that as memories of her dead husband began to fade he might stand a chance of a brief fling at least. She looked like she could be fun given a bit of encouragement. Spending so much time on the road, which had initially made for an interesting and varied career, over time had become tedious. One hotel was pretty much like another, the dining room in the evening full of people sitting one to a table, usually reading a newspaper, occasionally a book, and trying hard not to meet the eyes of fellow diners. He was only in Bishop's Wood for a couple of nights, but even before he arrived he'd made tentative plans to make his stay as enjoyable as possible and now they'd been well and truly scuppered.

In the short intervals when he wasn't with his sales team, Tom spent time talking to any member of the hotel staff who had time to listen. The atrocious weather became an opening gambit and after a few minutes of futile chat about the state of the roads and the difficulty in getting about he would finally get onto the subject of staff and how the weather was affecting their transport. Then he'd mention as casually as possible that he hadn't seen Mrs Hirsch around the place. The readiness of the staff to impart information genuinely surprised him and by the time he left he not only knew that Liz had moved to Wiltshire but that 'someone' had heard that she was working at a hotel in Salisbury. He filed the information away for future reference.

The weather still showed no signs of warming up by the beginning of March and Liz began to think that spring would never come. She'd been at the cottage for nearly three months and was slowly getting used to being there without Paul. She knew the isolation must be difficult for Maria and promised to arrange driving lessons for her, but the roads were so atrocious they both felt it wasn't a good time to be learning to drive and opted to wait until the weather got warmer.

She'd managed to find a job as assistant manager in a hotel in Salisbury. It was larger and consequently busier than Bishop's Wood and Liz was grateful that the combined efforts of work and family left little time to feel sorry for herself. She'd begun to make plans for improving the cottage, which was fine as a weekend bolt-hole, but had shortcomings as a permanent home. It was frustrating to look out at the garden every day knowing that there were weeds under the snow which needed pulling out and soil that needed turning. Before leaving Bishop's Wood she'd picked up the urn containing Paul's ashes from Oscar thinking to scatter them in the garden at Ivy House. When he was alive it had been the one place where they could be alone and some of Liz's happiest memories were of times they'd spent here together. Now with everything shrouded in snow she reconciled herself to waiting until the thaw before she could finally scatter them.

With the garden off-limits she concentrated her efforts on the interior and had already managed to replace some of the older and more faded curtains and planned a programme of re-decoration when the weather improved. Fortunately the roof was sound, so there was no need to worry about leaks, and it was therapeutic to be planning ahead, even if it was only décor.

She'd enrolled Marcus in a nursery school in the village. Liz usually managed to drop him off on her way to work and a neighbouring farmer picked him up when he collected his own child, frequently using the Land Rover as the best form of transport on the frozen roads. On one occasion on the way home from work Liz had to leave her car in the village as the snow made it impossible to drive it up the hill. She'd struggled home on foot, slipping and sliding on a new fall of powdery snow.

It was the middle of June before Tom Merton found the opportunity to visit Salisbury. He'd phoned the three major hotels in the town to find out which, if any, Liz was working in and timed his arrival for early evening when the shift would be changing and with any luck she'd either be clocking on or off. As it happened she was walking across the foyer as he arrived.

'Well, well, what a surprise! I didn't expect to see you so far away from home,' he lied, neatly covering up his expectation of seeing her.

The encounter wasn't one that Liz wanted, but she gave him a swift update on her new job, her move and finally how tough it had been to relocate in the awful weather. Tom listened as if he was hearing everything for the first time, but he couldn't help but notice that the staff at Bishop's Wood had been considerably more forthcoming than Liz herself.

Liz inched her way in small steps towards the door as she spoke, trying to transmit the message that she was in a hurry, knowing that, sooner or later, he was going to invite her to have a drink with him. When the invitation came she used the same reply she used with all male guests who'd issued similar invitations, and there had been plenty since she'd started work in the hotel. 'Thank you, it's nice of you to ask, however I don't think it's good for staff morale to see me fraternising with the guests.'

'I presume there are other establishments in Salisbury where one may buy a drink?'

Liz had underestimated his ability to think on his feet and was left floundering about in her mind for a reply, at the same time cursing her own dull-wittedness.

'Just give me a moment to check in and I'll be with you,' he said, seeing her hesitation and deciding to capitalise while he still had the chance. Liz was lost. She watched helplessly as he crossed to reception checked in and then left his luggage with the concierge.

'I mustn't be long,' she said as he rejoined her. 'Remember I have a family and an au pair waiting at home. I like to give Maria the opportunity to have some time off in the evening as she's been looking after the children for most of the day.'

Tom appeared not to hear. Once they were out of the hotel he turned sharply to the right and walked in the direction of a rival establishment, taking the outside of the pavement and steering Liz lightly along with a guiding hand under her elbow. Although still wearing her business suit, she was acutely aware of both the pressure and the warmth of his hand, remembering with distaste the clammy feel of his fingers the last time they'd met.

'Here we are,' he said, pausing at the entrance to the Mitre, a larger hotel than the one in which Liz worked and with which she was unfamiliar. They walked up a short flight of steps to the entrance. The door was opened for them by the hall porter.

"Evening Mr Merton,' he said. Tom acknowledged the greeting with a smile, which left Liz wondering if he'd stayed here before or if this was where he brought colleagues or stray women like her on a regular basis. He seemed to know his way around and crossed the foyer decisively, pausing only when he reached the top of a short flight of stairs tucked away in a corner diagonally opposite the entrance. The stairs led down to a small bar and Tom Merton held open the door to allow Liz to enter.

The room in which she found herself was so dim it took a few seconds for her eyes to adjust to the gloom. It was furnished with banquettes upholstered in red plush, which absorbed much of the very little light coming from the small lamps shaded in crimson silk and placed on tables in front of each banquette. Liz had never been inside such a place before and her first thought was how Paul would have hated it.

Tom Merton chose a seat furthest away from the door. 'What's your poison?' he asked as the waiter, who'd been hovering by the bar, approached their table. 'I'll have a gin and tonic please,' Liz said and then quickly, 'a single, remember I'm driving.'

'And remember how small a pub measure is,' Tom said, before ignoring her request and ordering two doubles. Liz tried to conceal her annoyance, resolving to drink as slowly as possible. When the drinks arrived, Tom put a mere splash of tonic in her glass, but she reached for the bottle and filled it to the brim.

'Cheers,' he raised his glass. 'Lovely to see you again.'

'Cheers,' Liz was determined not to reciprocate the rest of his greeting, already reproaching herself for being here at all. She fished in her bag for a cigarette, needing a diversion. 'I started smoking again after Paul died,' she explained. 'I find it helps me to cope with the stress.'

Tom Merton didn't comment but reached forward, took the lighter from her hand and lit the cigarette for her. Liz found her irritation growing and wondered why she was always bumping into him and why he annoyed her so much.

'The evenings seem to drag when one's away from home,' he

began. It was a conversational gambit to which Liz felt unable to respond. 'I can imagine,' was all she could manage as she drew deeply on her cigarette.

'What do you find to do with yourself in the depths of Wiltshire?' he asked, helping himself to peanuts.

Liz set about filling her diary twenty four hours a day, seven days a week. Was he really so clueless or was he just trying to make conversation? 'With a young family, a cottage to care for and a full time job, my days seem pretty well occupied,' she said. 'I try to keep as busy as possible. It stops me thinking about Paul. And to be honest, working irregular hours, as one does in the hotel industry, whenever I get a free moment I'm usually trying to catch up on sleep. With a baby just over a year old I can never be quite sure that I won't be woken during the night, so I make the most of every opportunity. Do you have children?' she asked.

'We have two; Christopher is twelve and has just started at my old school and Charlotte is ten.'

'And your old school is?'

'Stowe.'

'And does Christopher enjoy it? Is he settling down?' *At least with children's schools we're on safe ground,* Liz thought, stubbing out her cigarette and immediately wanting another. She stretched out a hand and took a couple of peanuts, determined not to appear hungry in case he suggested dinner.

'Happy enough, I suppose. It's not always easy to tell with kids, is it? They tend to put a brave face on things, don't they? I know I did.' He took a long pull from his drink and helped himself to more peanuts.

Liz pounced joyfully on another conversational opportunity. 'So were you unhappy at school then?' she asked, thinking back to her own joyful days at grammar school and wondering how many boarding school boys tried to 'put a brave face on things'.

'There were times when the bullying was hard to take.' He didn't meet her eyes as he spoke, looking instead rather absently into his glass. 'Small boys can be unbelievably cruel when they gang up.'

'And yet you send your own son to the same establishment.' Liz realised that she was mentally notching up points against him.

'He'll probably be able to stand up for himself rather better than I did. I'm sure he'd tell me if he was really unhappy and I pride myself on being more sympathetic than my father.'

Liz looked at him over the top of her glass. So he was bullied at school and had an unsympathetic father. What effect had that had on his life? For the first time that evening she was interested to hear his reply. She asked the question.

'I felt I always had to prove myself. Try to be a tough guy. Big boys don't cry and all that stuff. Would you like another drink?' he said, draining his glass.

'No, I'm fine thanks.' Liz held on to her glass tightly in case he felt compelled to buy her another. She watched him signal to the waiter and, shortly after that, his second double of the evening appeared. He moved closer to her. She felt the warmth of his thigh against her own and moved slightly away from him trying to gauge how much leeway she had before she reached her end of the banquette. A surreptitious glance at her watch told her that it was seven o'clock. 'I really must go. The family will wonder where I am. Normally I'd be home by now.'

'I was hoping you'd have dinner with me. I've nothing booked this evening.'

'Unfortunately *I* have.' Liz jumped to her feet and held out her hand formally. 'Thank you very much for my drink. I don't often hang around once my shift has finished.'

'Perhaps next time I'm in the area we could have dinner together?' There was an expression in his eyes which she could only describe as pleading and, for the first time that evening, Liz began to feel sorry for him.

'Perhaps,' she raised her hand in a farewell salute and left him to his gin and tonic. She hadn't had a drink alone with a man since Paul's death, unless she counted the time she'd had tea with him in Bishop's Wood. It felt like disloyalty to Paul's memory and she was glad she'd resisted the invitation to dinner. *The next time he asks me I'll be busy*, she told herself climbing into her car to begin the drive home.

During the journey she thought back to the first time Paul had taken her out. They'd talked non-stop and she smiled as she remembered the joy of finding out about him. Her discovery that he liked Chopin, a composer with whom she'd had a long love affair. The story about his escape from Vienna sounded like a Boy's Own adventure rather than the life and death exit which was the reality. Her interest had been so easily kindled, her heartbeat quickened and her pulse raced every time he came anywhere near. Surely she wasn't becoming too old for that kind of excitement? Would any man ever make her feel that way again?

For the life of her she couldn't understand what constituted the magic of chemistry; why one man had the ability to enslave you for life without even trying and another merely succeeded in repelling. Yet another, Oscar for instance, could be a good friend with whom you could relax and whose company you could enjoy in the knowledge that he wouldn't try to make a pass, given the opportunity. She was no nearer to finding either a solution, or a satisfactory explanation when she finally drew up outside the cottage.

There was, however, one decision which she felt couldn't be delayed for much longer. Ever since the transition from Bishop's Wood she'd avoided doing anything with Paul's ashes. Every time she went into the cellar her eyes were drawn to the urn, which still sat on a shelf just above the wine rack where she'd placed it when they moved. She had thought about taking them to Austria and scattering them over one of his beloved mountains, but then argued to herself that if she did that the last tangible evidence that he'd ever existed would be the best part of a thousand miles away. Perhaps she should have sprinkled them in the woodland around the hotel where he had spent so much of his working life? This idea was dismissed almost as soon as she asked herself the question, thinking that perhaps he might not rest in peace so close to his working environment.

Almost without realising it she'd reached a decision on the

drive home. In the spring of last year they'd planted a camellia in the garden of Ivy House. It survived the winter, much to her surprise, and she felt now that if she were to place Paul's ashes under the tree and fork them in, whatever was left of him would somehow transmute into sustenance for the shrub, which in its turn would give him shelter.

Not an entirely wasted evening then, she told herself as she locked the car door. The next fine day she would finally lay Paul to rest. It was a comforting feeling.

CHAPTER TWENTY ONE

Antonia was doing a spot check on the bedrooms on Amy Jones' day off. Normally she wouldn't bother, but they'd had a few changes of staff recently and she wanted to be certain their standards weren't slipping. In one room the bedside lamp failed to light when she tried it, although on checking the wall plug it was quite clear the lamp was connected. There was a half used tablet of soap in the bathroom which she removed. In the third room she could swear the carpet hadn't been vacuumed and went in search of the room maid and found her, looking hot and bothered, changing the sheets in yet another bedroom.

'Would you mind coming with me to check on some of the bedrooms?' Antonia asked, thinking that to show the woman the evidence of her mistakes might leave a more lasting impression than simply talking about them.

The woman looked pointedly at her watch. 'I hope you'll square it with Miss Jones,' she said, 'only I have to clean ten rooms in five hours and I already had to wait for clean linen, so I'm a bit short of time.' Antonia was taken aback, unaware that the hotel set tight time limits on room cleaning. Tomorrow she'd have a word with Amy. In the meantime, here was an opportunity to point out what she considered to be important for guests.

The public rooms had also lost some of their usual sparkle, although Gaston LeGrange assured her that it was just a matter of time before the new recruits came up to standard. Normally when going about the hotel she came face-to-face with people who'd worked for them for many years. She knew their family history and had helped some of them with their problems in the past. Now there were more and more people she didn't know and the hotel felt less and less like the place in which she'd invested half a lifetime.

And then one morning in mid-September she walked down the stairs from her flat to her office with the distinct feeling that somehow or another this morning was different. Everything looked the same as usual and it was some time before the change filtered through to her. There seemed to be a lightening of the atmosphere. The receptionist on duty smiled broadly when she appeared and George, who was studiously arranging fliers for various local events, looked up and called, 'Good morning Miss Antonia. Lovely morning!'

Antonia walked over to the cubby hole that served as George's office. 'Something feels different, have you any idea what it can be?' George beamed at her. 'Well, I thought I'd wait until you appeared before I told you. Fact is, our Monsieur LeGrange has gone.

'Gone, George. What do you mean, gone?' Antonia felt the faintest prickle of anxiety and her heart began to thump.

'He left in the small hours of this morning. John, the night porter told me when I came on duty. Saw him loading his bags into Mr Paul's car and then he left. We thought he might have gone on holiday, but then I took the liberty of checking out the flat and it's empty. It looks as if he's done a runner.'

Antonia's energy drained away and she clutched the edge of George's counter, afraid that she might fall over if she didn't have support. Just when she thought things couldn't get any worse . . .

'Shall I have some coffee sent to your office while you decide what you're going to do?' George asked.

'That would be kind, George. Thank you.'

Antonia walked slowly towards her office knowing she would have to inform the police of Paul's stolen car. They didn't need adverse publicity at the moment, but it was unthinkable to let that dreadful, smooth Frenchman get away with theft. Then she had a second thought. Was the car the only thing he'd stolen? It would be better to check his flat before informing the police. Just in case . . .

She collected her spare keys and walked upstairs to the flat. It still felt strange when she entered it. The childish chatter was missing, together with the clutter in the hallway that had been a vital part of it in the days when Paul and his family lived there. She went into the sitting room and was met by a scene of disorder as if Monsieur LeGrange had left in a hurry. Desk drawers were open, the stopper was off the whisky decanter, newspapers scattered on the floor. Antonia restored the stopper to its rightful place, picked up the newspapers, closed the desk drawers and then walked through to the main bedroom. All the cupboard doors were open, but at first glance nothing seemed to have changed. And then she noticed a pale square on the wall where a picture had been taken down.

When Liz left the flat, Antonia had brought a landscape from her own sitting room and hung it in the bedroom. It wasn't particularly valuable, worth a few hundred perhaps, but her father had bought it in the days when he'd been helping her to run the hotel and to Antonia it was priceless. Without walking down to her office she picked up the phone and called the police.

Next she summoned all the heads of department, told them what had happened, asked them to look out for Paul's car whenever they were out and about and finally requested a list of any items that might have gone missing during the past few weeks. By the time the police arrived there was an inventory of 'lost' property on the desk in front of her, which included a couple of cases of wine, three bottles of whisky and about four hundred cigarettes. Aileen had checked through the telephone accounts and reported long distance calls to France totalling £150.

Antonia was still talking to the police three quarters of an hour later when there was a knock at the door and, before she could say 'come in' it opened a fraction and a head appeared. It was the barman. 'Thought I ought to let you know straight away that unless my till's been emptied after last night someone's helped themselves to the takings.'

There was a small residential course staying in the hotel, only ten people, but before and after dinner they'd pretty well taken over the bar and the returns had been particularly good.

Steve the barman had checked the till roll and reckoned he was about £220 down. Antonia thanked him and the police added the missing cash to their list of stolen items.

'Any idea where he might have gone?' The police inspector asked Antonia as he concluded the interview. Antonia confirmed she had none, explaining that Gaston LeGrange had been with them just over ten months acting as manager and came highly recommended from one of the most reliable staff agencies in London. 'Best give us the name of the agency,' the inspector said, 'in case they've found him another post.' Antonia pulled out a card from a well-organised index system and handed it to the inspector who noted down the name and number.

She sat on in her office after the police left, thoughts flying about her head like leaves in a whirlwind. *Oh Paul, where are you?* The same question came up every time there was a crisis. It irked her to think that Liz could have easily taken over from him, but her harsh words forbidding Antonia any contact with the children were too sharply etched on her memory to make that a possibility.

The hotel hadn't totally picked up after the fall-off in business during those terrible winter months. The cold spell had taken another toll in raised fuel bills and burst pipes. At the end of the financial year she discovered they'd made a loss and was terrified that if things got any worse they wouldn't be able to meet the repayments on the loan they'd taken out to refurbish the public rooms. What if at some time in the future she couldn't meet the wage bill? Then she'd really be in trouble. What if they were unable to pay their suppliers? Things wore out and needed replacing; then there were cleaning materials, garden maintenance. The thoughts went on and on.

How had Paul made it seem so effortless? The capital investment alone was huge when you considered buildings, fixtures and fittings. Perhaps they should have waited to refurbish? Perhaps if she didn't replace Gaston LeGrange and gave every head of department responsibility for running their own sector of the hotel that would give her dual benefits? Not only would she save one fairly generous salary plus all the perks, allowable and stolen, but she'd also boost the confidence of the heads of department by increasing their responsibility.

If they ever recovered Paul's car she would sell it. Every time she saw it reminded her of Paul driving it, together with treasured memories of the many miles they'd covered together. But she couldn't afford to be sentimental about a mere car. The sale would give her an added windfall and she could begin to forget all the times she'd been a passenger in it. Perhaps after all things might not be as bad as she feared.

☙

Two weeks later Antonia had just gone up to her flat for the evening, refusing dinner saying she wasn't particularly hungry and would make herself some scrambled eggs. She was tempted to ignore the phone when it rang, but knew that it would probably ring again if she didn't answer or, worse still, someone from reception would come up to try to find her.

'Antonia? It's Celia.' Her sister's voice sounded urgent.

'Oh hello,' Antonia's voice came out without enthusiasm. Celia, who was never put off by her sister's moods, pitched in with no preamble. 'Look, you're not going to believe this, but last night I saw that French manager of yours.' Antonia's grip on the telephone receiver tightened. 'You mean Gaston LeGrange?'

'You know I have a terrible memory for names.'

Unless the owners are going to be useful to you, Antonia thought. 'Where did you see him?' she asked reaching for the pad and pen she always kept by the phone.

'Why in Moncton's Hotel. He's working for Eloise.'

'What! Since when?'

'Not sure exactly. Eloise said something about his contract with you coming to an end.'

'Well that might be her story, or his for that matter, but I've already told you what really happened. I must get on to the police straight away and have him picked up. I don't suppose you saw the car?'

'I asked Eloise. She hasn't seen it, but he's hardly likely to park it near to the hotel, is he?'

'I suppose not. Well thank you for your detective work. I must say I'm rather mystified. How did he know that Eloise owned a hotel, I wonder? She hasn't been near Bishop's Hall since Paul's memorial service.'

'Search me. You know Eloise. Always one to be seduced by a handsome face. Maybe she got in touch later. Offered him a job. Maybe they bumped into each other? Maybe they knew each other before he came to you? Who knows?' Now that she'd passed on her piece of news, Celia saw no reason to linger and, before Antonia could quiz her any further, she'd said goodbye and hung up.

After Antonia had informed the police she picked up Omar and sat stroking him, listening to his gruff purr, finding it comforting. Suddenly she felt extremely tired and admitted to herself she no longer had the energy or the will to carry on running the hotel. What to do instead? Bishop's Hall had been her home for more years than she could remember. She'd built it up from scratch; first with her father and then with Paul. If she was really honest she'd only kept it going during the last few years for Paul's sake, expecting one day to use the place as her home and hand over all the responsibility for day-to-day operations to him. And now her carefully laid plans had crumbled away to nothing. Tears of self pity slipped down her face.

It was early November and Liz was back in Bishop's Wood for the first time in almost a year. Peter Kilby had requested a meeting. He'd prepared what he described as interim executorship statements and wanted Liz to go through them with him so that he could explain the finer details. Oscar, in his capacity as an executor, was also present. He and Sarah had invited Liz to spend the night, but she'd declined the offer explaining she didn't want to leave Maria alone with the children any longer than necessary.

The heading **Paul Hirsch Deceased** jumped out at Liz when Peter Kilby handed over her copy of the statements. For a few seconds the print swam in front of her eyes and the columns of figures merged uneasily with each other as she tried to get a grip on her emotions, telling herself silently that this afternoon was merely another stepping stone and therefore a journey worth taking.

'Are you alright, Mrs Hirsch?' Peter Kilby asked, leaning forward slightly as if to offer some physical assistance.

'I'm fine, thank you,' Liz said quickly, wanting more than anything to get on with this dreadful business so that she could get out into the real world again. 'It's just that I still find it difficult to think of Paul as 'deceased',' she explained.

Peter Kilby looked embarrassed, 'I'm afraid it's accepted legal and official language; there is no other way I can express . . .' His voice tailed off.

'I understand, and forgive me for being so sensitive.' Liz opened the document hoping to signal her readiness to continue.

She watched Oscar's eyes flicking rapidly up and down the columns and envied his facility with figures. Before she was halfway down the first page, Oscar had turned over rapidly and she began to see why Paul had chosen him as an executor. 'I don't see any profits from the hotel listed,' he said as he reached the end of the document.

Liz heard Peter Kilby clear his throat. 'I'm afraid there aren't any,' he said. 'Of course, I'm not acting for the hotel any longer, but they did take out quite a substantial loan when Mr Hirsch was still alive and I'm assuming that interest and perhaps capital repayments have swallowed up any surplus income from the hotel. You know, of course, that the new manager absconded,' he continued. 'One doesn't wish to gossip, but it was reported in all the local papers at the time and one cannot help but hear . . .'

Liz turned sharply towards Oscar. 'Did you know Gaston LeGrange had left?'

Oscar shifted in his seat. 'Yes, I knew. I just haven't got around to telling you. A change of manager is not going to affect the value of the business significantly in the short term. There have been several new staff recently, but that's quite normal following a major change at the top.'

'Do you have any questions? Or is there any point you'd like me to clarify whilst we're all together?' Peter Kilby turned his attention to Liz, sensing the slight tension in the air. Liz shrugged her shoulders slightly before turning to Oscar, willing him to take the initiative.

'Well,' Oscar began. 'It's obvious there isn't going to be a share dividend in the foreseeable future. Obviously I'll keep an eye out for any changes in the hotel that may affect profitability. I've built up quite a relationship with the barman and I find dropping in for the odd pint usually brings me up to date with the latest information, particularly if I buy him a drink at the same time.'

'Quite.' Peter Kilby waited.

'In view of the fact that Mrs Hirsch, and perhaps more importantly the children, have lost their major source of income and have depended largely on her earnings for the past twelve months, can I take it that any surplus cash in Paul's estate will be transferred to her name some time soon?' Now that he knew the score, Oscar was just as keen as Liz to wrap up the interview.

'Indeed. I'll be putting that in hand just as soon as the executorship statements have been agreed.'

'Good. I see that Mrs Hirsch has been charged for accommodation and food for the whole of November and December last year. I would expect to see a refund for the five days in November when Mrs Hirsch was still in Rome and also for the Christmas period, which she and her family spent with us. Perhaps you'd like to pursue that with Miss Harvey, unless of course you've already done so and had a negative response.'

Peter Kilby looked uncomfortable. 'I'm afraid the matter of reimbursement completely slipped my mind,' he admitted. 'Thank you for bringing it to my attention. I will, of course, follow it up on Mrs Hirsch's behalf.'

'Excellent.' Oscar folded his copy of the statement neatly in half, signalling his satisfaction that everything was in order. He turned towards Liz. 'Is there anything else you need to know?'

'How long do you think it will be before . . .' she hesitated, not wanting to appear like a grasping beneficiary keen to get her hands on the cash.

'Oh, I think we can safely say that in two to three weeks everything will be finalised, unless there are any last minute glitches. I shall, of course, write and advise you.'

'Thank you for all your help,' Liz said, rising to her feet and holding out her hand.

'If there's anything else I can do, you only have to call.' Peter Kilby spoke with the confidence of a man who knows that a trust fund for minors will generate income, albeit a modest one, for many years to come.

'Well, that didn't hurt too much, did it?' Oscar said as they walked back to the car.

'I guess I'm slowly getting used to the fact that however much I dislike it I've got to take an interest in our financial future. Thank you for spotting the lack of a rebate for our food and the flat. I'm afraid that, left to my own devices, I wouldn't have queried it.' Now tell me about Gaston LeGrange. Did Antonia give him the sack?'

'He did a runner.' Oscar wasn't going to stand on ceremony. 'Piled all his own stuff as well as some property and cash belonging to the hotel into Paul's car and left in the small hours of the morning. Rumour has it he's working for Eloise Moncton.'

'You're joking!' Liz turned to Oscar in astonishment. 'Well you have to hand it to her, she doesn't waste time does she?'

'I'd say they deserve each other, wouldn't you?' Oscar smiled as he unlocked the car and held the door open for Liz.

Liz couldn't help but laugh. 'Well, I must admit I didn't see that one coming. A petty crook and a potential blackmailer. What an interesting combination!'

'It only remains to be seen who'll come out on top.' Oscar started the engine and put the car in gear.

'I'll lay you five to one in favour of Eloise Moncton.' Liz settled back in her seat.

CHAPTER TWENTY TWO

Liz had the whole day to spend with the children. Maria had borrowed the car and driven off to see a college friend and, for once, she had a precious Sunday away from the hotel. The weather, although cool and crisp, was bright and sunny. There wouldn't be many more days like this before the end of the year and she decided to take advantage and take the children outdoors.

For some weeks now she'd been trying to find the time to trim the beech hedge that separated her property from the road. Every time she drove in and out, the shaggy strands waving in the breeze reminded her that time wasn't on her side. She bundled the children up in warm clothes and rubber boots, promising them a bonfire once the hedge had been trimmed. Marcus was given a small wheelbarrow and a toy rake with which to collect dead leaves. Emma had a tiny basket and Liz urged her to fill it with the few beech husks that lay scattered about the lawn where they'd been blown over from a large tree on the Perkins' property.

Once the children were occupied, Liz, armed with a sharp pair of secateurs, set about tidying up the hedge. She worked on the garden side to begin with until happy that the children could be left to their own devices and then walked around to begin on the other side. Fortunately there was a short bank leading up from the road and once Liz had scrambled up to the top she was able to reach the stray branches easily and keep an eye on the children at the same time. They were in their element piling up leaves and a few, very few, beech husks with which to start the bonfire.

Within half an hour Liz had removed most of the stray branches and jumped down from the bank to survey her handiwork, feeling the warm glow of satisfaction that comes with the achievement of a task long postponed. She stepped back a yard or two intending to look for any branches she might have missed, but before she'd had the time to focus properly there was the sound of a car horn and, acting purely on instinct, she flung herself back towards the hedge. She heard the squeal of brakes followed by the sound of a car door banging. Footsteps approached. Liz opened her eyes and turned around to face the driver who was sprinting up the road towards her.

'Thank your lucky stars I wasn't driving any faster or you'd be splattered all over the road by now! Are you all right?'

'Well, I don't think anything's broken. I'm sorry if I scared you, I was just checking the hedge. It's easier to see from a distance. I hope there's no damage to your car.' Liz looked over his shoulder to the grey Aston Martin that was now slewed across the entrance to her drive.

'As I said, I wasn't driving fast. I'm Adam Broadbent by the way.'

'Liz Hirsch.' Before she could elaborate, she heard screams of protest coming from the other side of the hedge. 'And that awful noise you can hear is the sound of my children enjoying themselves!' Liz threw the remark over her shoulder as she ran towards the drive and the relative safety of her garden.

'She's pinched my rake!' Marcus said as Liz appeared.

'I'm sure Emma only wants to borrow it. Anyway, I've just about finished trimming the hedge, so we're nearly ready to start the bonfire.'

'I don't care, I want my rake back!'

Liz saw that Emma was carefully raking all the leaves that Marcus had collected, away from the site of the fire and reckoned they'd be all over the garden again if she continued unchecked. She walked across to where Emma stood, panting with exertion after her strenuous efforts to undo Marcus' good work. 'We're going to use those leaves to start the bonfire,' she said, taking the rake firmly but gently from Emma's hand, 'would you like to help?'

Emma considered for a moment and then said, 'Who's that?' as she spotted Adam Broadbent striding across the lawn with his arms full of branches.

'Hello. I'm Adam. Who are you?' He grinned down at her as he began breaking up branches and laying them across the leaves.

'I'm Emma. Can I help?'

'Sure.' He handed her a couple of the smaller branches before turning to Liz. 'I could clear up more quickly if I had a wheelbarrow.'

'I think you've just made a friend for life,' Liz said. 'There's a wheelbarrow in the shed.' She began walking across the lawn.

'I'll show you! I'll show you!' said Marcus, jumping up and down with excitement.

Liz stopped in her tracks and watched her son and Adam Broadbent walk towards the shed, or more accurately Adam walked, Marcus ran. When he reached the shed door he jumped up to try and un-latch it, but the handle was about six inches too high for him. Adam bent down, lifted Marcus up and held him while he opened the door. *That's exactly what Paul would have done,* Liz thought and then, with a sudden revelation realised that until that moment she hadn't thought of Paul all day.

Adam parked the wheelbarrow at the bottom of the drive and urged Marcus to keep an eye on it whilst he picked up the branches. Once it was full, he persuaded Marcus to stand in front of him so they could push it together. He looked, Liz thought, like a man who spent a lot of time in the open air. His face was tanned and when he smiled his eyes crinkled at the corners as if he smiled a good deal. He was lean without being thin and dressed for a country weekend in corduroy trousers and a chunky sweater over a checked shirt. Both children appeared to be quite captivated and Liz began to feel redundant for the first time in a year. It was a surprisingly good feeling.

'Would you like some coffee?' she asked. 'Or are you expected somewhere?'

'Coffee would be marvellous. I'm having lunch with my

brother, but I've got plenty of time. Anyway, I can always give him a ring to say I'll be late, if you don't mind my using your phone. If I'm staying for coffee I think it might be a good idea for me to move the car, if that's OK with you.' The Aston Martin still stood where he'd stopped it and was partially obstructing the entrance to Liz's drive.

'Well, our au pair's out with the car and I'm not expecting her back until later, but I guess it would be safer to drive in.' She picked up Emma and slung her around her right hip. 'I'll take this young lady with me, it's just about time for her nap,' Liz said, feeling an unaccustomed exhilaration as she went off to make their coffee

'Would you like to help me park the car?' Adam looked down at Marcus whose beaming face gave him the answer to his question. 'Right, let's go.' He laid an arm lightly across Marcus' shoulder as they made their way towards the Aston Martin.

'Papa had a sports car,' Marcus confided as they reached the car and Adam opened the door.

'Did he now?' Adam picked up on the past tense. 'Was it like this one?'

'Not exactly. Papa's was black. I think it was a TR. He doesn't need it now. He's in Heaven.'

Adam rumpled Marcus' hair. 'That's pretty tough for you.' What else could he say? The boy had just dropped a minor bombshell, but in such a matter of fact way that, or so it seemed, he'd accepted his father wasn't around any more. He settled himself into the driving seat, pulled Marcus onto his lap and placed his hands carefully on the steering wheel at twenty to four. He started the engine and gave it a few extra revs in a passable imitation of the starting grid of a grand prix racing circuit before placing his own hands at ten to two. 'Now, let's see if we can park this baby a bit more tidily.' He straightened the car, drove forward and parked on the left hand side of the drive, close to the cottage.

'That was a great piece of driving,' he said as the two of them climbed out. 'But you must remember never to get into a car unless you have a grown up with you because they can be very dangerous. Now, shall we start that bonfire?'

Adam pulled out his lighter and, cupping the flame with his hands, applied it to a bundle of leaves at the base of the fire. 'Don't stand too close,' he said to Marcus. 'If you get smoke in your eyes it will sting like anything.' Marcus stepped back with the obedience of a child who is having a good time and doesn't want it to end. Within a few minutes the branches from the hedge were blazing, helped by the stiff autumn breeze.

'It's a wonderful smell, isn't it?' Liz appeared and stood sniffing the smoke now whirling all around the garden. 'It might be as well to have your coffee in the kitchen, unless you want to end up smelling like a kipper.'

'Lead the way,' Adam said before turning to Marcus. 'I think the bonfire will look after itself for a while. Are you coming with us?' Marcus needed no second invitation.

'I hope you don't mind if we stay in the kitchen. I was so keen to get on with the hedge trimming that I didn't get around to lighting the sitting room fire this morning and I wasn't expecting visitors.'

Adam ducked his head as he followed her through the kitchen door, his nostrils quivering with pleasure at the smell of fresh coffee. There was a plate of what looked like homemade shortbread standing next to the coffee pot. 'I wasn't expecting to be given coffee. It seems like an unfair reward for someone who almost ran you over a while ago!'

'Look at it as a fair reward for your efforts in the garden,' Liz said, almost filling a cup with black coffee. 'Help yourself to milk and shortbread if you like it.' She poured orange juice for Marcus and pulled out a chair for Adam.

'Do you mind if I take advantage of your Rayburn?' Adam said, taking his mug in one hand and a biscuit in the other and leaning against the rail in front of the stove. 'It should be mandatory to have these things in all kitchens.' He set down his mug, rubbed his hands together and held them over the hotplate. He looked, Liz thought, completely at home; at ease with himself and the world.

'Do you live in Wiltshire?' she asked, knowing that she hadn't seen him around either in the village or in Salisbury.

'Sadly not. My brother's just bought a house in Broadstone. I'm afraid I still live in London. My father owns a central heating company and I help him to run it. Now that money is a bit easier people are beginning to update their homes and after the cold winter we were inundated with requests for heating systems. I'm sure it won't be many years before everyone in the country has it.'

Liz was glad she'd asked him to stay in the kitchen. If Adam Broadbent was used to central heating he'd find her cottage sadly lacking. It had taken her a while to get used to having no central heating after the warmth and comfort of the hotel and when the winter was at its height there were times when she felt she'd never be warm again.

'You mentioned phoning your brother earlier,' she said. 'The phone's just through that door in the hallway.' She waved a hand towards a door on the opposite side of the kitchen. 'It's unheated, I'm afraid,' she apologised as Adam put down his mug and walked across the kitchen floor.

'I guess I'll survive.' He closed the door carefully behind him and Liz sat down and began to drink her own coffee.

'Well, that's all fixed,' Adam said as he returned to the kitchen. 'Sunday lunch is a fairly moveable feast in our family, so nobody gets in a sweat if the guests are a bit on the late side. Have you lived here long?' he asked.

'I came down almost a year ago, although I've had the cottage for about five years now. It belonged to my grandmother and, as her only descendant, I inherited it when she died.'

'Living in a flat as I do, I envy you your garden. It looks pretty generous by London standards.'

'I have a lot more work to do on it. I've spent most of my spare time trying to make this cottage into a home. Previously we only used it for weekends and now that I have a job, and with two small children, you can imagine life is a bit hectic.' Liz felt disinclined to talk about Paul and her real reason for moving to Broadstone, not wanting to present herself as a needy female looking for a replacement for the man she'd lost.

'I shouldn't think there are many opportunities for work in this neck of the woods.' Adam pulled out a packet of cigarettes. 'Do you mind if I smoke?'

'Not at all,' Liz said. She reached for her own, declining Adam's proffered packet as too strong a brand for her. 'I work in Salisbury,' she offered, once they'd finished the business of lighting cigarettes. 'I manage a hotel, so a Sunday off is quite a treat for me.'

'And *very* lucky for me,' he said.

Liz felt herself blush, something she hadn't done for a long time, and realised with a shock it had been months since anyone had paid her a compliment.

Adam turned his attention to Marcus. 'Do you think we should have a last look at our bonfire?' he asked. 'Then I'll be on my way and leave you in peace. There are limits even to my brother's patience.'

Liz followed the two of them back into the garden. The bonfire had now died down. 'Perhaps I should sling some soil on the embers,' Adam said as a sharp wind blew a flurry of sparks around the immediate area of the fire.

'That's OK, we'll do it when you've gone. Won't we Marcus?' Liz reached down and took Marcus' hand, which he promptly withdrew. 'I want Adam to do it,' he said.

'Adam is going out for lunch,' Liz said firmly smiling across at him, signalling that she was happy for him to leave.

'It won't take a minute,' Adam said, much to her surprise. 'I'll help myself to a spade, I'm sure I spotted one in the shed.'

'You realise you now have two friends for life? I guess you're used to children and their demands.' He'd been so natural with both the children Liz guessed he'd had plenty of practice.

'I've a couple of rowdy nephews, they keep me up to speed.'

If Liz was relieved that he hadn't practised on his own children she chose not to show it, but instead continued to watch as he shovelled soil onto the dying embers of the fire. Although it slowed his progress, he was careful to let Marcus help him and they wielded the spade together.

Finally, when he was satisfied there were no more stray

sparks, he replaced the spade in the shed, dusted off his hands on the seat of his trousers and came back to say goodbye.

'Thank you for the coffee,' he said to Liz. 'And thank you for helping me,' he turned to Marcus and rumpled his hair before climbing into the car, executing a swift three-point turn and, with a last wave, driving away.

'He let me drive his car,' Marcus said to Liz as they walked back to the cottage.

'That was kind of him, but you mustn't get into a car and try to drive it on your own because it could be dangerous.'

'Adam said that as well. Do you think he'll come again?' Marcus asked.

'I really don't know,' Liz answered, not wanting to make any rash promises to Marcus in case he should be disappointed later on. 'I hope so,' she added, surprising herself.

Well, what an interesting and unexpected morning, Adam thought as he drove down the hill towards his brother's house on the other side of the village. Who'd have thought that in the middle of a country road in deepest Wiltshire you could meet someone so intriguing! Interesting she hadn't mentioned her dead husband once. Perhaps the memories of him were too painful to share? He wondered if an accident or an unexpected heart attack had carried him off. It was a good thing Marcus had alerted him or he might have inadvertently put his foot in it. He felt in the right hand pocket of his trousers and was relieved to find that the paper he'd torn from Liz's telephone pad, on which he'd scribbled her phone number, cribbed from the dial at the front of the instrument, was still there. He smiled to himself as he trod on the accelerator and roared off to have lunch with his brother.

Liz and Adam didn't meet again until the day after Boxing Day. He'd called to invite her to a party that his brother was giving the week before Christmas, but as it was a Saturday evening Liz was busy with pre-Christmas functions in the hotel and didn't feel she could take time out. Like most hotels they put on a special programme over the Christmas break and she drove the family in to share in it, thinking that, although not ideal, it would be more fun for all of them than staying at home.

When the official celebrations were over she gave Maria the day off and invited Adam for a lunch she'd stayed up late the previous night to prepare. Marcus was overjoyed when she told him and spent most of the morning running to the window every time he heard a car passing the end of the drive. When Adam finally arrived he brought presents for the children and a bottle of wine as a contribution towards lunch.

His gift to Marcus was a toy Aston Martin with a remote control. Leaving Liz to put the finishing touches to lunch, he showed Marcus exactly how it worked. By the time Emma woke up the two of them had mastered all the technicalities. With two children around, conversation over lunch was limited. Liz had half expected Adam to leave before the children were in bed, but he seemed in no hurry and when finally Liz said that she should make their tea he offered to do the washing up, which Liz had left in the kitchen when they finished lunch.

'Well, I've been working over the holiday, so I'm not going to refuse an offer like that,' she said. 'The children ate such a huge lunch that I'm just going to give them boiled eggs and then they'll be ready for bed. I really miss Maria when she isn't around, but she's been looking after them over the holiday and I think she needs a break.'

'Do *you* ever have a break?' he asked.

Liz shrugged her shoulders and laughed. 'A couple of hours after the children have gone to bed and before I'm ready to fall asleep. As you can imagine, hotel hours are irregular; sometimes I have very early starts, at other times late finishes. Having Maria makes it all possible.'

It wasn't until the children were tucked up that she felt able to talk about Paul. By this time they'd retreated from the kitchen and were drinking wine in front of a roaring log fire in Liz's sitting room. 'I suppose you're wondering why I'm down here on my own,' she began, feeling that the time was right to put Adam in the picture.

'Marcus already told me his father was in Heaven,' Paul confessed. 'Obviously I didn't press him for details. It must have been a tough time for all of you.'

'I don't mind admitting that when it happened I thought I'd never smile again, but having survived the first awful year when there seemed to be so many problems, I think there's a good chance I might be able to rebuild my life.'

'I'll drink to that,' he said, raising his glass and then, feeling that he should return the compliment, and bring her up to speed with his own life, he continued. 'At the moment I'm trying to extricate myself from an affair which has run its course. She's a lovely lady, but too demanding for my taste. I have a strong suspicion that whatever I do for her it will never be enough. If I feel that way now what will I be like in five years time? I think it's kinder to end it. Unfortunately, the woman in question doesn't agree.'

Liz found herself sympathising with 'the woman in question'. Adam was charming, easy going, good looking and not short of cash, if the Aston Martin was anything to go by. What woman wouldn't want to hang on? 'Surely love must be the deciding factor,' she said. 'After all, if you really love someone you're prepared to go to almost any lengths to ensure that the relationship will not only survive but flourish. I don't think I could live with someone who beat me up or regularly came home drunk or womanised excessively, but then I'm lucky enough not to have had a relationship with anyone who behaved in that way.'

Adam laughed. 'You do realise that you've just excluded about fifty per cent of the male population, don't you?'

Liz joined in the laughter. 'What a cynical view you have of your own sex!'

'I'd prefer to call it realistic.'

Liz thought for a moment about Tom Merton and all the other 'men on the road' that she'd met whilst working in the hotel industry and conceded that he might just have a point.

Adam drained his glass and looking at his watch saw to his surprise that it was nine o'clock. He jumped to his feet. 'I'm really sorry to stay so late. You must be exhausted after your busy weekend. Thank you for asking me to lunch, I've really enjoyed it.

'And thank you for being so nice to my children, particularly Marcus. He was so excited when I told him you were coming. I'm afraid he misses his father.'

Adam shrugged. 'He's an engaging young man. It isn't difficult to be nice to children when they're so receptive. It's the little monsters I can't stand!' He paused briefly as if trying to make a decision before he said, 'I'd like to return your hospitality. Will you let me give you dinner some time soon?'

Liz hoped he wouldn't notice she was blushing. 'That would be lovely.'

'Good. I'll ring you.'

He hadn't kissed her goodbye. Why not? Adam admitted that he was afraid of scaring her off. How ironical life could be at times. Back in London was a woman he couldn't shake off for love nor money and down here was what? A woman who'd suffered the pain of loss and who might just possibly be trying to fend off unwanted attention if he knew anything about men on their own staying in hotels away from wives or girlfriends. What's more, she had responsibilities and was, by her own admission, only just beginning to rebuild her life. *Patience Adam*, he told himself. *Patience.*

CHAPTER TWENTY THREE

Five Months Later

All the windows of the cottage were wide open and warm air from the garden drifted inwards. Liz was putting up the hems on a pair of curtains she'd been making for Emma's bedroom; one of the final tasks in her refurbishment programme. The children and Maria were playing on the swing that Sid Perkins had put up for them. Their laughter coming from the garden was one of the most profoundly comfortable sounds she'd heard during the nightmare of the last eighteen months.

She had the whole weekend off and planned to take the children on a picnic to the coast tomorrow, but was keeping it as a surprise in case a last minute crisis in the hotel meant she would have to sacrifice her Sunday.

Tonight she was meeting Adam. They planned to visit a new restaurant attached to one of the local pubs, which Adam's brother had recommended. They'd met a few times since their first lunch together, but the combination of her job and his location meant they didn't see each other as frequently as Adam would have liked.

The sound of the telephone shrilled through the summer afternoon and startled Liz so much that she pricked her finger. 'Please God, don't let it be the hotel,' she said and, for a moment, was tempted not to answer, but then thought it could be Adam with a last minute change of plan.

'Hello Liz. It's Oscar. I was beginning to think you weren't at home.'

'Oscar! How are you? Sorry to take so long to answer. I'm enveloped in curtains at the moment. Just trying to finish them before Emma's bedtime.'

'I know how precious weekends are, but I've just had a call from George and thought I'd better ring you as soon as possible.'

'George?' Liz was so immersed in her own world that the name didn't strike a chord.

'George as in hall porter, Bishop's Hall Hotel. Remember?' Oscar was using his patient voice. 'Come on Liz, it hasn't been that long, surely.'

'Oh, Oscar, I'm sorry. I was just hoping it wasn't a call from my employer, asking me to go in either tonight or tomorrow. You know what it's like. Is there a problem?'

'Well, I hope not, but George tells me Antonia hasn't been seen around the hotel for the last three days. Apparently she's been trying to manage the place herself since Gaston LeGrange left. Suddenly she's taken to her room and whenever one of the staff phones to ask if she's all right they're assured that everything's fine. She's refusing food, and tells everybody she's making her own meals. If anyone knocks at the door she pretends not to hear and none of them knows what to do. I don't relish going there on my own and I wonder if you could possibly come up? I know your time off is precious and I hate to ask you, but I'm out of my depth and I'd really appreciate it. In the normal course of events I wouldn't care, but let's not forget it's the children's future that's involved.'

Liz saw her precious weekend disappearing in the space of a few moments. Would that dreadful woman never stop dogging her footsteps? 'Aren't you forgetting Antonia's sister in London,' she said to Oscar, 'surely she's the one you should be talking to.'

'I've been down that road already,' Oscar replied. 'Celia's in France with some friends at the moment. Antonia mentioned it to one of the staff before she went into hibernation. They're travelling and there's no way of contacting her unless we alert Interpol and that might be a bit extreme, don't you think?'

Liz felt a wave of disappointment. There'd been so much heartache and so little pleasure over the past eighteen months that she was greedy for every last moment when she could escape for a while and start to forget. But, as Oscar already pointed out, the future for her children was currently tied to the hotel and she owed it to them to put her own needs on hold. 'All right, Oscar, I'll come. Maria's here, so I don't have to worry about the children. I'll try and leave early this afternoon, so I should be with you about five. May I spend the night with you and Sarah?' she added. As neither of them knew the likely outcome of the proposed visit to Antonia, it was as well to be prepared to stay in Hertfordshire for as long as necessary.

'Consider it done. See you later.' Oscar terminated the call.

Liz replaced the receiver and looked at her watch, eleven forty five. She hoped and prayed she'd catch Adam before he left London, otherwise it would mean leaving a message with his brother. It was a relief when he answered her call.

'I'm sorry, Adam, but I'm going to have to change our plans for this evening,' she began and explained the reason as quickly as she could.

Adam took the news philosophically. 'That's OK, I guess I'll stay in London,' he said. 'I'll save the trip to my brother for your next free weekend. I hope you manage to sort things out. Give me a call and let me know how you get on.'

It was half past six on Saturday evening when Oscar and Liz drew up outside Bishop's Hall. Oscar had already called George to let him know they were on their way and he walked forward to meet them as they entered the foyer. 'Nice to see you again, Mrs Hirsch,' he said. 'How're the two kiddies?'

'We're all fine, George, thank you. The children are growing fast. Marcus will be going to school next summer.' Liz wished this was just a social call and they could have a drink and a leisurely dinner and then just as quickly silently chastised herself for being selfish.

'We'd best get on,' Oscar said. 'Do you have a spare set of keys for Miss Harvey's flat?'

George disappeared into his office, produced a master set of keys, riffled through them and selected one. 'I think you'll find that will open Miss Antonia's front door. If you need any help just give me a shout.'

Oscar crossed the hall briskly and took the stairs two at a time. When they reached the door of the flat he knocked loudly. There was no answer. He knocked again. Still no response. 'Right, let's get it over with.' Oscar fitted the key in the lock and opened the front door.

They were met by an overpowering smell of cats, made worse by the almost suffocating heat. Oscar pulled a face, 'I take it Omar and Khayyam are in residence. God Almighty, what a stink.'

Liz pulled out a hanky and held it to her nose. 'Just until I can open a few windows,' she said.

'Miss Harvey, are you there?' Oscar called. There was no reply. He shrugged and then turned to Liz. 'You're sure you're ready for this?'

'I'm not nearly as fragile as I look!' As she spoke she didn't know who she was trying to reassure, herself or Oscar. 'Let's try the sitting room first,' she suggested, indicating the door immediately in front of them. Oscar opened it and the smell of cats grew stronger.

Antonia sat immobile in a wing chair facing the door. For one awful moment Liz thought she was looking at a corpse and felt goosebumps on her forearms, but a second glance told her Antonia was still conscious. She sat bolt upright, her hands clasped tightly together and resting in her lap. Liz crossed over to her chair. 'Antonia, it's Liz. Do you recognise me? Can you hear me?' Antonia didn't respond, but gazed at Liz with unseeing eyes and continued to sit as if in a state of catatonia.

'I think she might have had some kind of breakdown,' Oscar whispered in Liz's ear. 'I'll go down to reception and get George to call the hospital. It's obvious she can't stay here in this state. Do you think you could put a few things in a bag for her? I expect they'll keep her overnight at least, if only for observation. In the meantime, where do you think those two damned cats are hiding? I'll take them with me. They obviously can't stay here.'

'I'll try the kitchen first,' Liz said, crossing the sitting room and opening the door. There were two bowls containing remnants of half-eaten cat food. The floor surrounding the dishes was littered with scraps of stale food, but there was no trace of either cat. She walked into the bedroom and found both of them asleep on Antonia's unmade bed. Omar opened an eye and surveyed her with mild interest before closing it again.

'You won't ignore me for long,' Liz told him and, after opening the window, shooed the pair of them into the hall. 'Right, mission accomplished,' she said to Oscar as she went back into the sitting room. 'When you've gone I'll open the rest of the windows and pack a bag for Antonia.'

Antonia still sat where they'd found her. Now that Liz had time to look at her properly, she could see how much weight she'd lost. Her eyes were dull and had sunk into her head. She looked scruffy and untidy as if she'd neither washed or combed her hair for several days. Liz left her and went back into the bedroom, making a mental list as she did so of the things that Antonia might require. After a few minutes she'd packed a wash bag, a dressing gown and slippers into an overnight case she found in Antonia's bedroom cupboard. There was a nightdress on the bed, presumably where Antonia had left it. It was grubby and covered in cat hairs. Liz opened the chest of drawers to find a clean one and, hearing Oscar return, she pulled out the first one that came to hand and put it on top of the rest of the stuff she'd packed into the bag.

'Thank God you're here,' Oscar said as she rejoined him. 'I wouldn't want any of the staff to see the flat in its current state and I'd never have managed to find the things Antonia might need. The ambulance will be here shortly. If I go with Antonia to the hospital do you think you could stay here and tidy the place up a bit? I'll come back for you as soon as I can.'

Liz began to collect the dirty crockery surrounding Antonia's chair and piled it on a tray. She felt uncomfortable having Antonia so close and immobile and retreated to the kitchen and began washing the dirty plates and cups. Ten minutes later there was a knock on Antonia's door and the sound of voices told her the ambulance had arrived.

She went back to the sitting room just in time to see two paramedics lift Antonia into a wheelchair. 'Thank God they didn't bring a stretcher,' Oscar said, 'At least she'll be able to leave the hotel with a little dignity.'

Liz could see nothing dignified about the emaciated wreck slumped in the wheelchair, but she smiled at Oscar in an effort to reassure him. 'I'll come with you if you like,' she offered.

'No, I'll be fine, thanks all the same. I think we'll be more productive if we split up, don't you?' Liz agreed and returned thankfully to the kitchen. Within an hour both kitchen and sitting room were restored to something like their normal order and she moved on to the bedroom where she pulled off sheets which were covered with cat hairs and muddy paw marks. She remade the bed, thinking longingly of the Saturday evening she could be spending with Adam.

In her haste to get to Antonia's nightdress, other items of underwear in the drawer had become disarranged and she set about refolding and tidying them up. She picked up a crumpled slip and, with a shock, recognised Paul's handwriting staring up at her from the front of a stark white envelope. Her own name leapt out at her making her heart beat faster and a momentary prickle of fear crawl up the back of her neck. For one wild moment it was almost as if Paul had returned and was standing silently behind her waiting. Her fingers shook as she picked up the envelope and read the contents.

'Oh Paul!' The words came out in a choking sob. He *had* said goodbye to her, after all. In her hand was the letter she'd been searching for and thought she'd never find. But in the letter he'd mentioned diamond earrings. Where were they? Liz went back to the drawer and moved aside piles of underwear. Right at the bottom was the box and a bundle of letters and cards which she recognised as those she'd previously sent to Paul and which he must have kept.

♥

❦272❦

It was nine thirty when Oscar returned to the hotel. He had a quick word with George to update him about Antonia and then went up to the flat and was surprised to find it in darkness. Surely Liz hadn't left without him? He went from room to room switching on lights until finally he reached Antonia's bedroom.

Liz was sitting on the floor, head bent, arms wrapped around her knees. 'Liz, what on earth . . .?' Without hesitating he sat down beside her. 'Liz, what is it? Tell me. What's happened?'

'Oh Oscar!' Liz lifted a tear-ravaged face. 'I found a letter from Paul. He's left me his mother's earrings.' She raised a hand to her right ear and showed him the cascade of diamonds which caught the light and sparkled as her head moved from side to side. 'I found them in Antonia's drawer,' she said. 'Aren't they beautiful?'

Oscar pulled out a handkerchief to replace the sodden ball of wet linen she held in her hand and then put both his arms around her and laid his cheek against her hair. He felt the pressure of her head against his shoulder as if she'd been waiting for someone to lean against for a long time. He held her for several minutes waiting for her sobbing to die away and then slowly and gently kissed her tear stained cheek.

'As far as the rest of the world is concerned, the last half hour never happened,' Liz scrambled to her feet and began to pick up pieces of clothing which were scattered randomly on Antonia's bedroom carpet.

'I'm sorry, Liz, I didn't mean to take advantage.'

'I know, Oscar. You gave me exactly what I needed at precisely the right moment and thank you, thank you dearest Oscar. I promise I'll never, ever cry all over you again!'

He groped around the carpet for his underpants, which were lying on top of Liz's knickers, which he held out to her. 'Here, I think these will look better on you!'

Liz giggled and then started to laugh hysterically when she remembered whose bedroom they were in and why. In spite of the laughter, she felt duty-bound to ask about Antonia. 'How is the old harridan?'

'The consultant thinks she might have had a breakdown brought on by a combination of stress and pressure of work. What with the bereavement following Paul's death and taking her age into account it's obviously all been a bit too much for her. There's a possibility she might have self-prescribed some kind of medication to try and ease the pain she was feeling. The hospital will carry out tests over the next few days and then we'll have some kind of prognosis.'

Liz had been brushing her hair and re-applying lipstick whilst listening to Oscar. When she was satisfied that she looked tidy enough to get past George, she removed the earrings and placed them carefully in their box. 'If Antonia weren't so wicked I'd feel sorry for her. As it is, I can't forgive what she's done to all of us. Please don't think too badly of me, will you?' She looked anxiously across at him.

'I could never think badly of you. You're an old and treasured friend and you've had a hell of a rough ride. If I've been of any help . . .' He shrugged.

Liz crossed the room and kissed him quickly. 'I could never have managed without you,' she said. 'Now let's get the hell out of here.'

Tucked up in the guest room next door to Sarah and Oscar, Liz felt unexpectedly calm. It was as if today had been a turning point, the first step towards rehabilitation and a new life. Oscar had made love to her and in an inexplicable way she'd stopped feeling guilty. Until today she'd felt disloyalty to Paul every time she'd spent any time at all with Adam.

The last eighteen months had been terrible; filled with shocks, unpleasant confrontations and previously unknown situations. All this had been made worse by the realisation that

Paul was gone forever. She'd been forced to make decisions not only for herself but for the future of her children and, although she'd undoubtedly made mistakes, began for the first time to tell herself that perhaps she hadn't done so badly after all.

Oscar had been a rock, always there, unfailingly helpful and practical. Making love to him had been as much an expression of gratitude to him as a fulfilment of her own needs. It had surprised her that she could make love to someone else, let alone enjoy it, and the fact that there was no question of a long term relationship didn't matter. Oscar had helped her to cross the Rubicon and for that she would always be grateful.

Soon she would have to make more decisions. Neither she nor Oscar were in a position to do anything about the hotel until they knew more about Antonia and what was to happen to her. That decision would depend largely on Celia and the action she took once aware of her sister's situation. *I won't try to influence that decision in any way,* Liz vowed, *I'll wait and see then discuss it with Oscar.* Since Paul's death she'd discovered she was capable of making decisions and knew instinctively that she would make the right choice at the appropriate time. Sleep, when it finally came, was deep, dreamless and untroubled.

'I've just called the hospital,' Oscar said when Liz appeared the next morning.

'And?'

'Antonia had a comfortable night. They're trying to persuade her to eat and will begin tests tomorrow.'

'Right, so there's nothing we can do for the time being.' Liz meant it as a statement rather than a question. A plan for the rest of the day was already forming in her mind.'

'Except perhaps have breakfast.' Liz hadn't seen Sarah join them.

'That's a wonderful idea, but may I make a quick phone call before we eat?'

Please be there, she prayed as Sarah and Oscar tactfully

withdrew to the kitchen, leaving her alone with the telephone. Her fingers quivered with an excitement she hadn't felt since Paul's death as she dialled, knowing that eight thirty on Sunday morning was an uncivilised time to phone anyone. She couldn't remember when she'd last felt this degree of urgency and knew that she'd keep on phoning the number until it was answered.

Adam's voice sounded sleepy when he finally picked up the phone. 'Hello, Adam Broadbent.'

'Good morning Adam Broadbent. How are you this lovely morning.'

'It's pouring with rain!' Adam said. 'It's also early for a Sunday. You'd better have a good reason for tearing me away from the sports pages!'

'It's Liz,' she smiled broadly at nothing in particular. 'And I haven't looked at the weather yet. It just feels like a lovely morning.'

It was Adam's turn to smile. The omens were looking good. When he replaced the receiver five minutes later his smile was even wider. 'I told you to be patient,' he said to the empty space as he set about restoring some kind of order to his normally untidy flat.

BIBLIOGRAPHY

Around the World in 80 Treasures Pub: Weidenfeld and Nicholson
Dan Cruickshank

Italy The Hilltowns   Pub: George Philip
James Bentley

Italy   Pub: BBC Books
Francesco da Mosto

How to Visit the Beauties of Florence   Bonechi Guide - Firenze

Frommer's Review of Galleria   New York Times
Nazionale Perugia

Let's Go Italy   Pub: Pan Books
Ed: Kathryn S Moffett

Life Beyond the Reach of Hope   Published in The College
Recollections of a Refugee 1938-1939   The St John's Review
Philipp P Fehl   St John's College, Annapolis,
                                                Maryland - Santa Fe,
                                                     New Mexico

Forgotten Voices of the Holocaust Pub: Ebury Press - Random House
Lyn Smith in association with
The Imperial War Museum

The Diving Bell & The Butterfly   Pub: Fourth Estate
Jean-Dominique Bauby
Translated by Jeremy Leggatt

How can I accept Christ?　　　　　　　An Islington Booklet
Rev. A. P. Wood D.S.C. M.A.　　　　　　Pub: A. Webb & Co.

Last Waltz in Vienna　　　　　　　　　Pub: Pan Books
The Destruction of a Family 1842-1942
George Clare

The Power of Art　　　　　　　　　　Pub: BBC Books
Professor Simon Schama CBE

The above books have provided valuable technical/artistic/architectural information.